Tree-House Comix Proudly Presents

DOG MAN
GRIME AND PUNISHMENT

WRITTEN AND ILLUSTRATED BY DAV PILKEY
AS GEORGE BEARD AND HAROLD HUTCHINS
WITH COLOR BY JOSE GARIBALDI

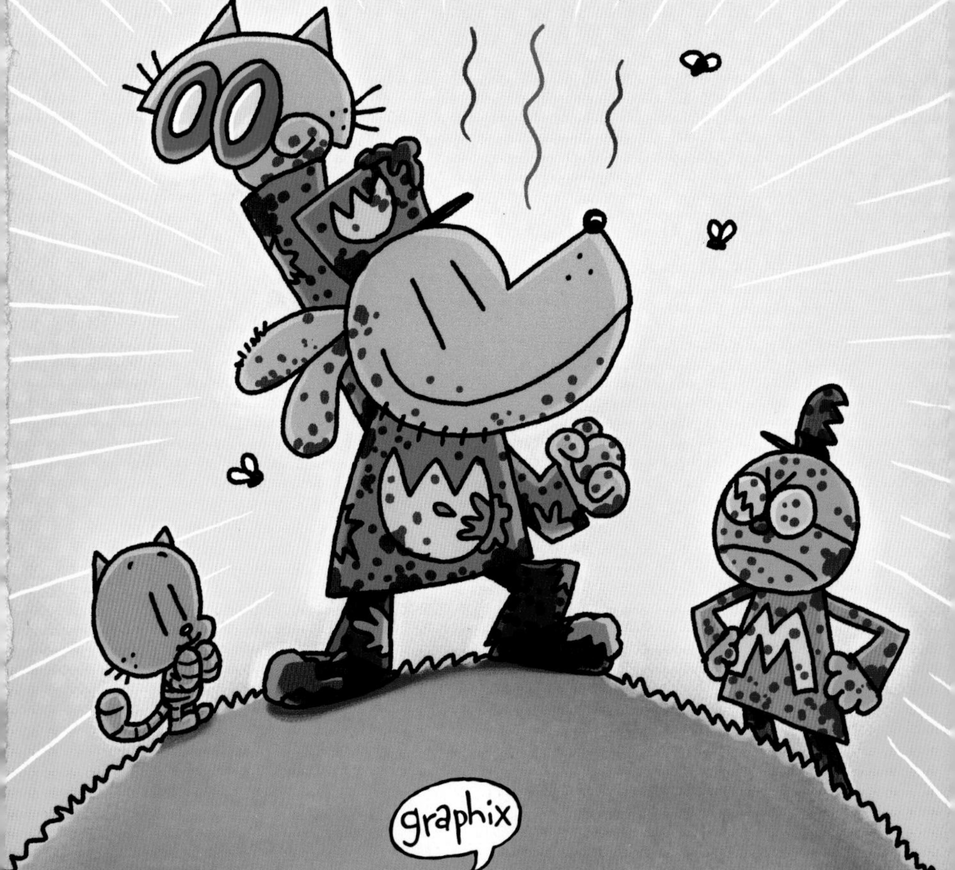

graphix
AN IMPRINT OF
SCHOLASTIC

TO AMY BERKOWER, WHO ONCE TOLD ME, "WRITE THE BOOKS THAT MAKE YOU HAPPY." THANK YOU FOR BELIEVING IN ME.

Library of Congress Control Number 2020930257

978-1-338-53562-4 (POB)
978-1-338-53563-1 (Library)

10 9 8 7 6 5 4 3 2 1   20 21 22 23 24

Printed in China   62
First edition, September 2020

Edited by Ken Geist
Book design by Dav Pilkey and Phil Falco
Color by Jose Garibaldi
Color flatting by Aaron Polk
Publisher: David Saylor

CHAPTERS

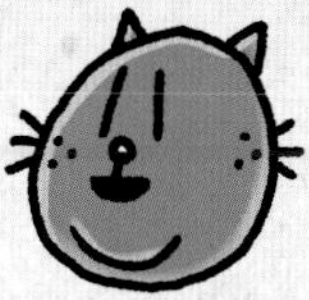

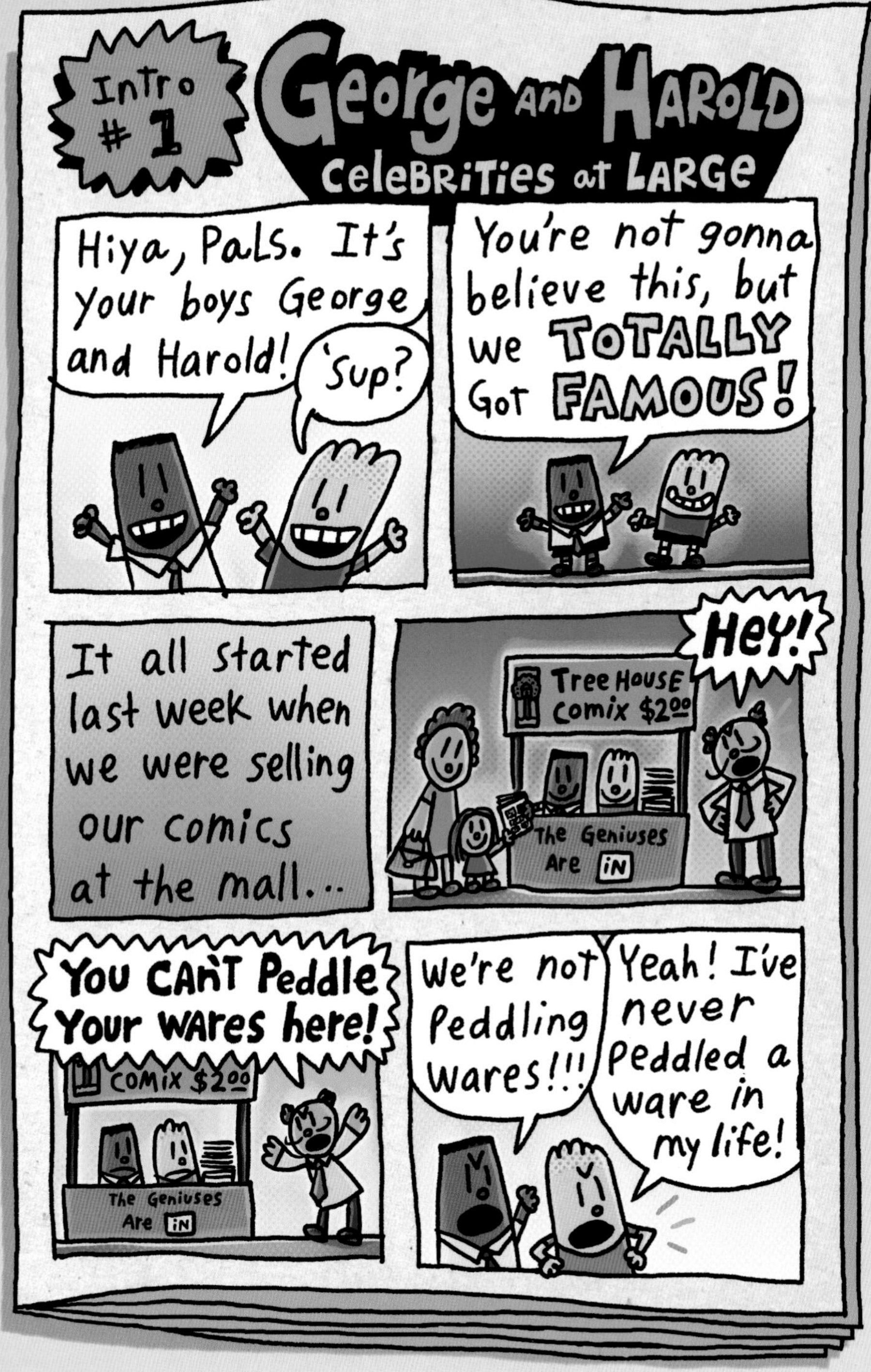
Intro #1
George and Harold
Celebrities at Large
Hiya, Pals. It's your boys George and Harold!
'Sup?
You're not gonna believe this, but we TOTALLY Got FAMOUS!
It all started last week when we were selling our comics at the mall...
Hey!
Tree House Comix $2.00
The Geniuses Are IN
You CAN'T Peddle Your wares here!
COMIX $2.00
The Geniuses Are IN
We're not Peddling wares!!!
Yeah! I've never peddled a ware in my life!

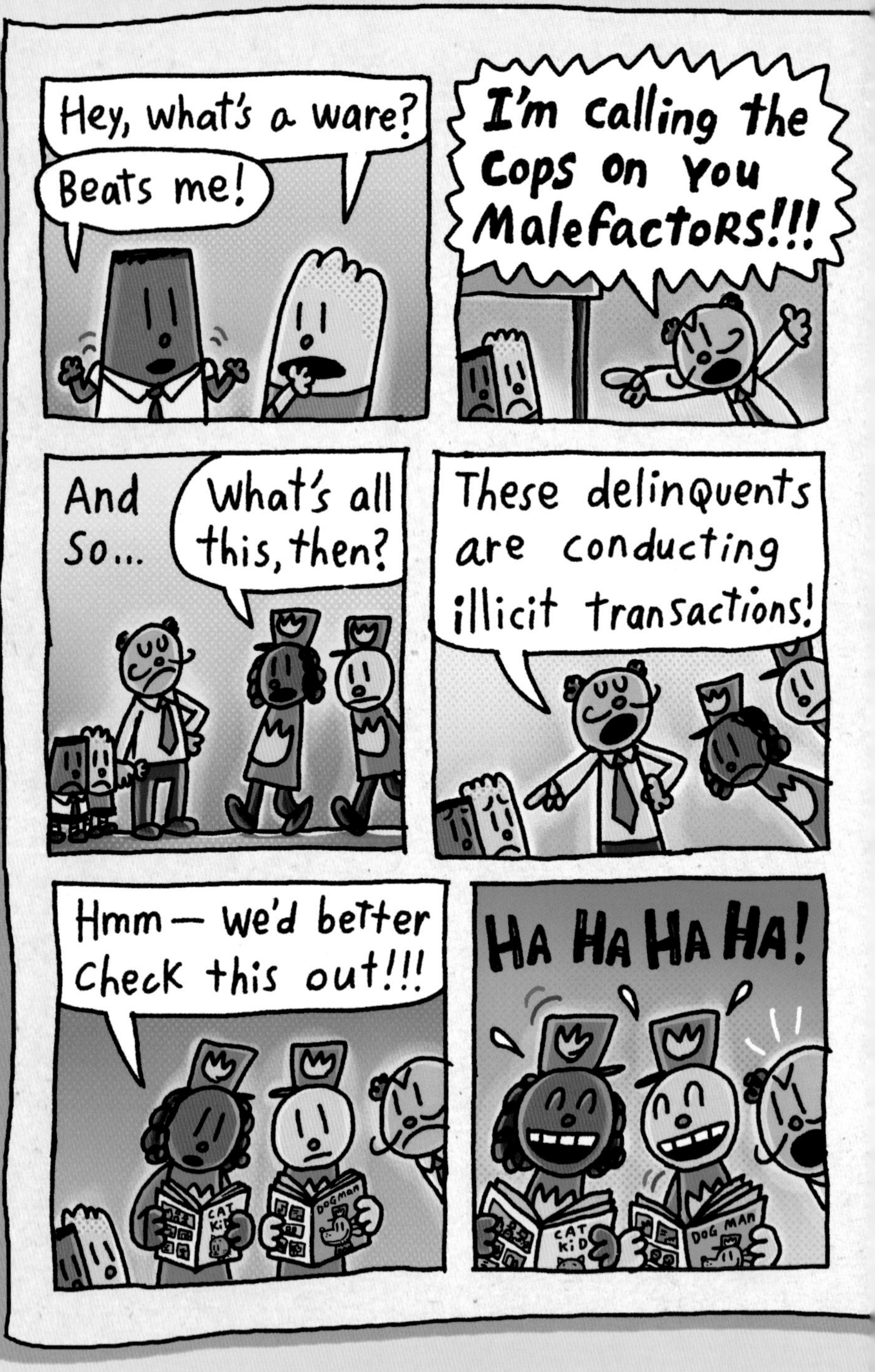
Hey, what's a ware?
Beats me!
I'm calling the Cops on You Malefactors!!!
And So...
What's all this, then?
These delinquents are conducting illicit transactions!
Hmm— we'd better Check this out!!!
HA HA HA HA!

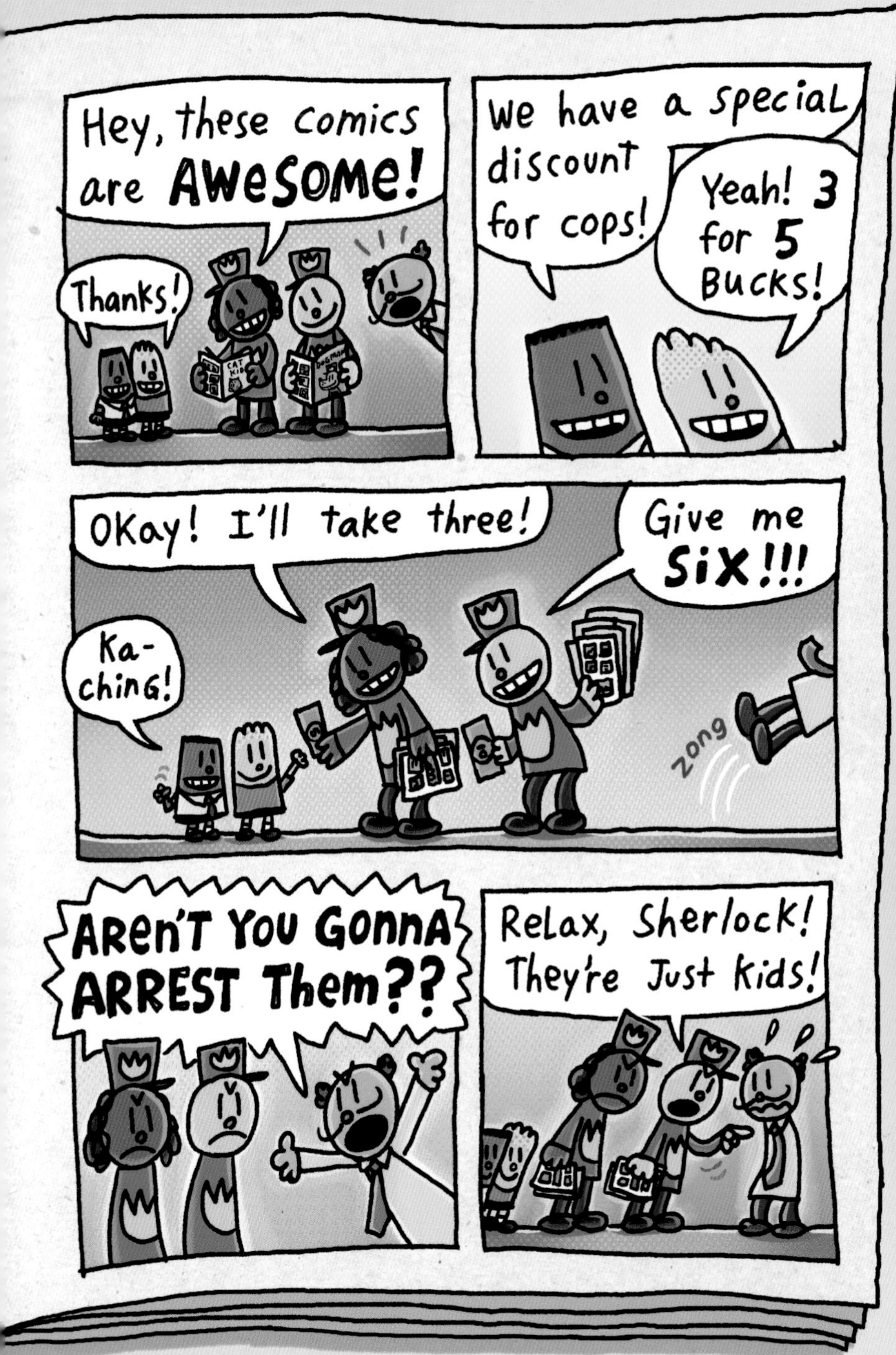
Hey, these comics are AWESOME!
Thanks!
We have a special discount for cops!
Yeah! 3 for 5 Bucks!
OKay! I'll take three!
Give me SIX!!!
Ka-chinG!
ZONG
AREN'T YOU GONNA ARREST Them??
ReLax, Sherlock! They're Just Kids!

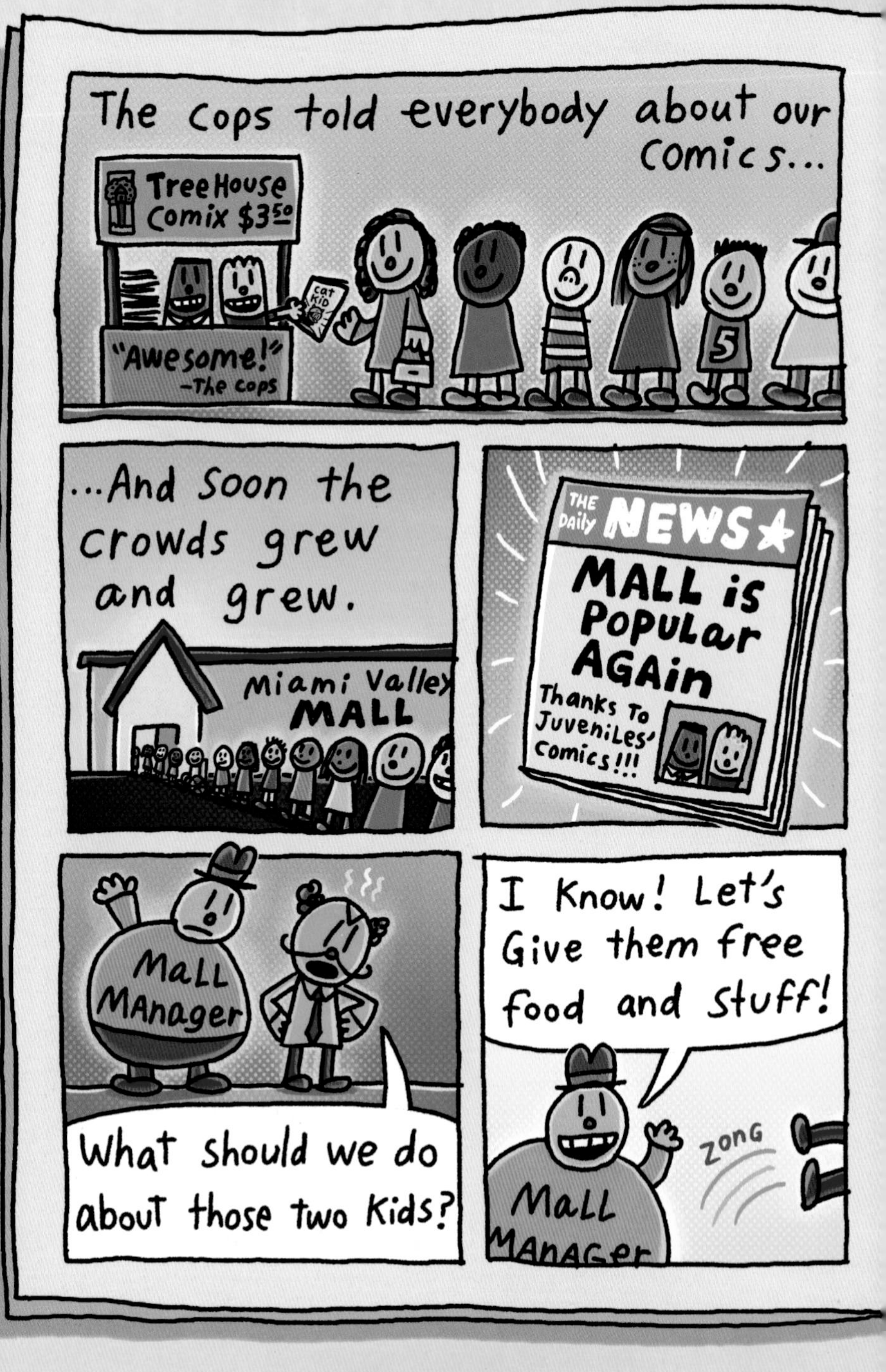
The cops told everybody about our comics...
Tree House Comix $3.50
Cat Kid
"Awesome!" -The cops
5
...And soon the crowds grew and grew.
Miami Valley MALL
THE Daily NEWS
MALL is POPULAR AGAIN
Thanks To Juveniles' Comics!!!
Mall Manager
What should we do about those two kids?
I Know! Let's Give them free food and stuff!
ZONG
Mall Manager

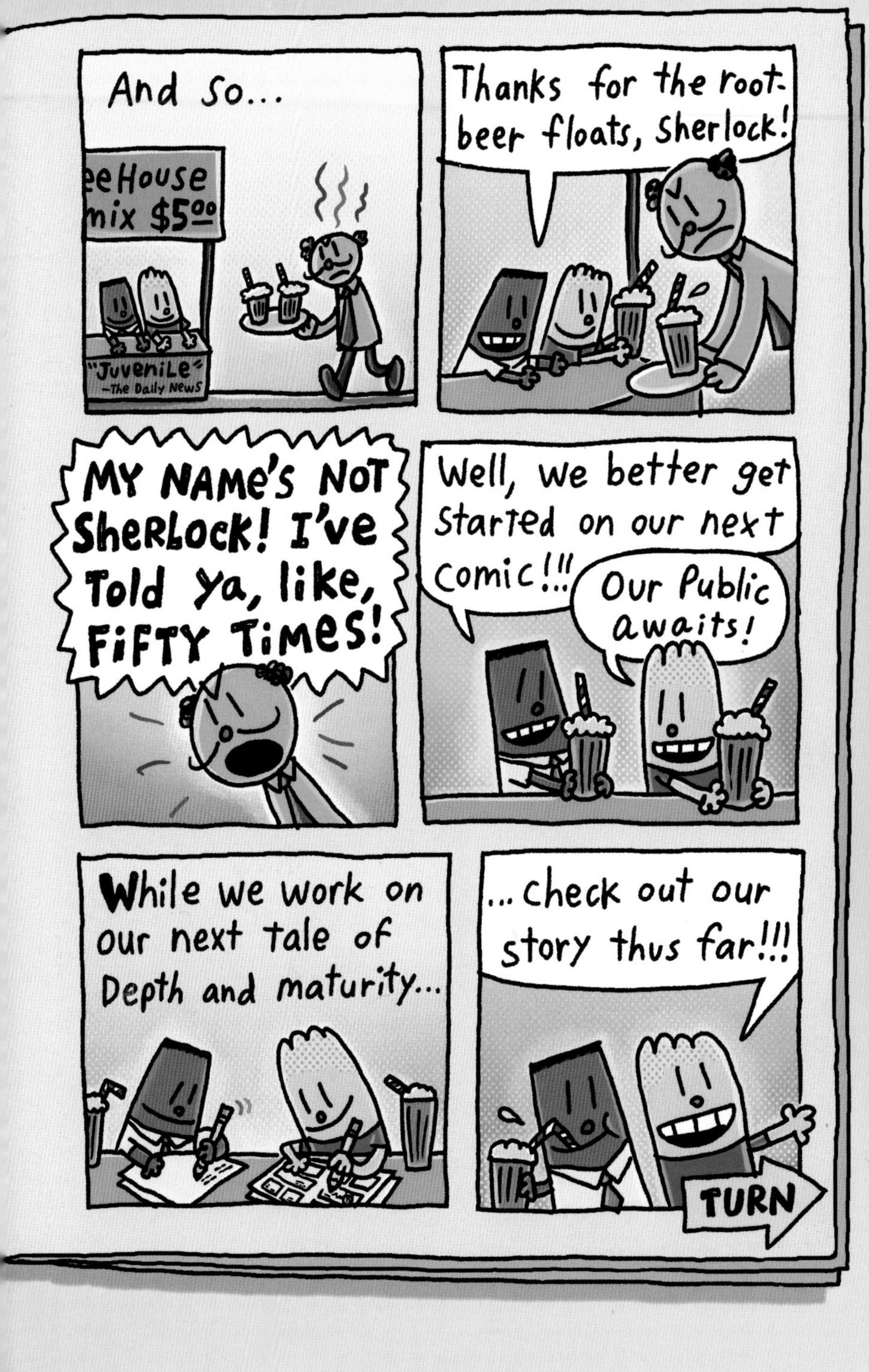

And so...
eeHouse
mix $5.00
"Juvenile"
—The Daily News
Thanks for the root-beer floats, Sherlock!
MY NAME'S NOT SHERLOCK! I'VE TOLD YA, LIKE, FIFTY TIMES!
Well, we better get started on our next comic!!!
Our Public awaits!
While we work on our next tale of depth and maturity...
...check out our story thus far!!!
TURN

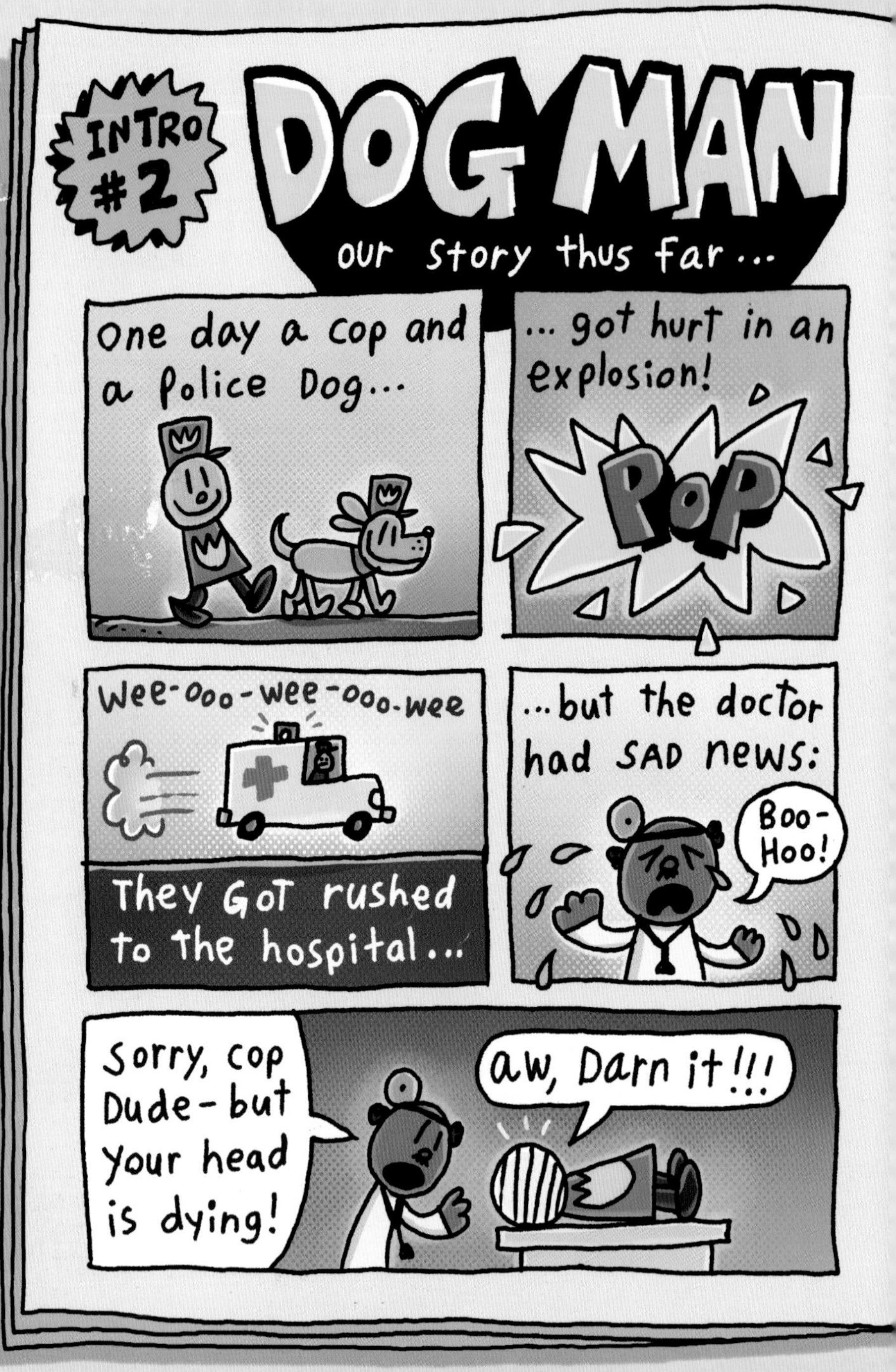
INTRO #2
DOG MAN
our Story thus far...
One day a cop and a Police Dog...
... got hurt in an explosion!
POP
Wee-ooo-wee-ooo-wee
They GoT rushed to the hospital...
...but the doctor had SAD news:
Boo-Hoo!
Sorry, cop Dude-but your head is dying!
aw, Darn it!!!

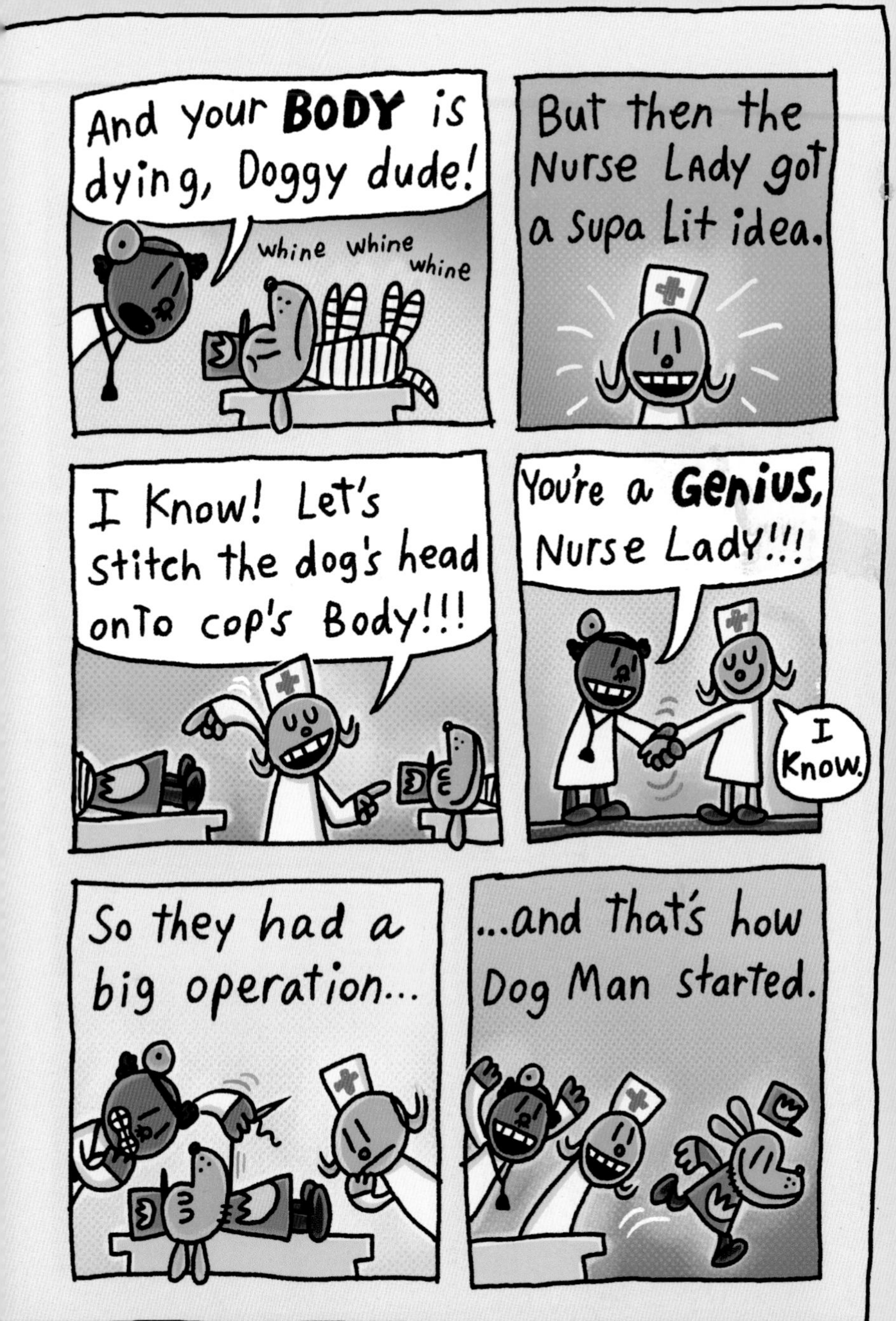
And your BODY is dying, Doggy dude!
whine whine whine
But then the Nurse Lady got a Supa Lit idea.
I Know! Let's stitch the dog's head onTo cop's Body!!!
You're a GENIUS, Nurse Lady!!!
I Know.
So they had a big operation...
...and that's how Dog Man started.

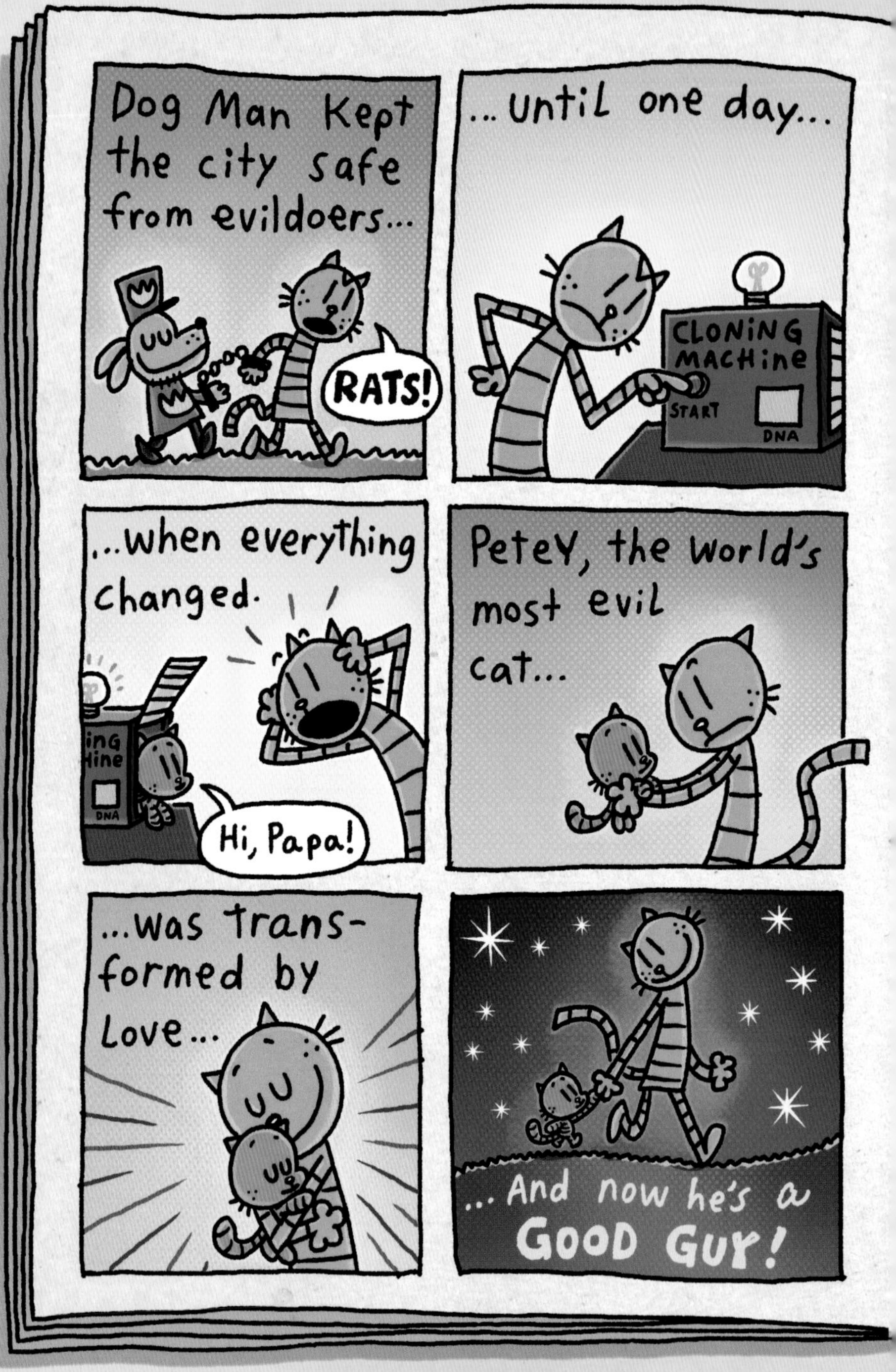
Dog Man kept the city safe from evildoers...
RATS!
...until one day...
CLONING MACHINE
START
DNA
...when everything changed.
Hi, Papa!
Petey, the world's most evil cat...
...was trans-formed by Love...
...And now he's a GOOD GUY!

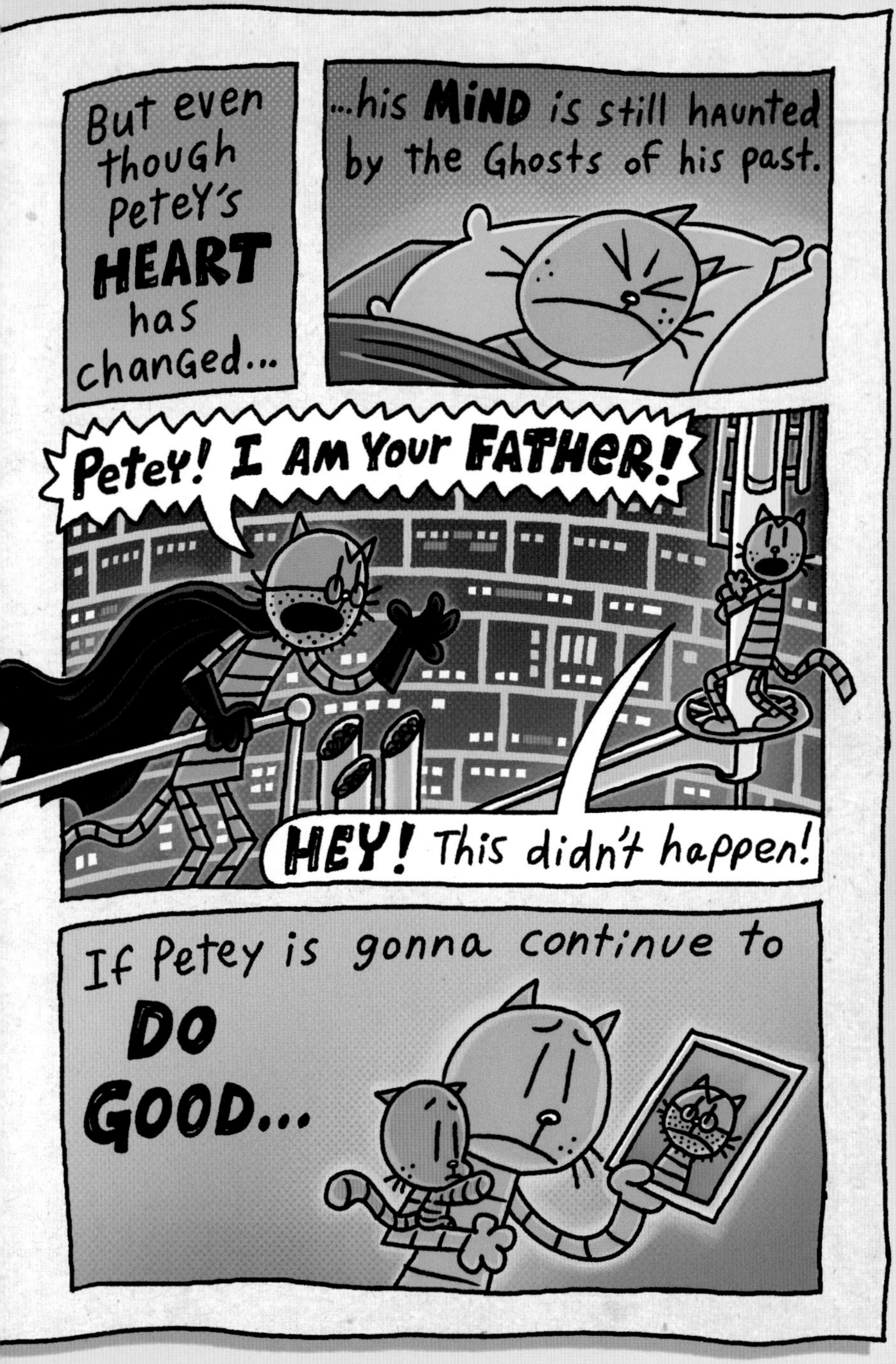
But even though Petey's HEART has changed...
...his MIND is still haunted by the Ghosts of his past.
Petey! I AM Your FATHER!
HEY! This didn't happen!
If Petey is gonna continue to DO GOOD...

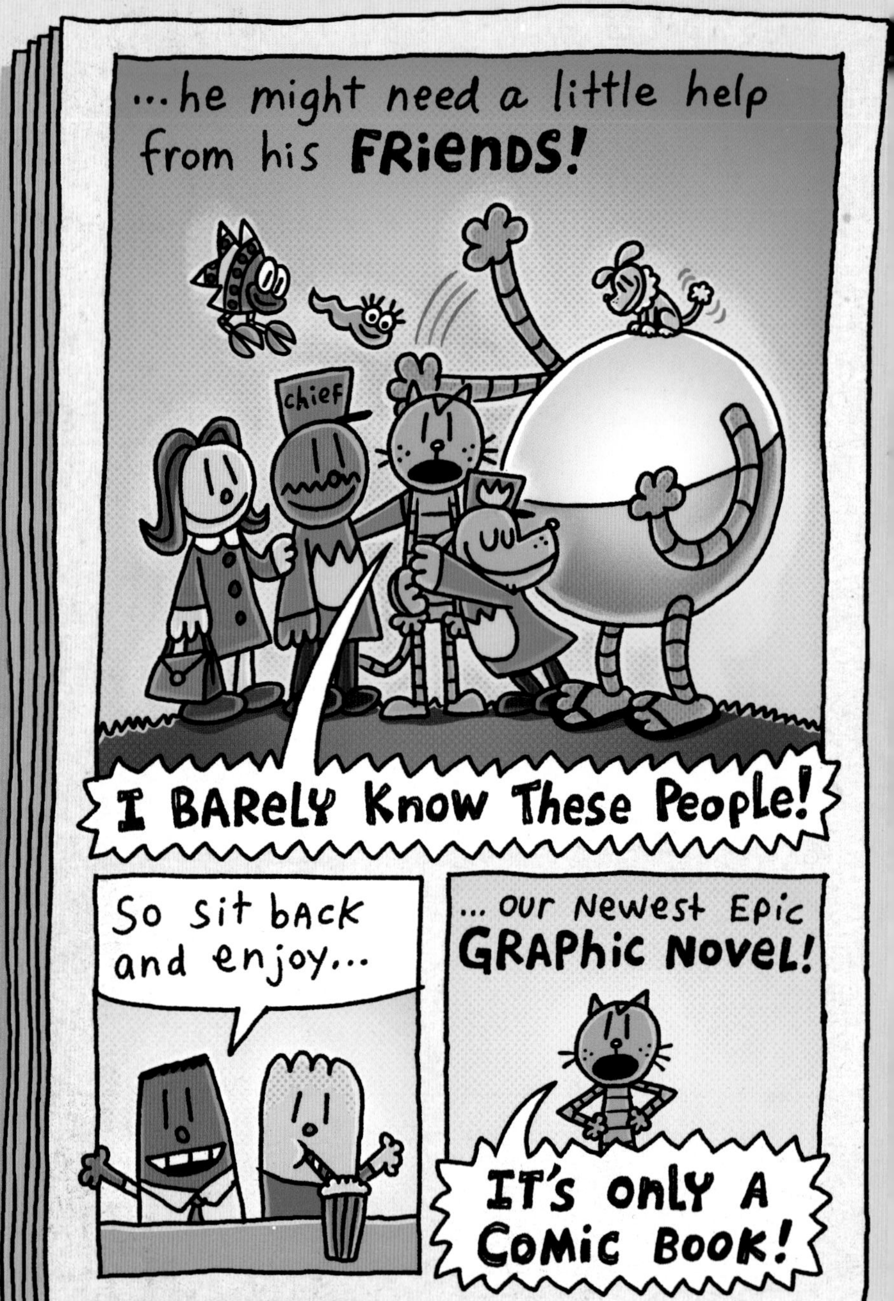
...he might need a little help from his FRIENDS!
chief
I BARELY Know These People!
So sit back and enjoy...
...our Newest Epic GRAPhic NoveL!
IT'S ONLY A COMIC BOOK!

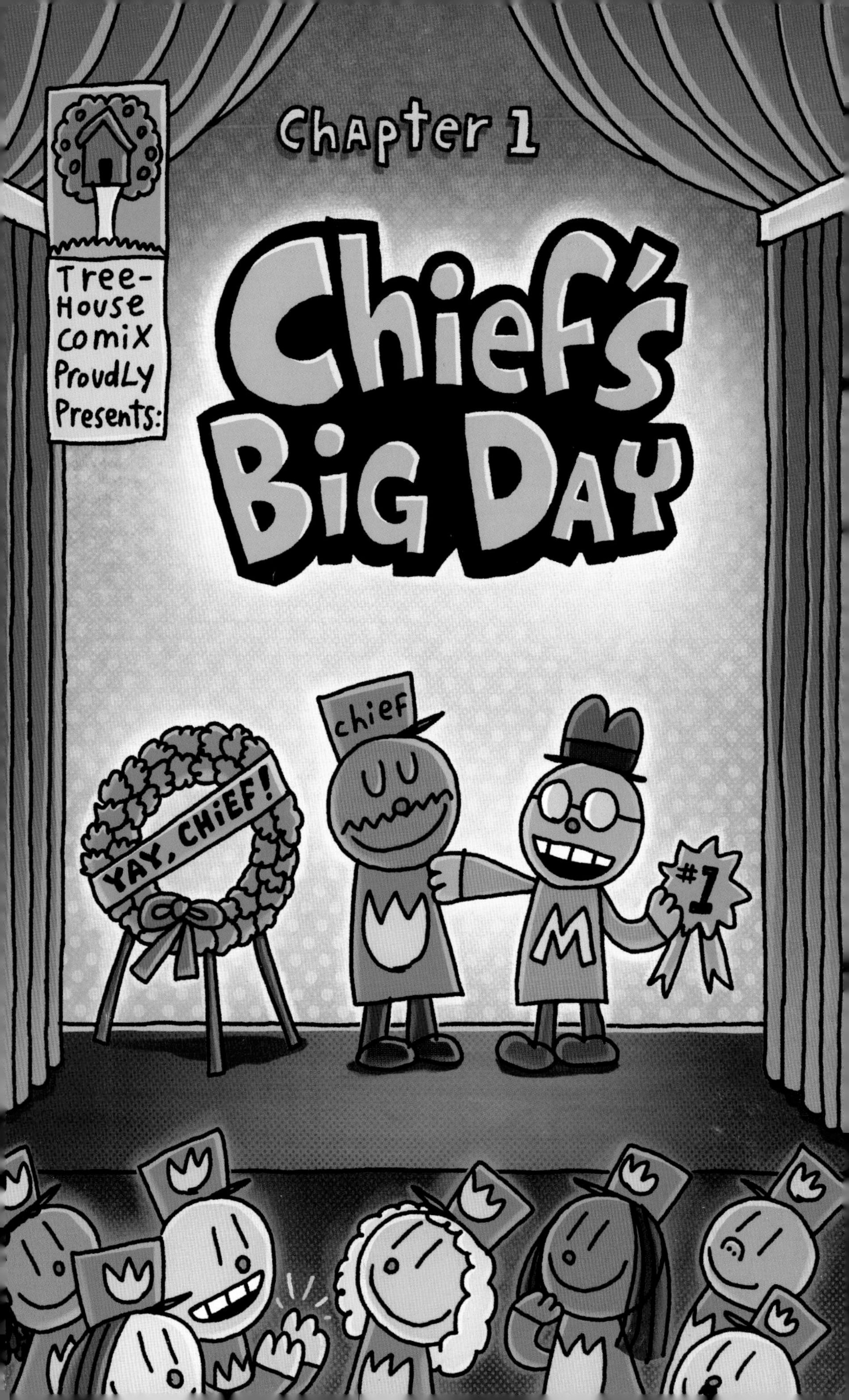
Tree-House Comix Proudly Presents:
Chapter 1
Chief's Big Day
chief
YAY, CHIEF!
#1

Good afternoon!
CITY HALL
I'm Mayor!
Thank you for Joining us on this ~~Auspitious~~ nice occasion!
chief
YAY, CHIEF!
We are here to honor CHIEF...
chief
...for being the BEST Chief in town!
chief
HOORAY!
Yippee!

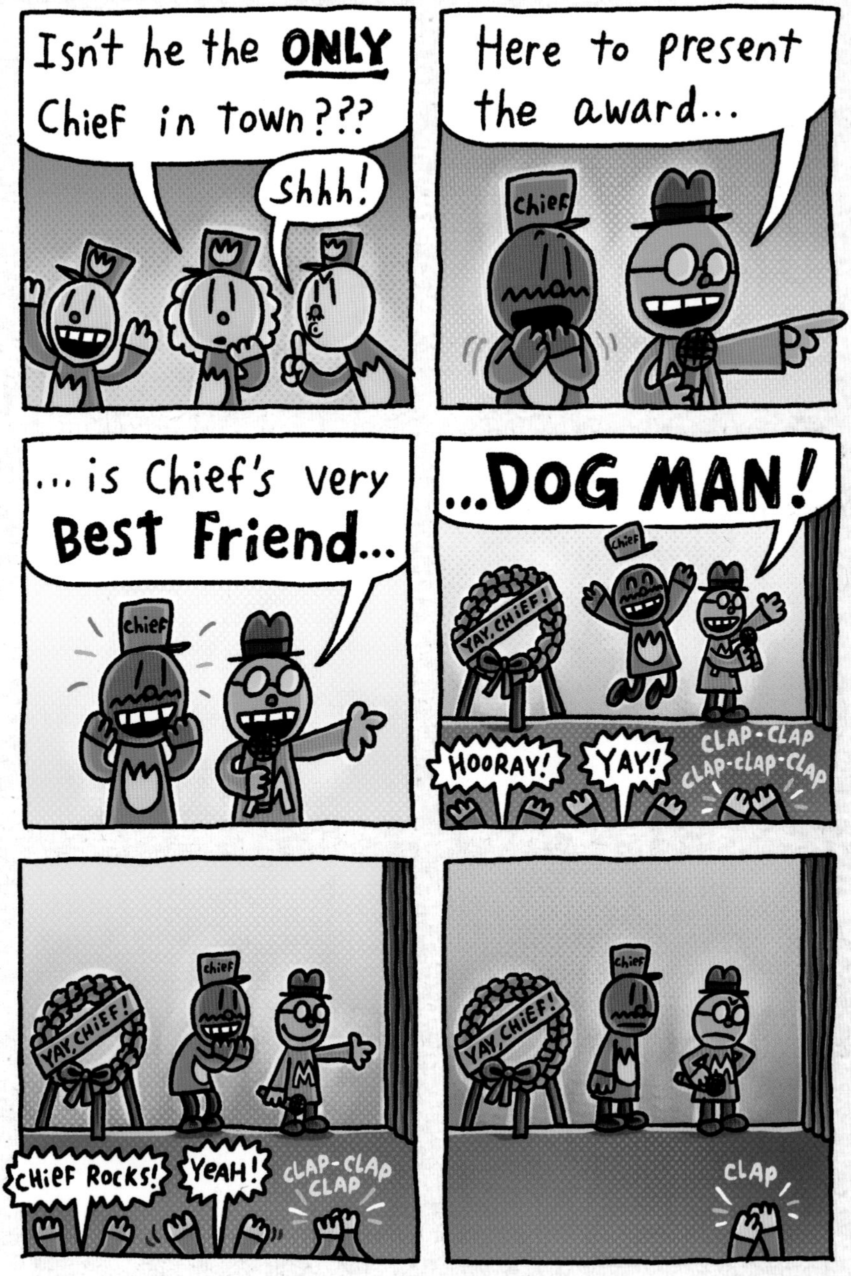
Isn't he the ONLY Chief in town???
Shhh!
Here to present the award...
Chief
... is Chief's very Best Friend...
chief
...DOG MAN!
Chief
YAY, CHIEF!
HOORAY!
YAY!
CLAP-CLAP
CLAP-CLAP-CLAP
YAY, CHIEF!
chief
CHIEF ROCKS!
YEAH!
CLAP-CLAP
CLAP
YAY, CHIEF!
chief
CLAP

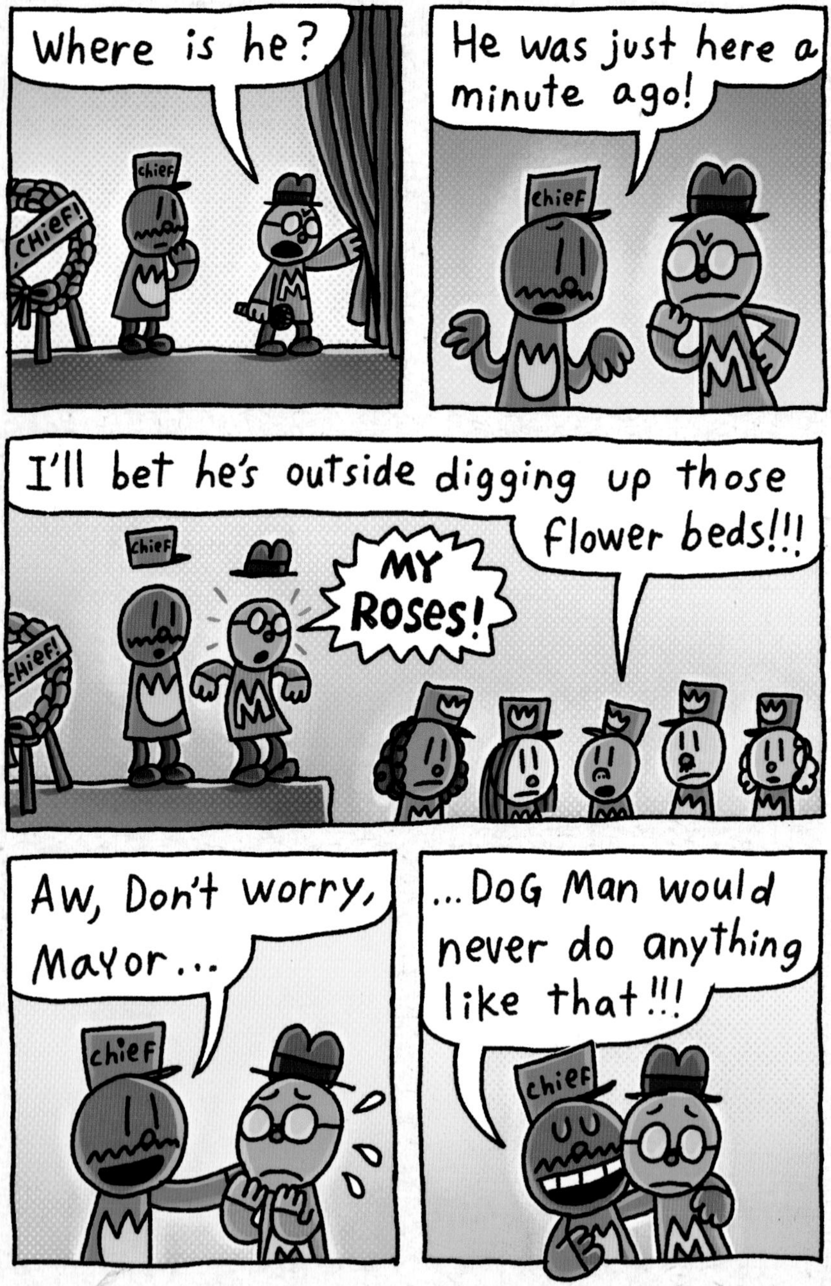
Where is he?
He was just here a minute ago!
I'll bet he's outside digging up those flower beds!!!
MY ROSES!
CHIEF!
Aw, Don't worry, Mayor...
...DoG Man would never do anything like that!!!

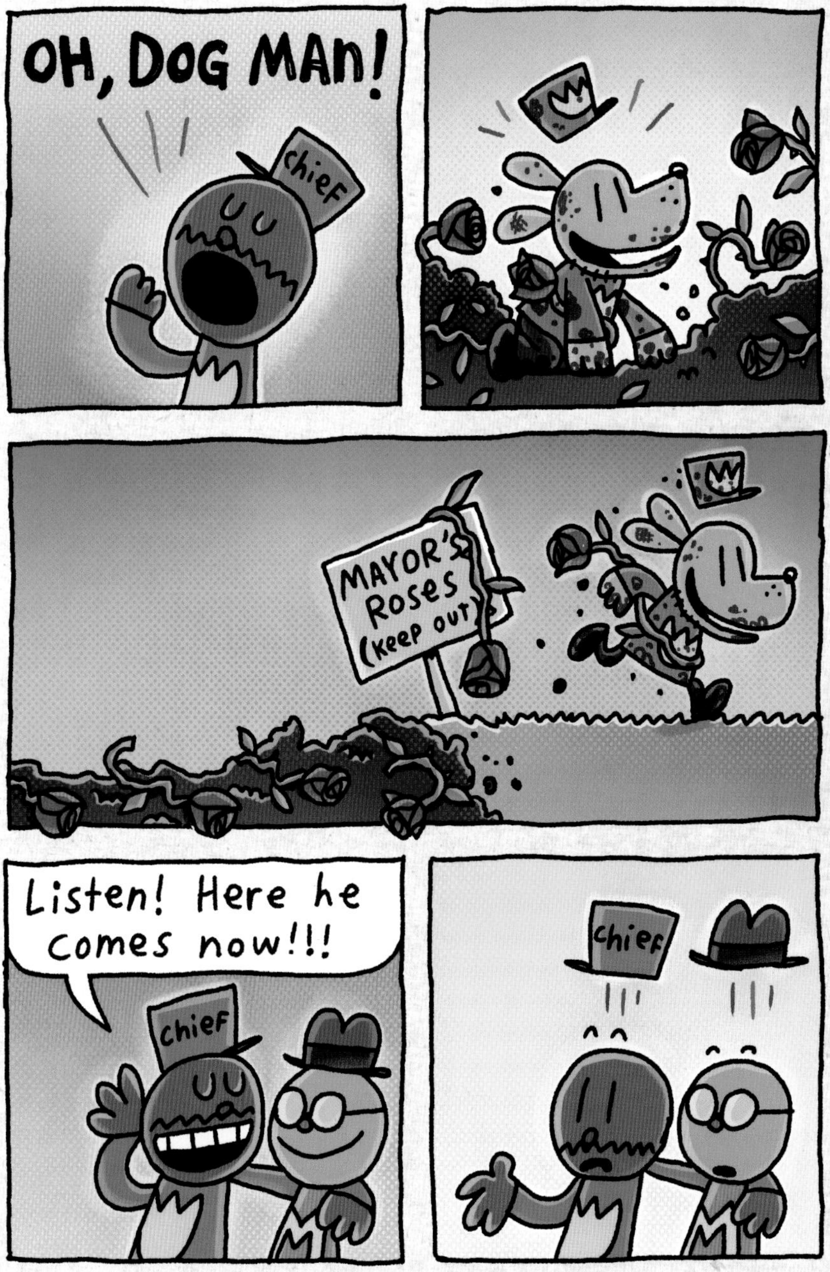
OH, DOG MAN!
chief
MAYOR'S Roses (Keep out)
Listen! Here he comes now!!!
chief
chief

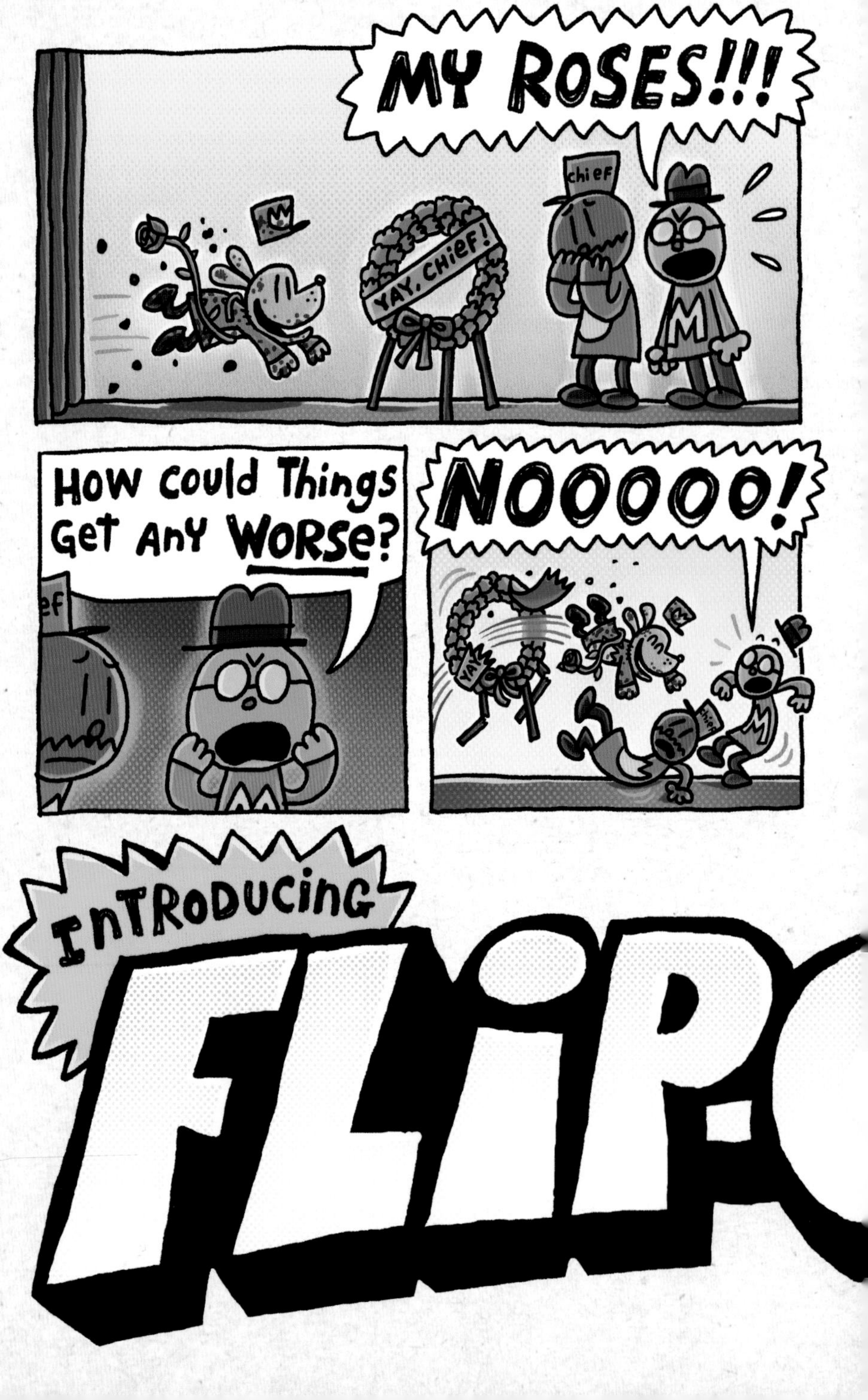

MY ROSES!!!
chief
YAY, CHIEF!
HOW Could Things Get Any WORSE?
NOOOOO!
YAY
chief
INTRODUCING
FLIP

STEP 1.
First, Place your Left hand inside the dotted Lines marked "Left hand here." Hold The book open FLAT!

STEP 2:
Grasp the right-hand Page with your Thumb and index finger (inside the dotted Lines marked "Right Thumb Here").

STEP 3:
Now QUICKLY FLIP the right-hand Page bACk and forth until the Picture appears to be Animated.

(for extra fun, try adding your own Sound-effects!)

O-RAMA

REMEMBER,

While you are flipping, be sure you can see the image on page **23** <u>**AND**</u> the image on page **25**.

If you flip quickly, the two pictures will start to look like **ONE** <u>**ANIMATED**</u> cartoon.

Don't forget to add your own sound-effects!!!

Left hand here.

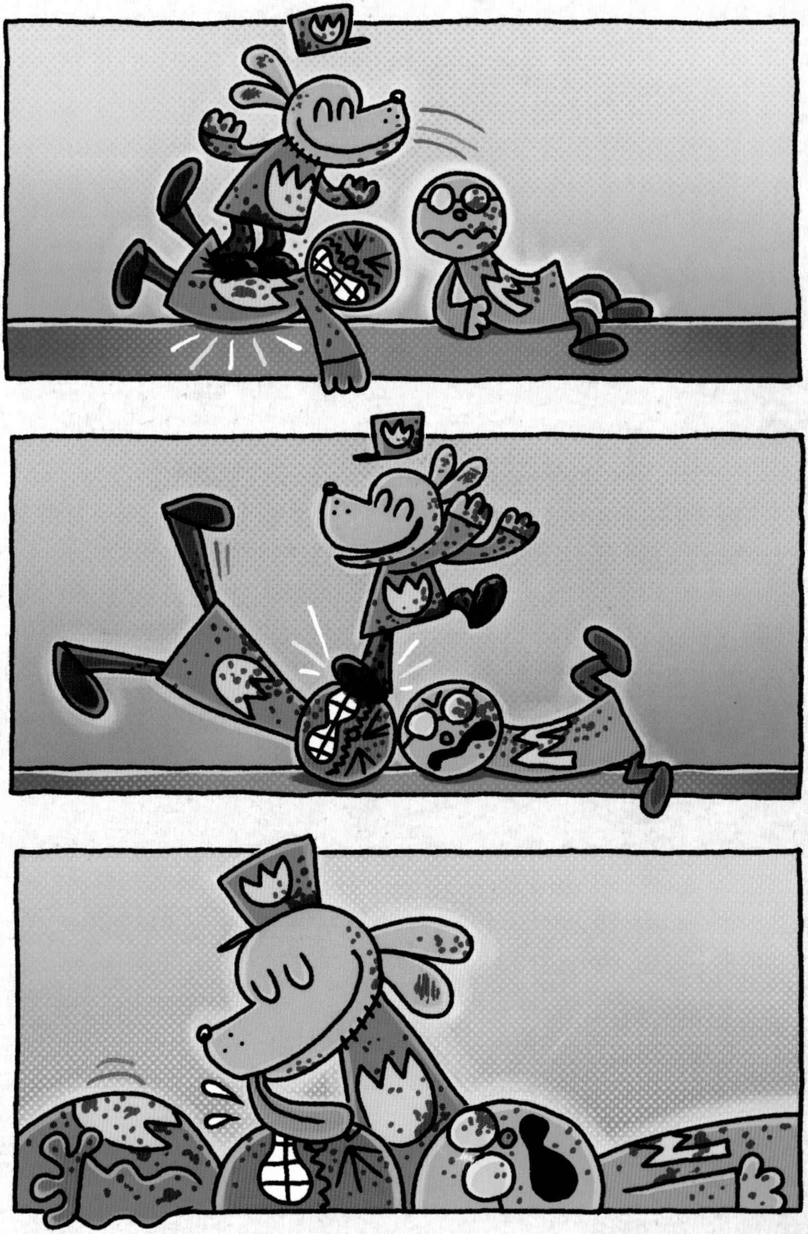

Right Thumb here.

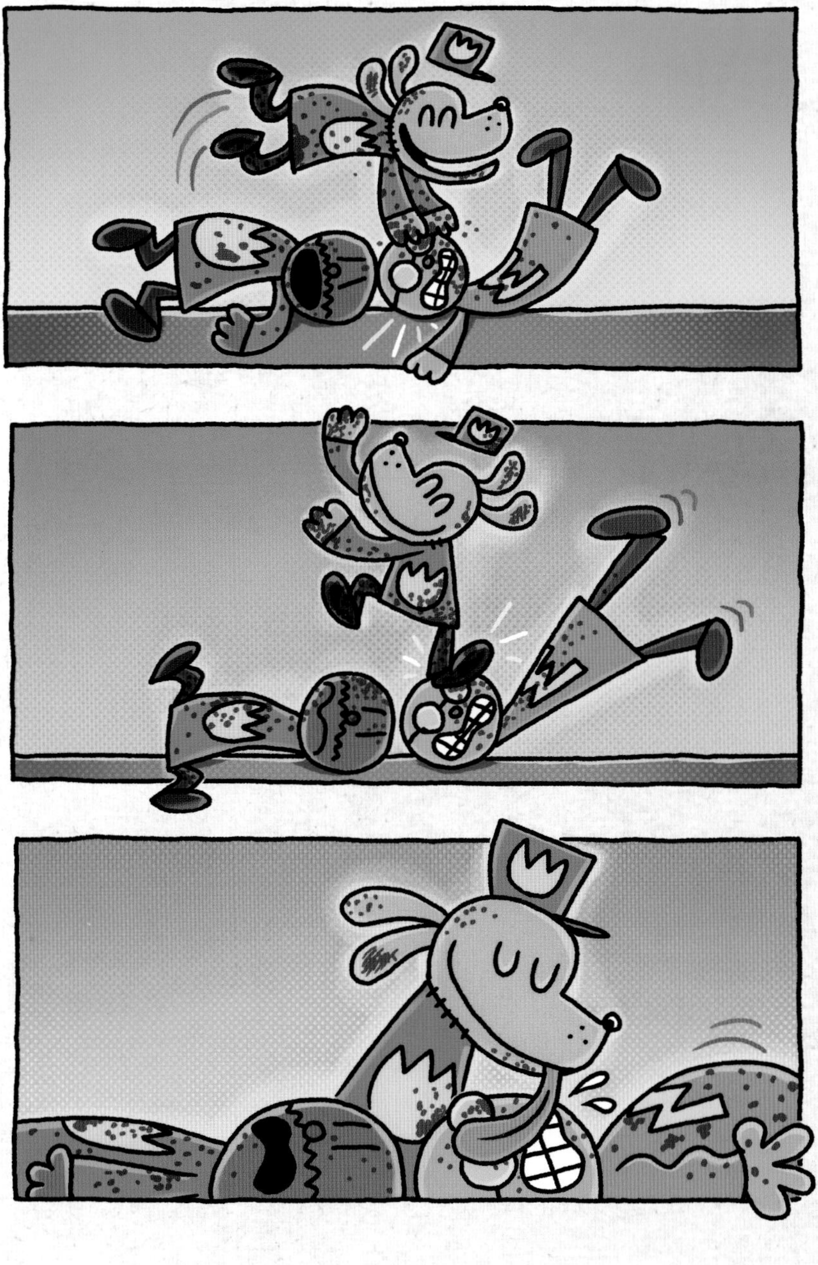

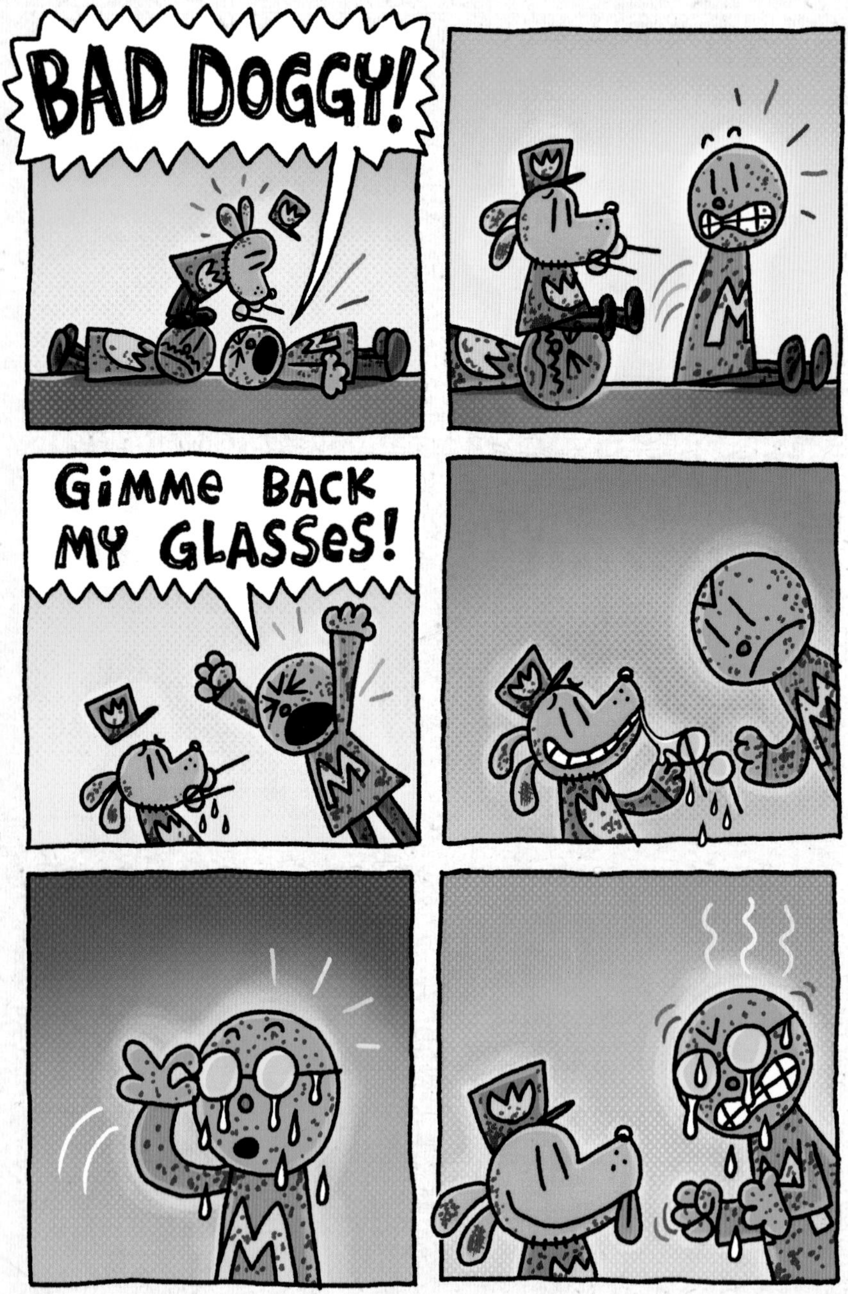
BAD DOGGY!
GiMME BACK MY GLASSES!

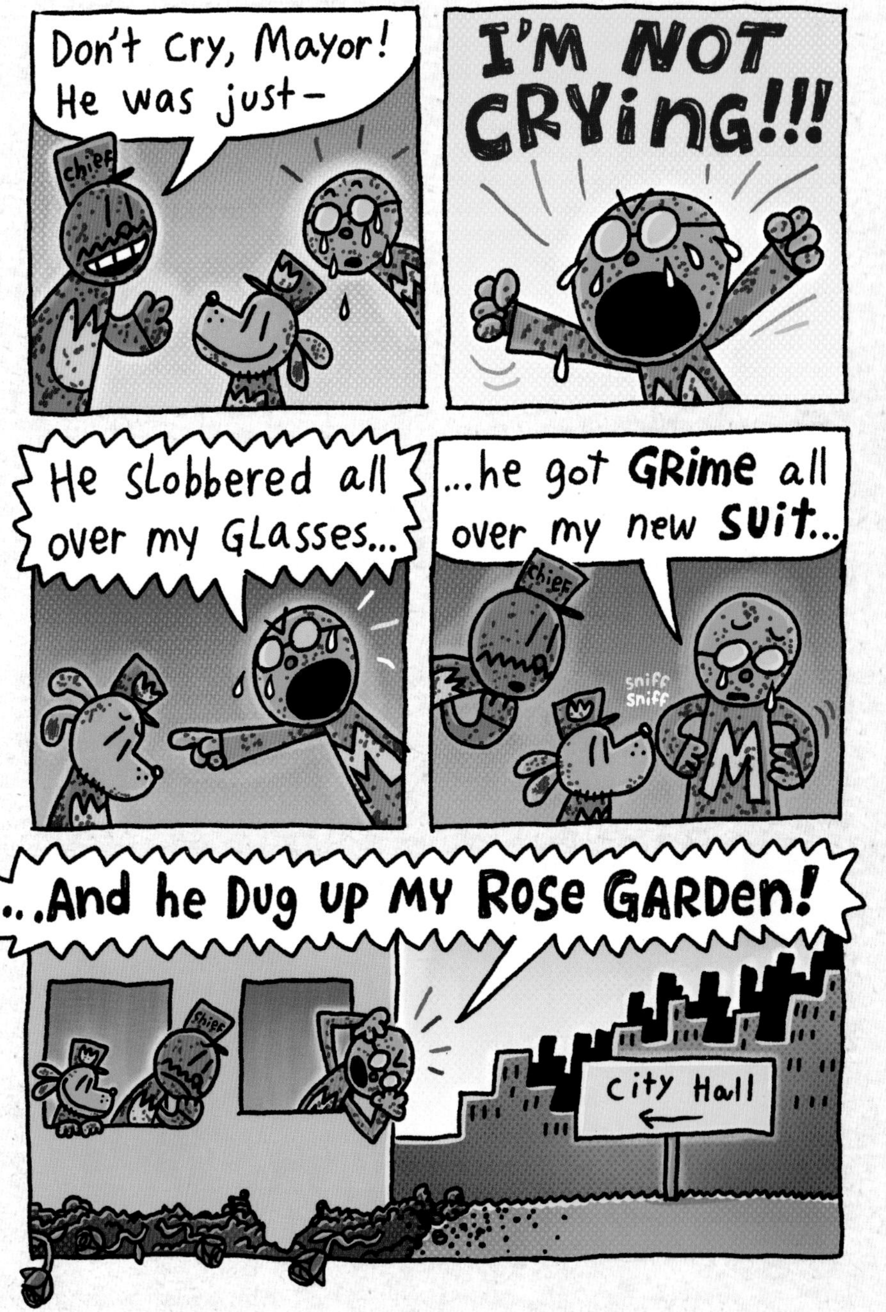
Don't cry, Mayor! He was just-
chief
I'M NOT CRYING!!!
He slobbered all over my Glasses...
...he got GRime all over my new SUIT...
chief
sniff sniff
M
...And he Dug up MY Rose GARDen!
chief
city Hall

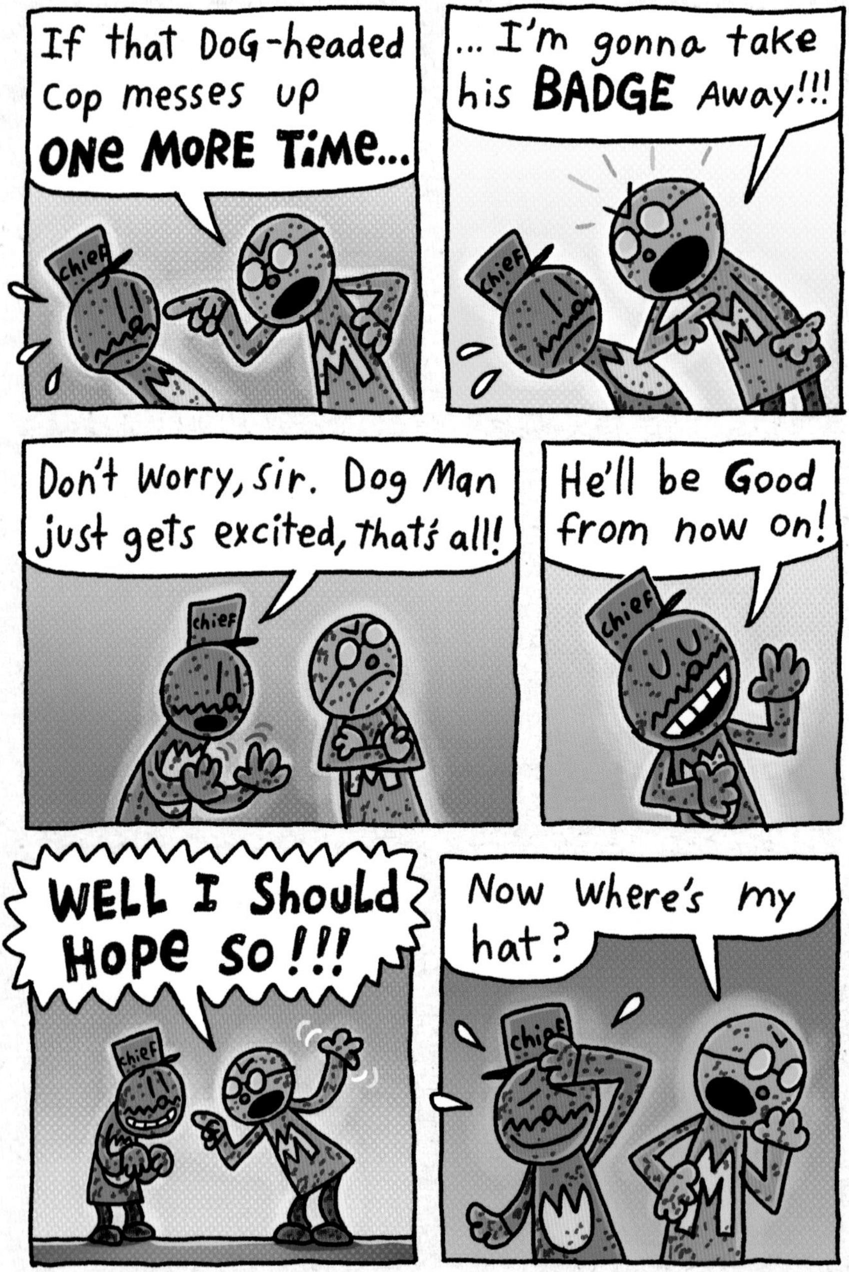
If that DOG-headed Cop messes up ONE MORE TIME...
... I'm gonna take his BADGE Away!!!
chief
Don't worry, sir. Dog Man just gets excited, that's all!
He'll be Good from now on!
WELL I Should HOPE SO!!!
Now Where's my hat?

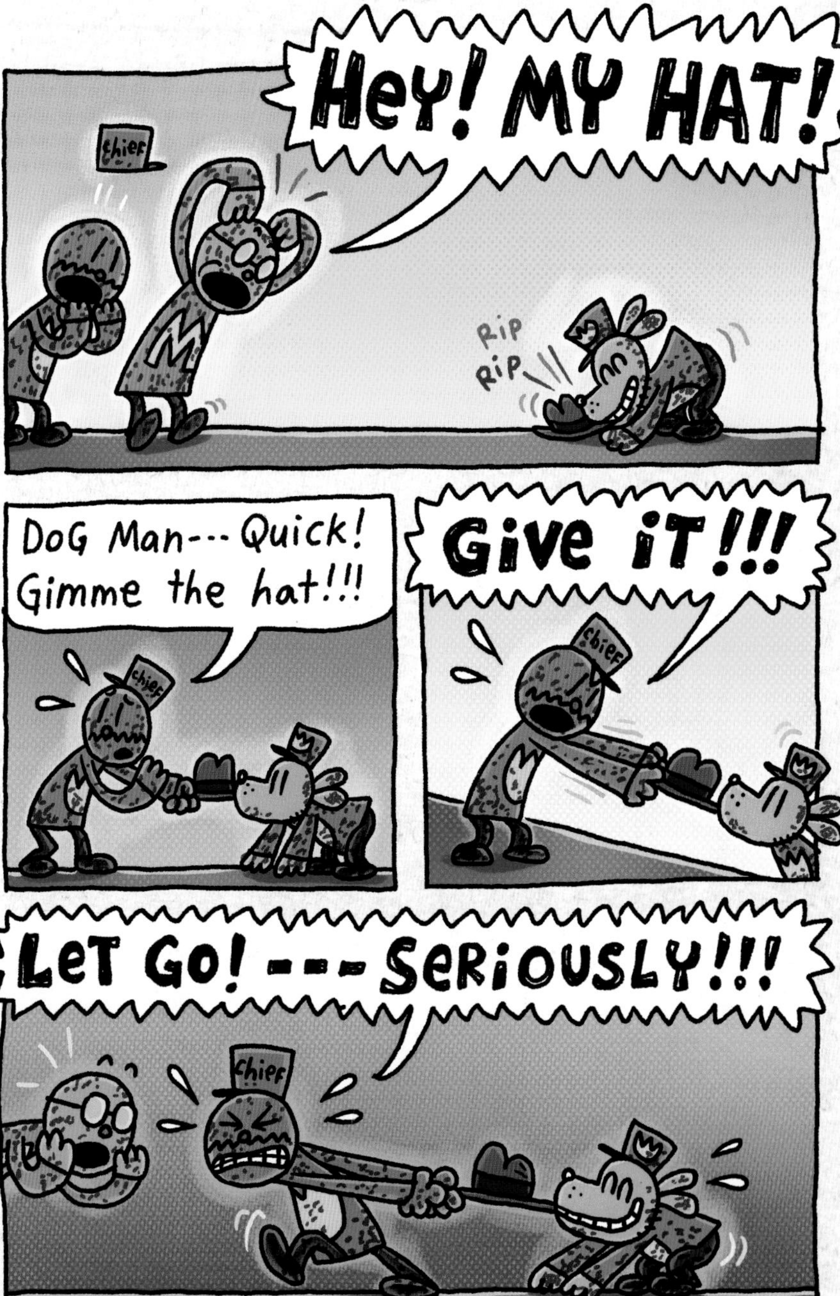
HEY! MY HAT!
Rip
Rip
Chief
DoG Man--- Quick! Gimme the hat!!!
Give iT!!!
LeT GO! ---SeRiOUSLY!!!

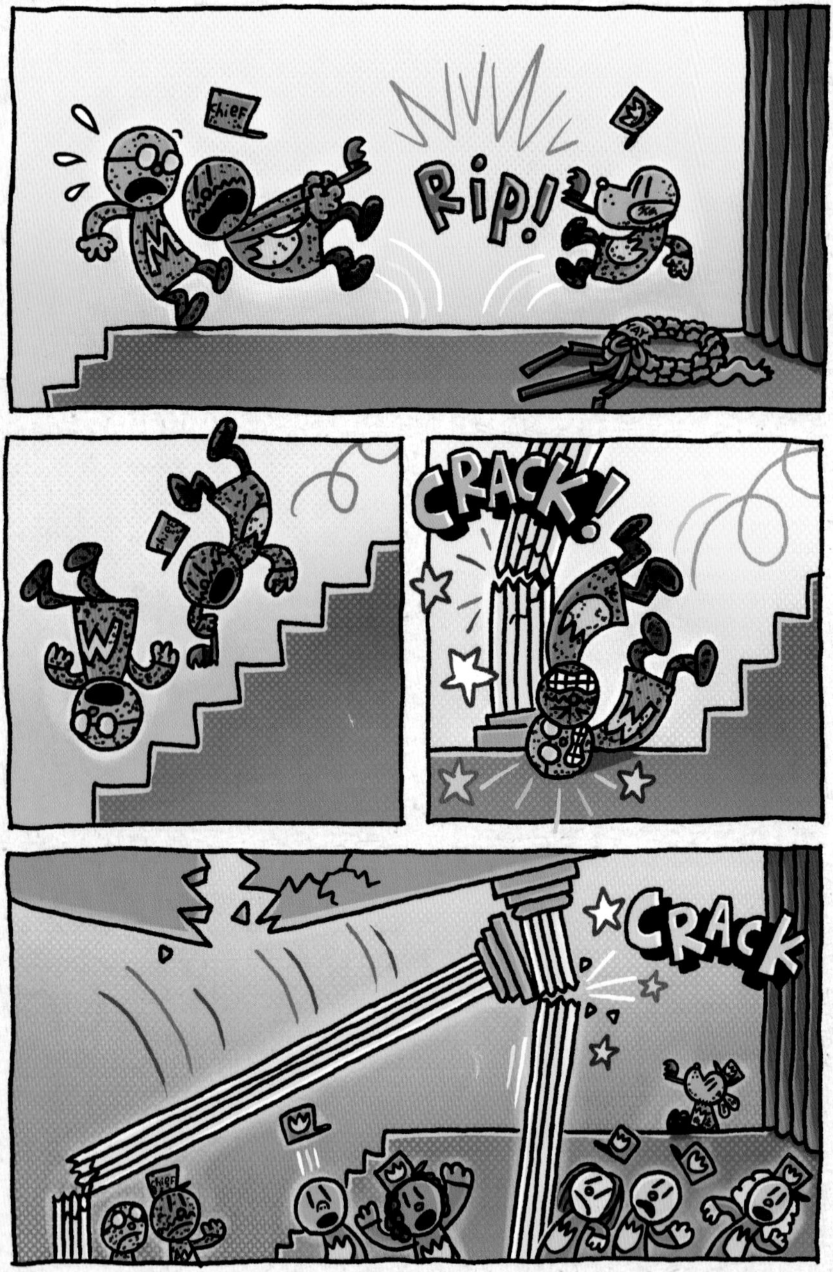
CHIEF
RIP!
CRACK!
CRACK

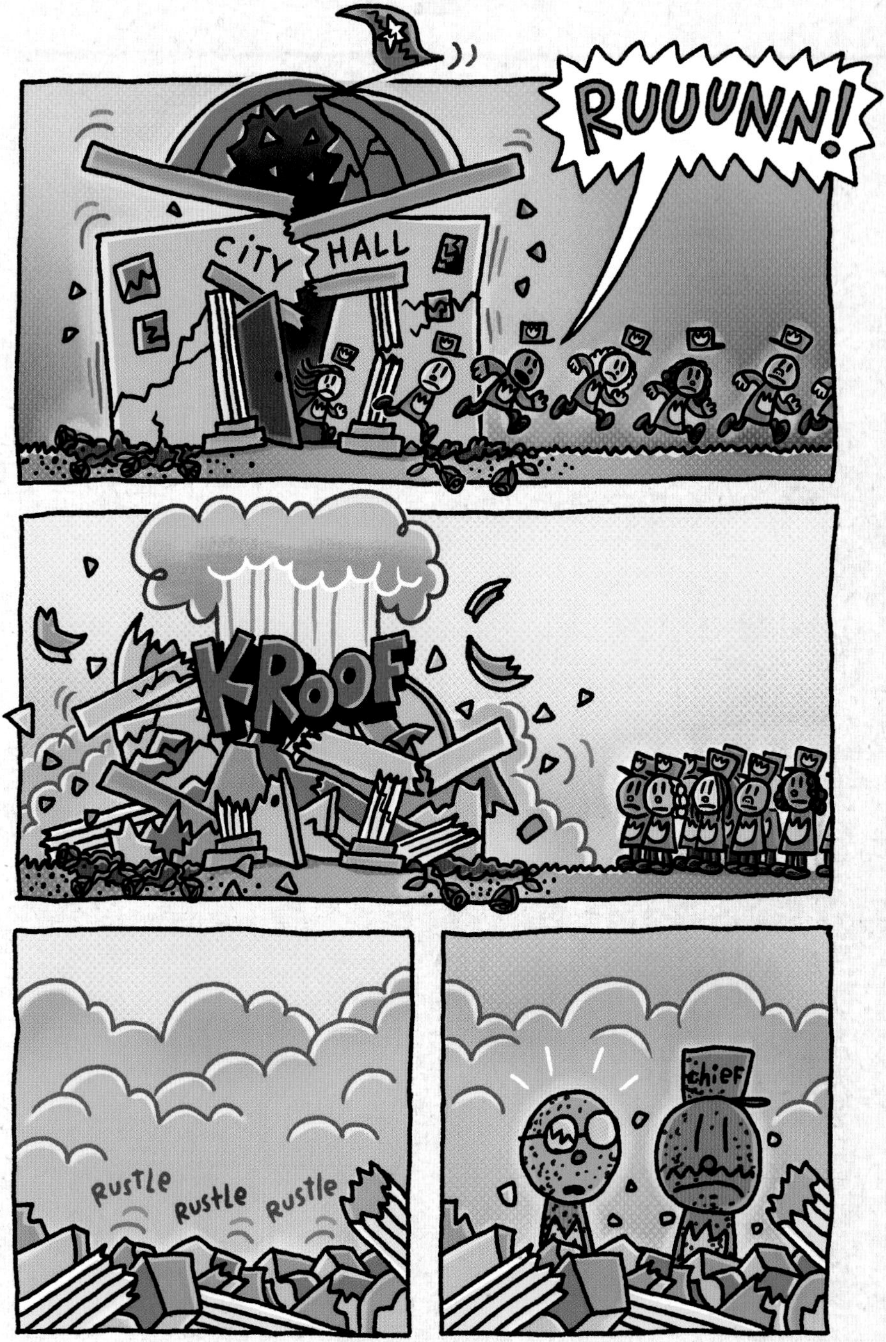
CITY HALL
RUUUNN!
KROOF
Rustle
Rustle
Rustle
chief

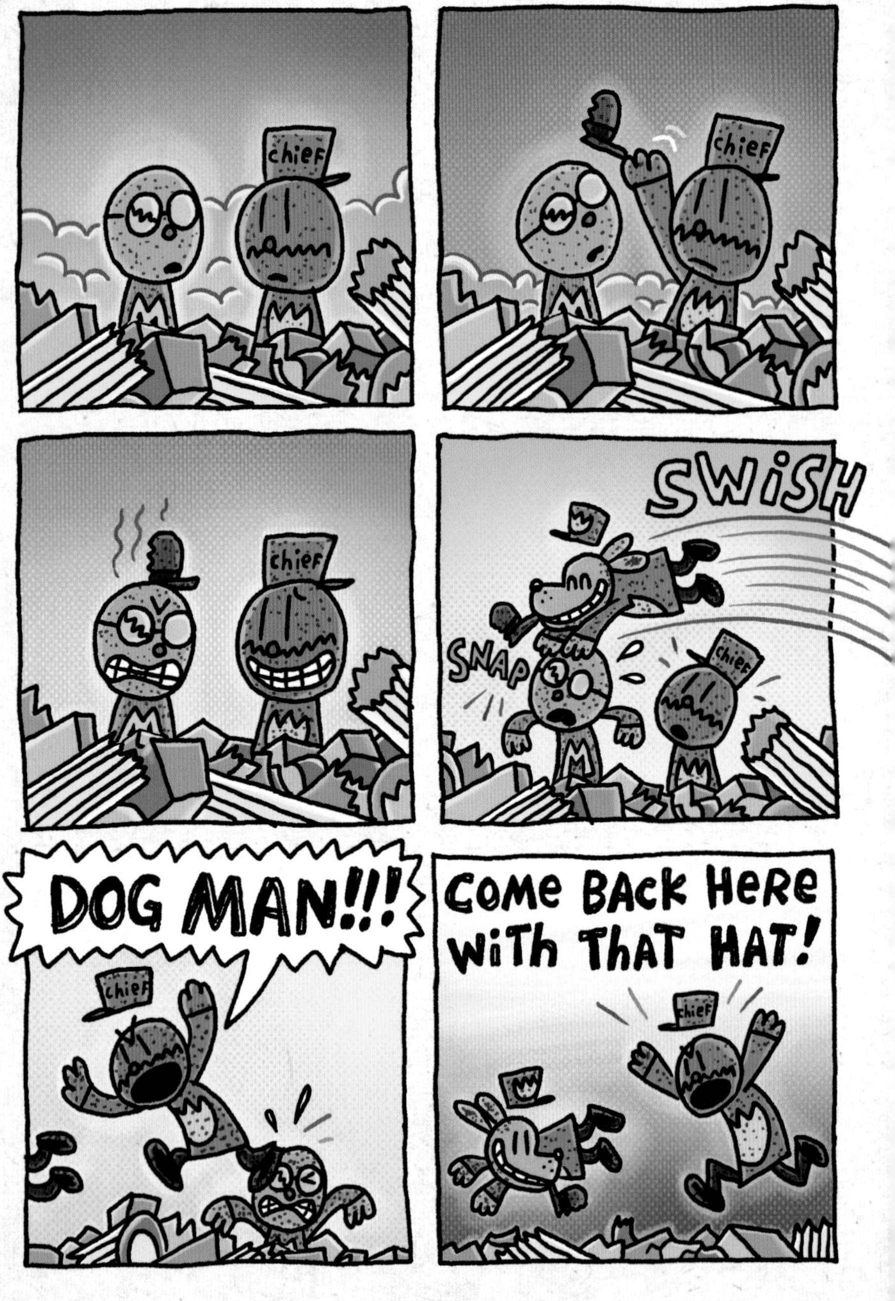
chief
chief
chief
SWISH
SNAP
chief
DOG MAN!!!
chief
COME BACK HERE WITH THAT HAT!
chief

CHAPTER 2

The Saddest CHAPTER Ever Written

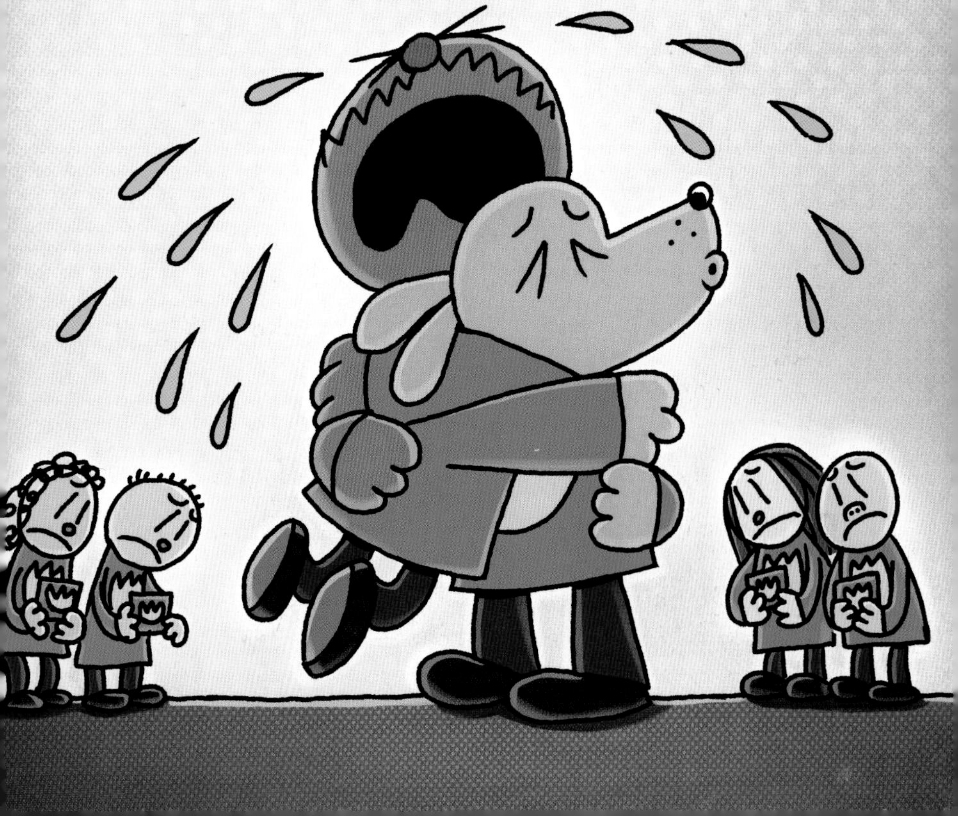

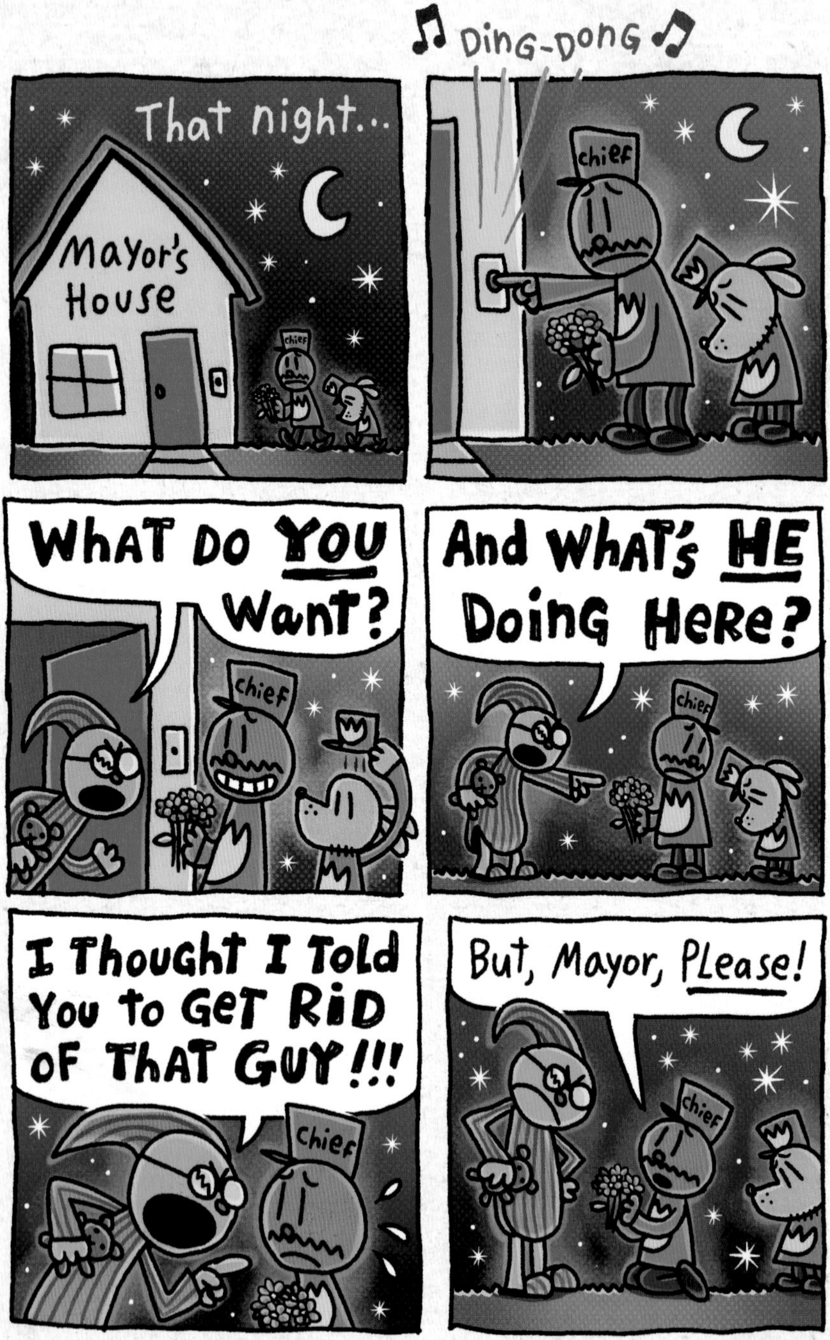
DING-DONG
That night...
Mayor's House
chief
chief
WHAT DO YOU Want?
chief
And WHAT's HE Doing Here?
chief
I Thought I Told You to GET RID OF THAT GUY!!!
chief
But, Mayor, PLease!
chief

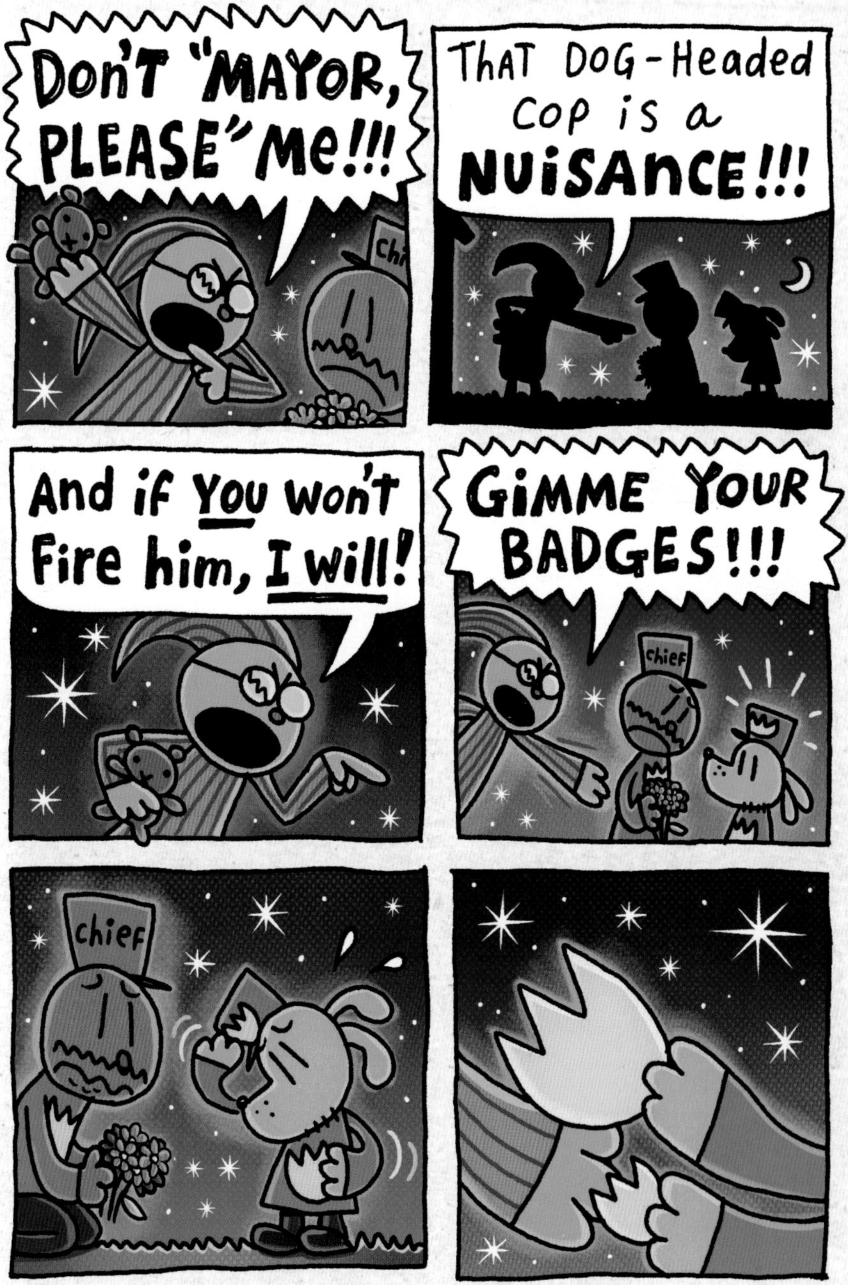
DON'T "MAYOR, PLEASE" ME!!!
THAT DOG-Headed Cop is a NUISANCE!!!
chief
And if YOU won't Fire him, I will!
GIMME YOUR BADGES!!!
chief
chief

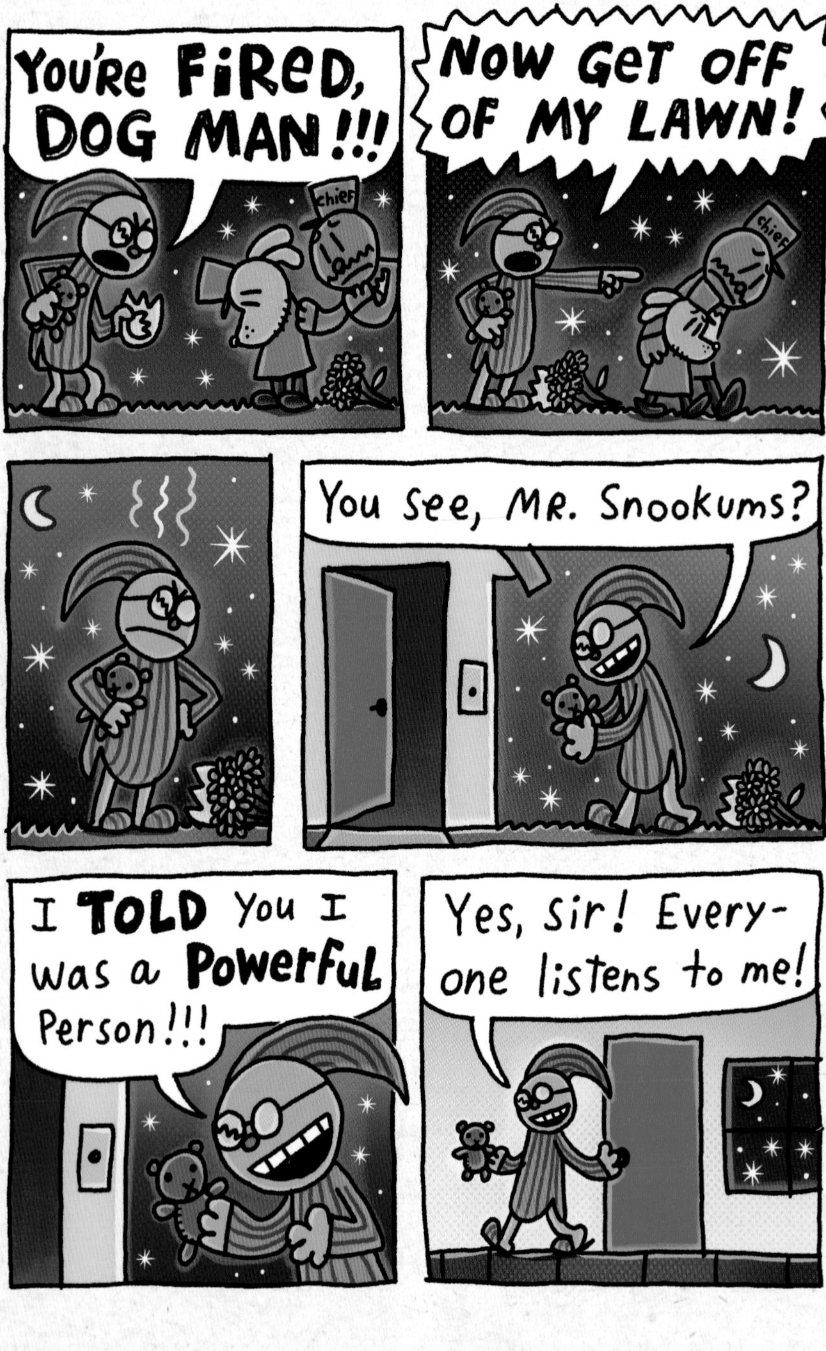
You're FIRED, DOG MAN!!!
chief
NOW GET OFF OF MY LAWN!
chief
You see, Mr. Snookums?
I TOLD you I was a POWERFUL Person!!!
Yes, Sir! Every-one listens to me!

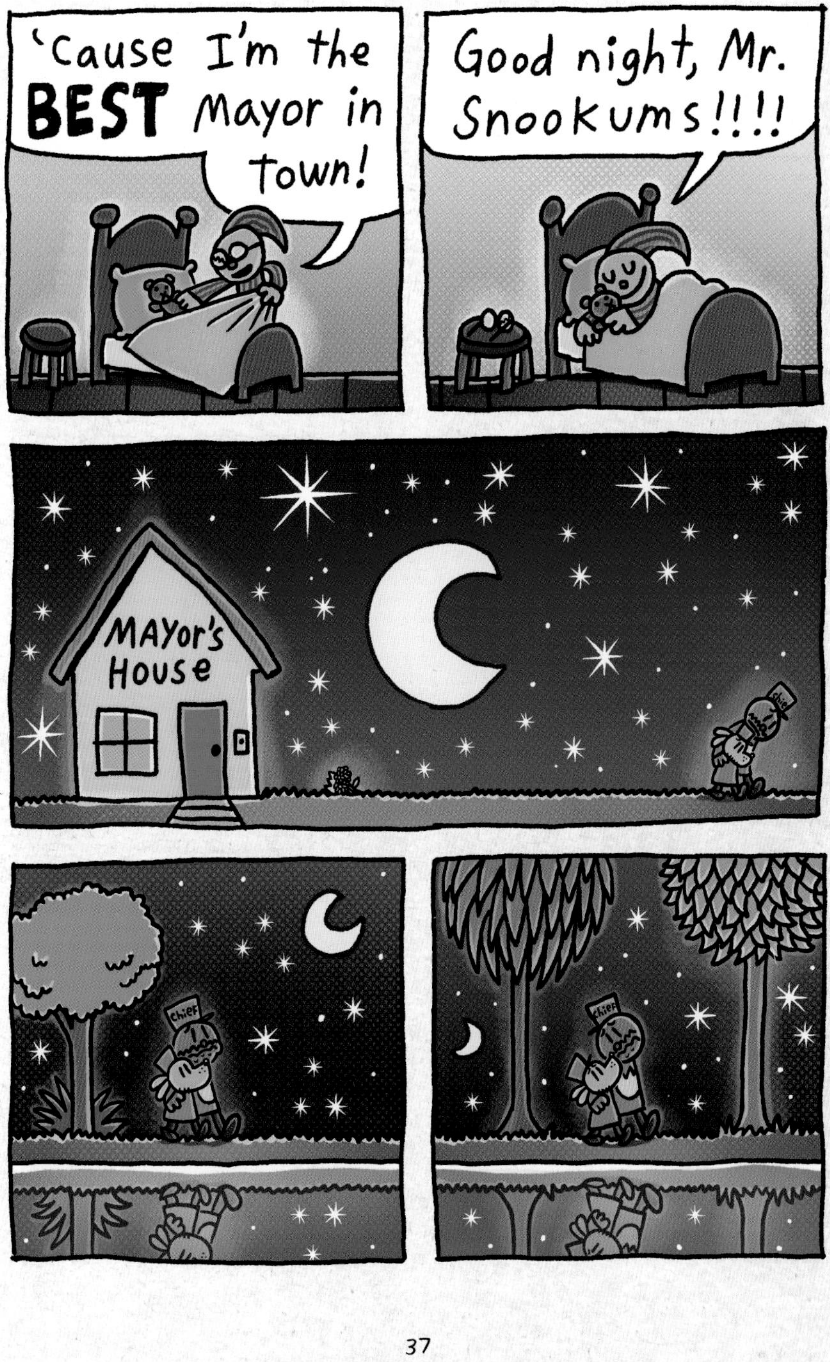
'Cause I'm the BEST Mayor in town!
Good night, Mr. Snookums!!!!
MAYor's House
chief

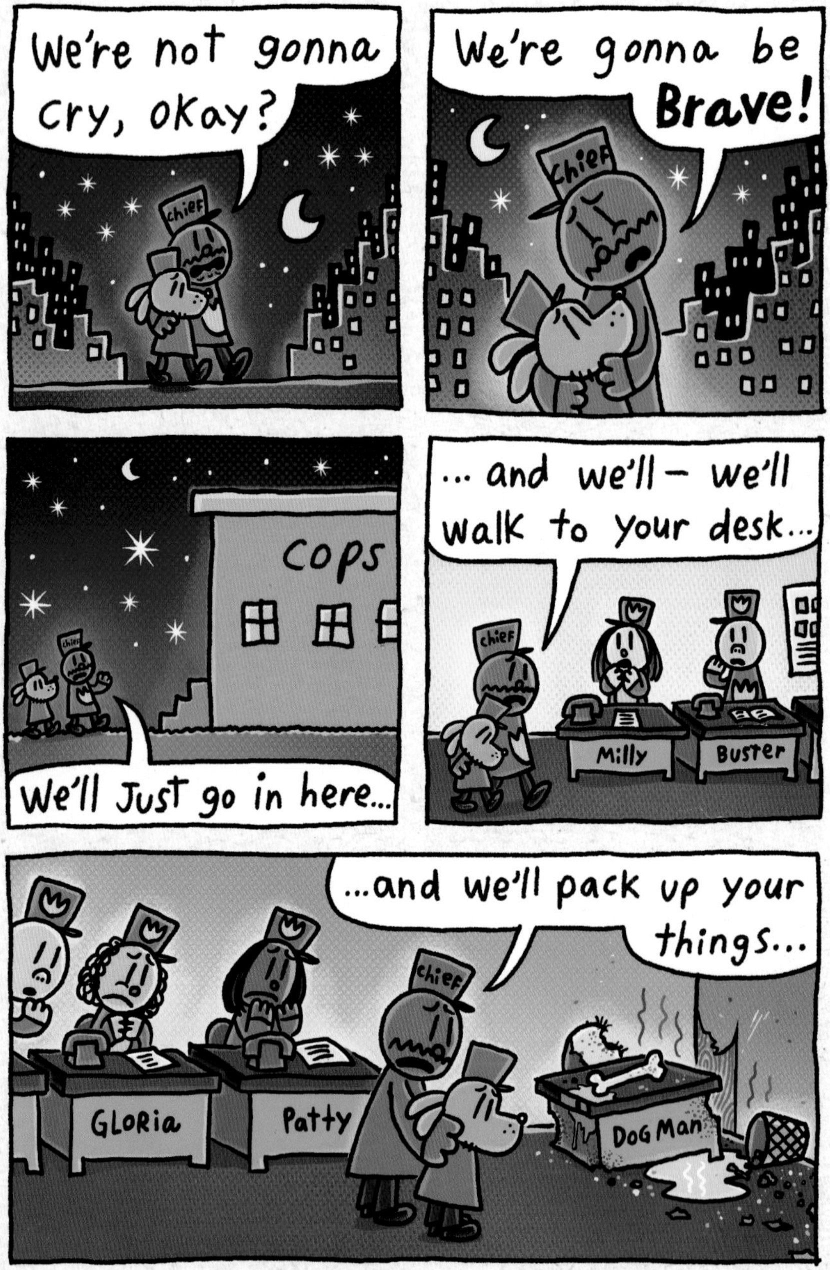
We're not gonna cry, okay?
We're gonna be Brave!
chief
COPS
We'll just go in here...
...and we'll— we'll walk to your desk...
Milly
Buster
...and we'll pack up your things...
GLORIA
Patty
DOG MAN

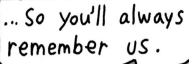
...So you'll always remember us.

Here's the bone that you like to chew.

Here's your squeaky toy telephone...

squeak squeak

...and here's the little ball you love to—

I'm not gonna cry. I'm not gonna—

I'm not gonna—

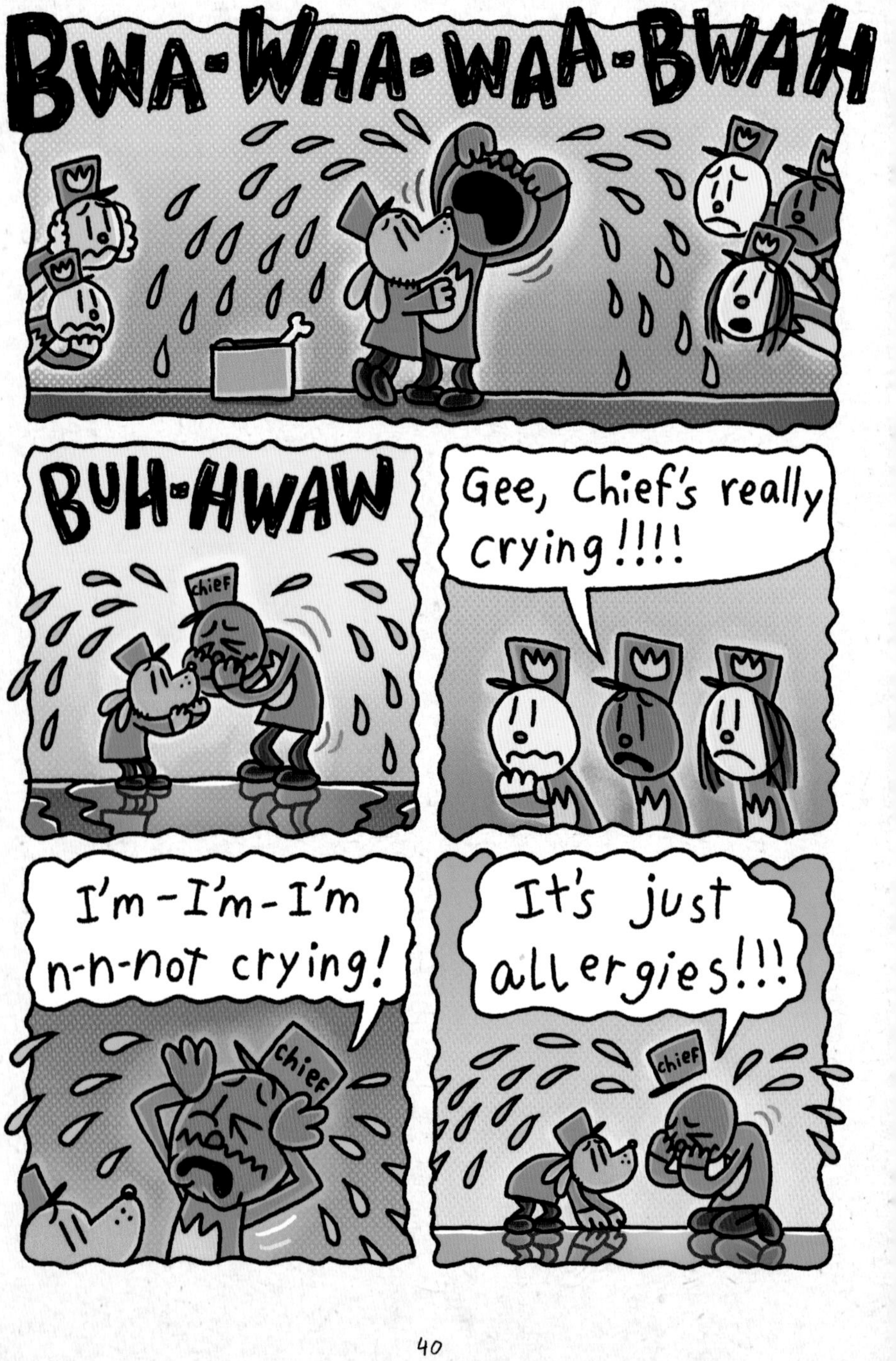
BWA-WHA-WAA-BWAH
BUH-HWAW
chief
Gee, Chief's really crying!!!!
I'm-I'm-I'm n-n-not crying!
chief
It's just allergies!!!
chief

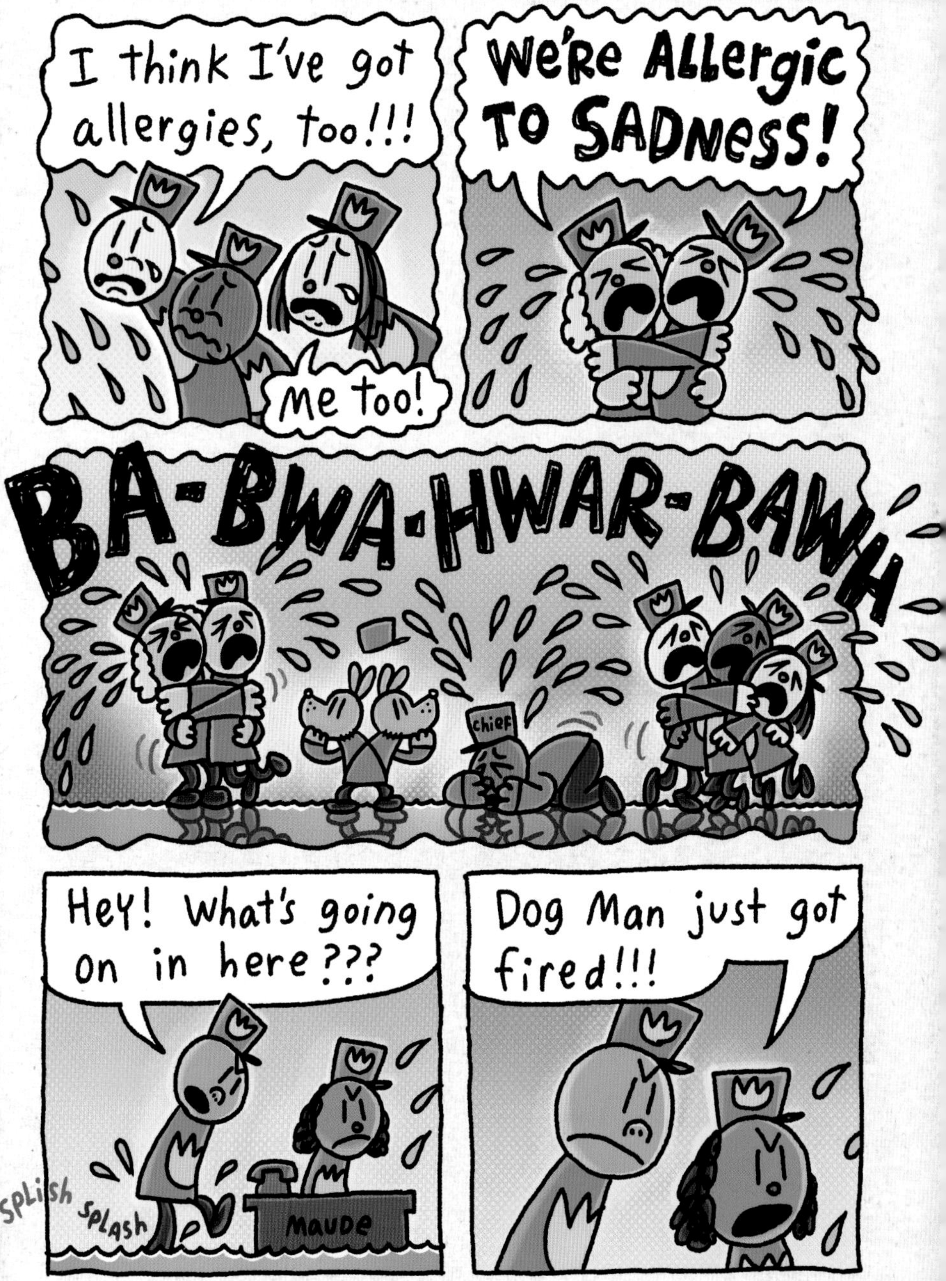
I think I've got allergies, too!!!
Me too!
We're Allergic TO SADNESS!
BA-BWA-HWAR-BAWH
CHIEF
Hey! What's going on in here???
SPLISH SPLASH
MAUDE
Dog Man just got fired!!!

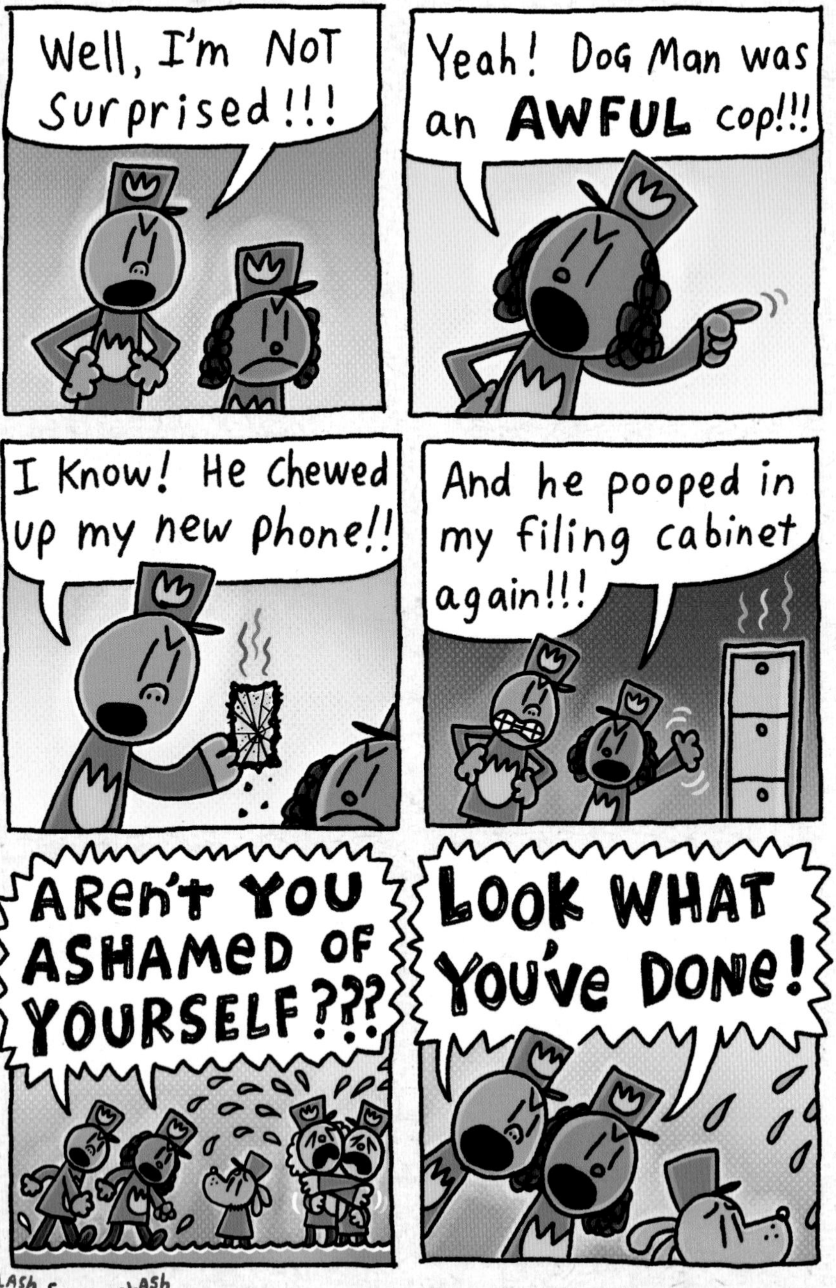
Well, I'm NOT Surprised!!!
Yeah! Dog Man was an AWFUL cop!!!
I Know! He chewed up my new phone!!
And he pooped in my filing cabinet again!!!
AREN'T YOU ASHAMED OF YOURSELF???
LOOK WHAT YOU'VE DONE!
Lish SPLASH SPLish SPLASH

YOU MADE Everyone CRY!

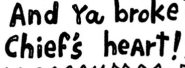

And Ya broke Chief's heart!

Get out of here, DOG MAN!

AND DON'T COME BACK!

SPLish SPLASH SPLish

COPS

SPLASH!

OW-WOOOO

OW-OW-OWOOOOOOOOOOOOOOOOOOOOOOO

OW-OWOOOO! OW-OW-OW-OWOOOOOOOOOOOOOOOOOOOO

CHAPTER 3

The Chapter That's Totally Not as Sad as The Last one

Meanwhile...

It's okay, 80-HD...

...You can make the tree red.

It's _our_ story. We can color it any way we want!

We Ruined Dog Man the house.

Hey, Look! Dog Man is home from—

What's wrong, Dog Man?

FLIP FLOP FLIP FLOP FLIP F

46

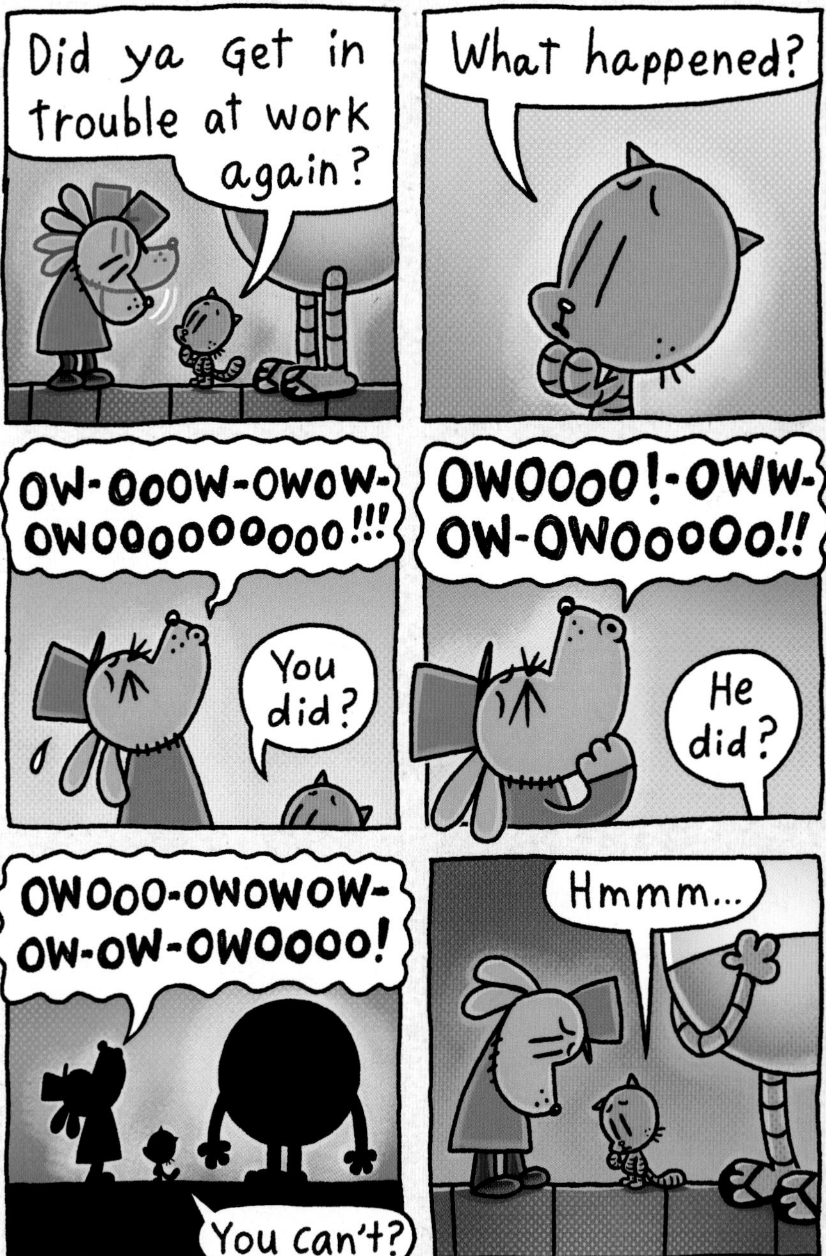
Did ya Get in trouble at work again?
What happened?
OW-OOOW-OWOW-OWOOOOOOOOO!!!
You did?
OWOOOO!-OWW-OW-OWOOOOO!!
He did?
OWOOO-OWOWOW-OW-OW-OWOOOO!
You can't?
Hmmm...

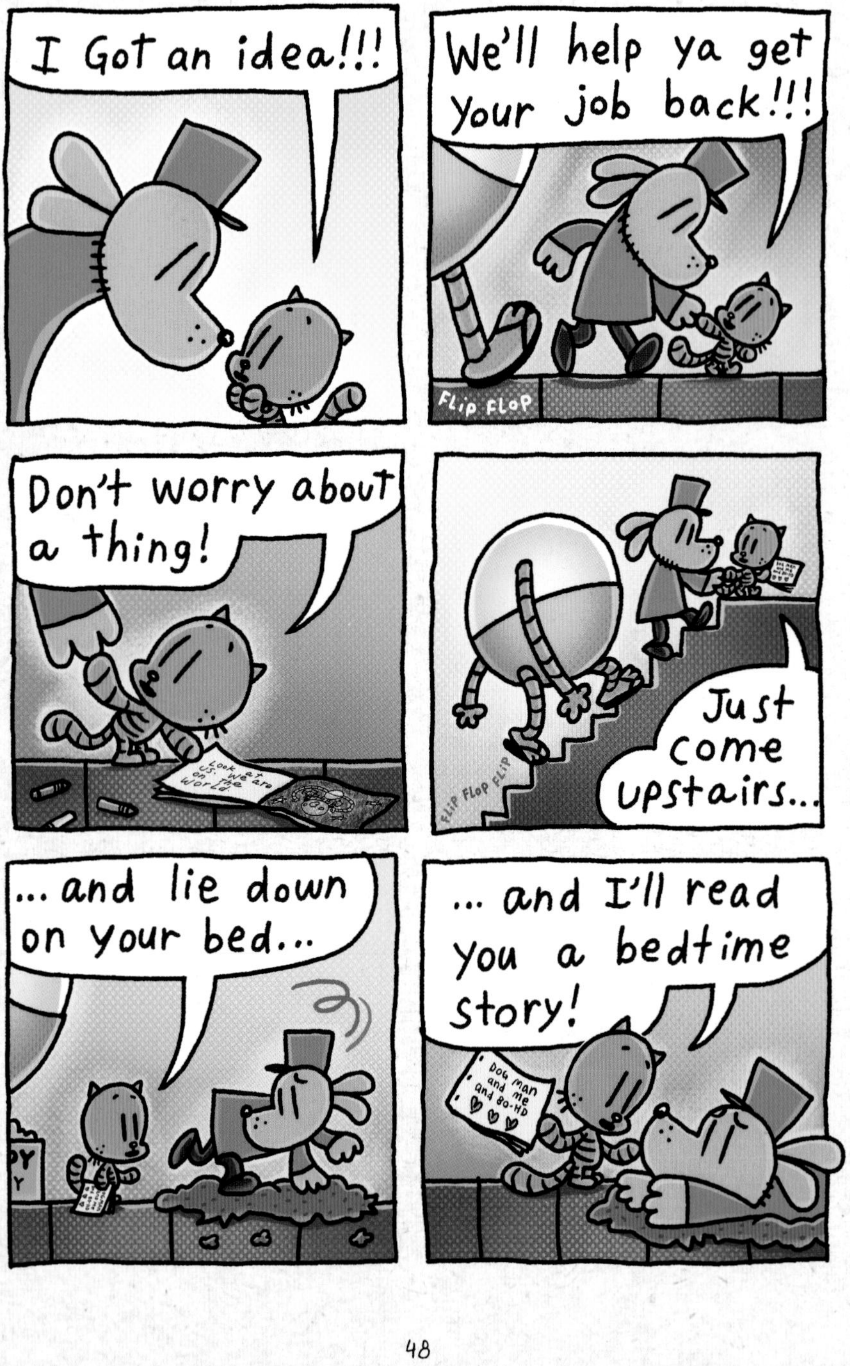
I Got an idea!!!
We'll help ya get your job back!!!
FLIP FLOP
Don't worry about a thing!
Look at US. We are on the World
Just come upstairs...
FLIP FLOP FLIP
...and lie down on your bed...
... and I'll read you a bedtime story!
Dog man and me and 80-HD

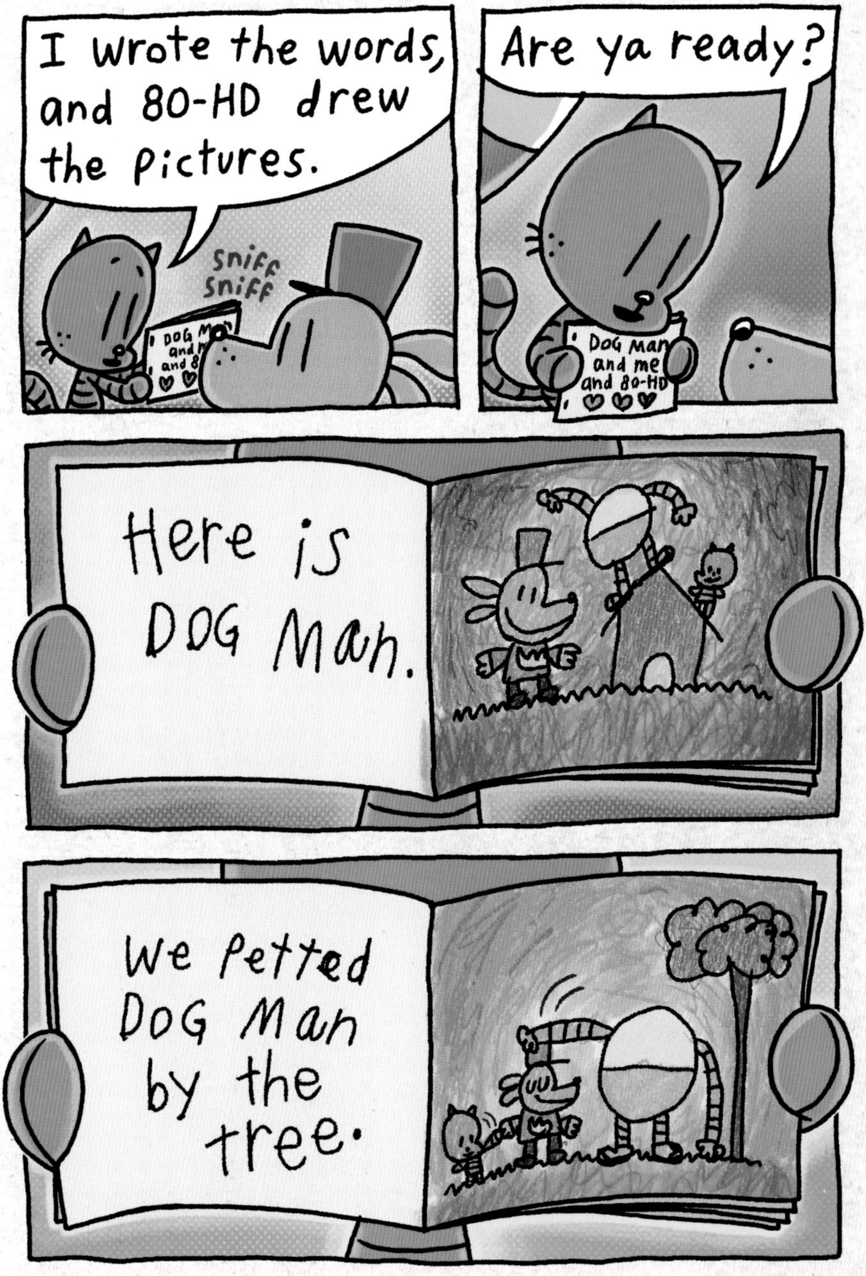
I wrote the words, and 80-HD drew the pictures.
Sniff Sniff
Are ya ready?
DOG Man and me and 80-HD
Here is DOG Man.
We Petted DOG Man by the tree.

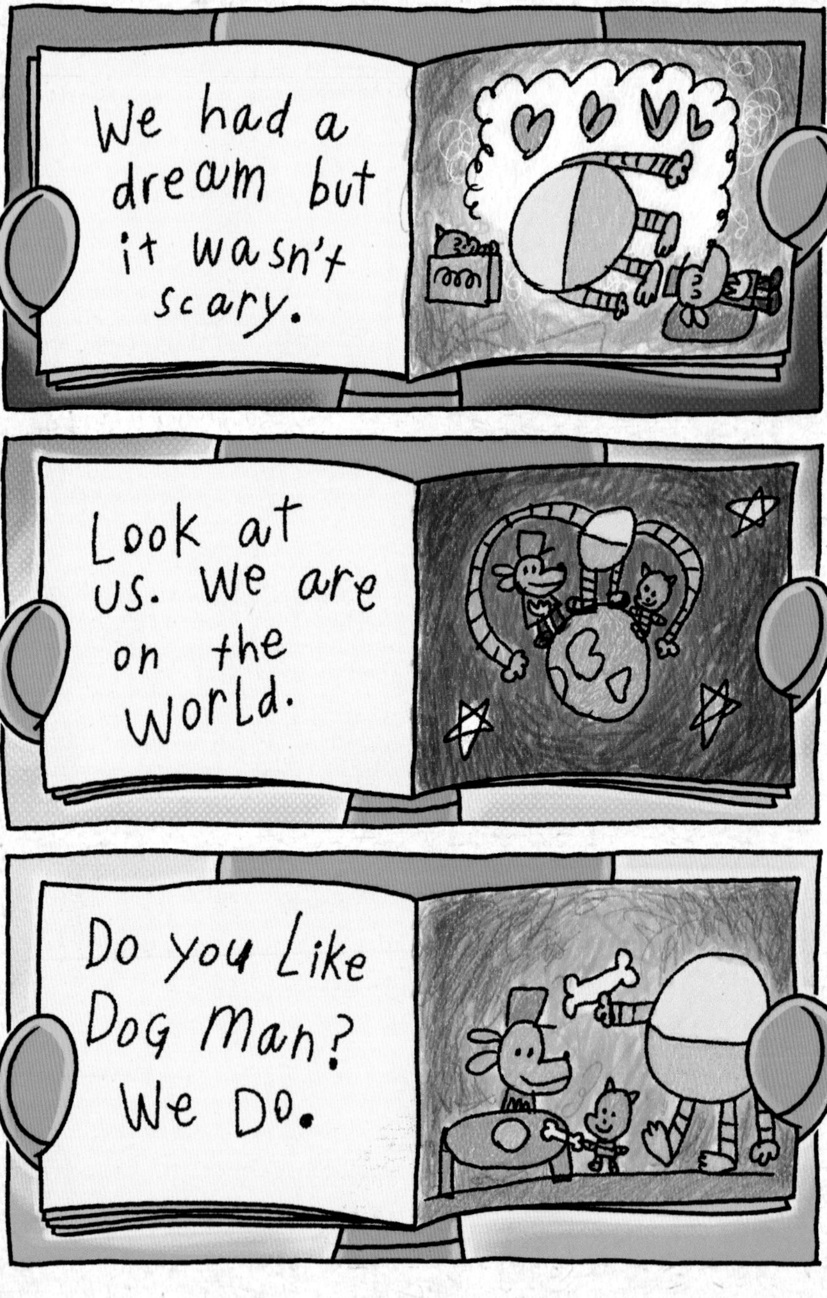
We had a dream but it wasn't scary.
Look at us. We are on the World.
Do you Like Dog Man? We Do.

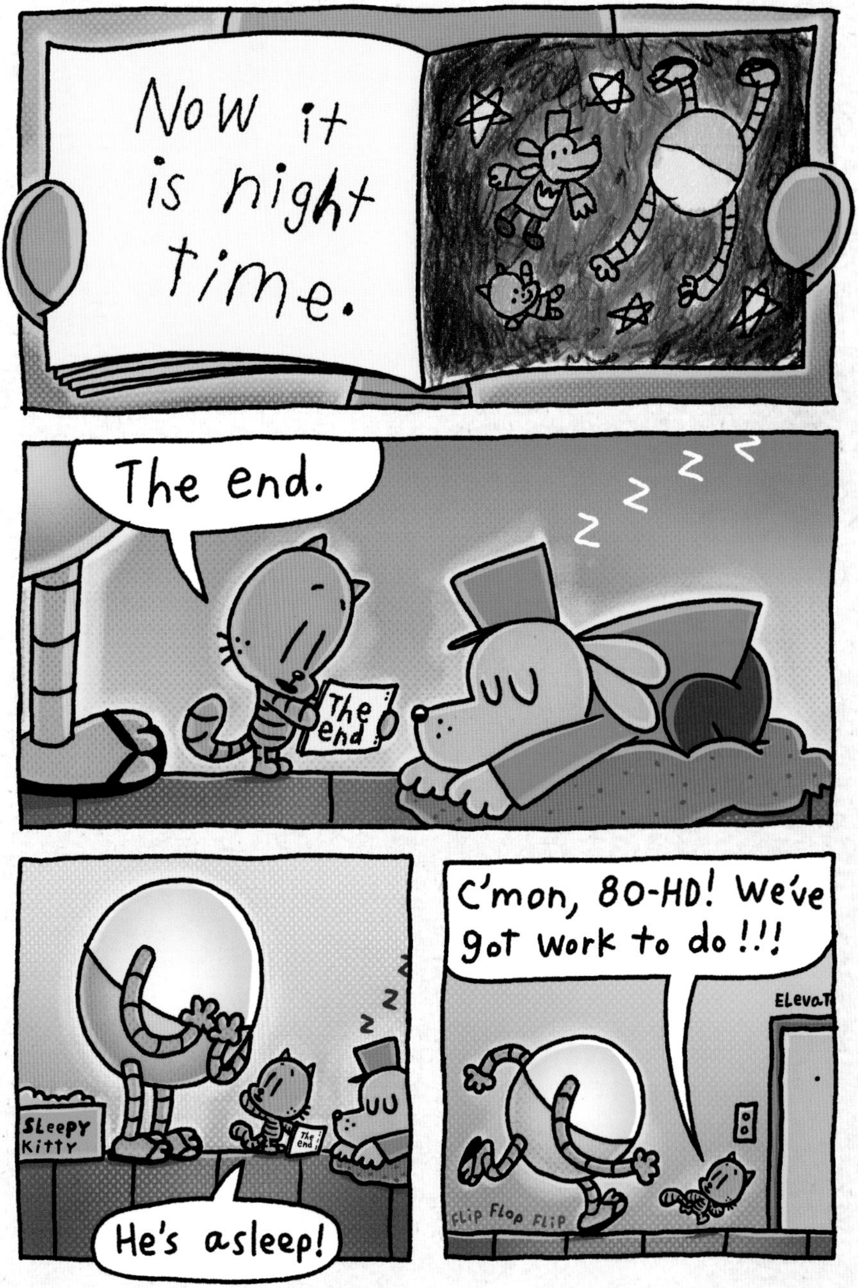
Now it is night time.
The end.
The end
Z Z Z Z
SLEEPY KITTY
The end
Z Z Z
He's asleep!
C'mon, 80-HD! We've got work to do!!!
FLIP FLOP FLIP

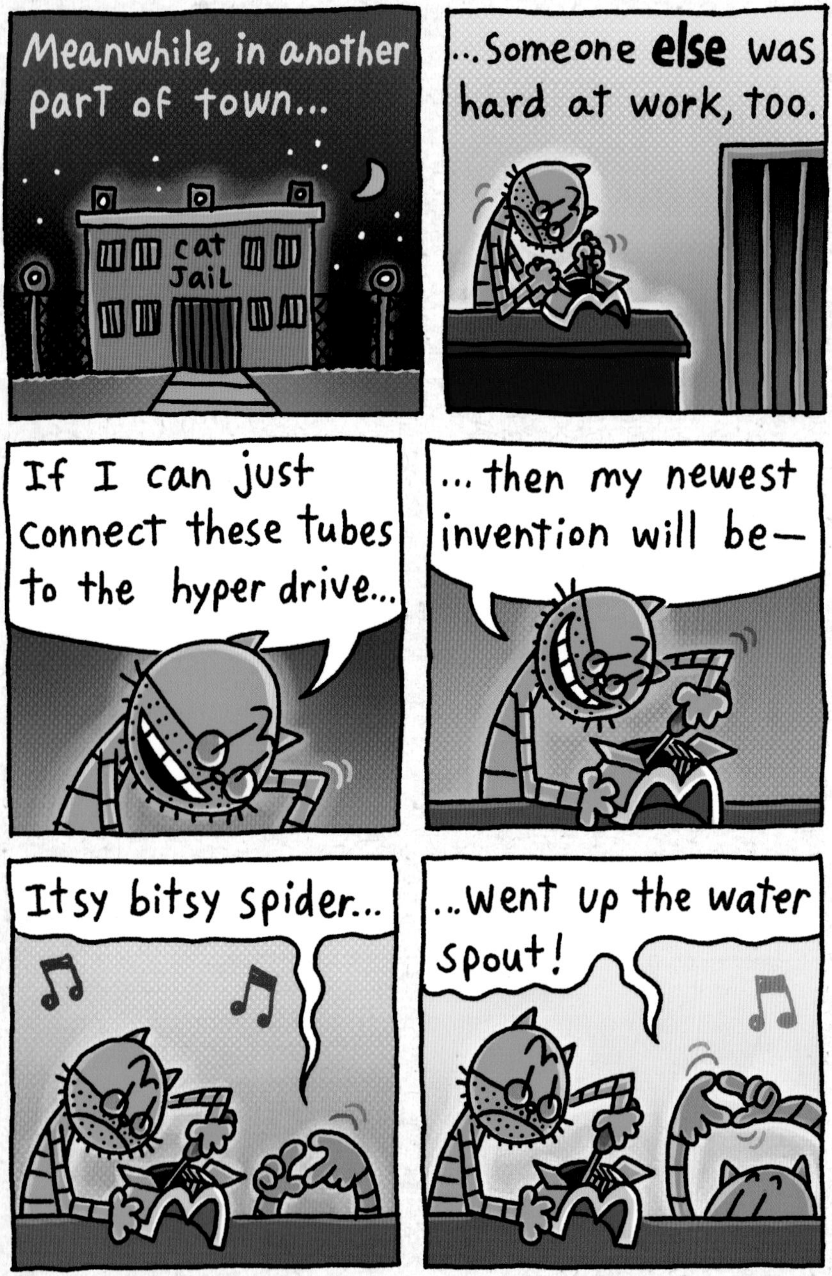
Meanwhile, in another part of town...
CAT JAIL
...Someone else was hard at work, too.
If I can just connect these tubes to the hyper drive...
...then my newest invention will be—
Itsy bitsy spider...
...went up the water spout!

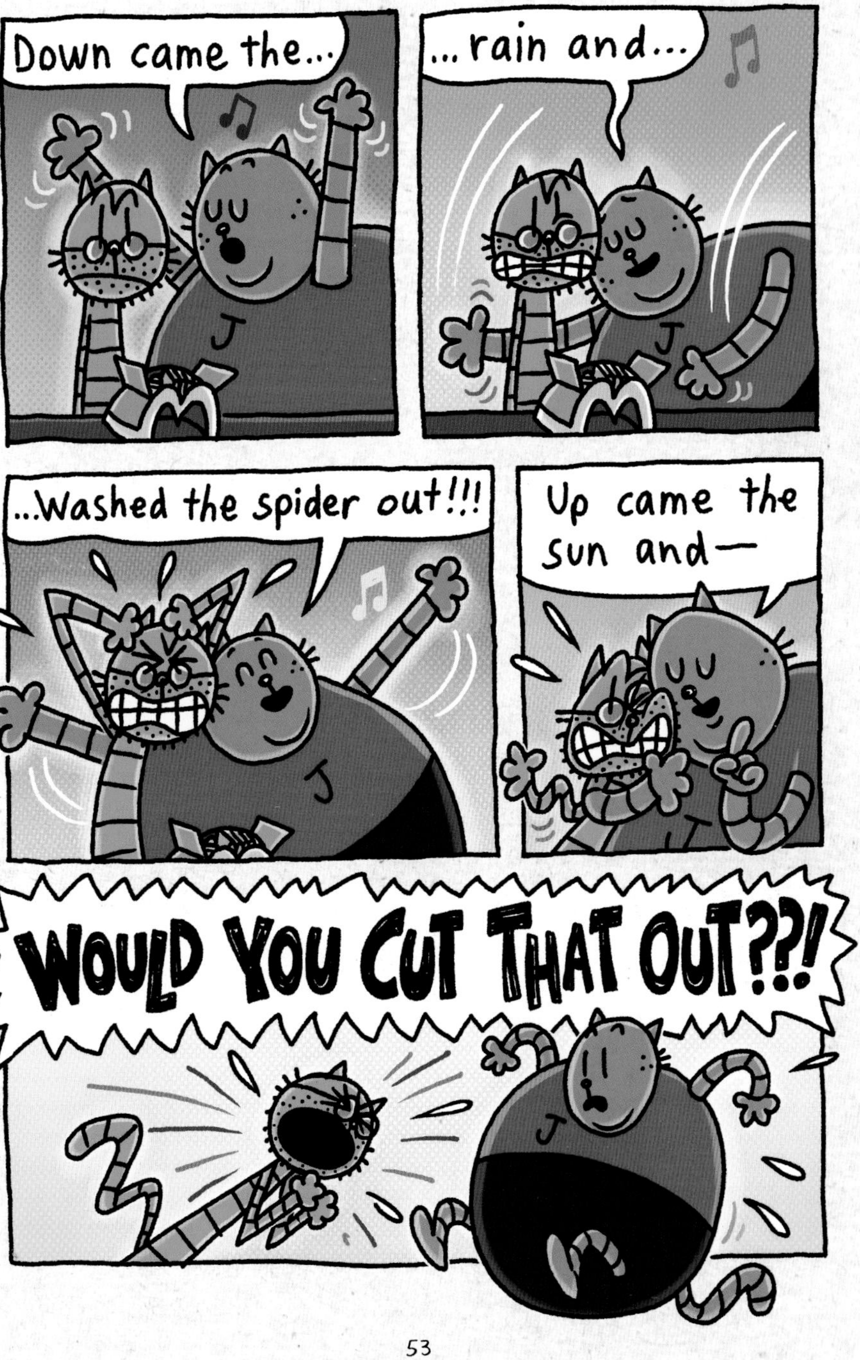
Down came the...
...rain and...
...Washed the spider out!!!
Up came the sun and—
WOULD YOU CUT THAT OUT??!

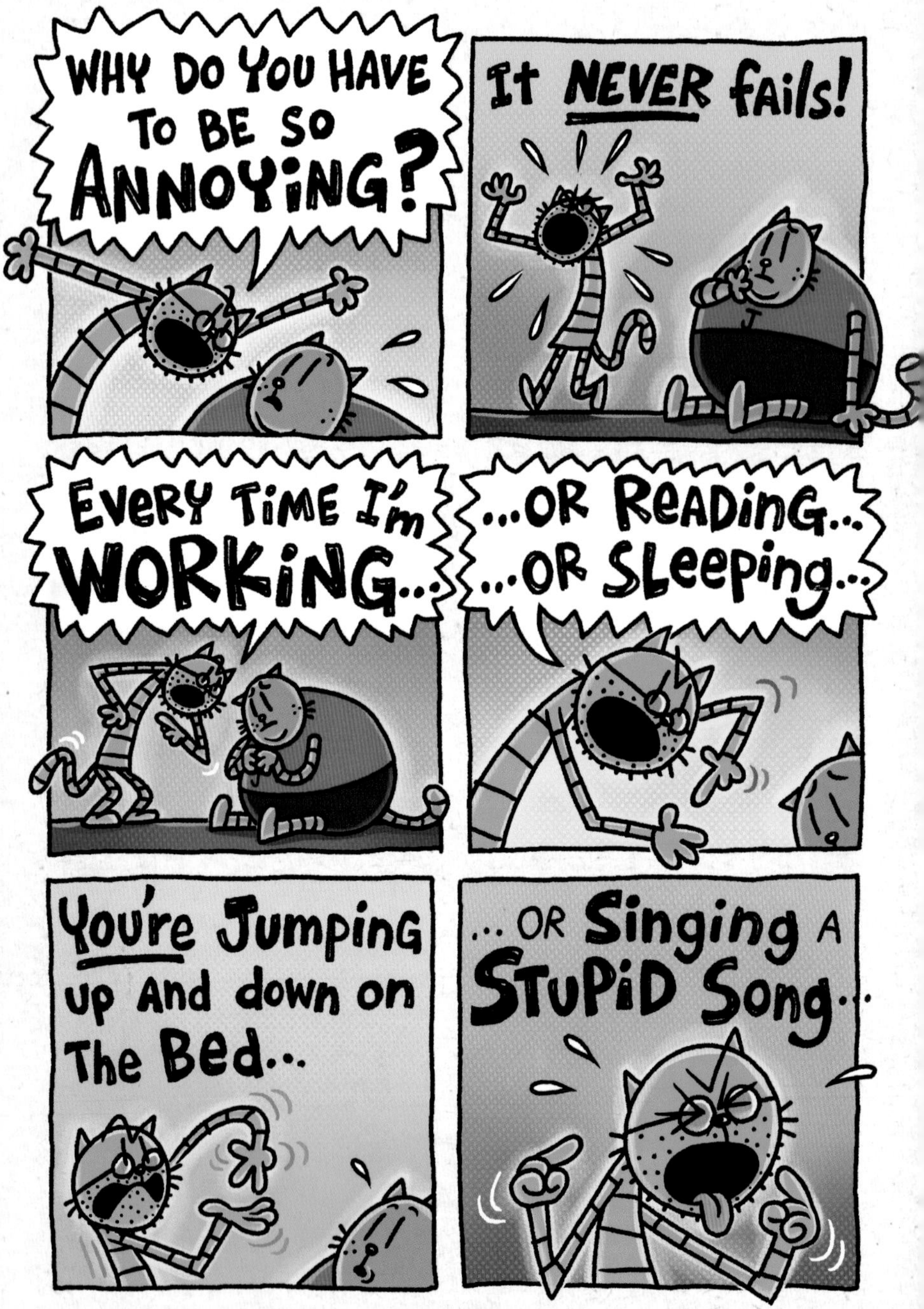
WHY DO YOU HAVE TO BE SO ANNOYING?
It NEVER fails!
EVERY TIME I'm WORKING...
...OR READING... ...OR SLEEPING...
You're Jumping up And down on The Bed...
... OR Singing A STUPID Song...

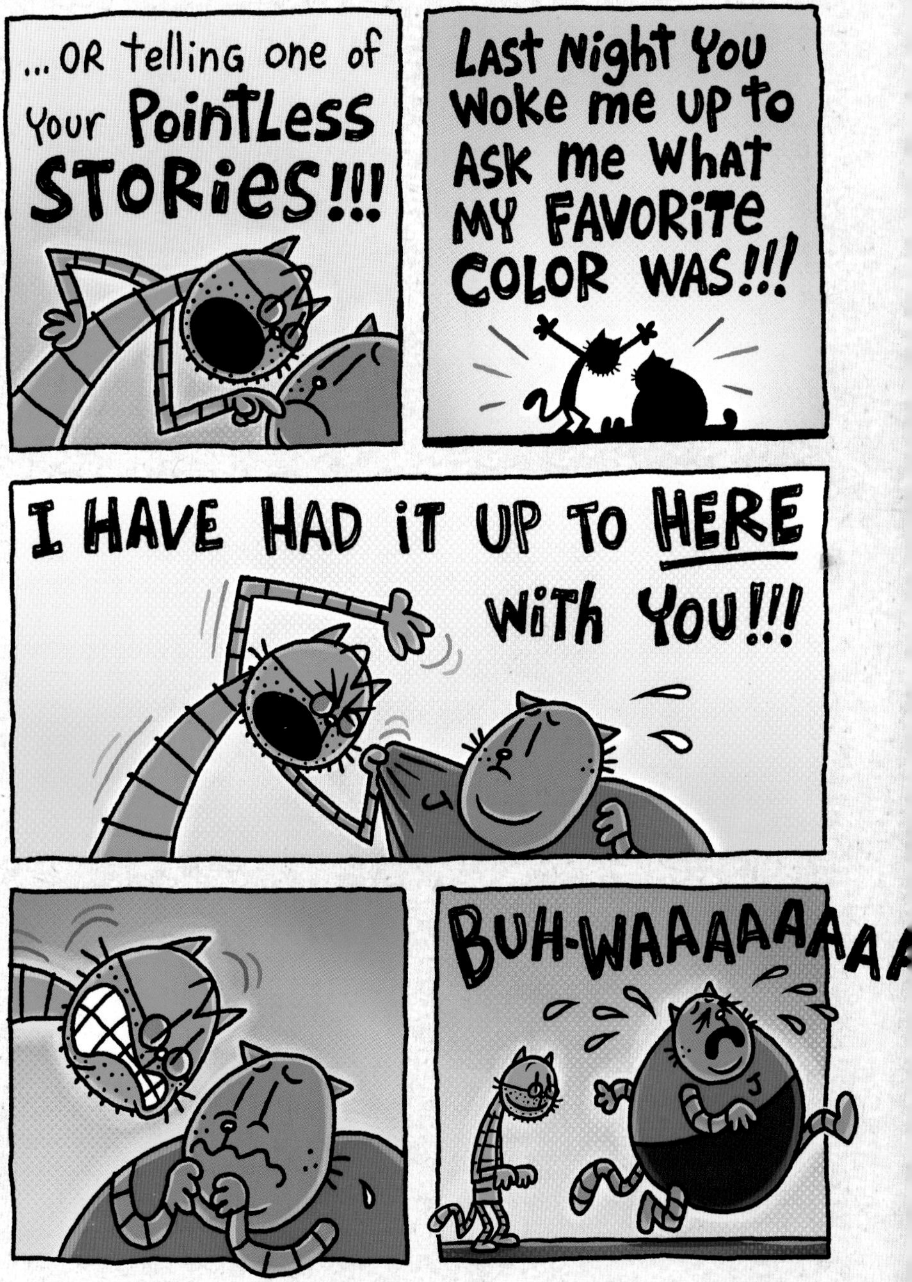
...OR telling one of your POINTLESS STORIES!!!
LAST NIGHT YOU WOKE ME UP TO ASK ME WHAT MY FAVORITE COLOR WAS!!!
I HAVE HAD IT UP TO HERE WITH YOU!!!
BUH-WAAAAAAAA

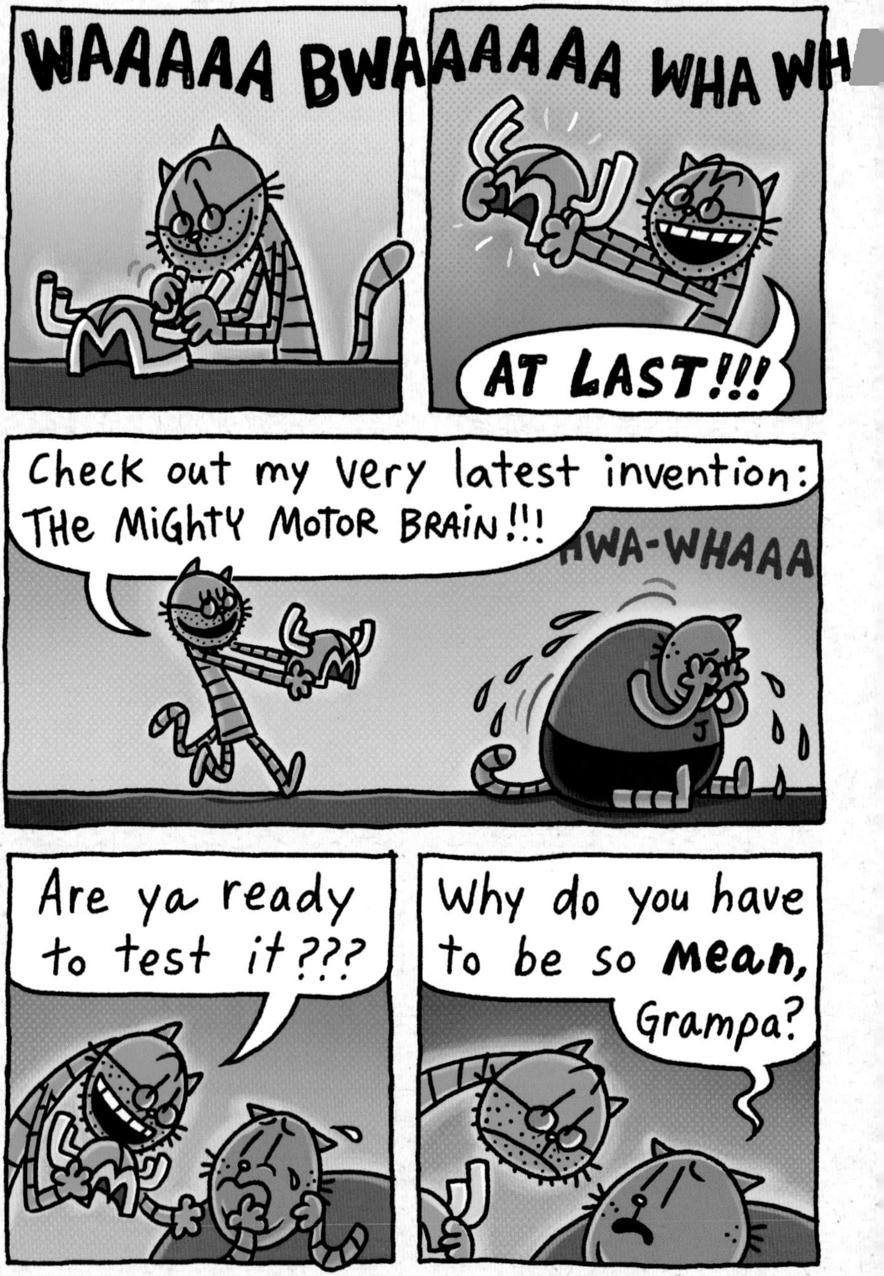
WAAAAA BWAAAAAA WHA WH
AT LAST!!!
Check out my very latest invention: THE MIGHTY MOTOR BRAIN!!!
WA-WHAAA
Are ya ready to test it???
Why do you have to be so mean, Grampa?

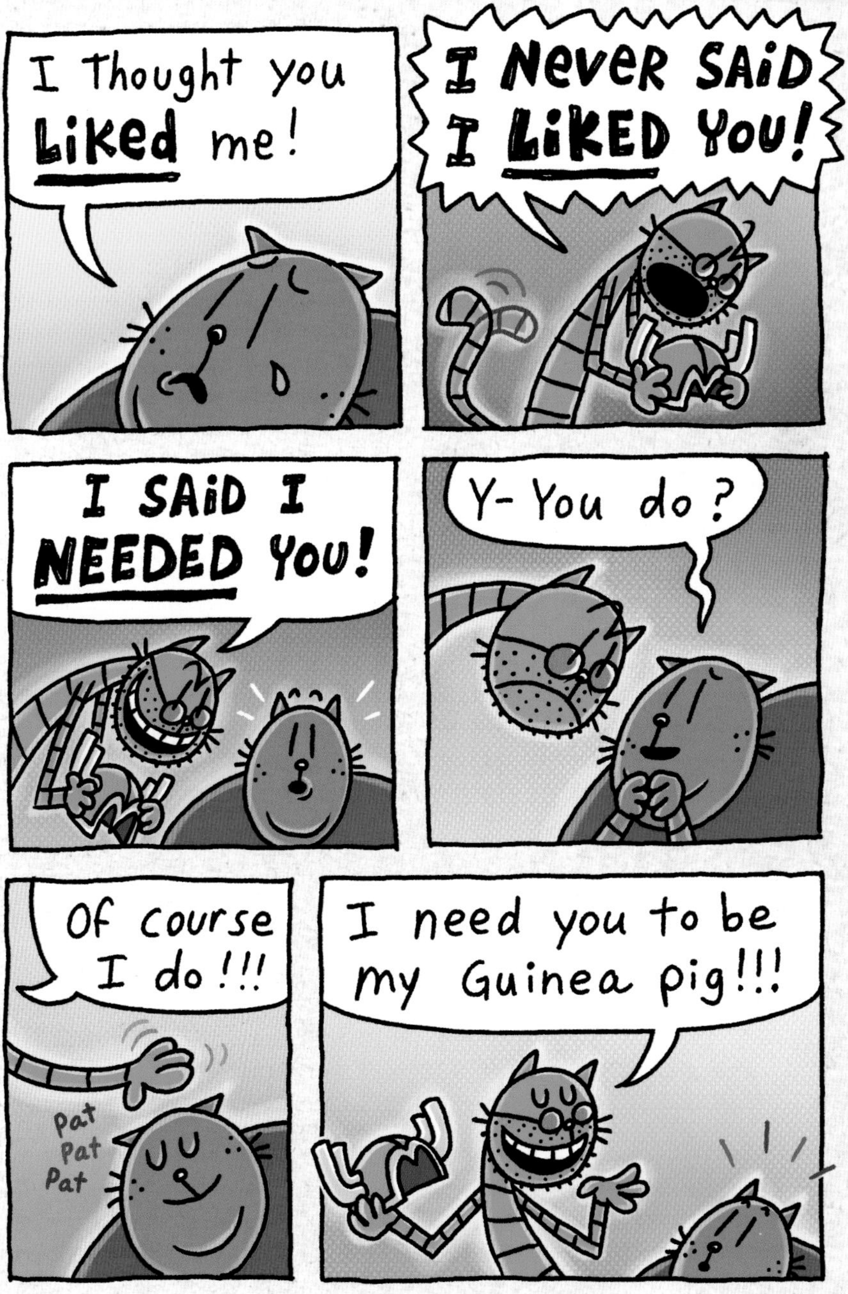
I Thought you LiKed me!
I NeveR SAiD I LiKED YOU!
I SAiD I NEEDED YOU!
Y-You do?
Of course I do!!!
Pat Pat Pat
I need you to be my Guinea pig!!!

Guinea pig?

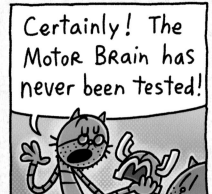

Certainly! The MOTOR BRAIN has never been tested!

It might be DANGEROUS!

That's why I need to try it out on **YOU!**

PLOP!

B-But, Grampa, is this thing **SAFE?**

Aw, don't worry, Big Jim. I'll be **fine!**

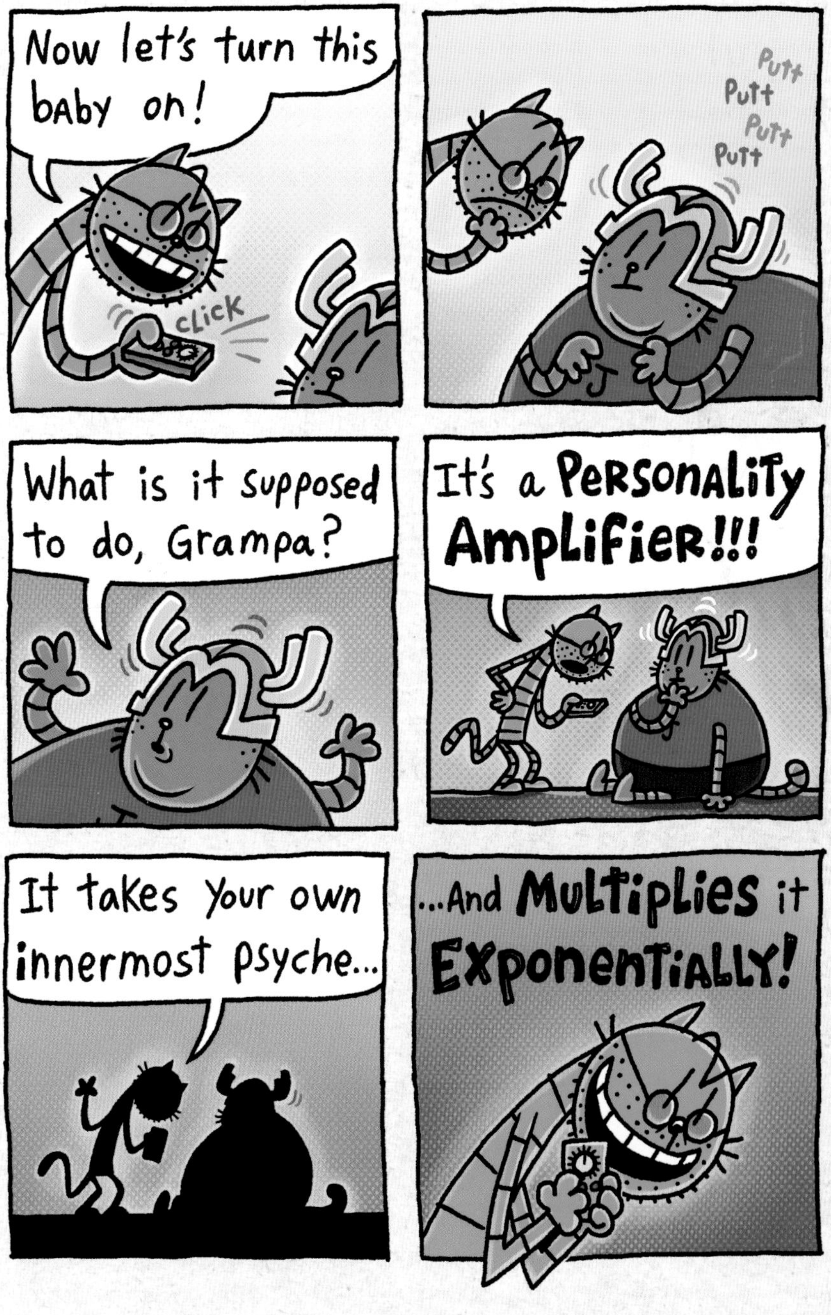
Now let's turn this baby on!
CLICK
Putt
Putt
Putt
Putt
What is it supposed to do, Grampa?
It's a PERSONALITY AMPLIFIER!!!
It takes your own innermost psyche...
...And MULTIPLIES it EXPONENTIALLY!

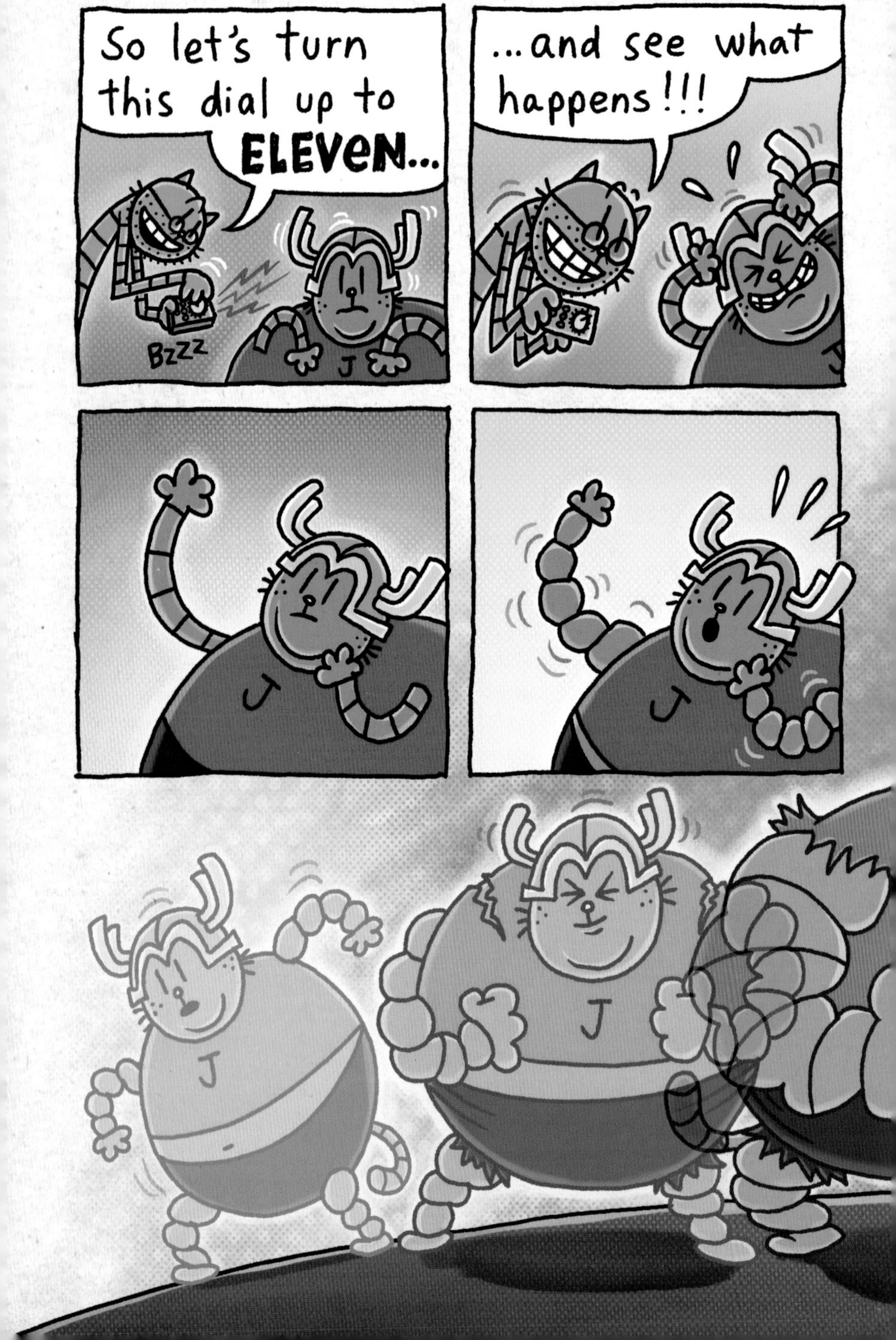

So let's turn this dial up to ELEVEN...
BZZZ
...and see what happens!!!

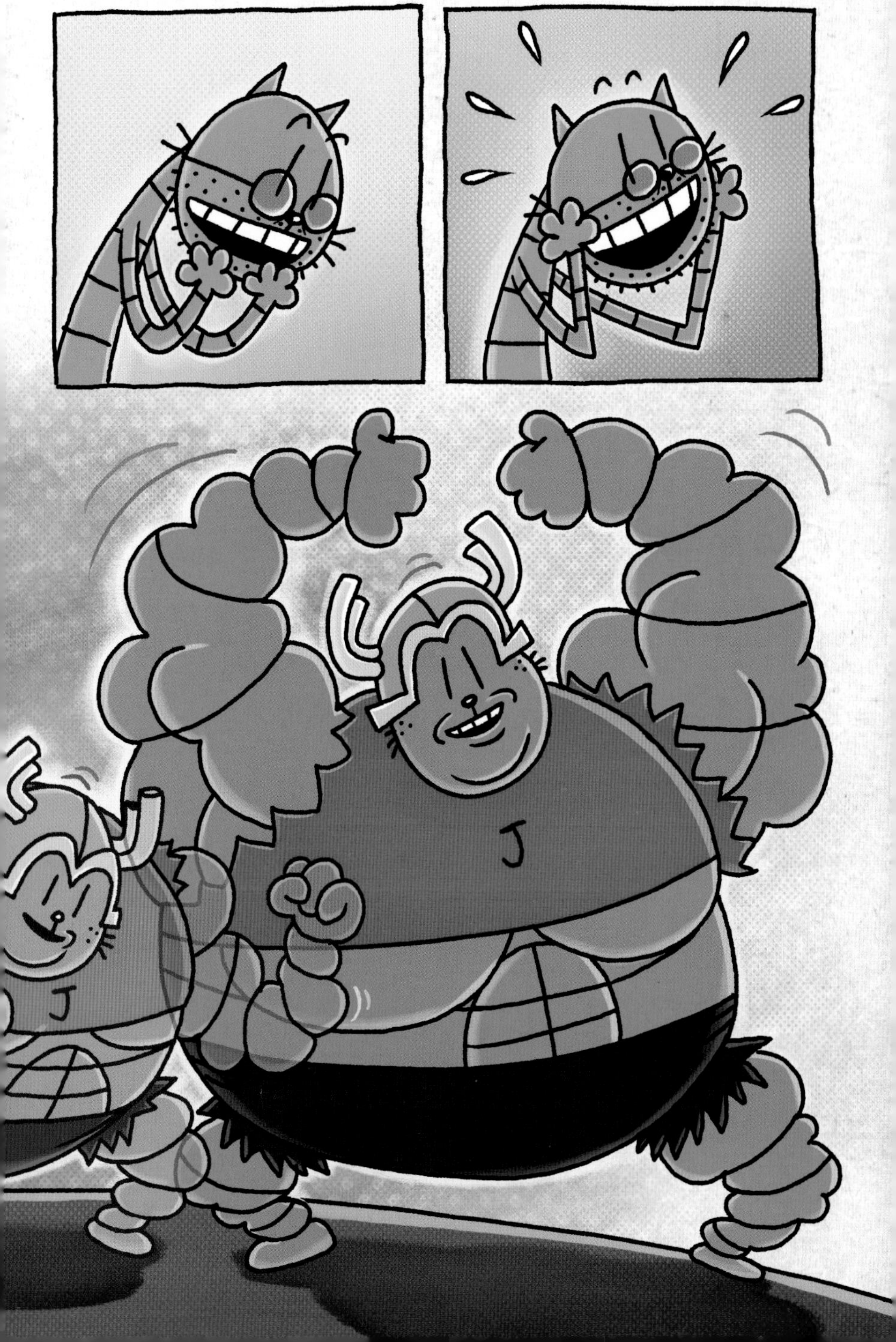

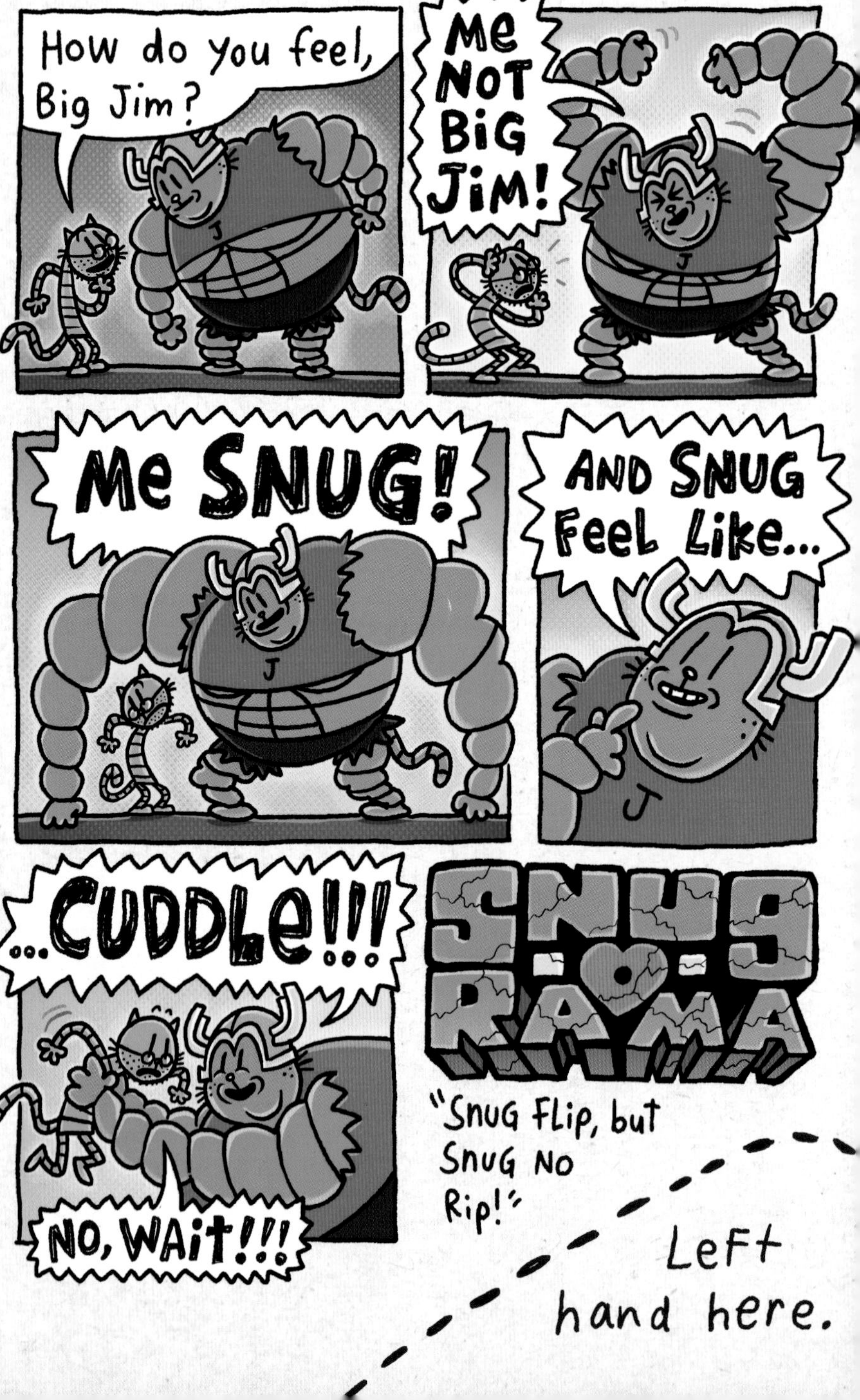
How do you feel, Big Jim?
Me NOT Big Jim!
Me SNUG!
AND SNUG Feel Like...
...CUDDLE!!!
NO, WAIT!!!
SNUG ♥ RAMA
"SNUG FLip, but SNUG NO Rip!"
Left hand here.

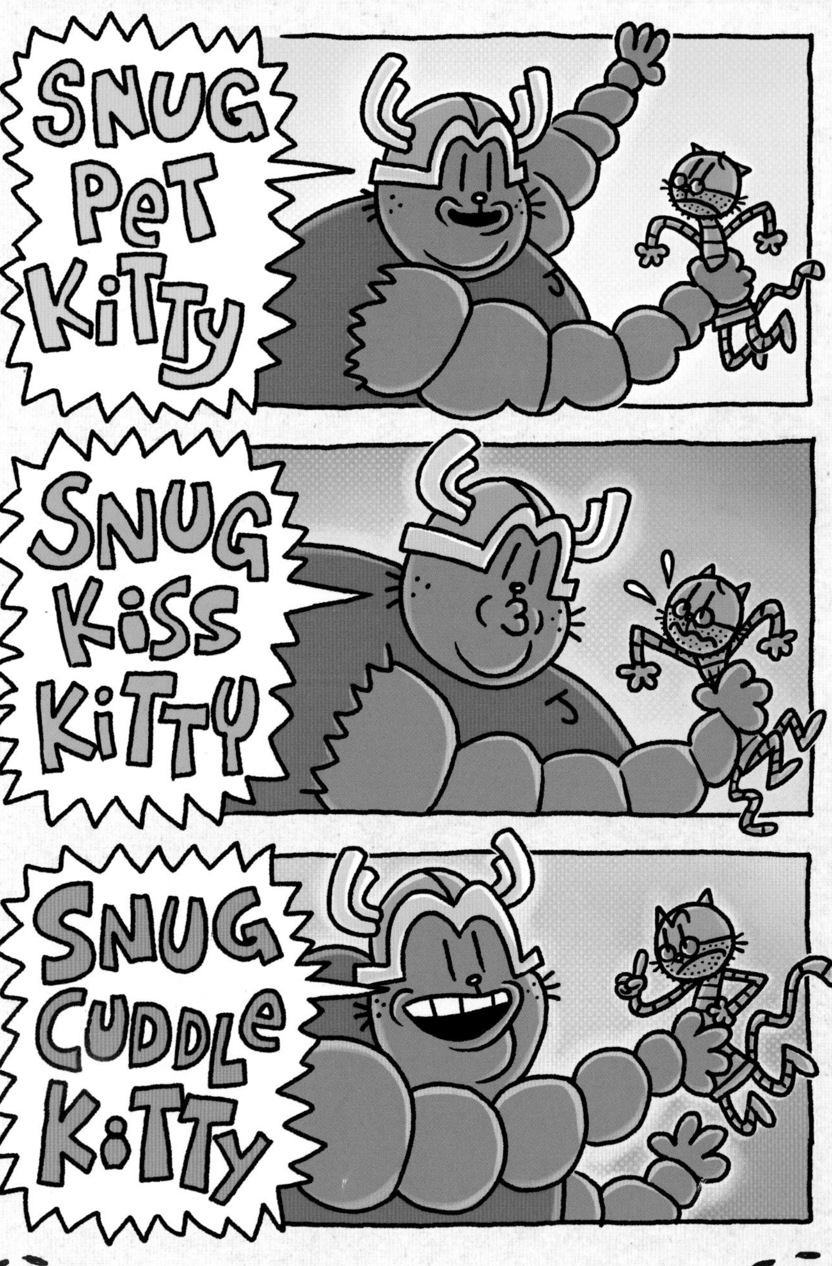

SNUG PeT KiTTy
SNUG KiSS KiTTY
SNUG CUDDLe KiTTy

Right Thumb here.

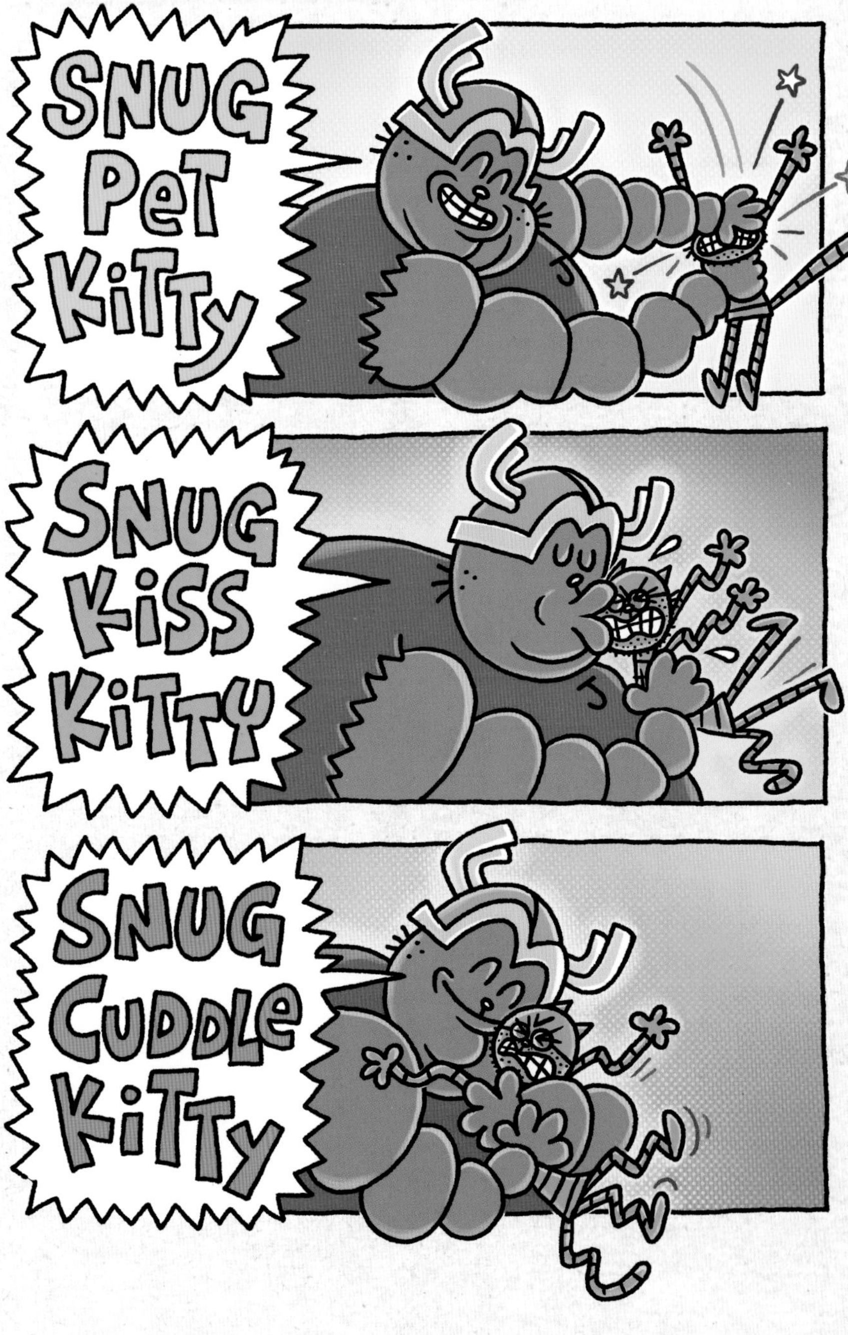
SNUG PET KITTY
SNUG KISS KITTY
SNUG CUDDLE KITTY

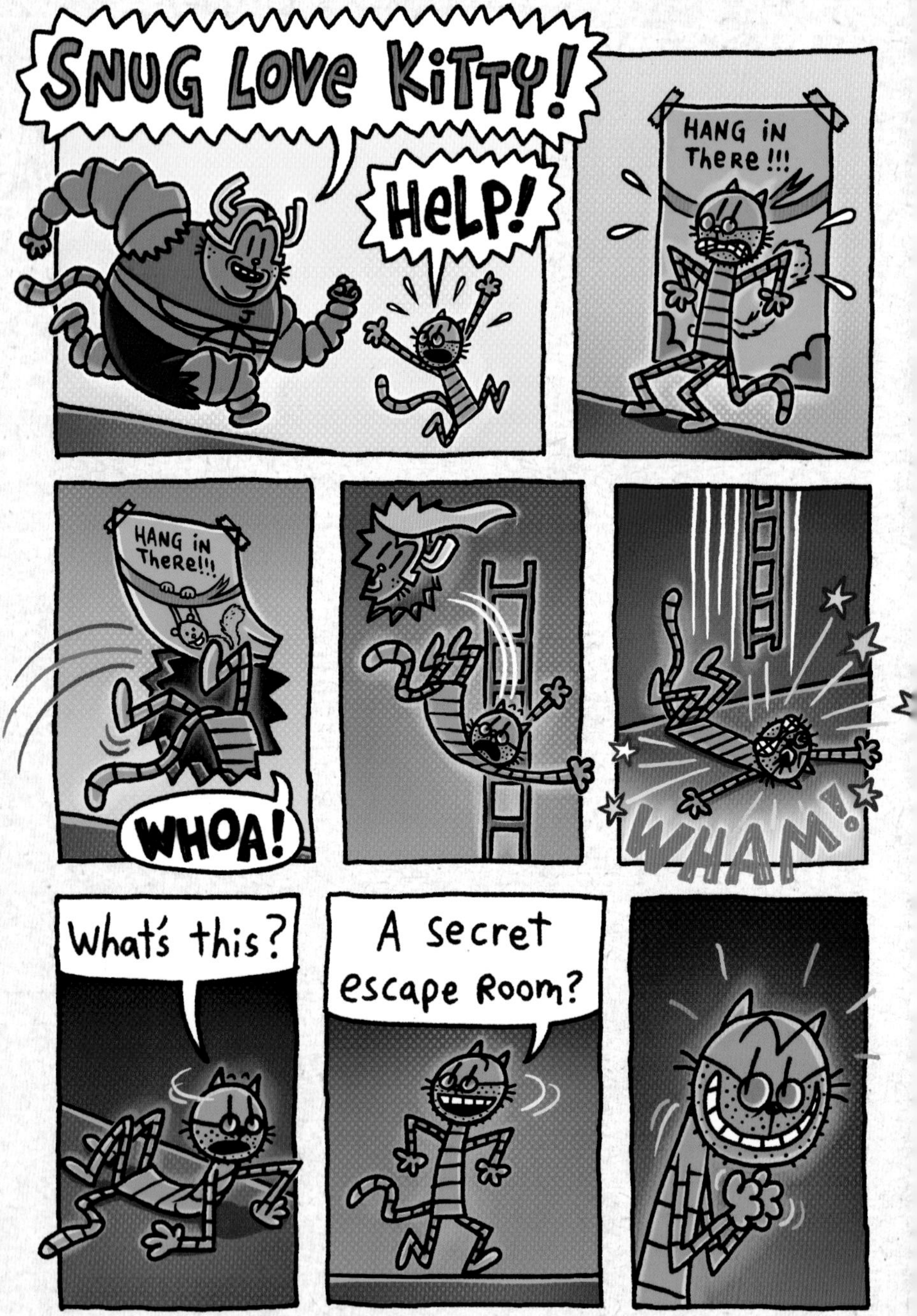
SNUG LOVE KiTTY!
HeLP!
HANG iN There!!!
HANG iN There!!!
WHOA!
WHAM!
What's this?
A secret escape Room?

CHAPTER 4

The DOG in The HAT

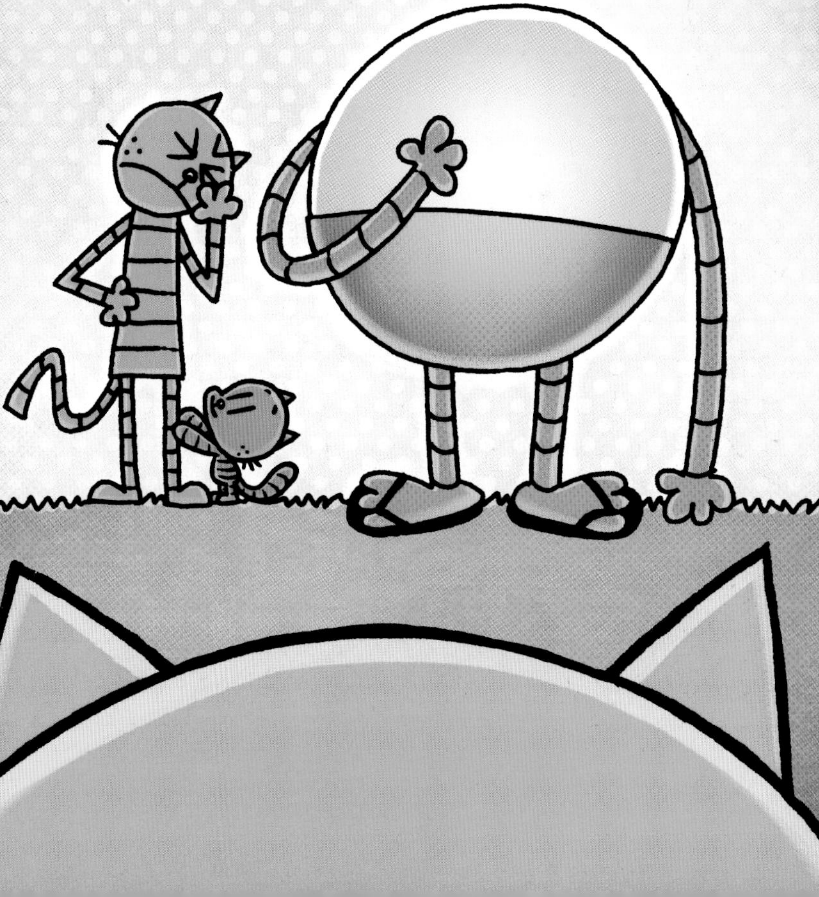

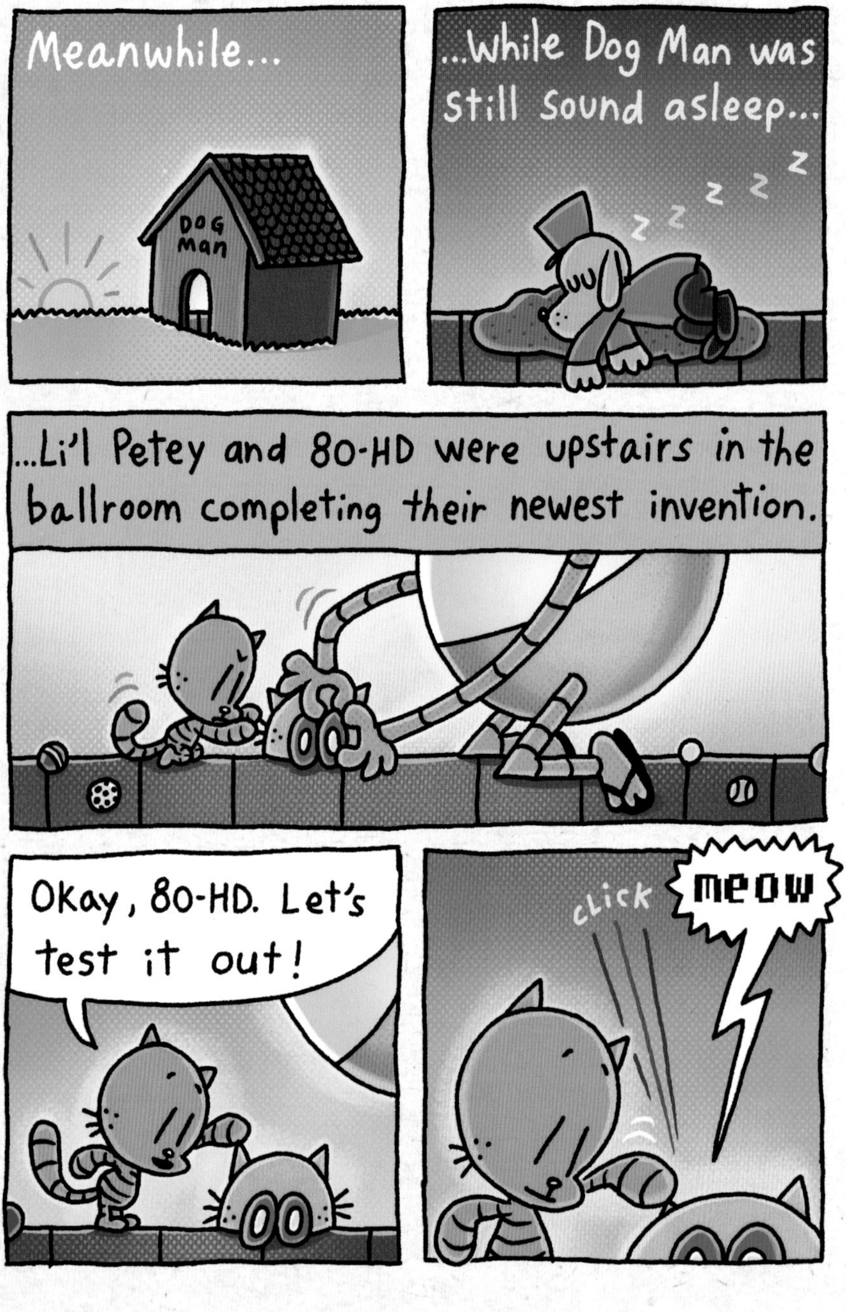
Meanwhile...
DOG Man
...While Dog Man was still sound asleep...
Z Z Z Z Z
...Li'l Petey and 80-HD were upstairs in the ballroom completing their newest invention.
Okay, 80-HD. Let's test it out!
CLICK
MEOW

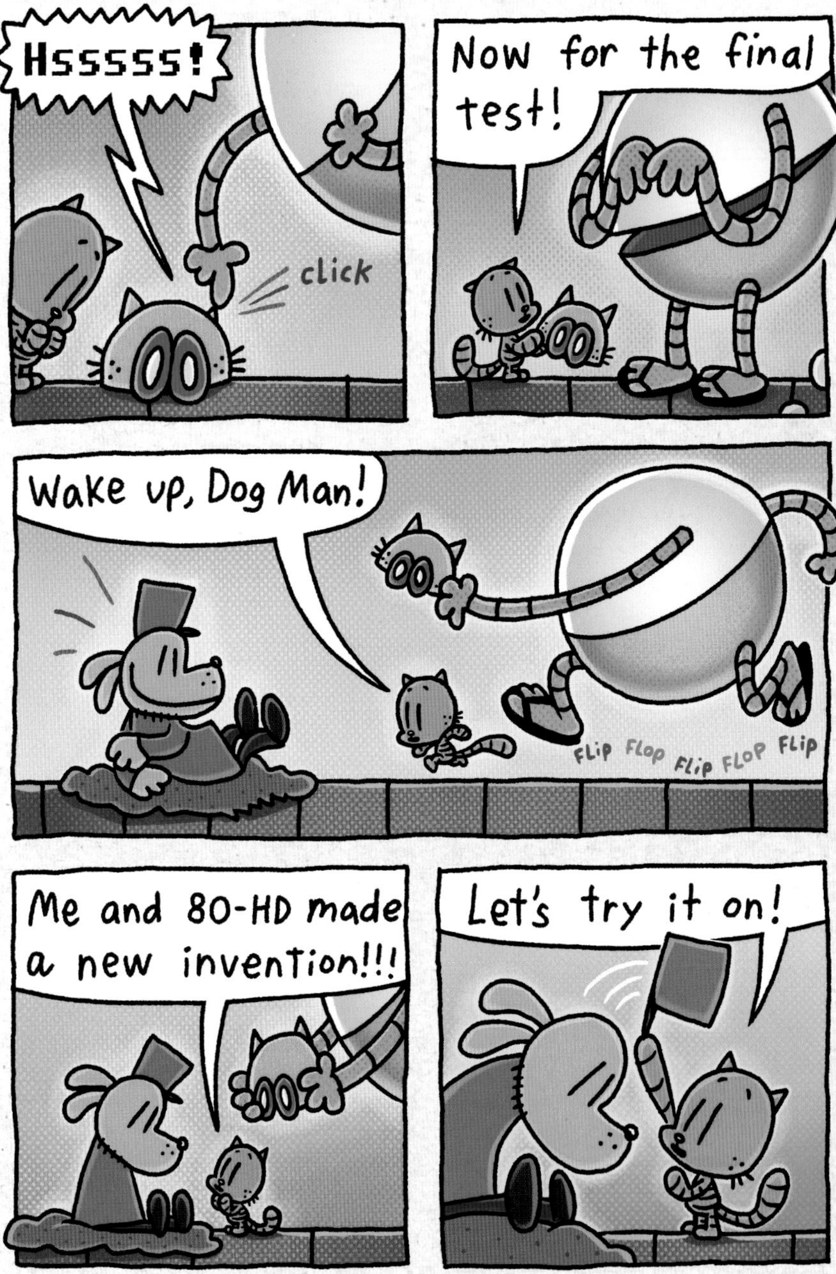
Hssss!
click
Now for the final test!
Wake up, Dog Man!
FLIP FLOP FLIP FLOP FLIP
Me and 80-HD made a new invention!!!
Let's try it on!

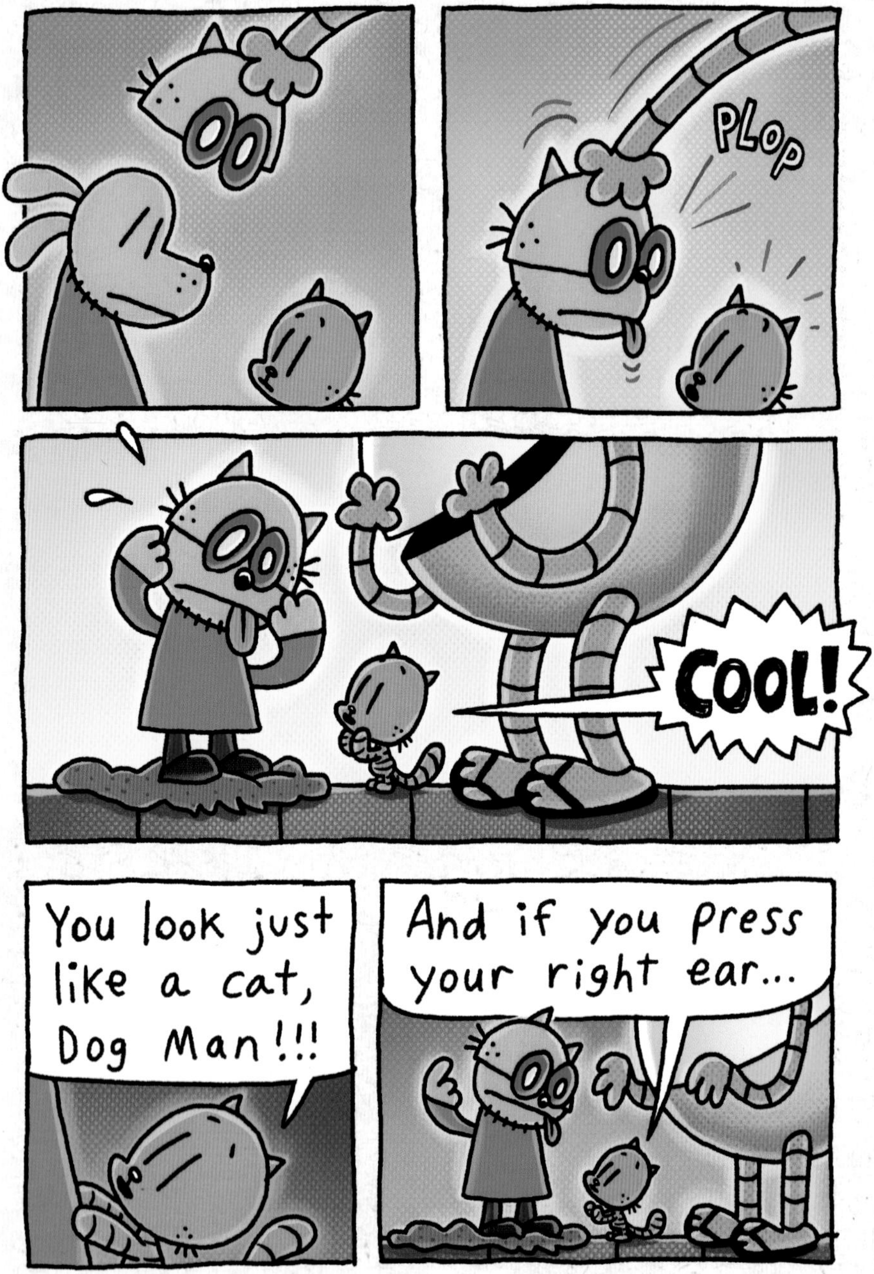
PLOP
COOL!
You look just like a cat, Dog Man!!!
And if you press your right ear...

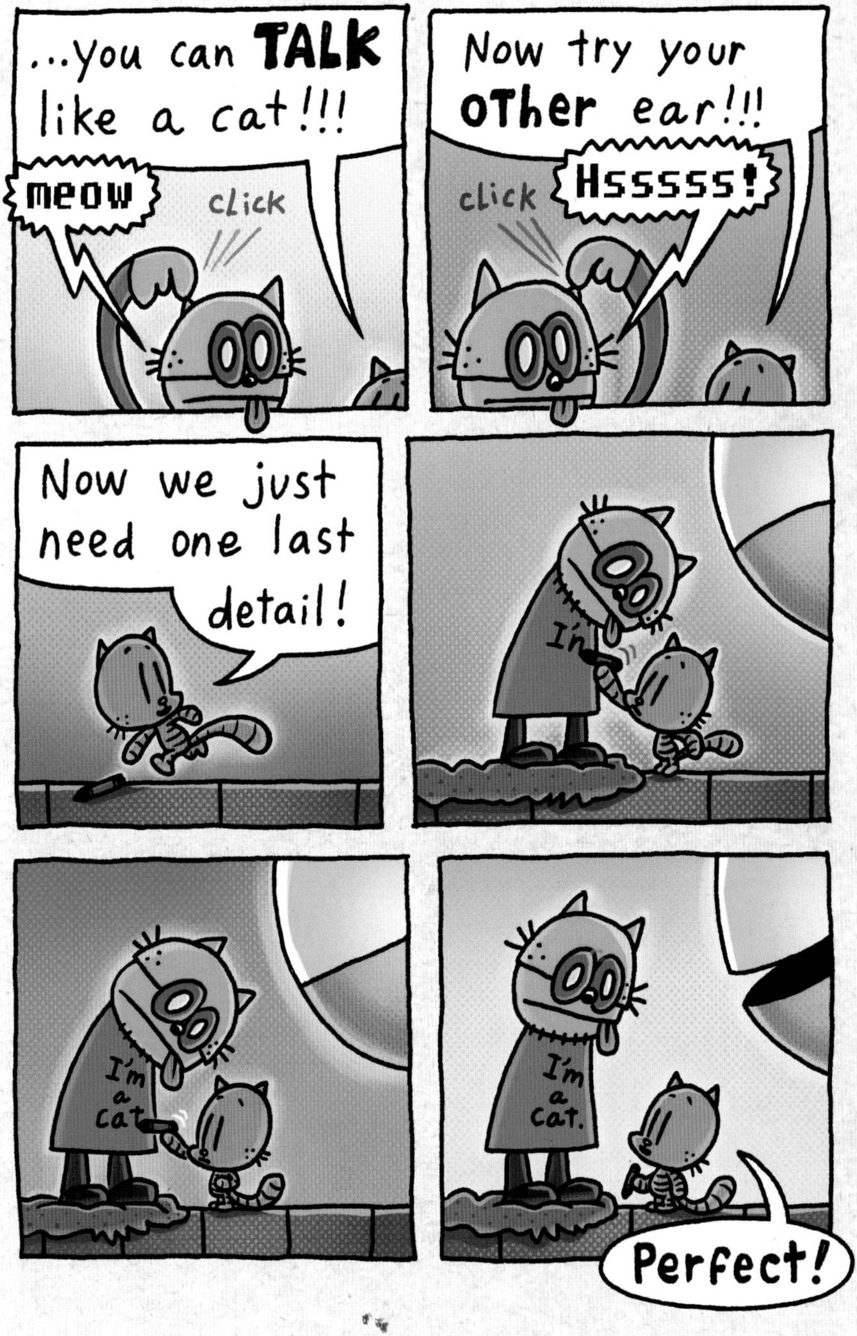
...you can TALK like a cat!!!
meow
click
Now try your OTHER ear!!!
click
Hsssss!
Now we just need one last detail!
I'm
I'm a cat
I'm a cat.
Perfect!

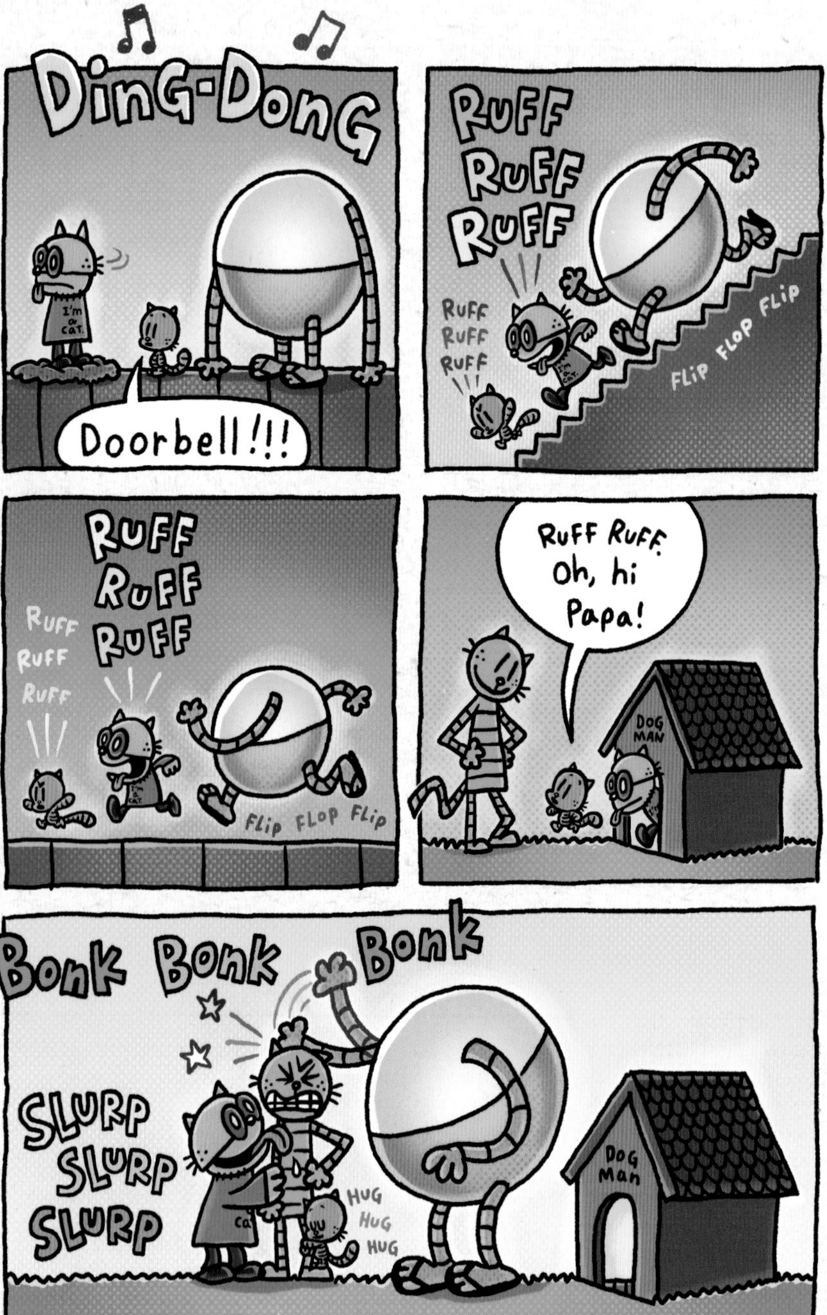
DING-DONG
Doorbell!!!
RUFF RUFF RUFF
RUFF RUFF RUFF
FLIP FLOP FLIP
RUFF RUFF RUFF
RUFF RUFF RUFF
FLIP FLOP FLIP
RUFF RUFF. Oh, hi Papa!
DOG MAN
Bonk Bonk Bonk
SLURP SLURP SLURP
HUG HUG HUG
DOG MAN

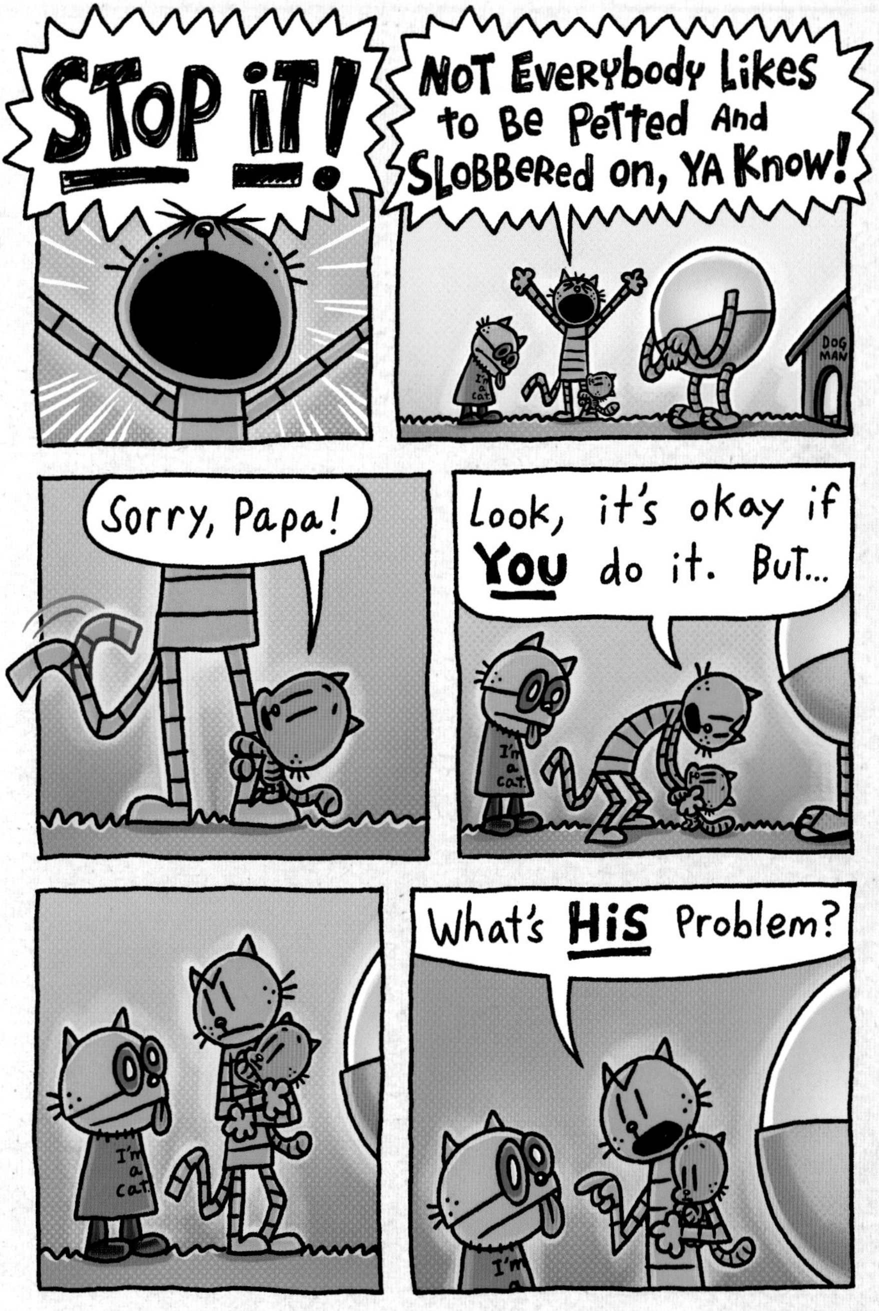
STOP IT!
NOT Everybody Likes to Be Petted And SLOBBERED on, YA Know!
DOG MAN
I'm a cat.
Sorry, Papa!
Look, it's okay if YOU do it. BUT...
I'm a cat.
I'm a cat.
What's HIS Problem?

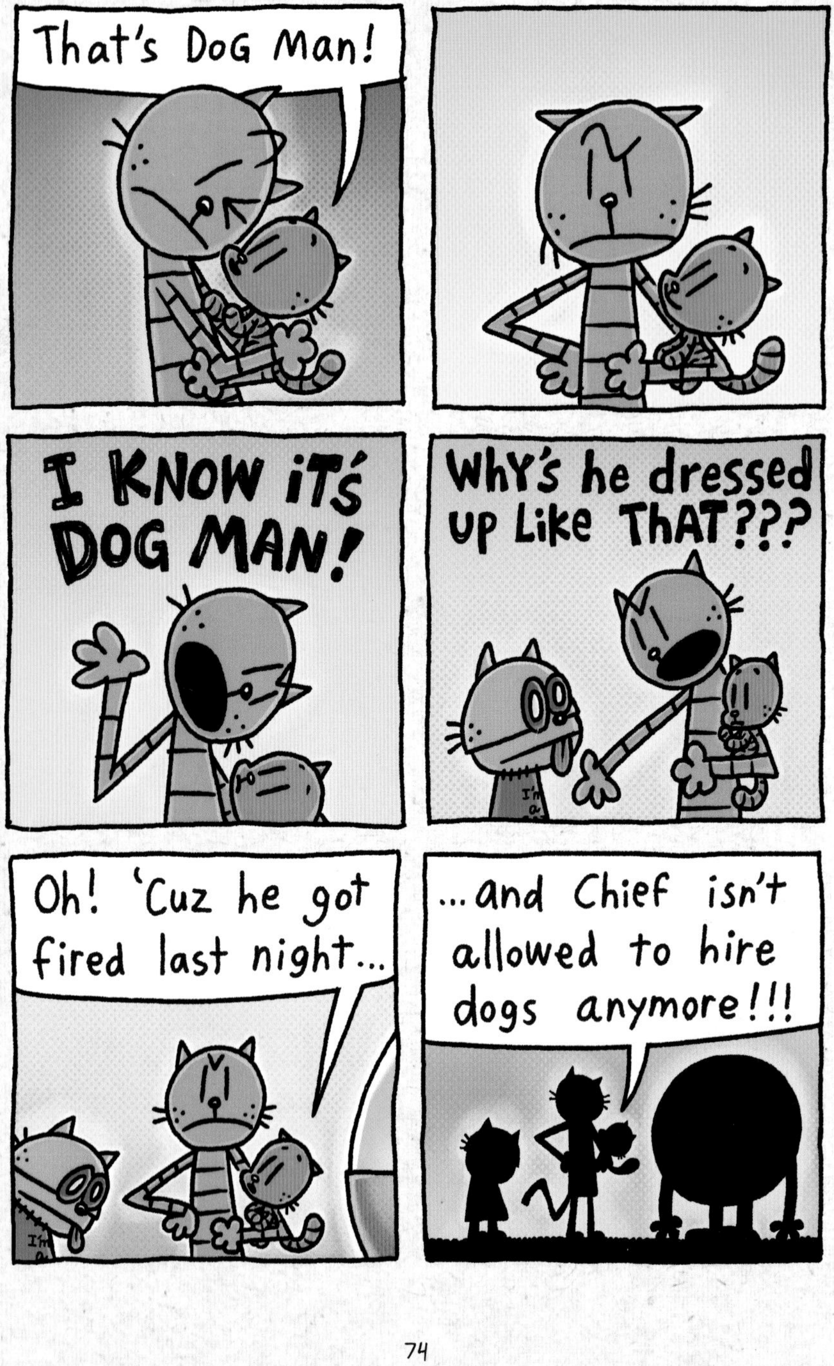
That's DoG Man!
I KNOW iT'S DOG MAN!
WhY's he dressed up Like ThAT???
Oh! 'Cuz he got fired last night...
...and Chief isn't allowed to hire dogs anymore!!!

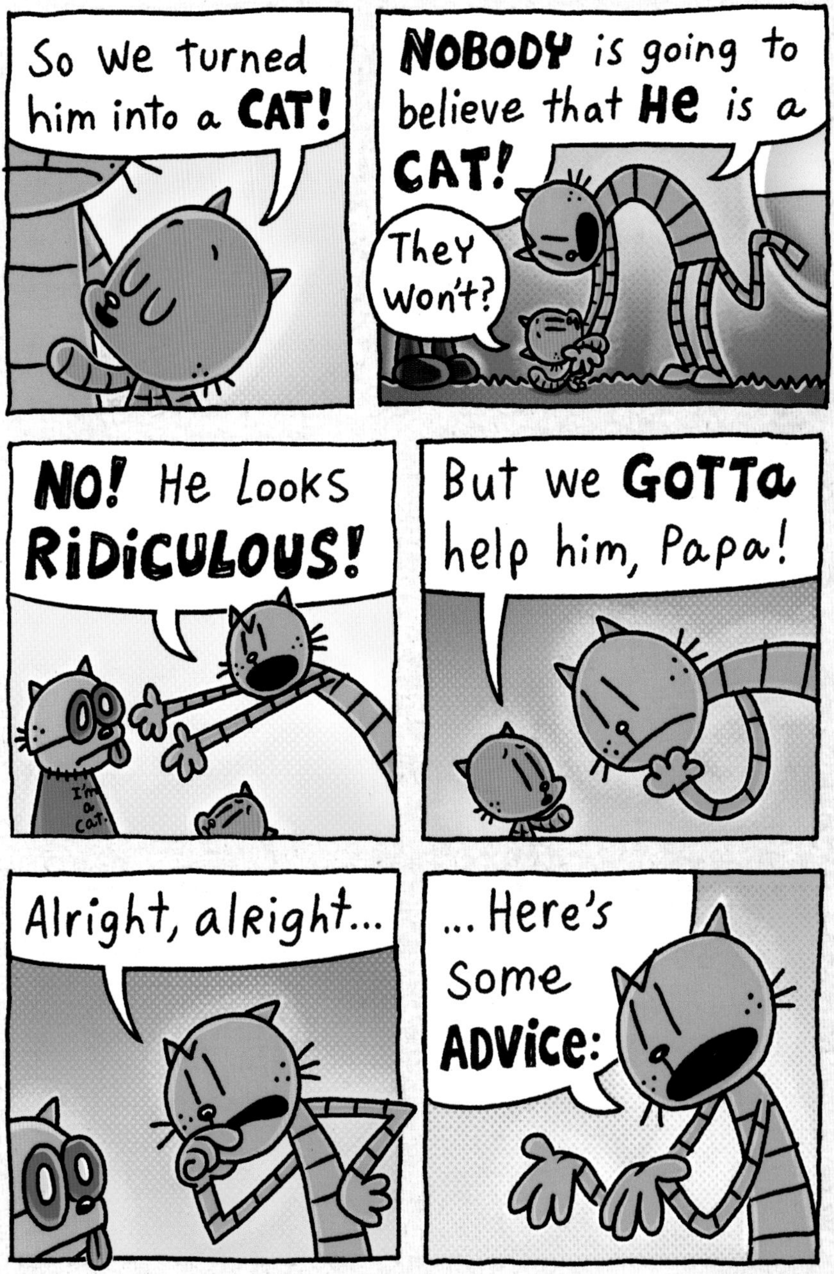

So we turned him into a CAT!
NOBODY is going to believe that HE is a CAT!
They won't?
NO! He looks RIDICULOUS!
I'm a cat.
But we GOTTA help him, Papa!
Alright, alright...
... Here's some ADVICE:

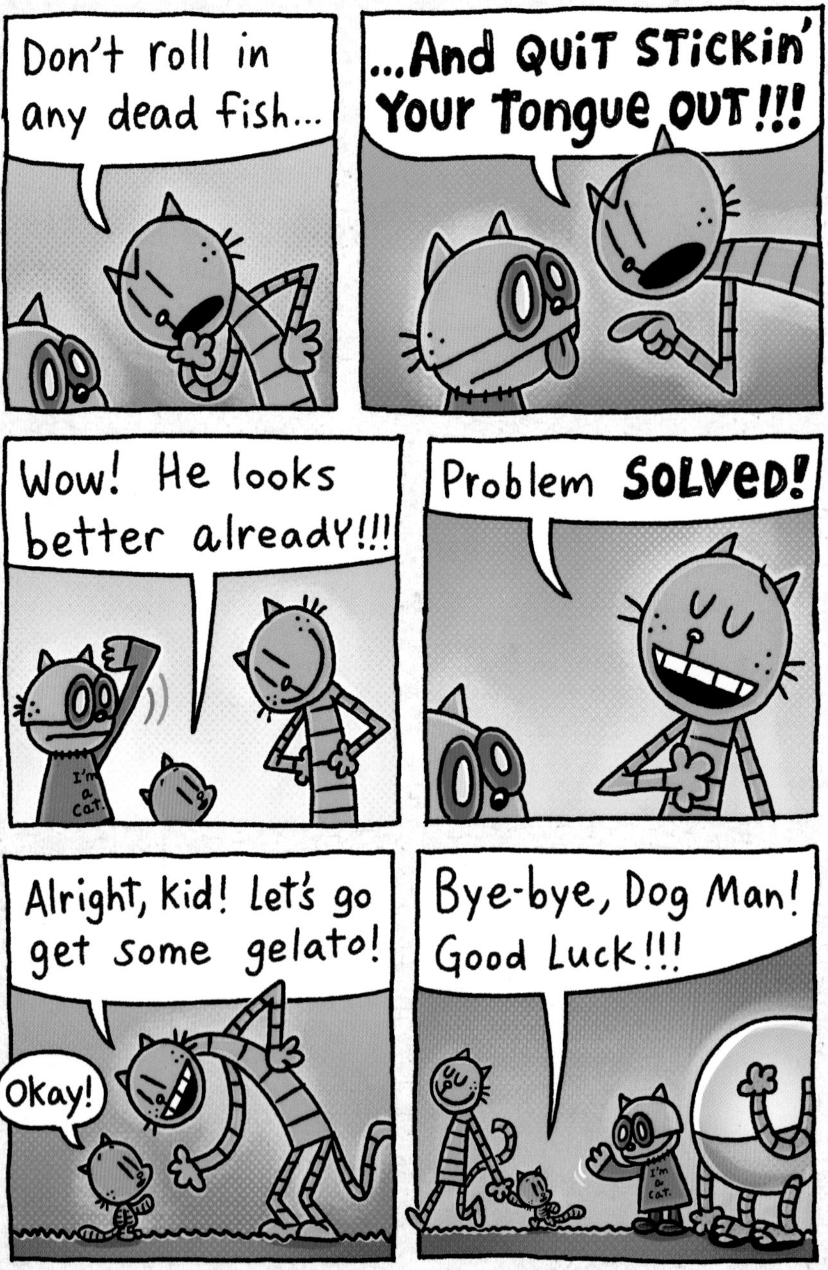
Don't roll in any dead fish...
...And QUIT STICKIN' YOUR TONGUE OUT!!!
Wow! He looks better already!!!
I'm a cat.
Problem SOLVED!
Alright, kid! Let's go get some gelato!
Okay!
Bye-bye, Dog Man! Good Luck!!!
I'm a cat.

CHAPTER 5

A Buncha Stuff That Happened Next

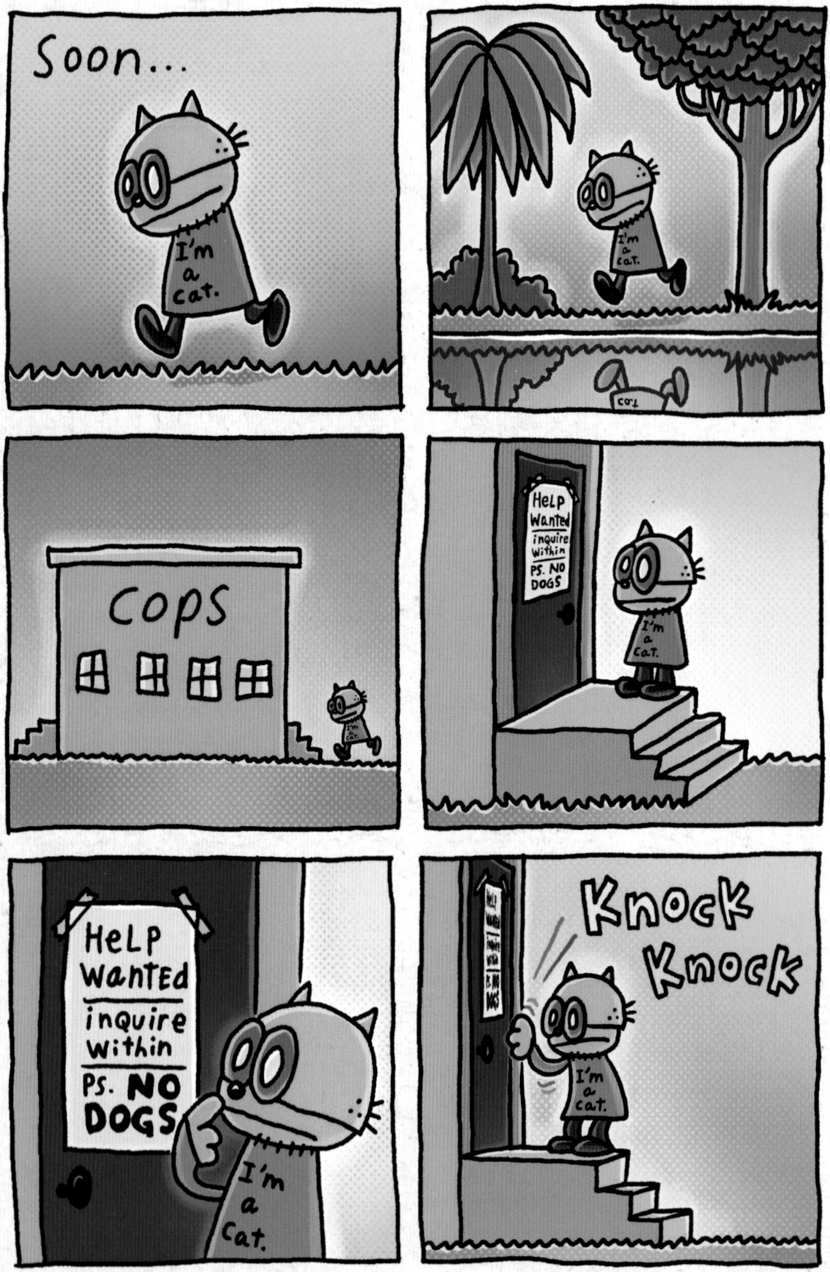
Soon...
I'm a cat.
I'm a cat.
COPS
HELP Wanted
inquire within
PS. NO DOGS
I'm a cat.
HELP WANTED
inquire within
PS. NO DOGS
I'm a cat.
Knock Knock
I'm a cat.

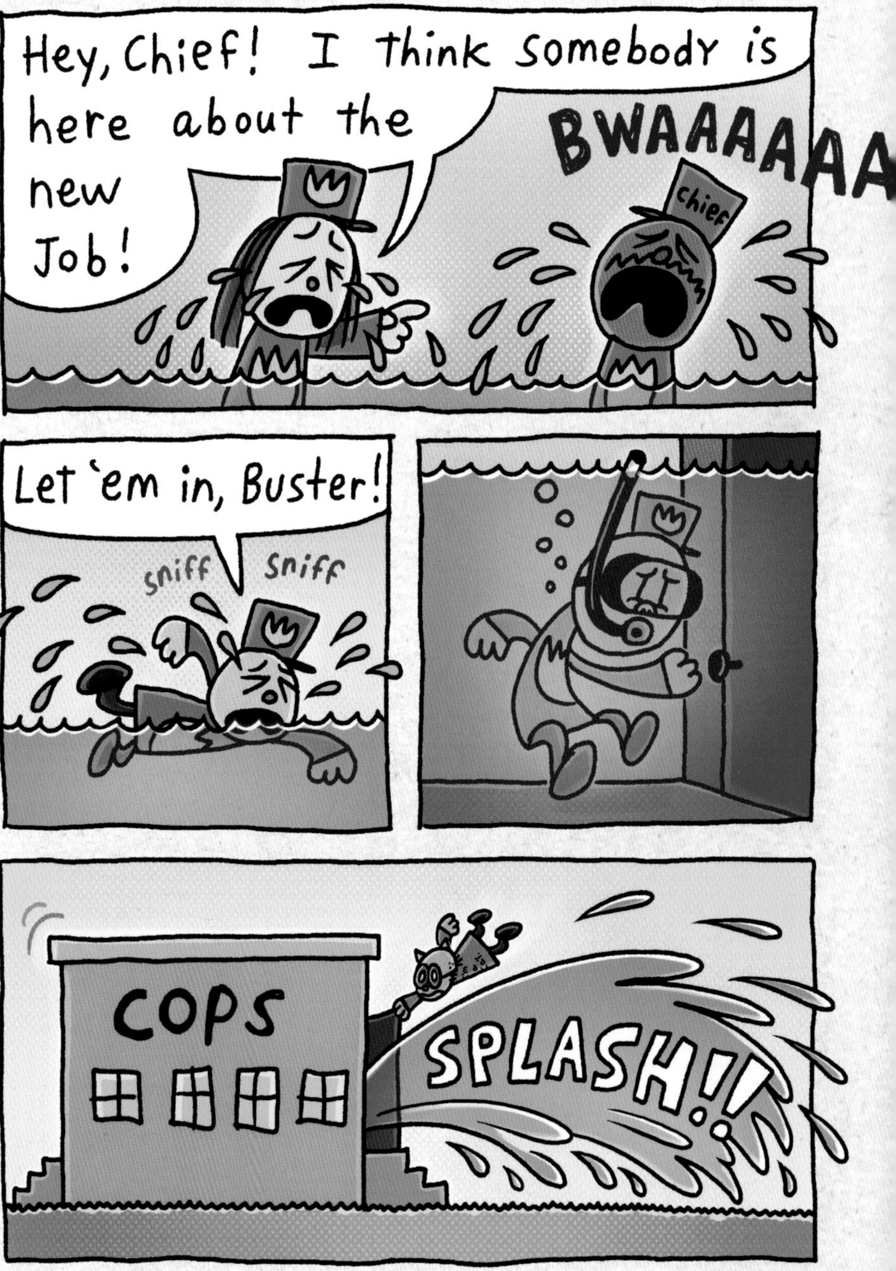
Hey, Chief! I think somebody is here about the new Job!
BWAAAAAAA
Chief
Let 'em in, Buster!
sniff
sniff
COPS
SPLASH!!

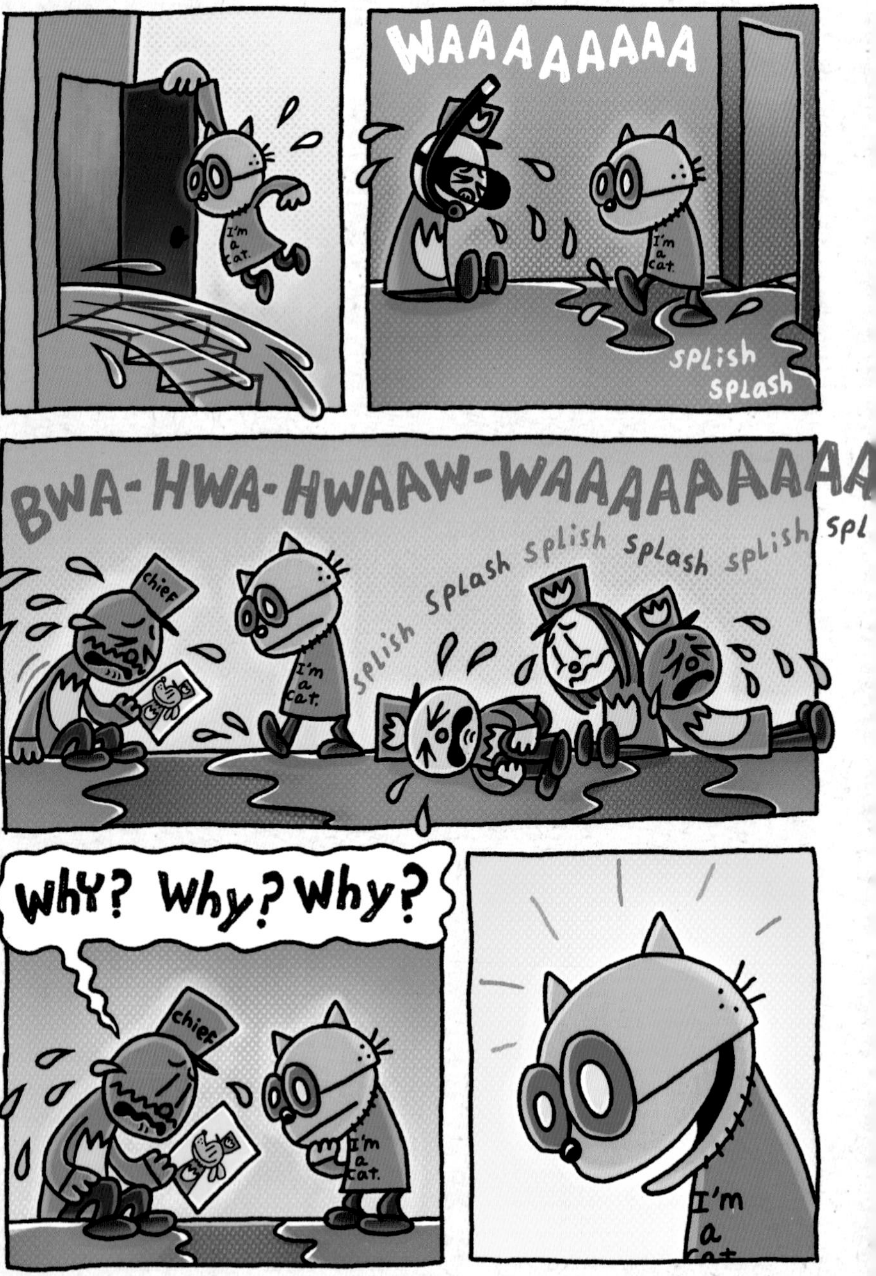
I'm a cat.
WAAAAAAAA
I'm a cat.
splish splash
BWA-HWA-HWAAW-WAAAAAAAAA
chief
I'm a cat.
splish splash splish splash splish spl
Why? Why? Why?
chief
I'm a cat.
I'm a

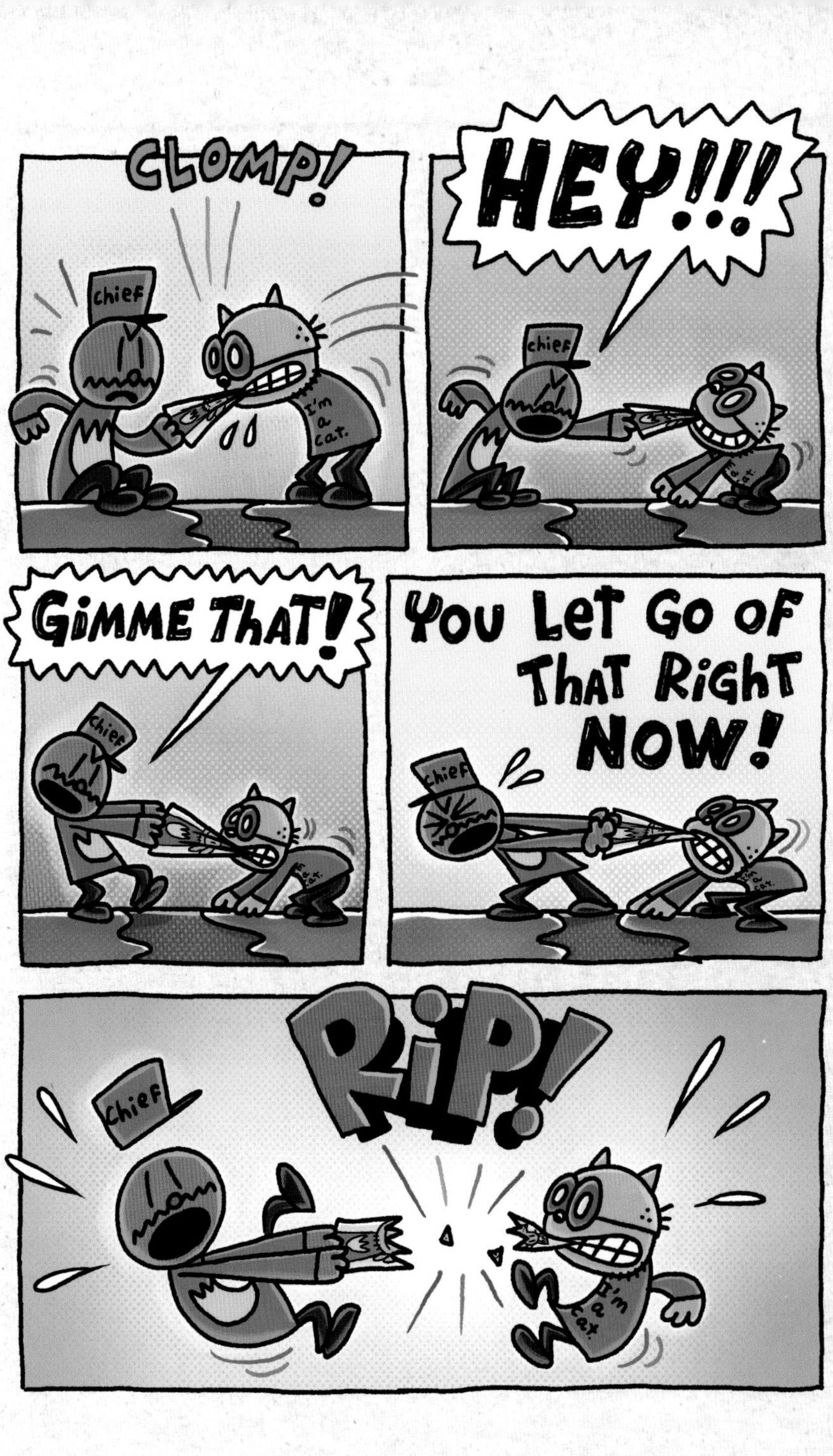
CLOMP!
chief
I'm a cat.
HEY!!!
GIMME THAT!
YOU LET GO OF THAT RIGHT NOW!
RIP!

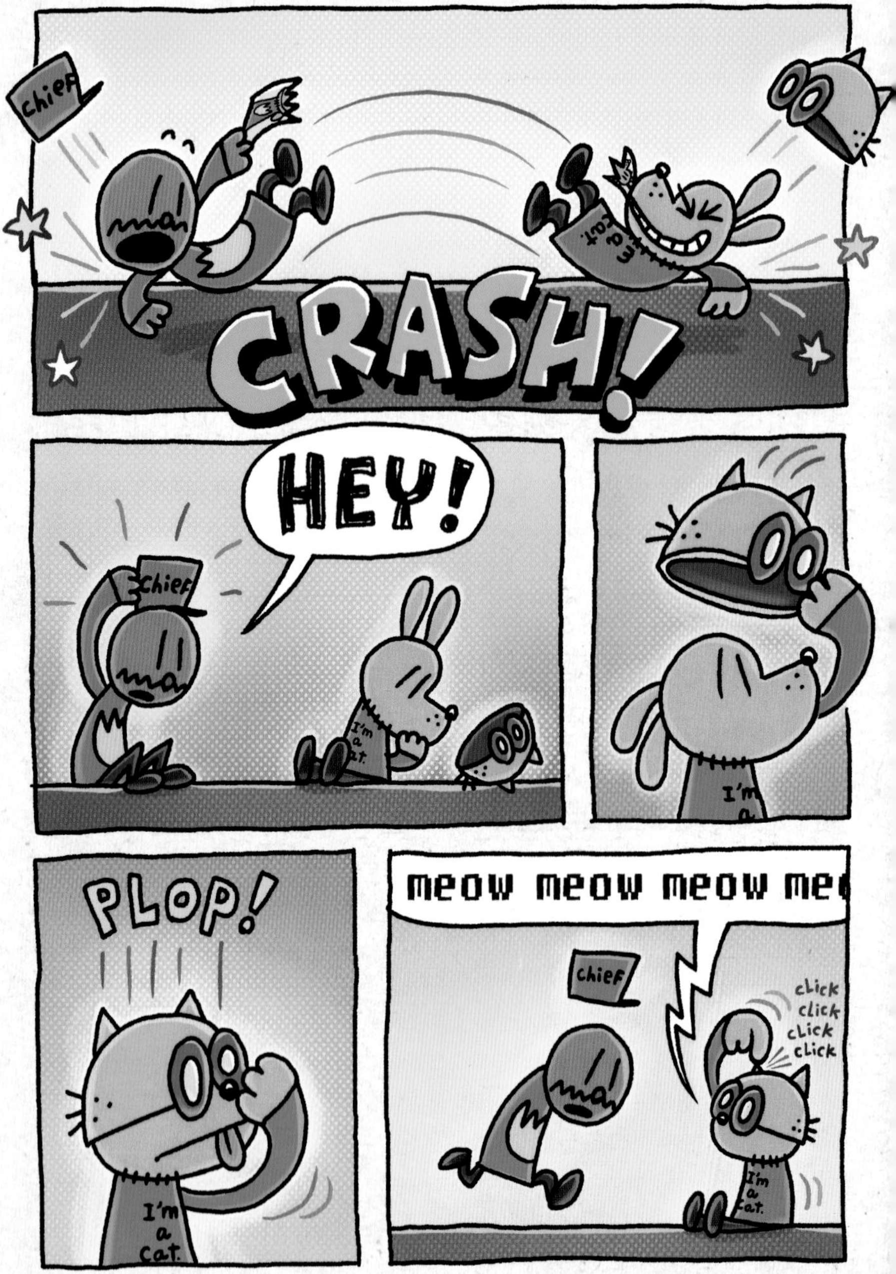
chief
Eat.
CRASH!
HEY!
Chief
I'm a cat.
I'm a
PLOP!
I'm a cat.
meow meow meow me
chief
click click click click
I'm a cat.

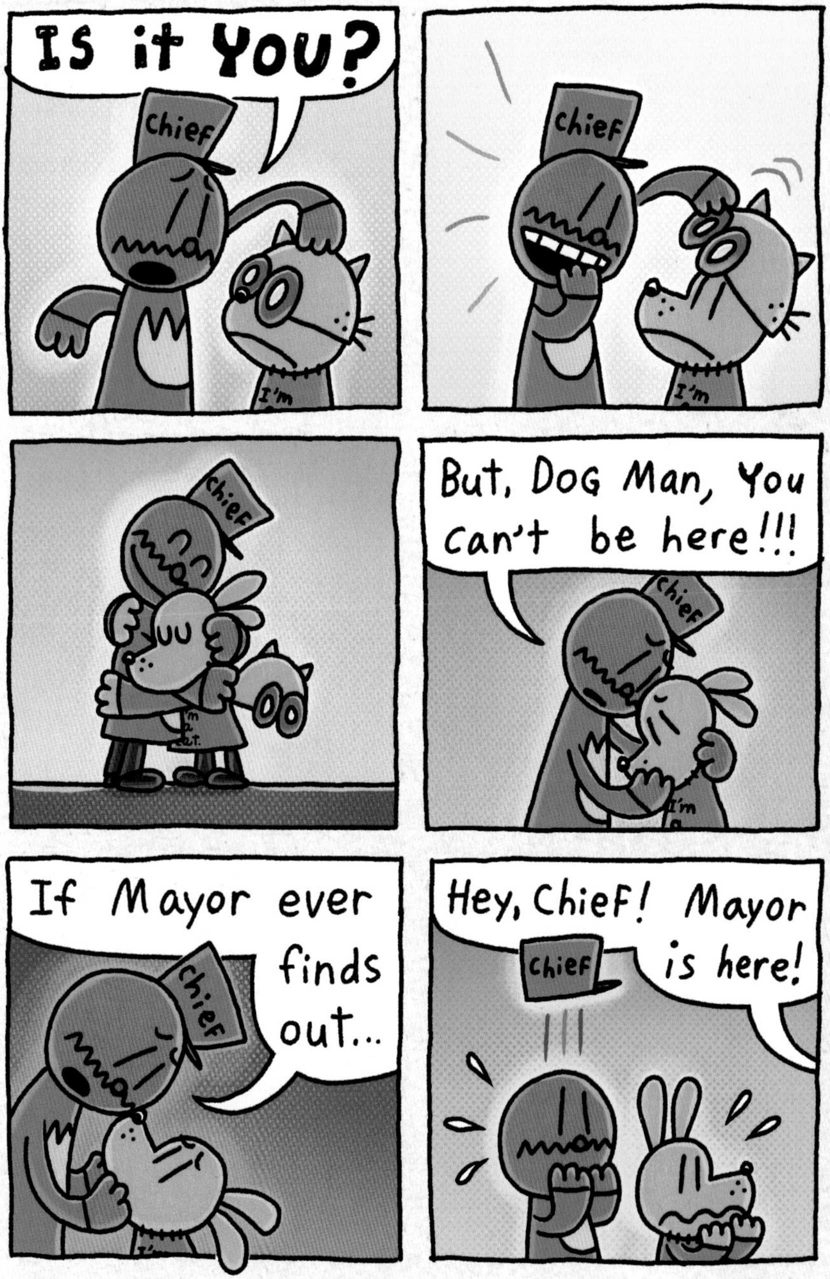
IS it YOU?
Chief
Chief
Chief
But, DOG Man, You can't be here!!!
Chief
If Mayor ever finds out...
Chief
Hey, Chief! Mayor is here!
Chief

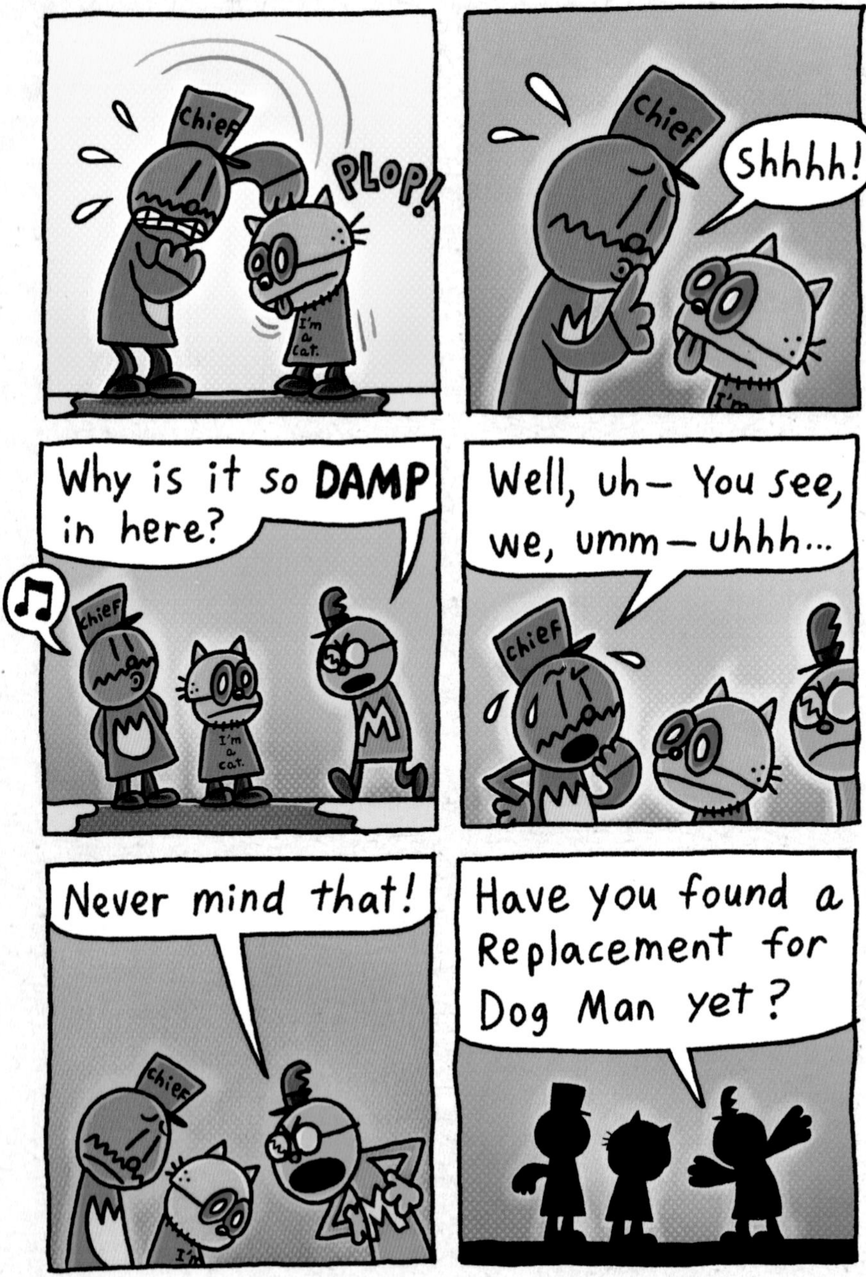
Chief
PLOP!
I'm a cat.
Chief
Shhhh!
Why is it so DAMP in here?
♫
Chief
I'm a cat.
Well, uh— You see, we, umm—uhhh...
Chief
Never mind that!
Chief
Have you found a Replacement for Dog Man yet?

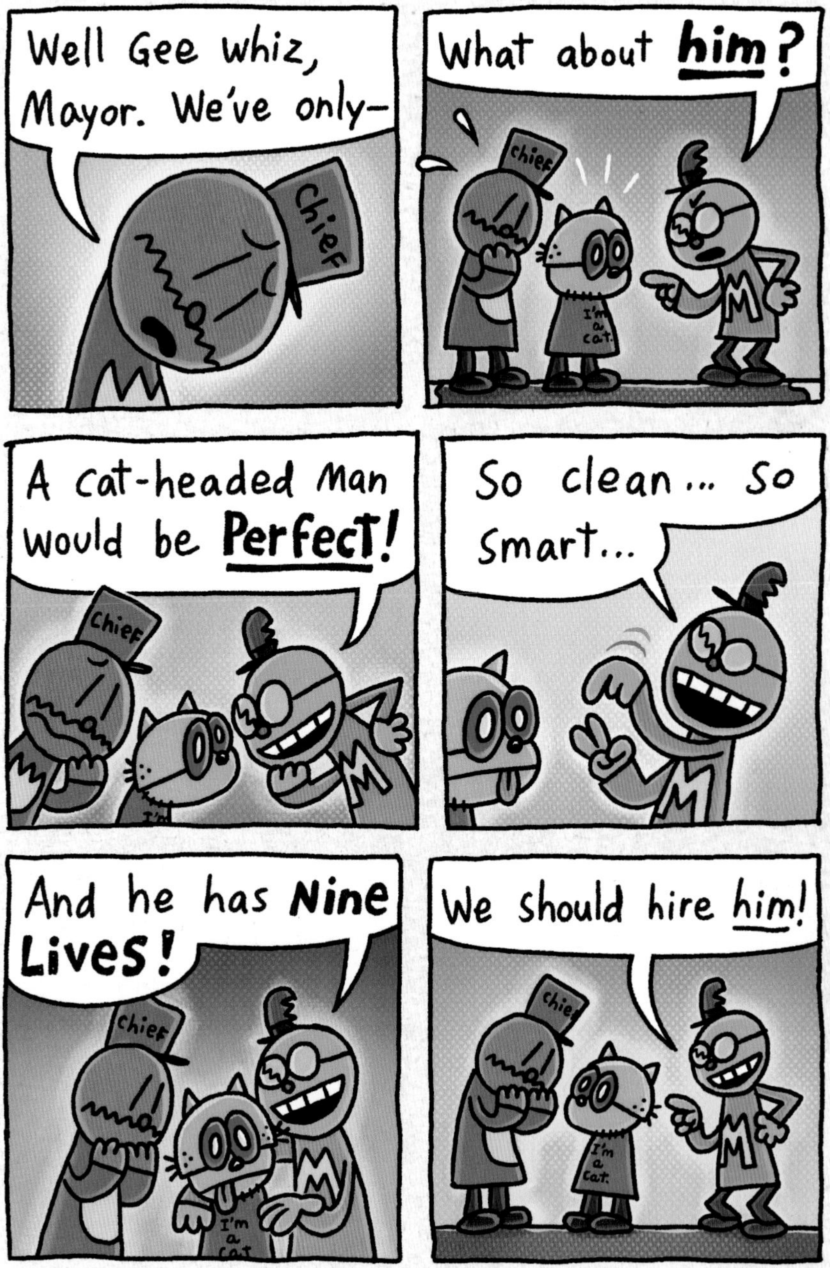
Well Gee whiz, Mayor. We've only—
Chief
What about him?
chief
I'm a cat.
A cat-headed Man would be Perfect!
Chief
So clean... So Smart...
And he has Nine Lives!
chief
I'm a cat
We should hire him!
I'm a cat.

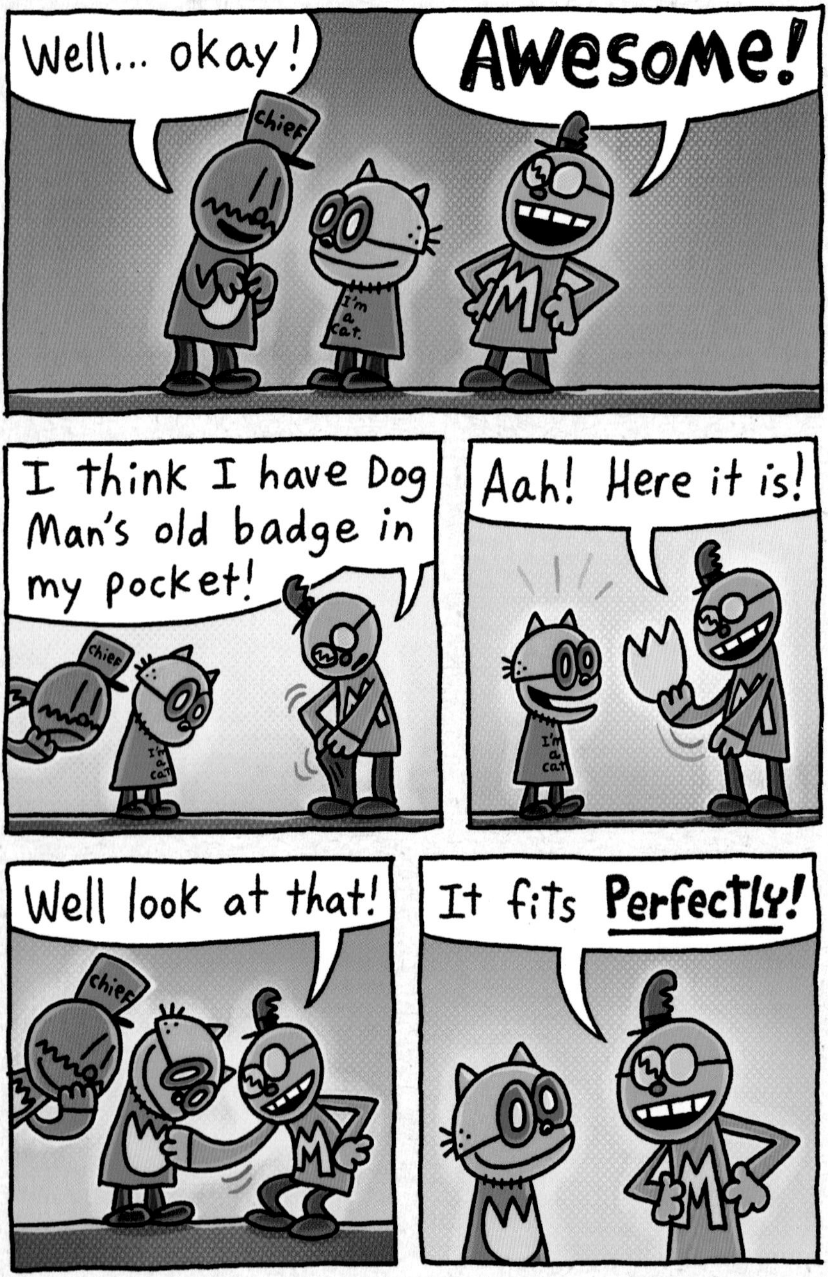
Well... okay!
AWESOME!
I'm a cat.
I think I have Dog Man's old badge in my pocket!
Aah! Here it is!
Well look at that!
It fits PERFECTLY!

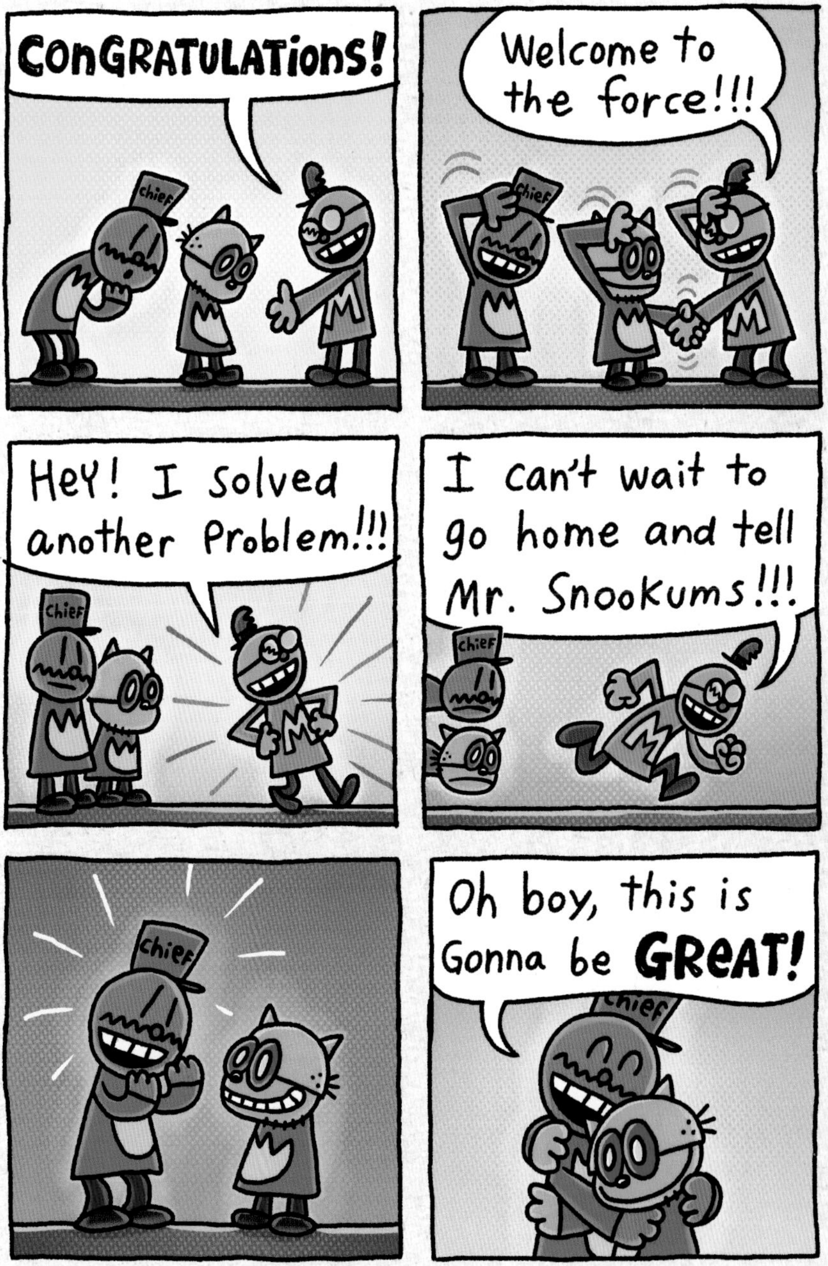
CONGRATULATIONS!
Welcome to the force!!!
Hey! I solved another Problem!!!
I can't wait to go home and tell Mr. Snookums!!!
Oh boy, this is Gonna be GREAT!

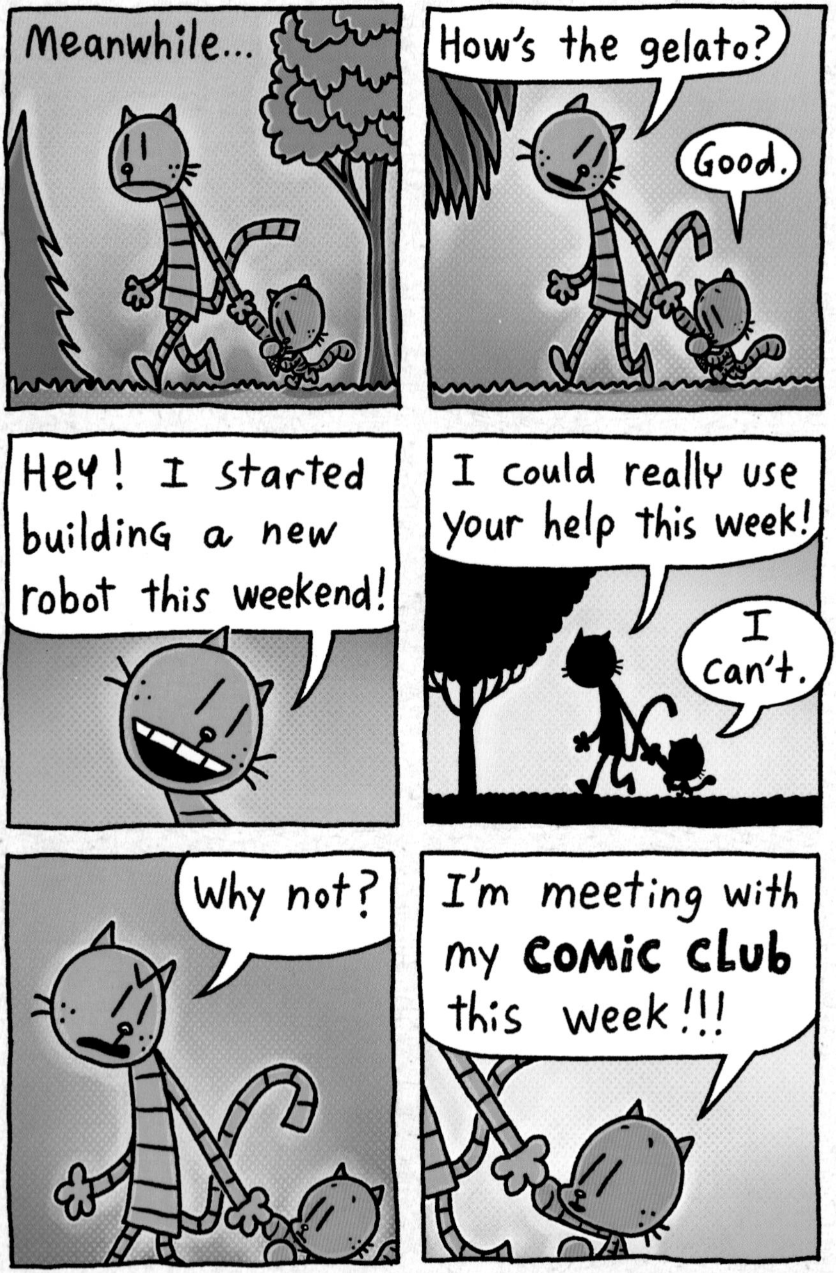
Meanwhile...
How's the gelato?
Good.
Hey! I started building a new robot this weekend!
I could really use your help this week!
I can't.
Why not?
I'm meeting with my COMIC CLUB this week!!!

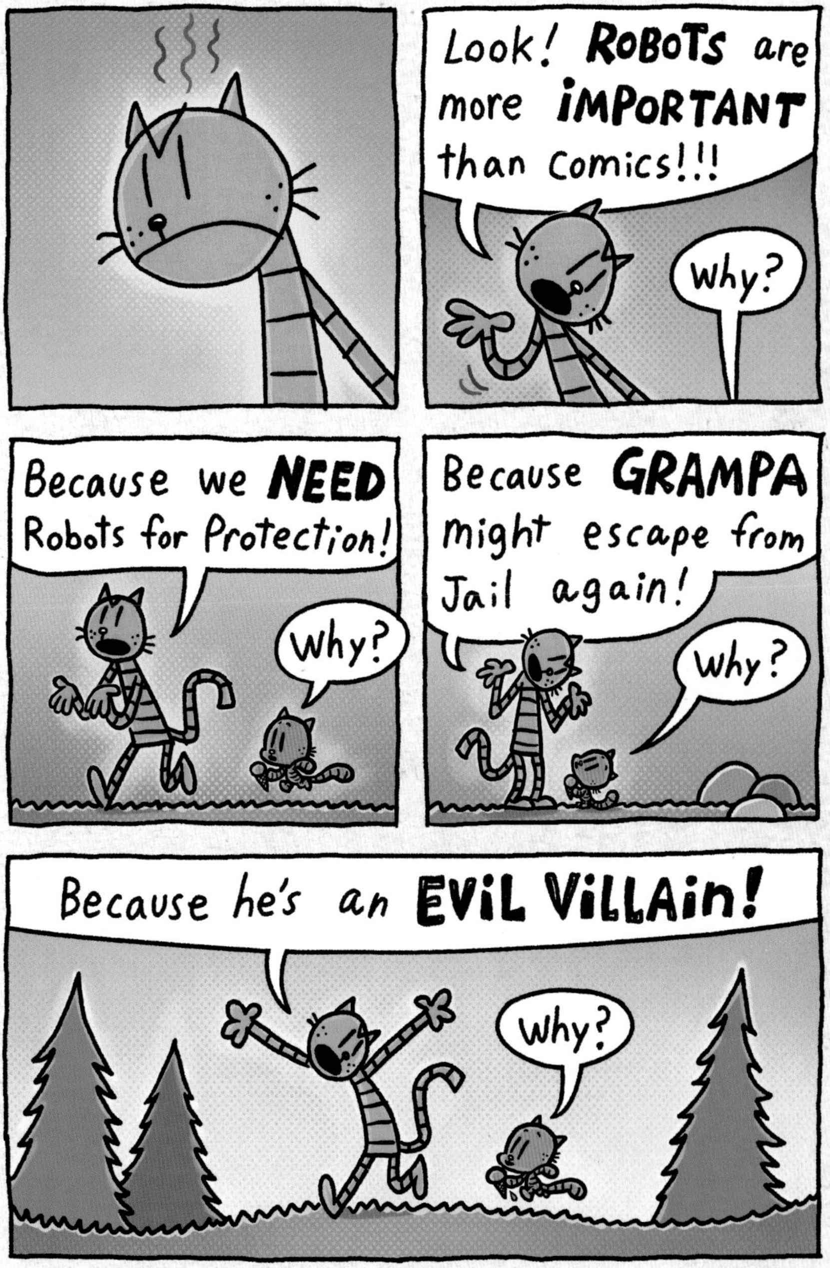
Look! ROBOTS are more IMPORTANT than comics!!!
Why?
Because we NEED Robots for Protection!
Why?
Because GRAMPA might escape from Jail again!
Why?
Because he's an EVIL VILLAIN!
Why?

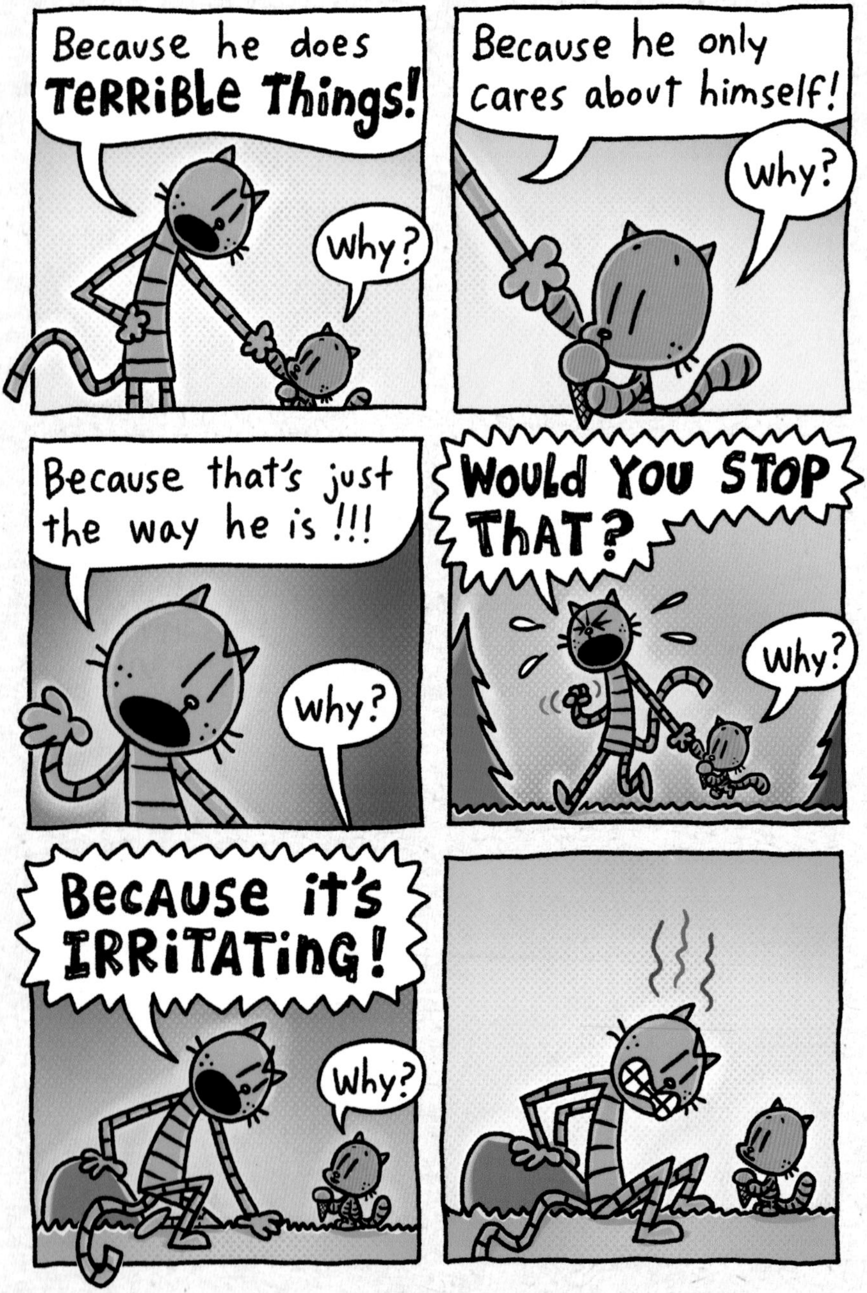
Because he does TERRIBLE Things!
Why?
Because he only cares about himself!
Why?
Because that's just the way he is!!!
Why?
WOULD YOU STOP THAT?
Why?
BECAUSE it's IRRITATING!
Why?

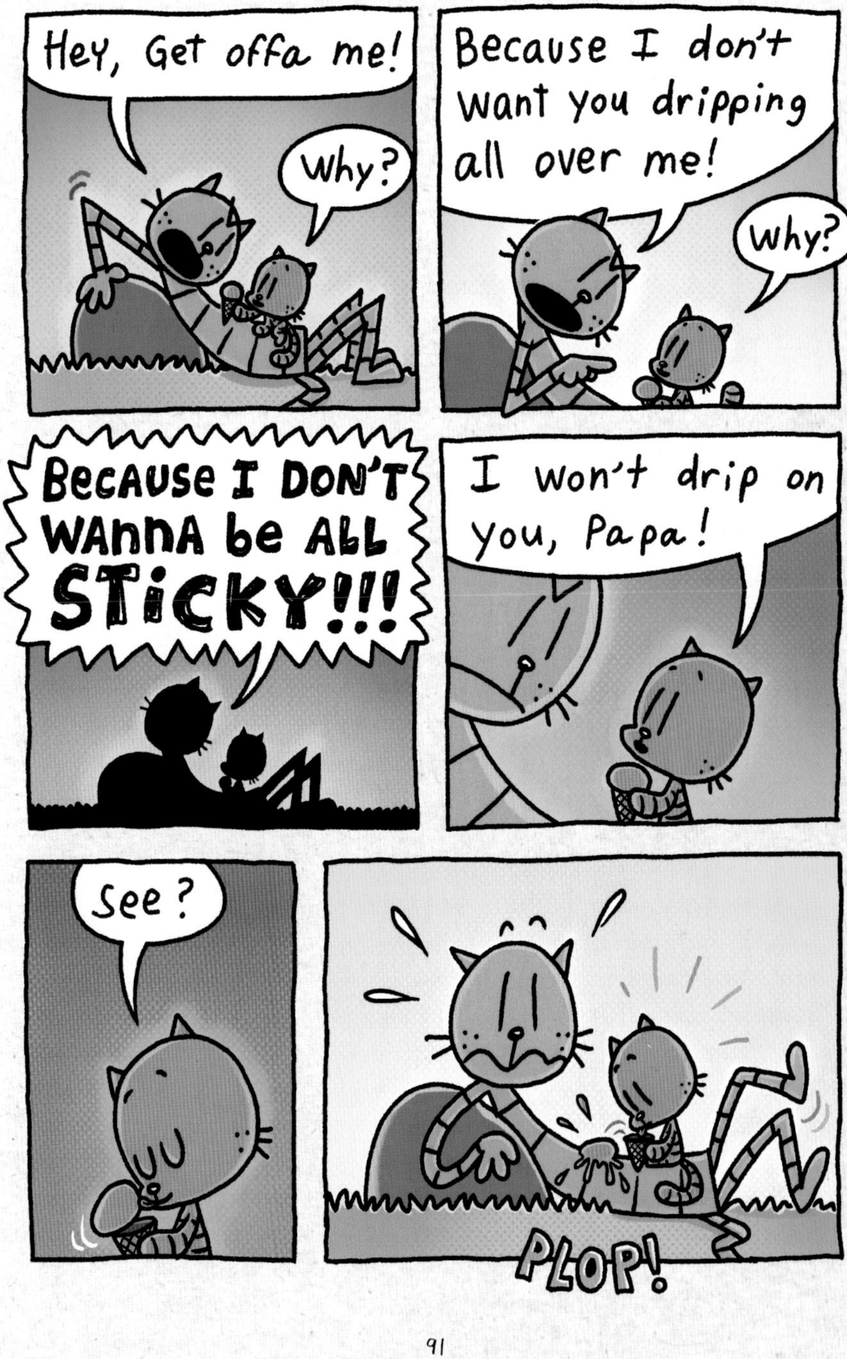
Hey, Get offa me!
Why?
Because I don't want you dripping all over me!
Why?
BECAUSE I DON'T WANNA be ALL STICKY!!!
I won't drip on you, Papa!
See?
PLOP!

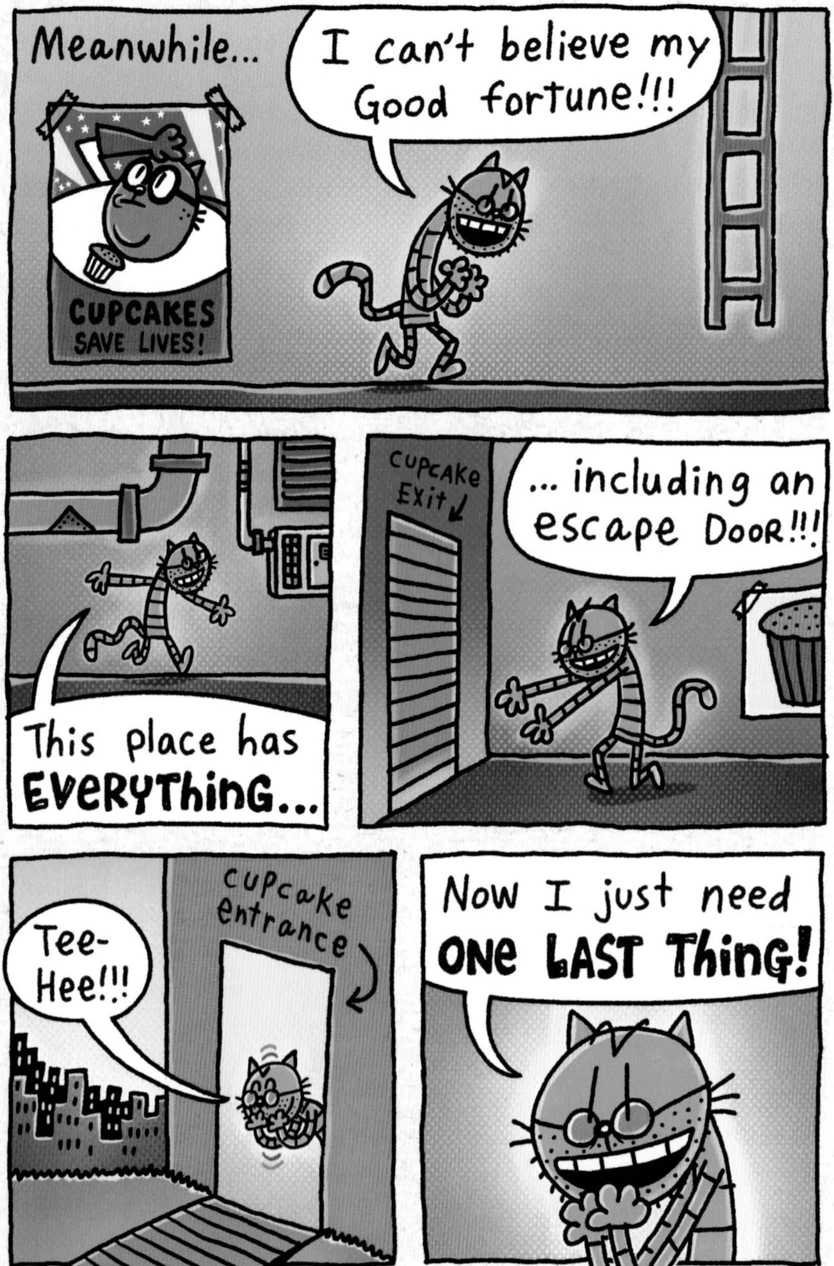
Meanwhile...
I can't believe my Good fortune!!!
CUPCAKES SAVE LIVES!
This place has EVERYTHING...
CUPCAKE EXIT
... including an escape DOOR!!!
Cupcake entrance
Tee-Hee!!!
Now I just need ONE LAST THING!

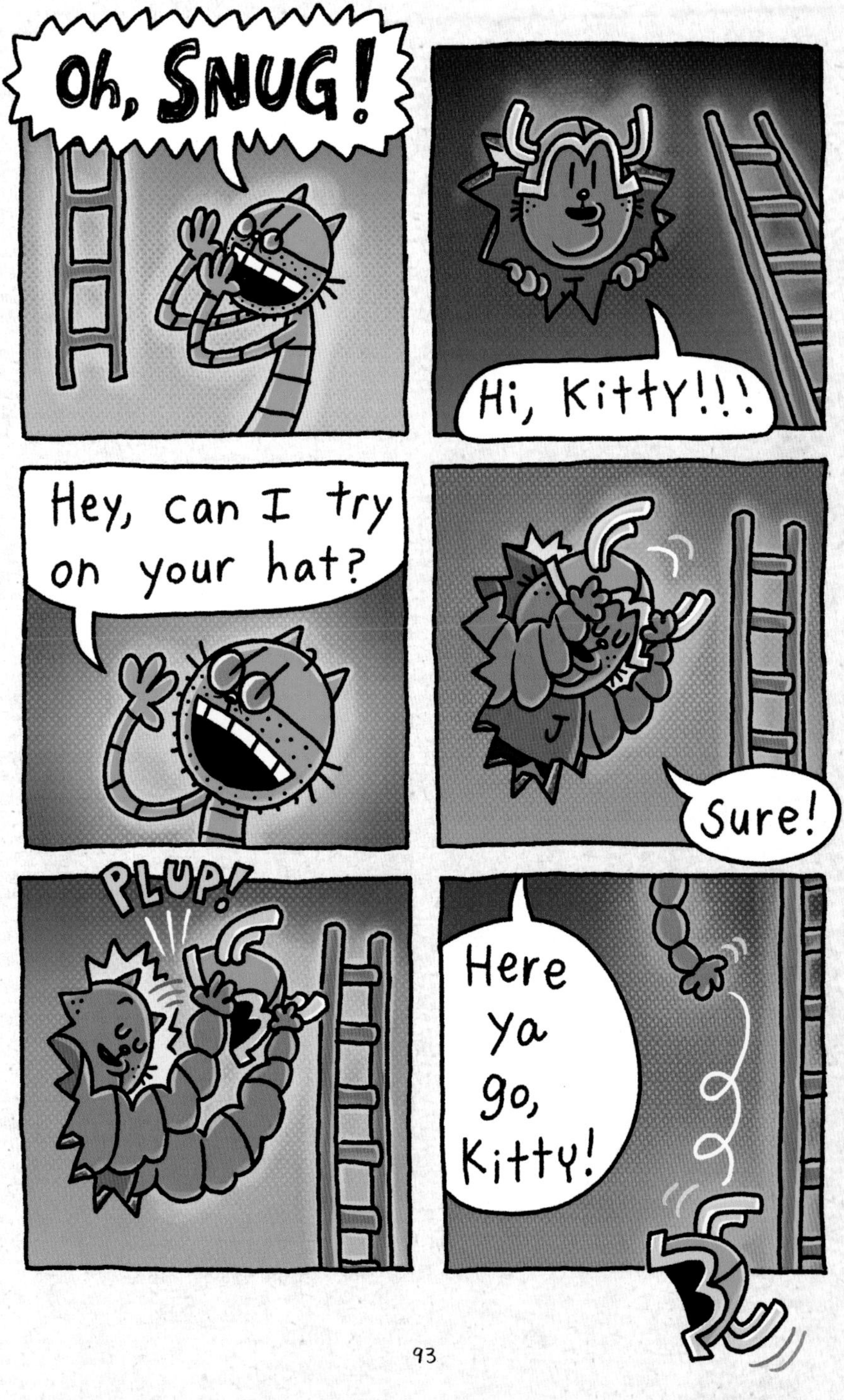
Oh, SNUG!
Hi, Kitty!!!
Hey, can I try on your hat?
Sure!
PLUP!
Here ya go, Kitty!

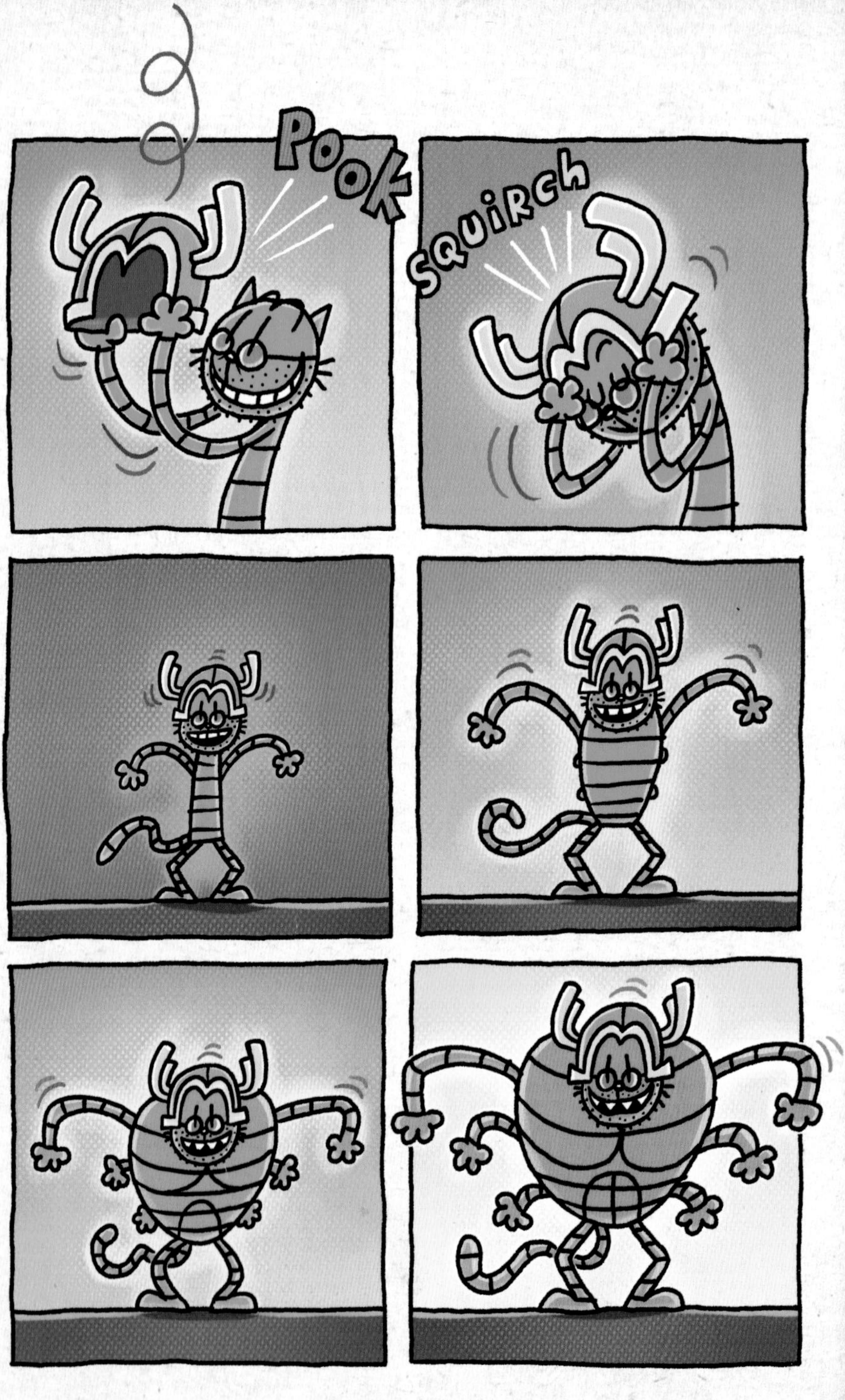
POOK
SQUIRCH

CHAPTER 6

THE INCORRIGIBLE CRUD

By George Beard and Harold Hutchins

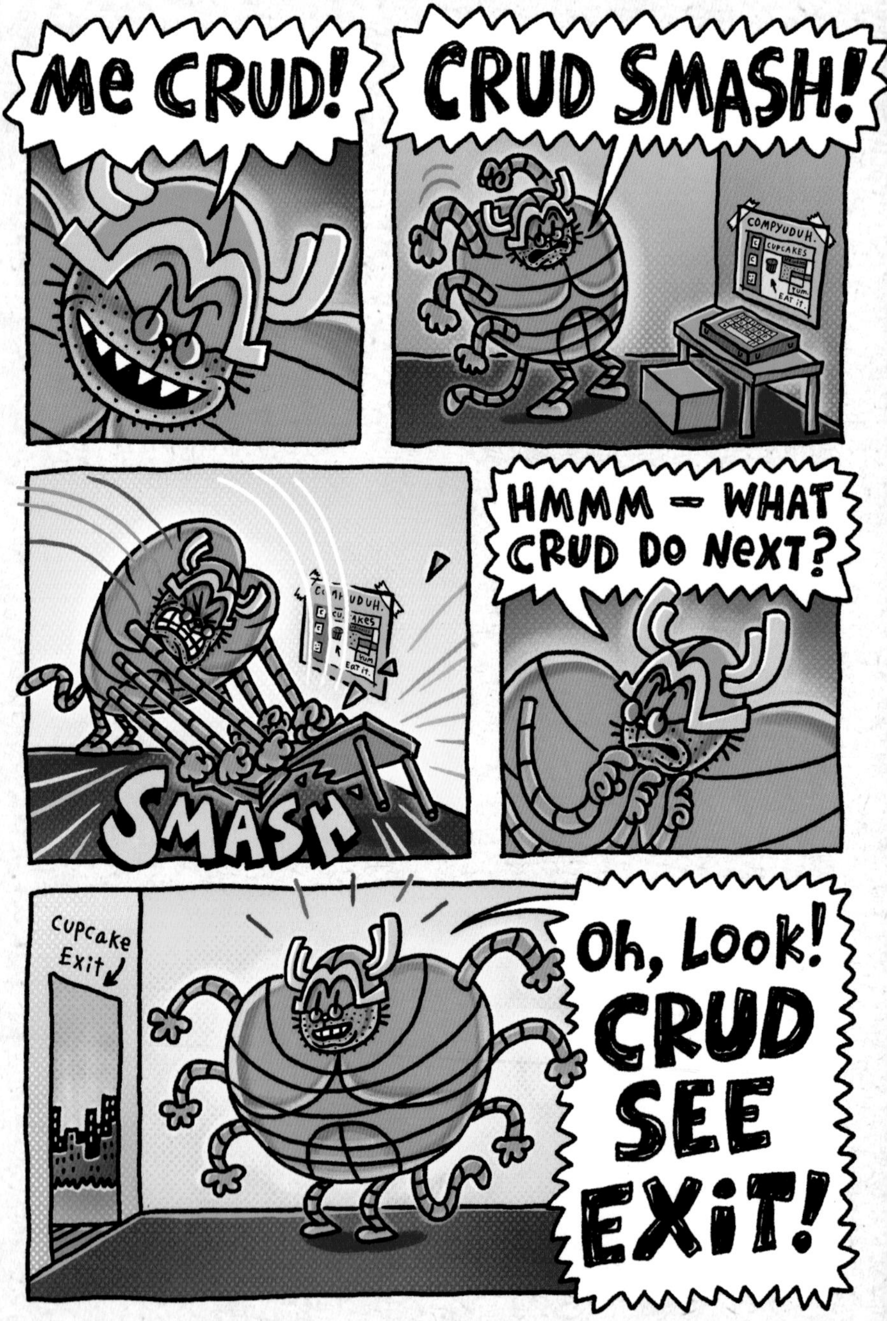
Me CRUD!
CRUD SMASH!
COMPYUDUH.
CUPCAKES
YUM.
EAT it.
SMASH
HMMM — WHAT CRUD DO NEXT?
Cupcake Exit
Oh, Look! CRUD SEE EXiT!

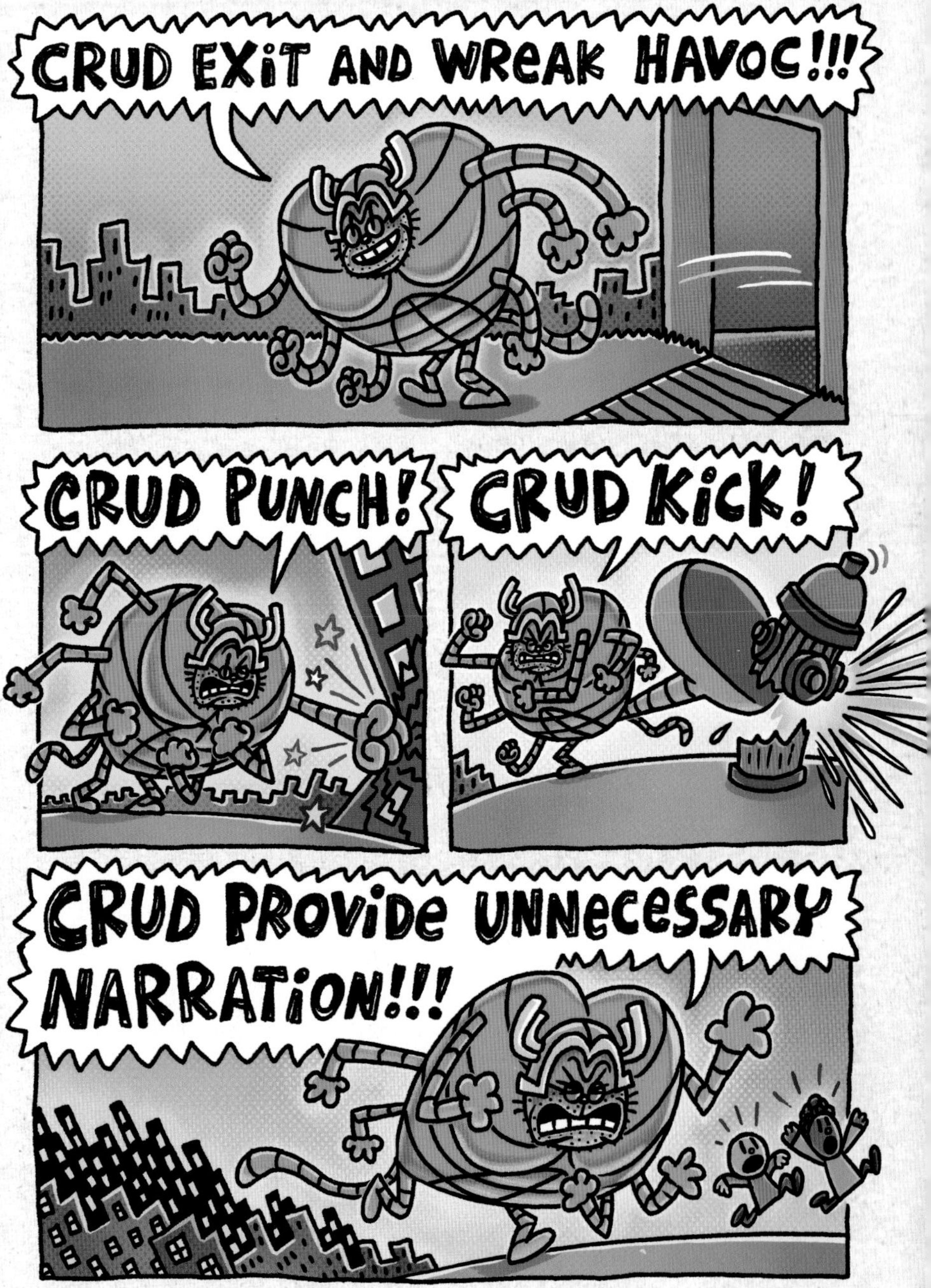
CRUD EXIT AND WREAK HAVOC!!!
CRUD PUNCH!
CRUD KICK!
CRUD PROVIDE UNNECESSARY NARRATION!!!

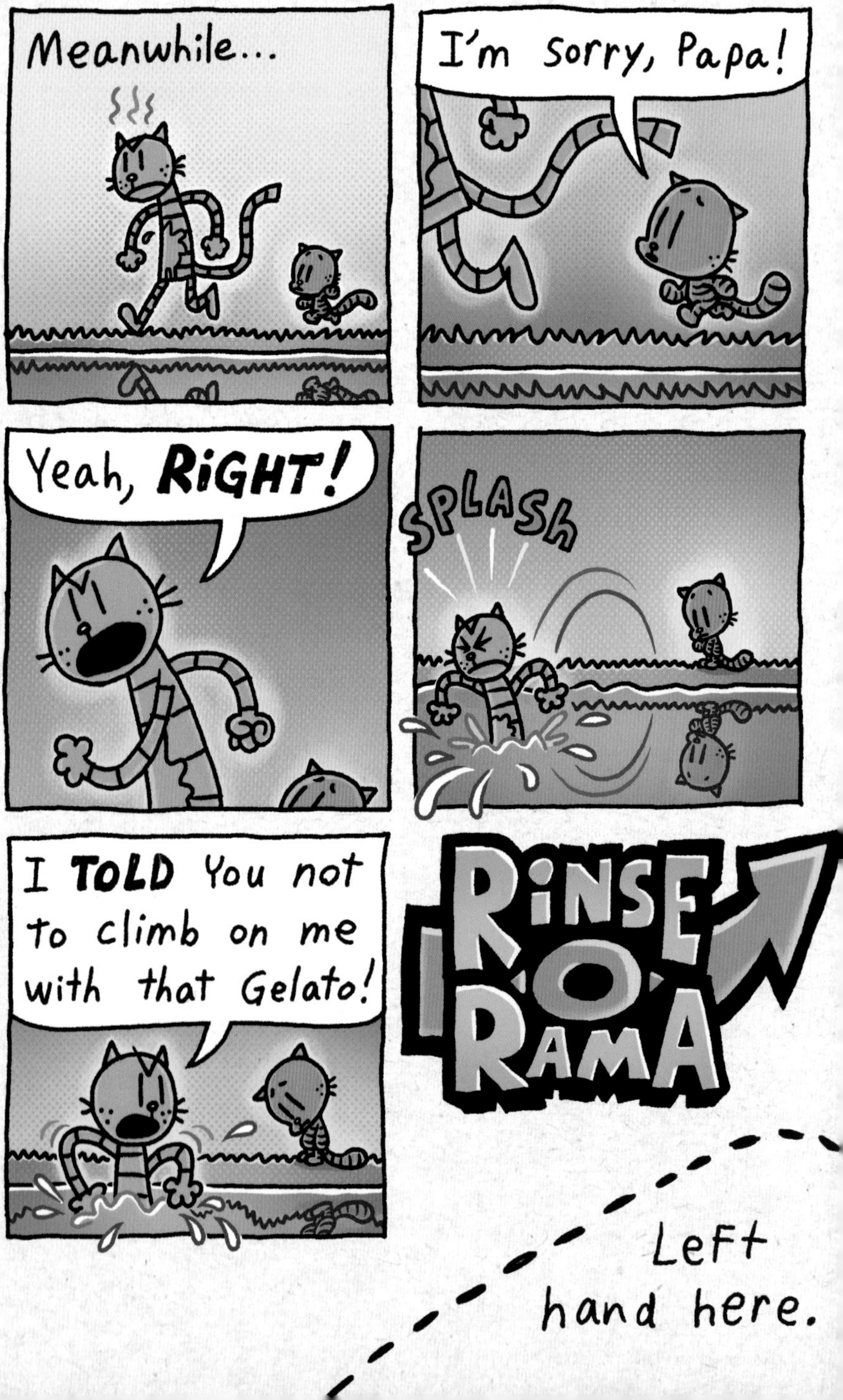

Meanwhile...
I'm Sorry, Papa!
Yeah, RiGHT!
SPLASh
I TOLD You not to climb on me with that Gelato!
RiNSE-O-RAMA
Left hand here.

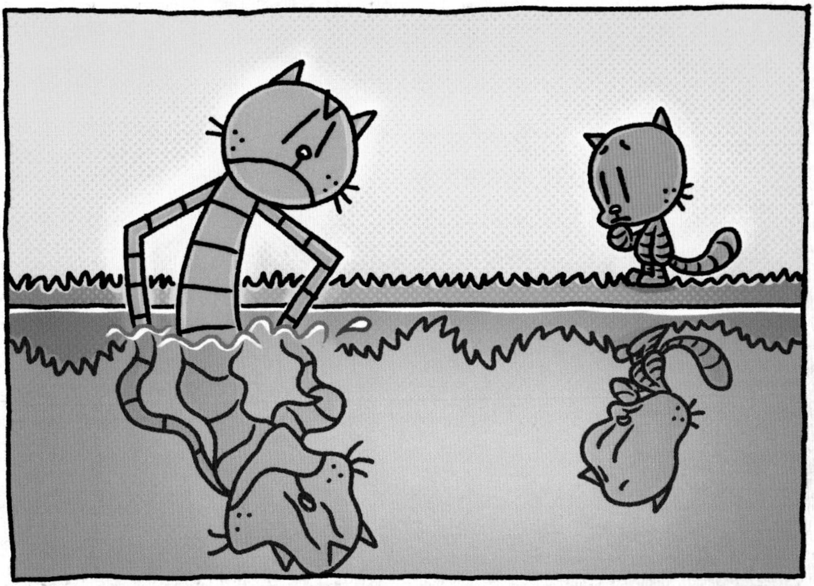

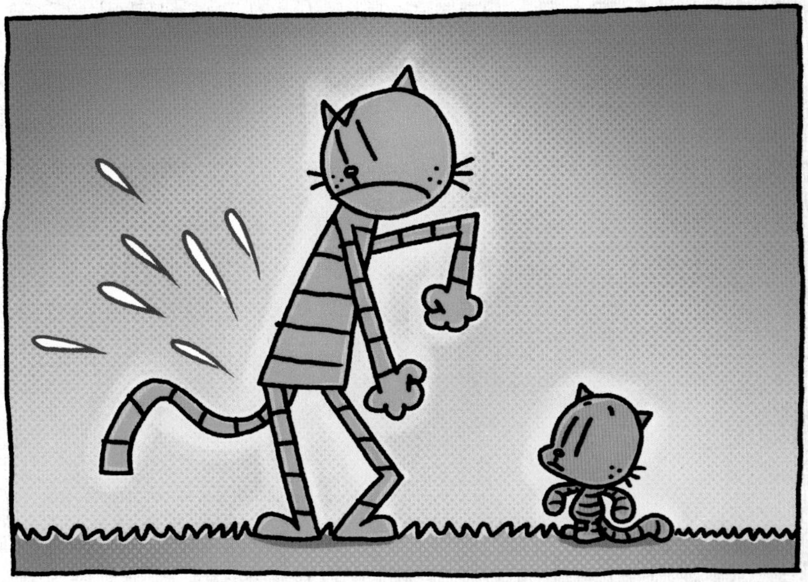

Right Thumb here.

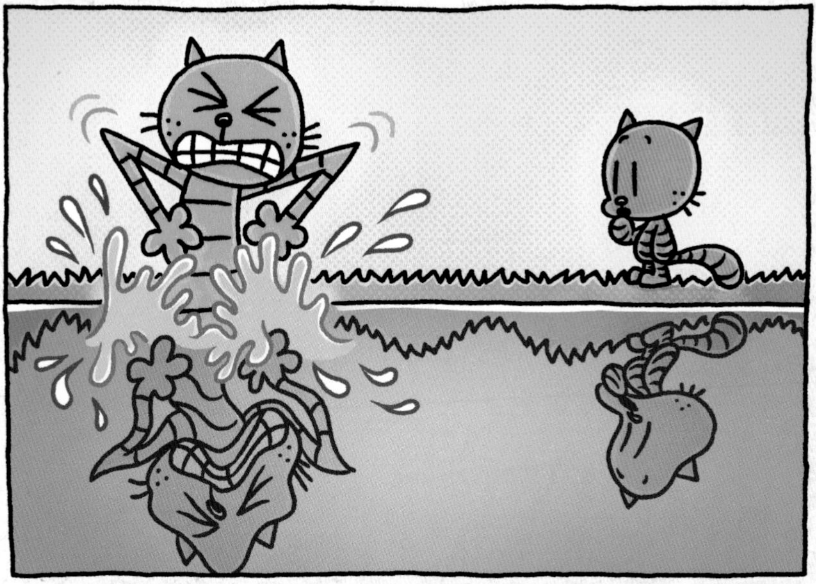

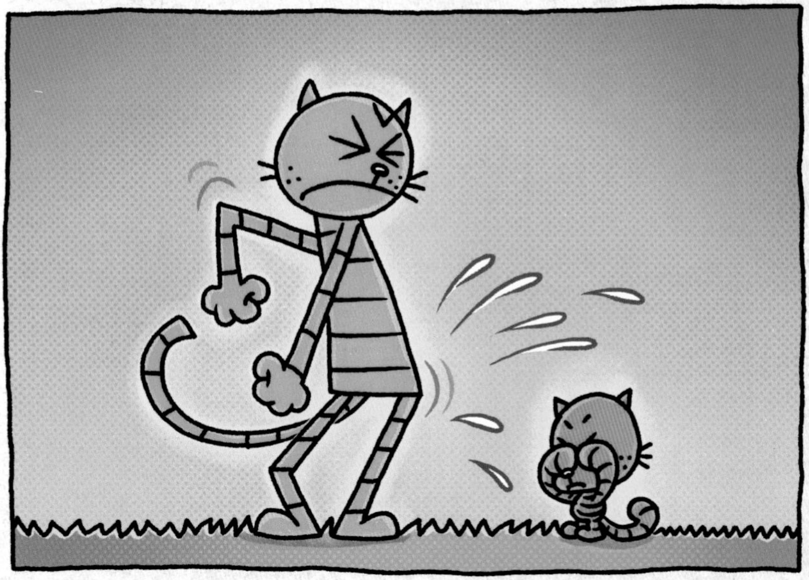

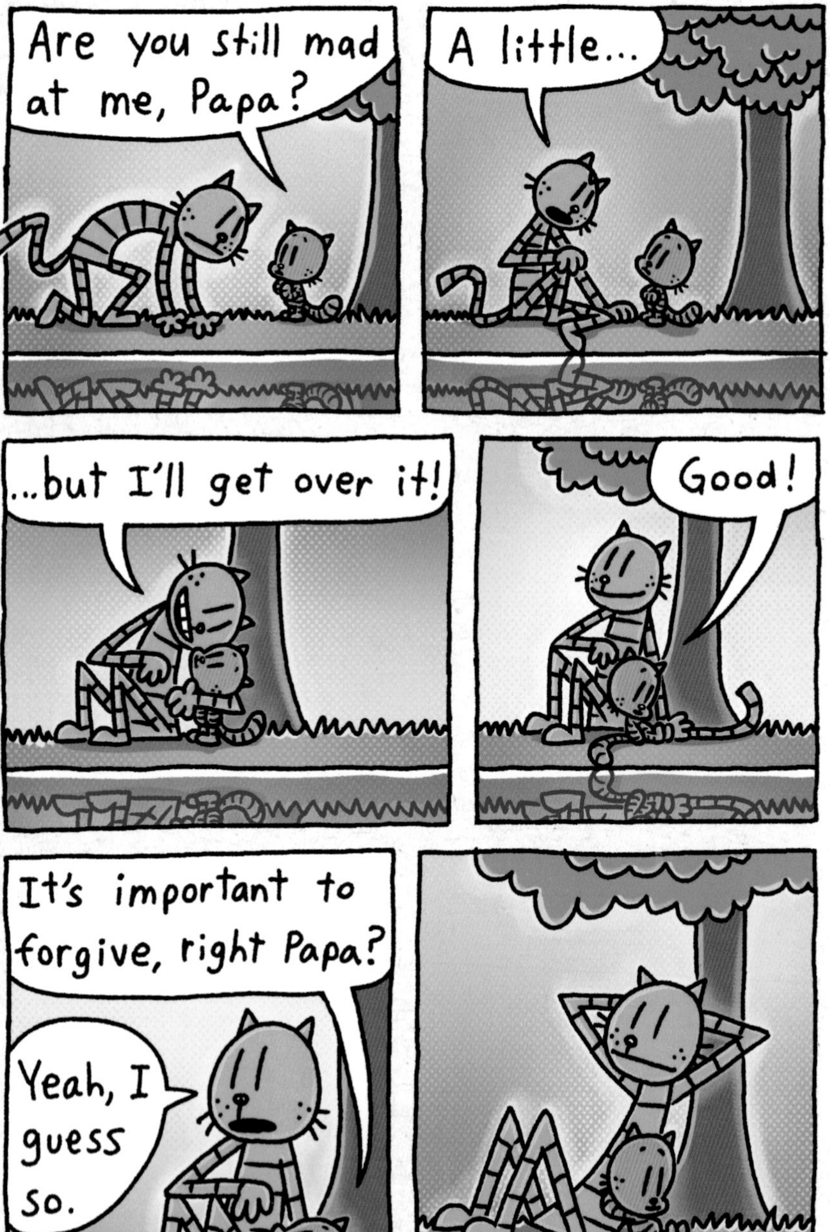
Are you still mad at me, Papa?
A little...
...but I'll get over it!
Good!
It's important to forgive, right Papa?
Yeah, I guess so.

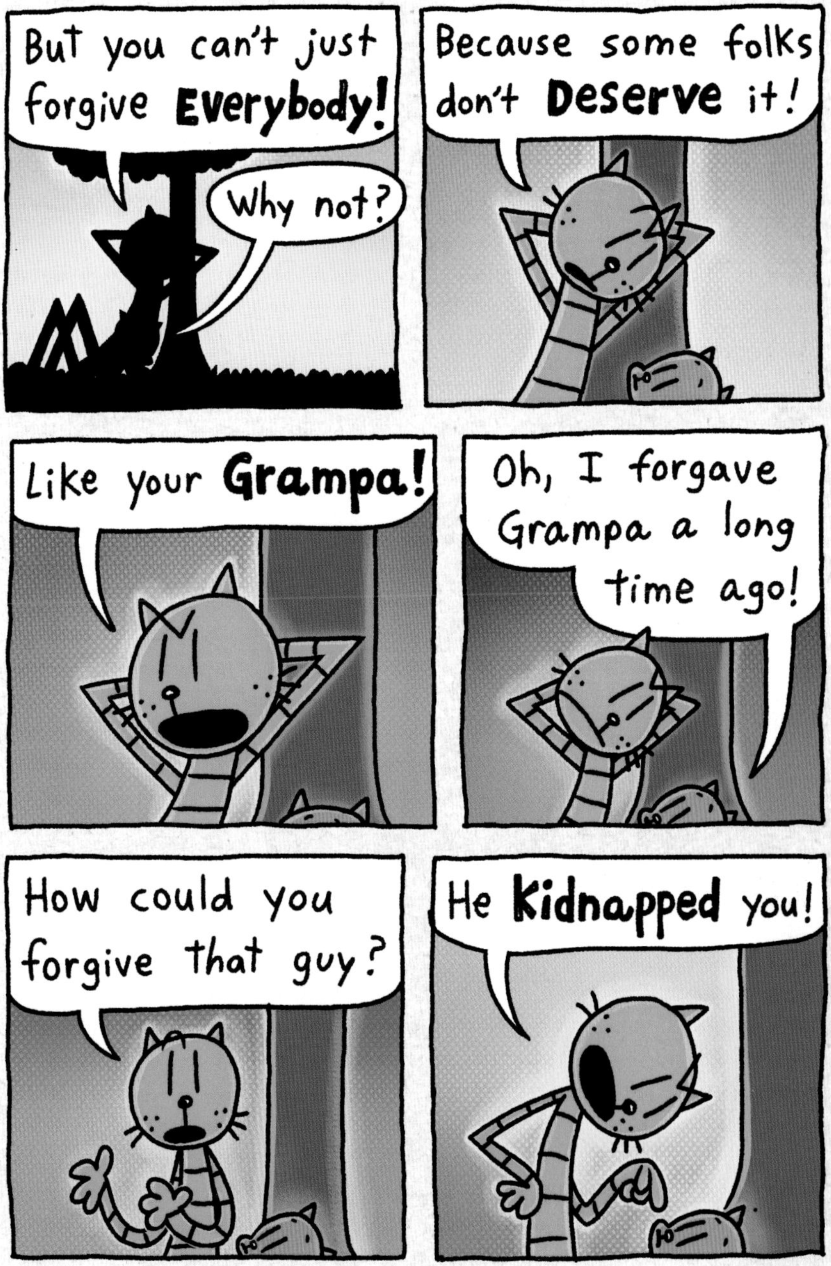
But you can't just forgive EVERYBODY!
Why not?
Because some folks don't DESERVE it!
Like your GRAMPA!
Oh, I forgave Grampa a long time ago!
How could you forgive that guy?
He KIDNAPPED you!

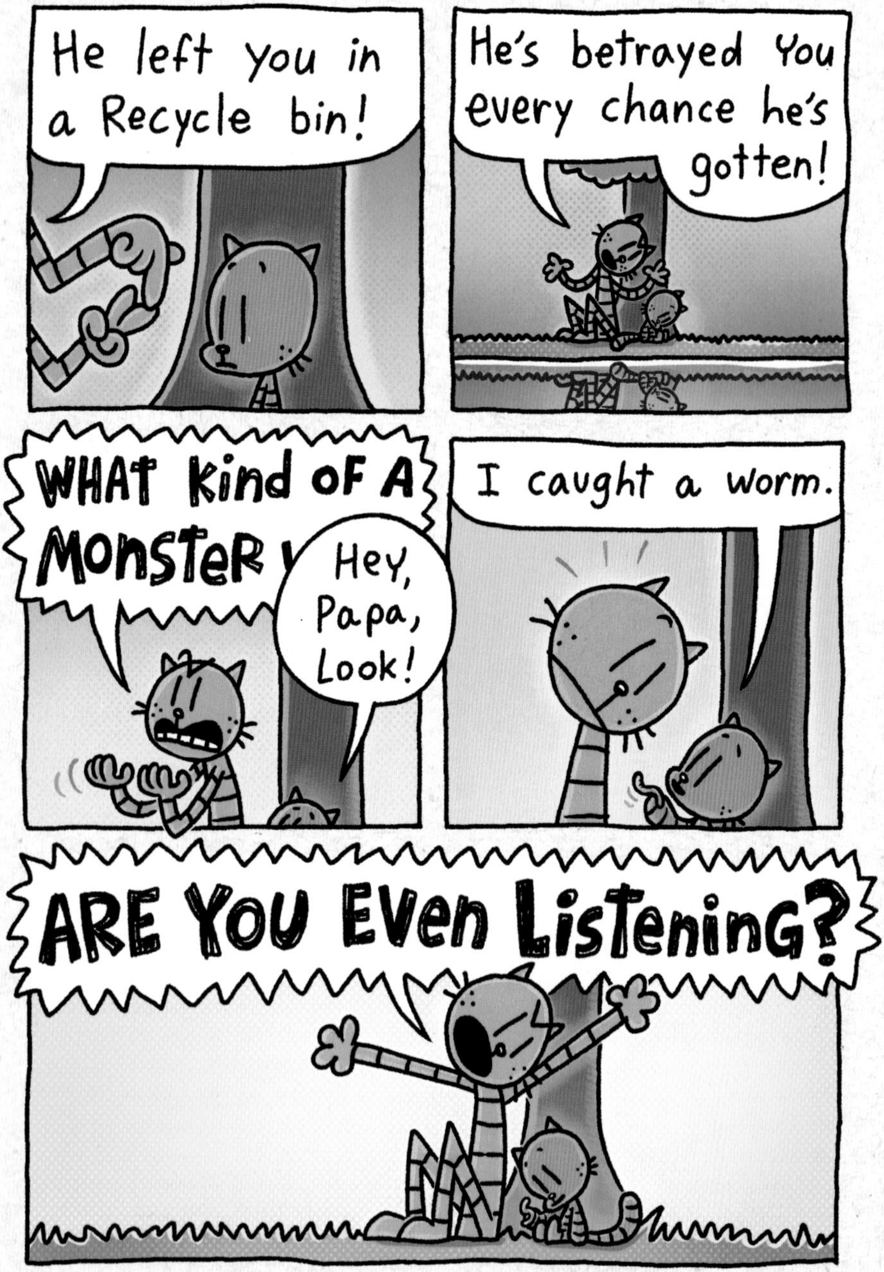
He left you in a Recycle bin!
He's betrayed You every chance he's gotten!
WHAT Kind OF A MONSTER
Hey, Papa, Look!
I caught a worm.
ARE YOU Even Listening?

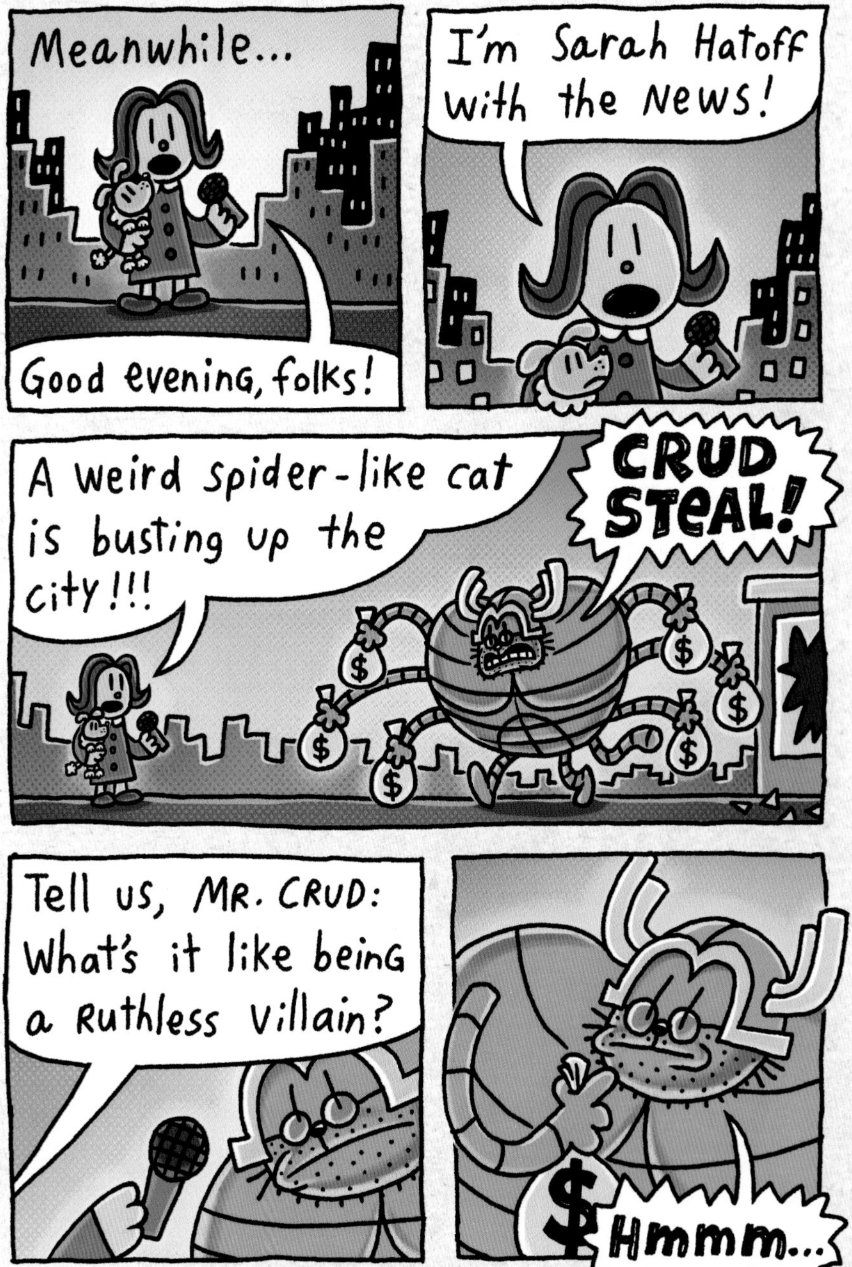
Meanwhile...
Good evening, folks!
I'm Sarah Hatoff with the News!
A weird spider-like cat is busting up the city!!!
CRUD STEAL!
Tell us, MR. CRUD: What's it like being a Ruthless villain?
Hmmm...

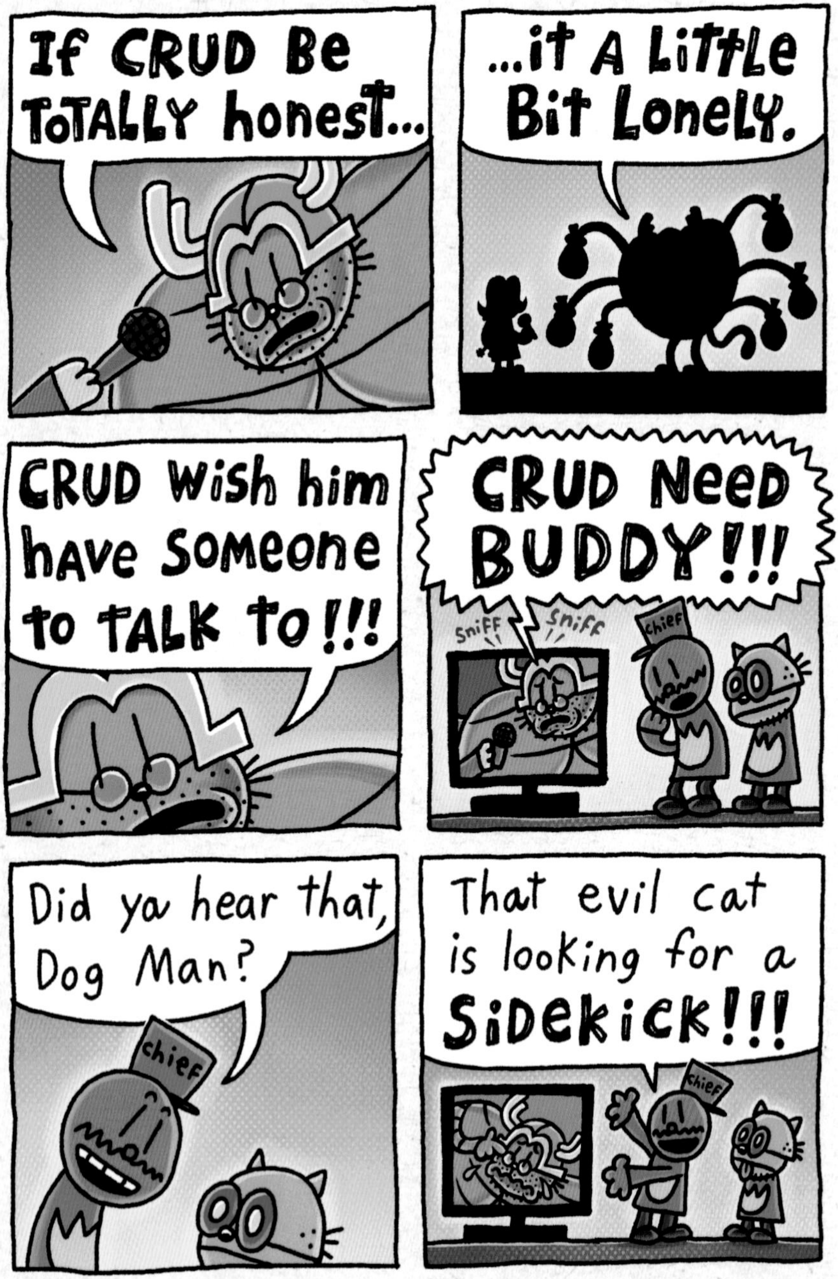
If CRUD Be TOTALLY honest...
...it A Little Bit Lonely.
CRUD Wish him have Someone to TALK To!!!
CRUD NEED BUDDY!!!
Sniff
Sniff
Chief
Did ya hear that, Dog Man?
chief
That evil cat is looking for a SIDEKICK!!!
Chief

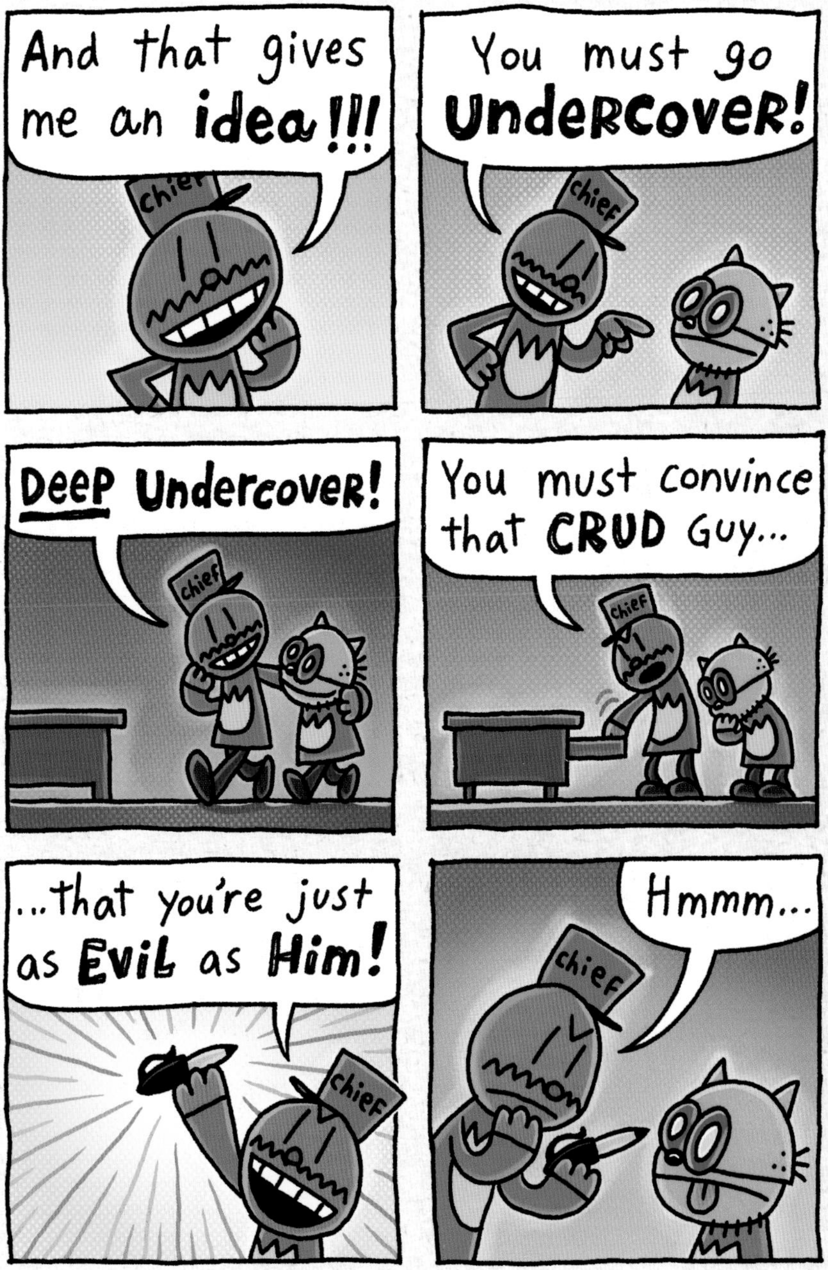
And that gives me an idea!!!
You must go UNDERCOVER!
DEEP Undercover!
You must convince that CRUD Guy...
...that you're just as EVIL as Him!
Hmmm...
chief

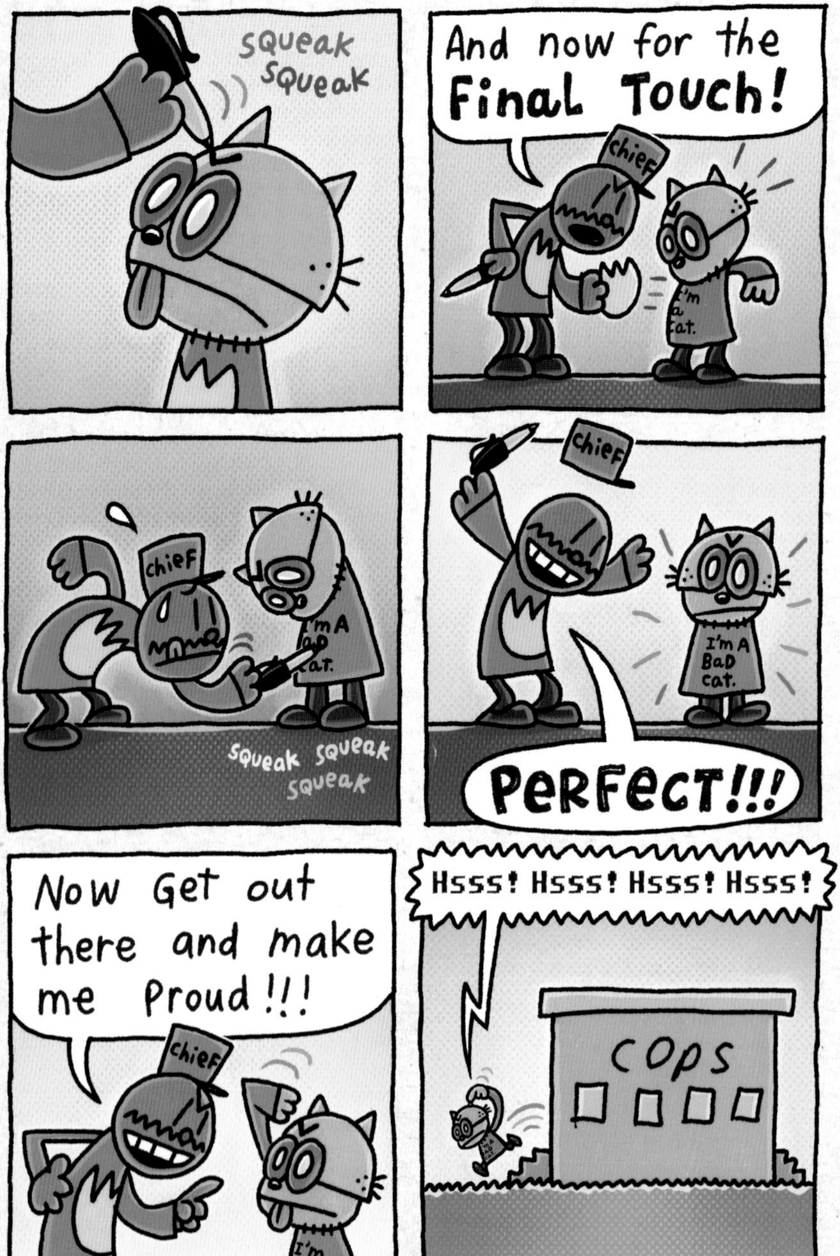

SQUEAK SQUEAK
And now for the Final Touch!
CHIEF
I'm a cat.
CHIEF
I'm A BAD CAT.
SQUEAK SQUEAK SQUEAK
CHIEF
I'm A BAD CAT.
PERFECT!!!
Now Get out there and make me Proud!!!
CHIEF
I'm
HSSS! HSSS! HSSS! HSSS!
COPS

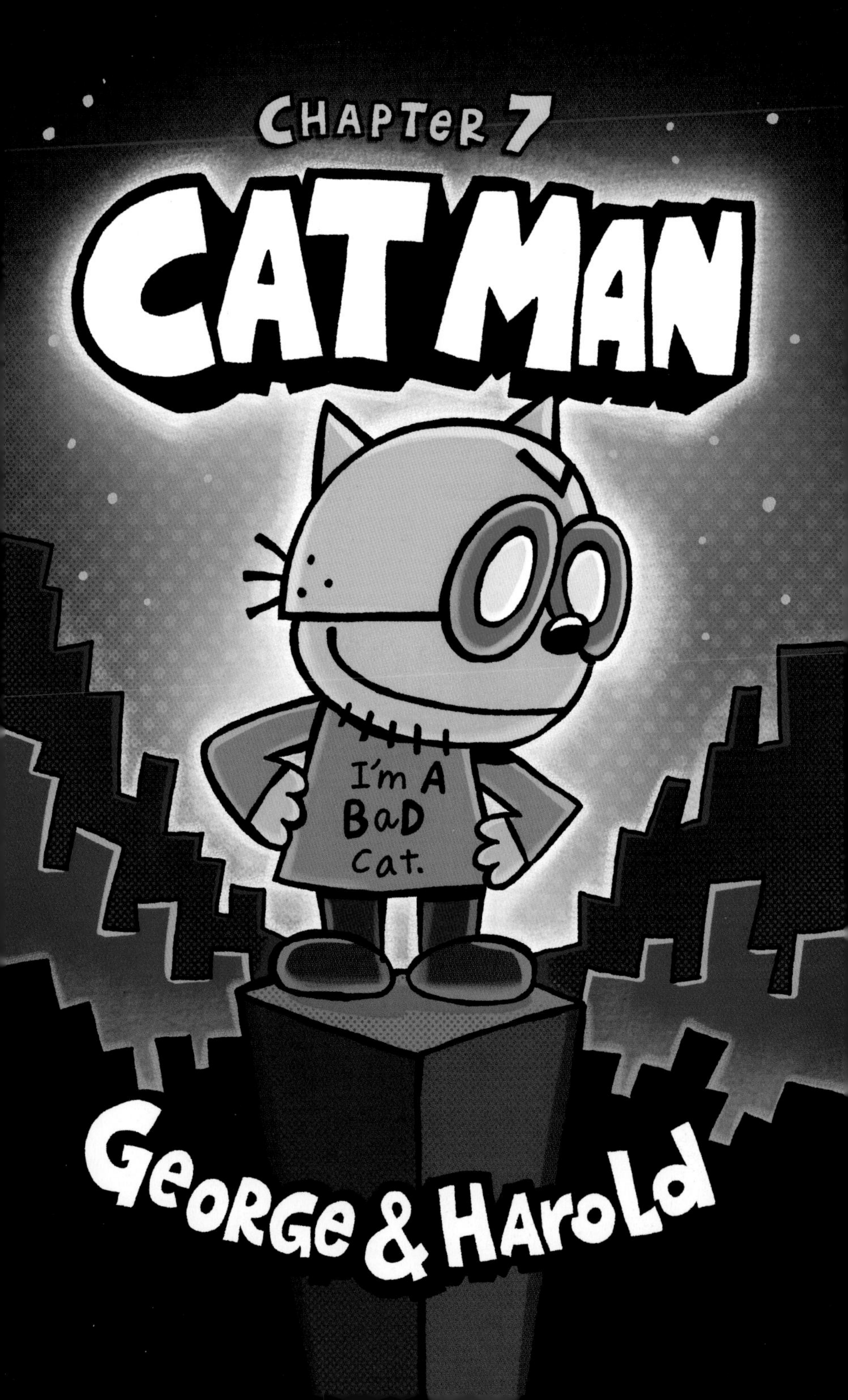
CHAPTER 7
CAT MAN
I'm A BaD Cat.
George & Harold

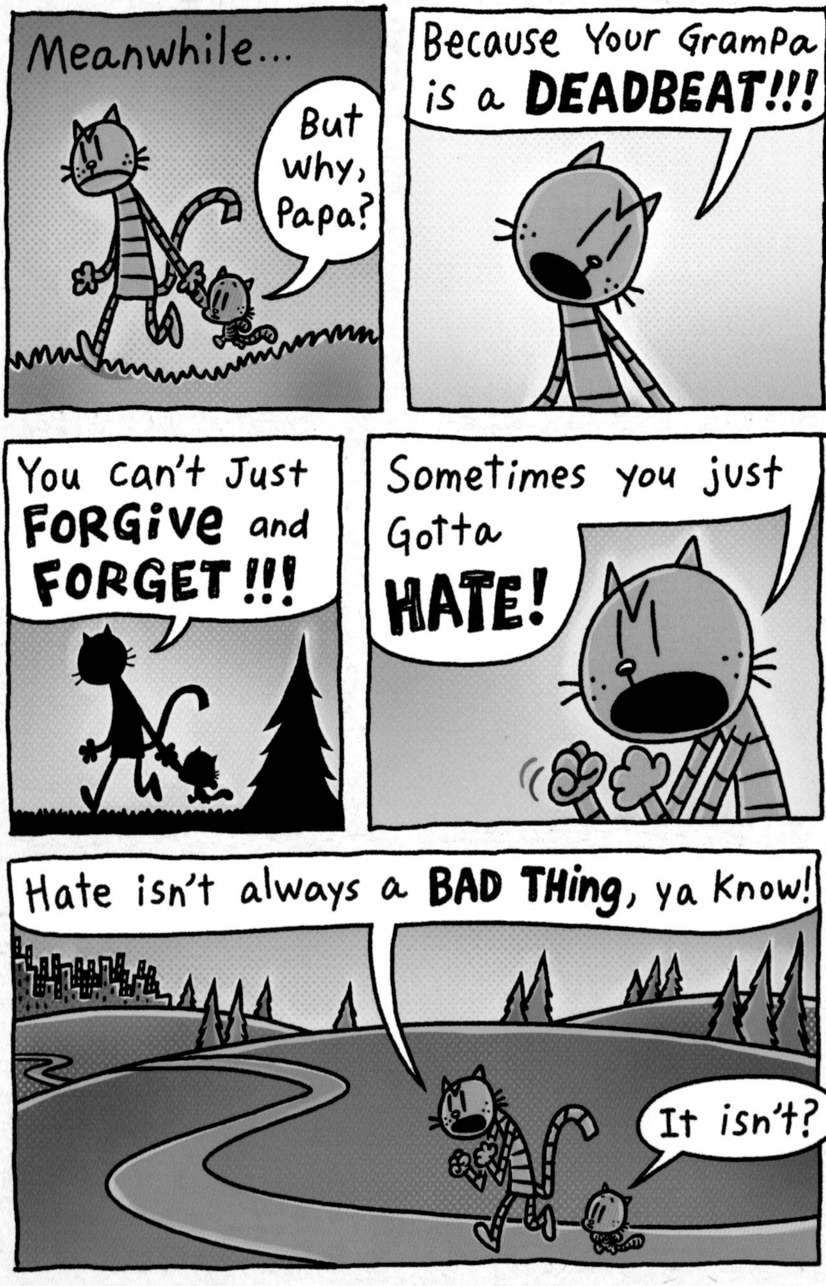
Meanwhile...
But why, Papa?
Because Your Grampa is a DEADBEAT!!!
You can't Just FORGIVE and FORGET!!!
Sometimes you just Gotta HATE!
Hate isn't always a BAD THing, ya Know!
It isn't?

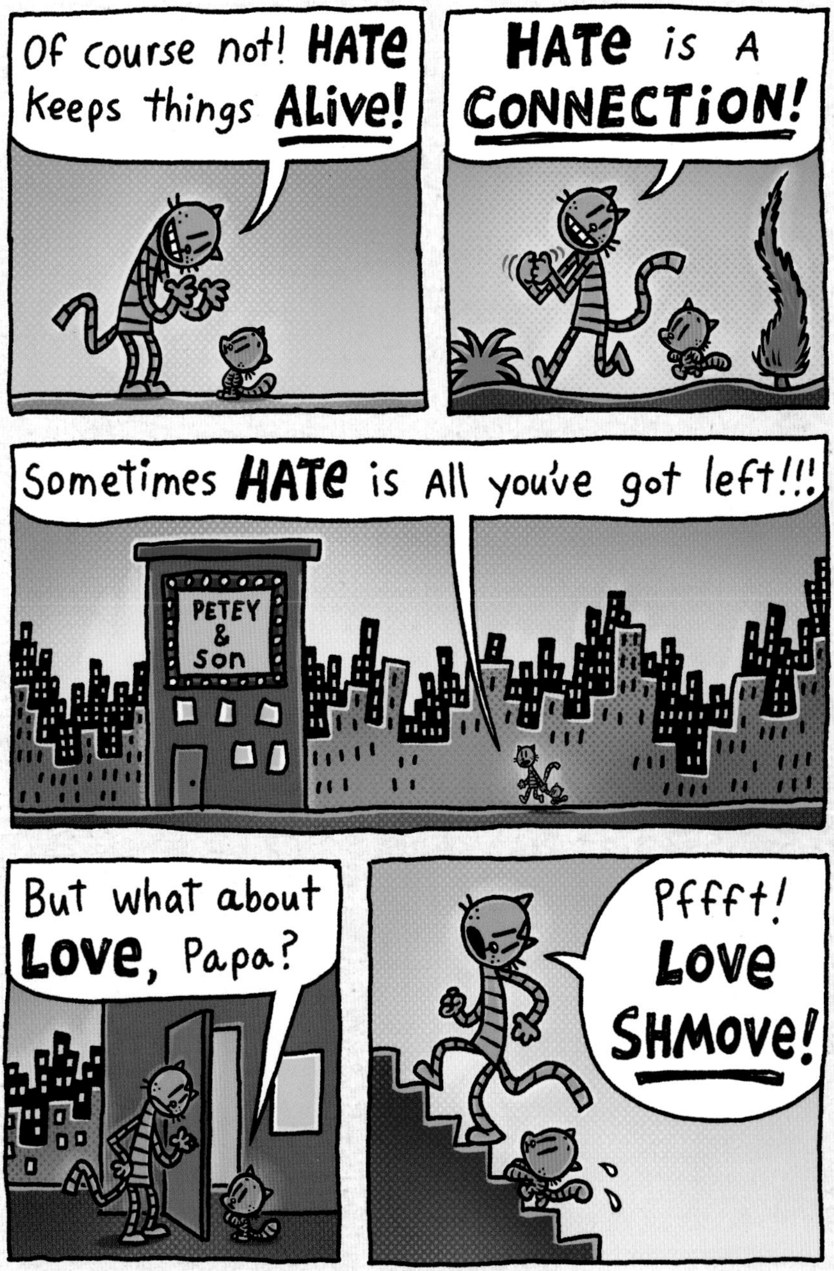

Of course not! HATE Keeps things ALive!
HATE is A CONNECTiON!
Sometimes HATE is All you've got left!!!
PETEY & Son
But what about Love, Papa?
Pffft! Love SHMOVE!

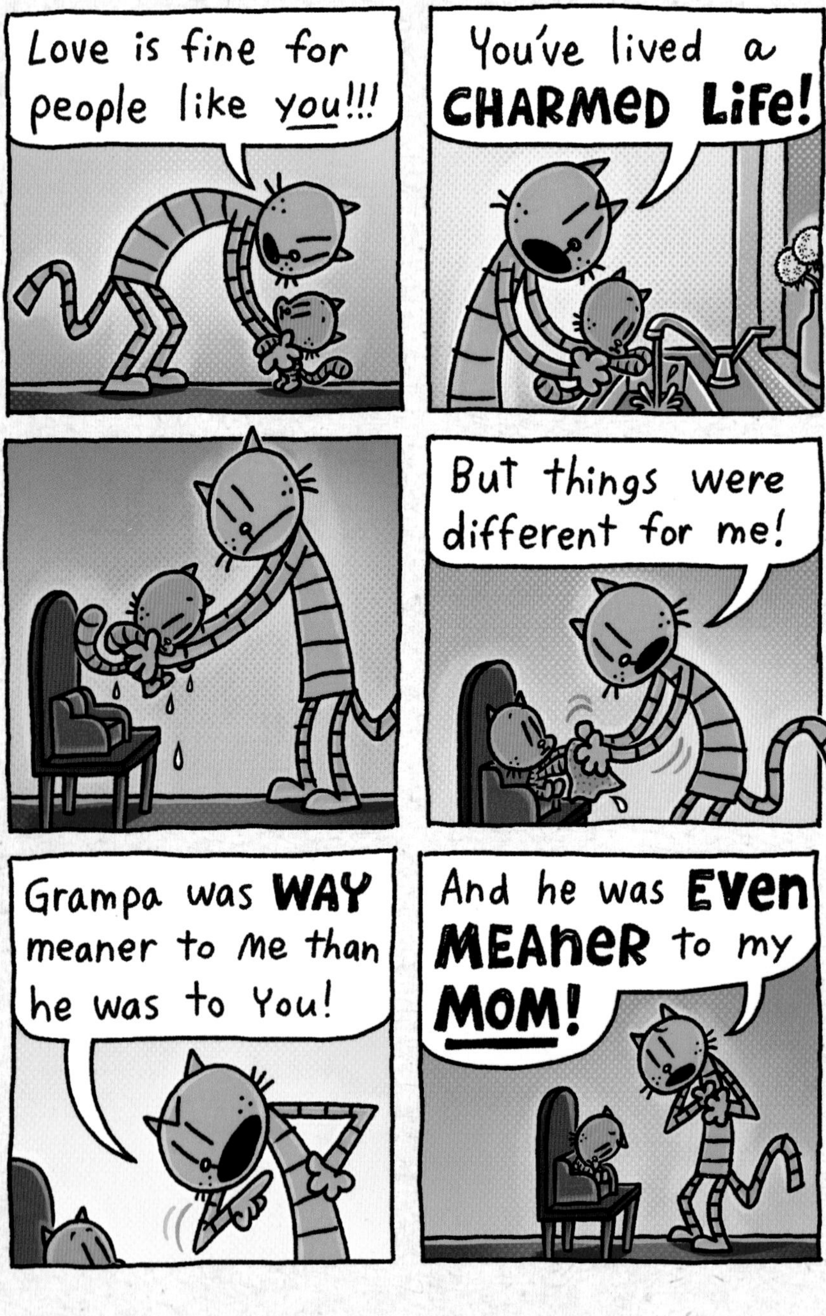
Love is fine for people like you!!!
You've lived a CHARMED LIFE!
But things were different for me!
Grampa was WAY meaner to me than he was to You!
And he was EVEN MEANER to my MOM!

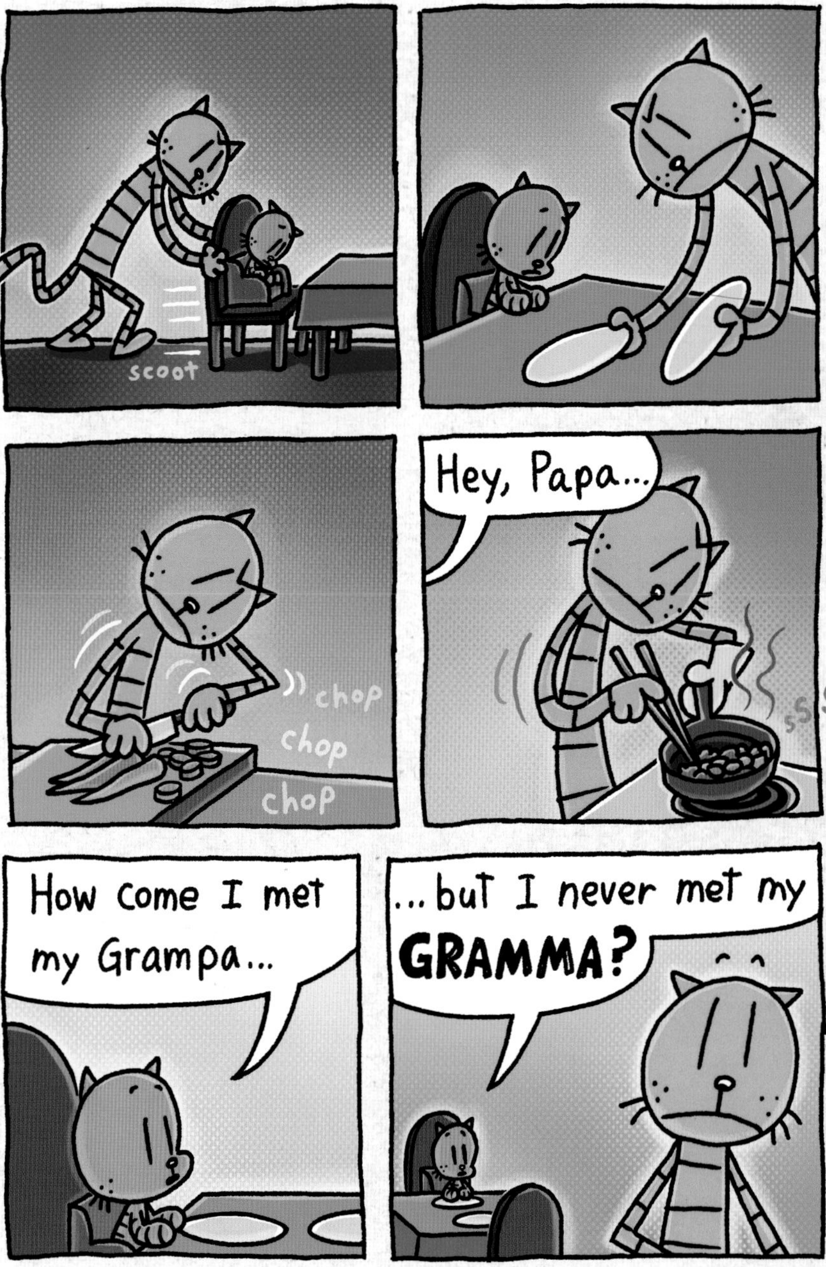
scoot
chop
chop
chop
Hey, Papa...
SSSSS
How come I met my Grampa...
...but I never met my GRAMMA?

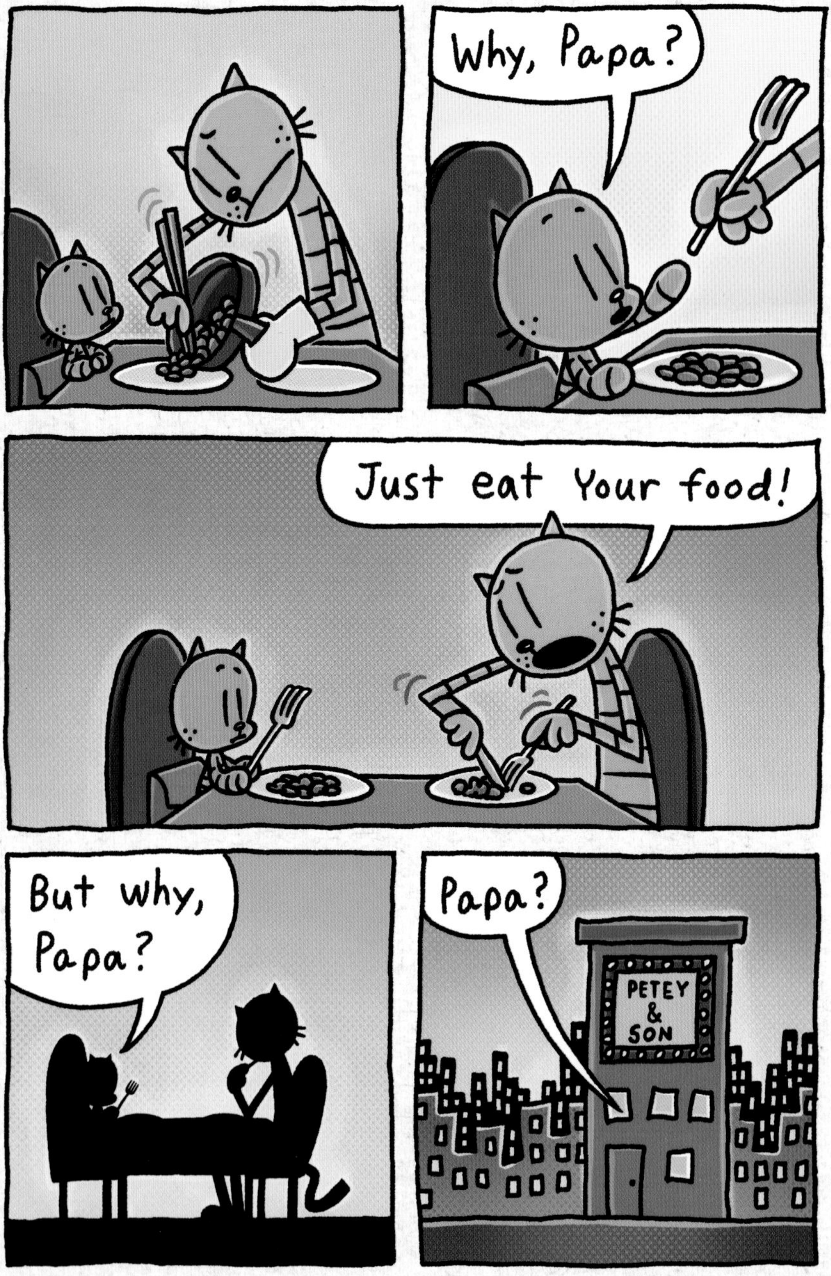
Why, Papa?
Just eat your food!
But why, Papa?
Papa?
PETEY & SON

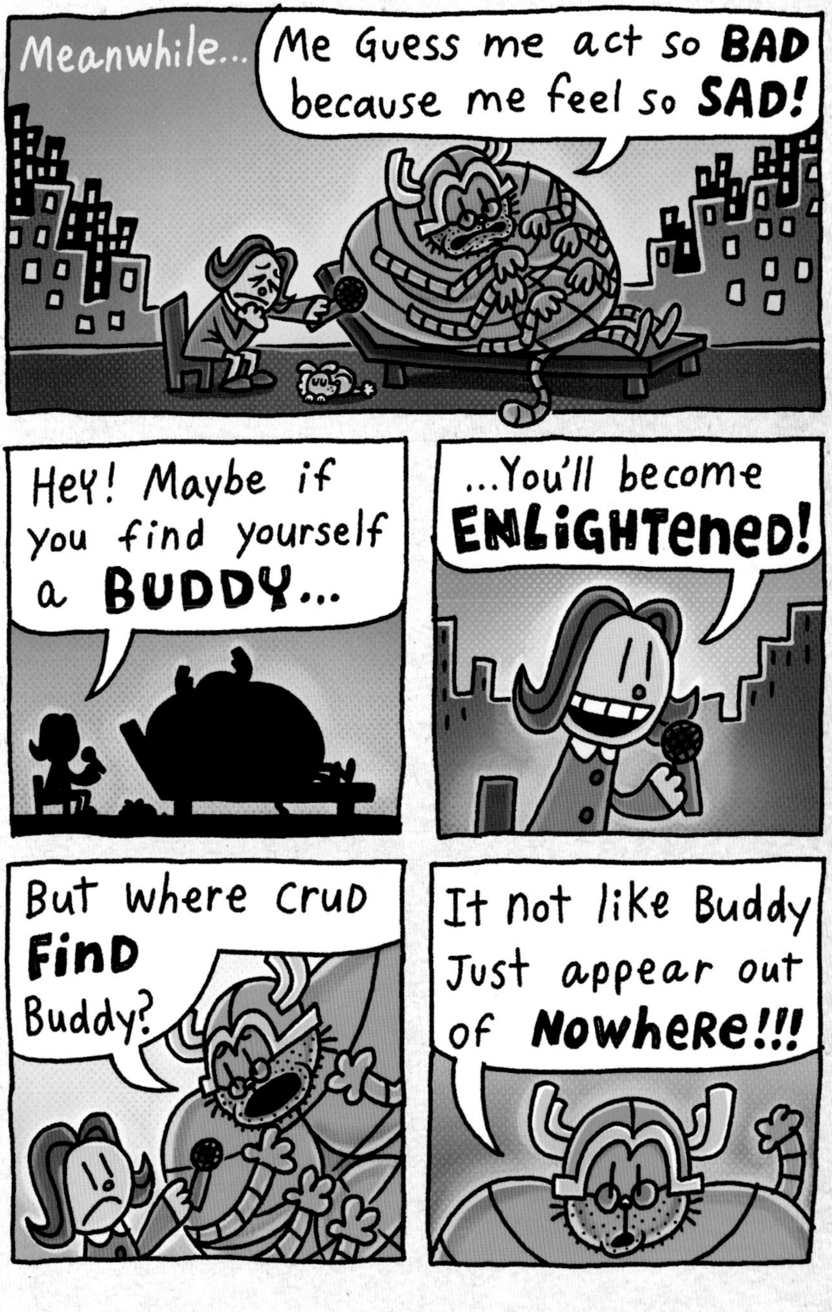
Meanwhile...
Me Guess me act so BAD because me feel so SAD!
Hey! Maybe if you find yourself a BUDDY...
...You'll become ENLIGHTENED!
But where CRUD FIND Buddy?
It not like Buddy Just appear out of NOWHERE!!!

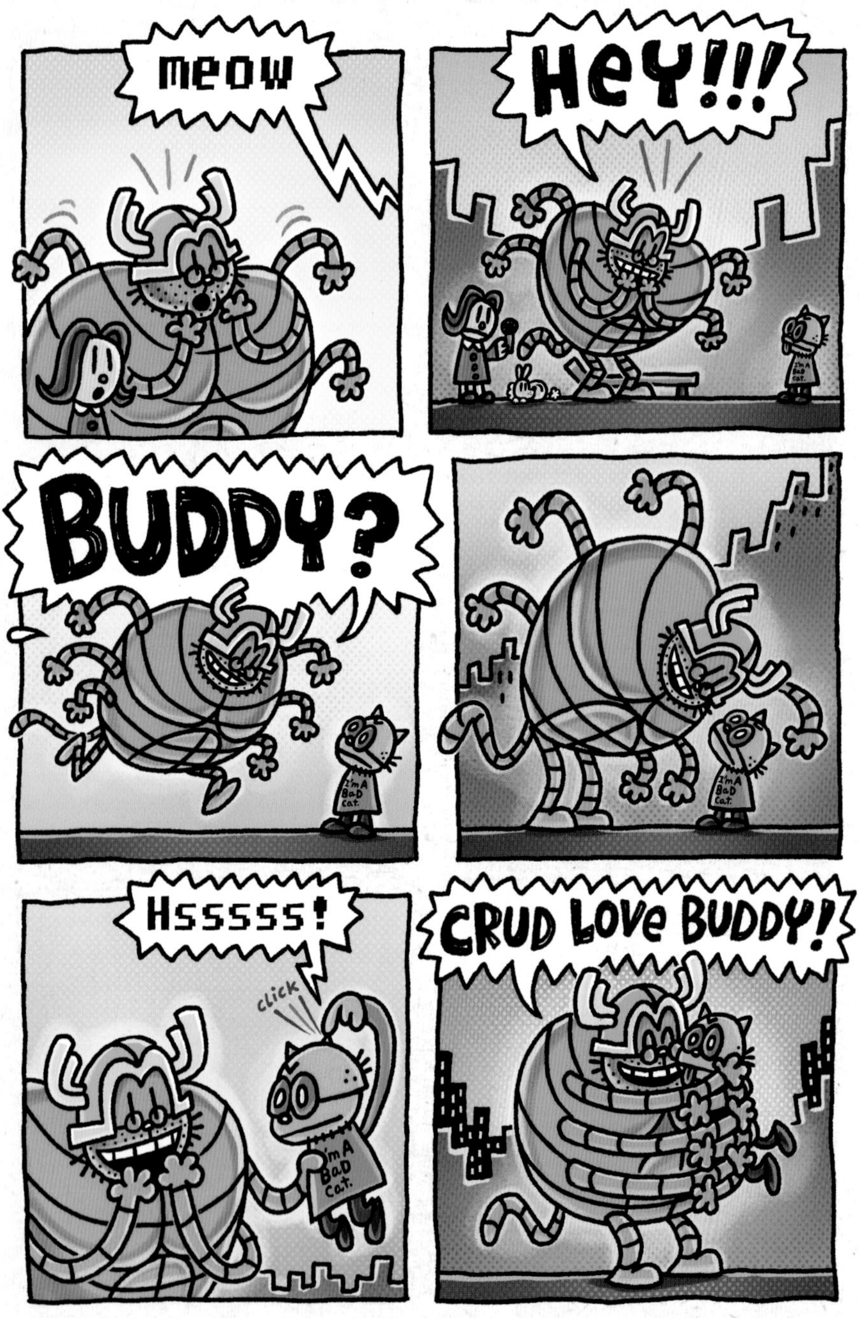
meow
HEY!!!
BUDDY?
Hsssss!
CLICK
CRUD LOVE BUDDY!
I'M A BAD CAT.

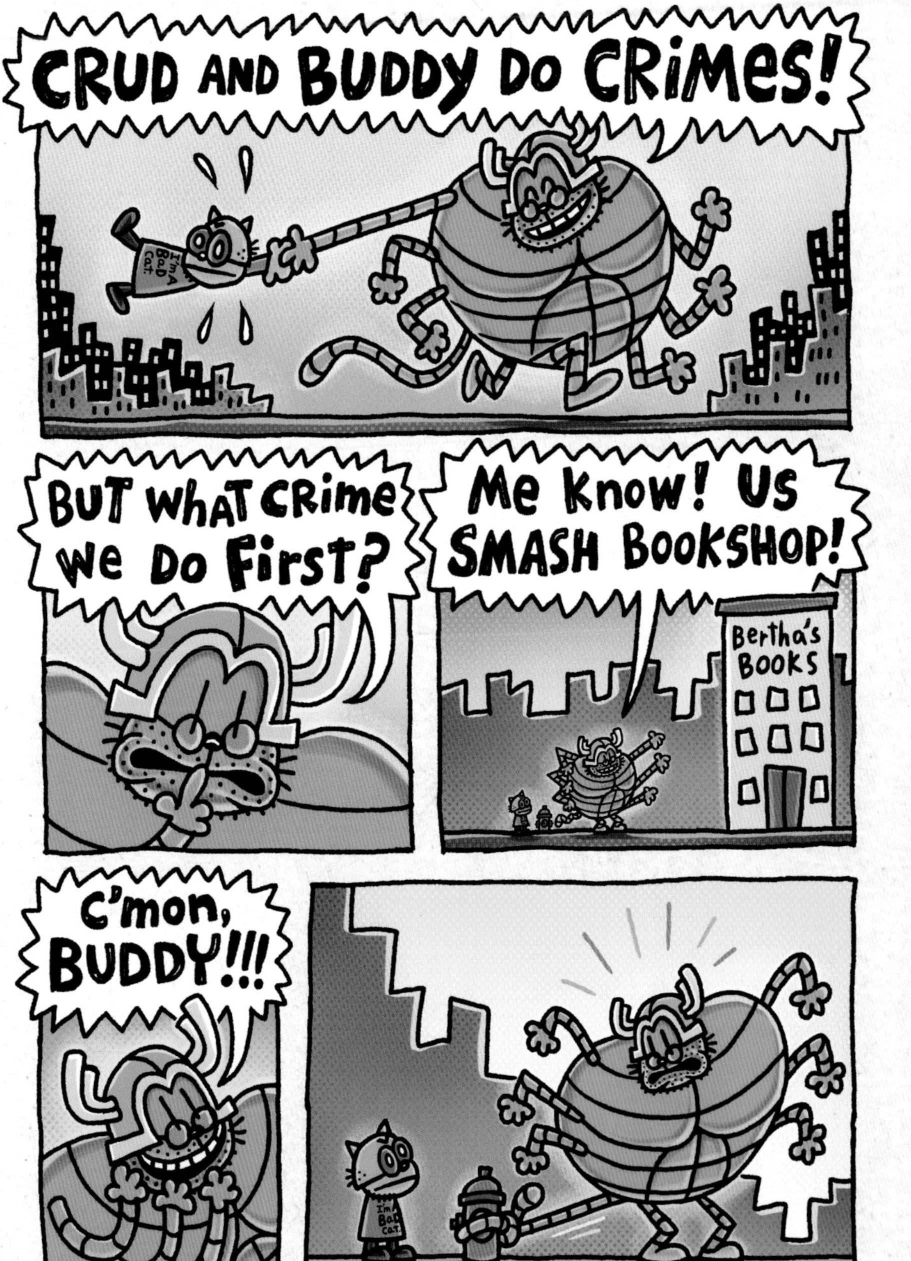
CRUD AND BUDDY DO CRIMES!
I'm A BaD Cat.
BUT WHAT CRIME WE DO FIRST?
ME KNOW! US SMASH BOOKSHOP!
Bertha's BOOKS
C'MON, BUDDY!!!
I'm A BaD Cat.

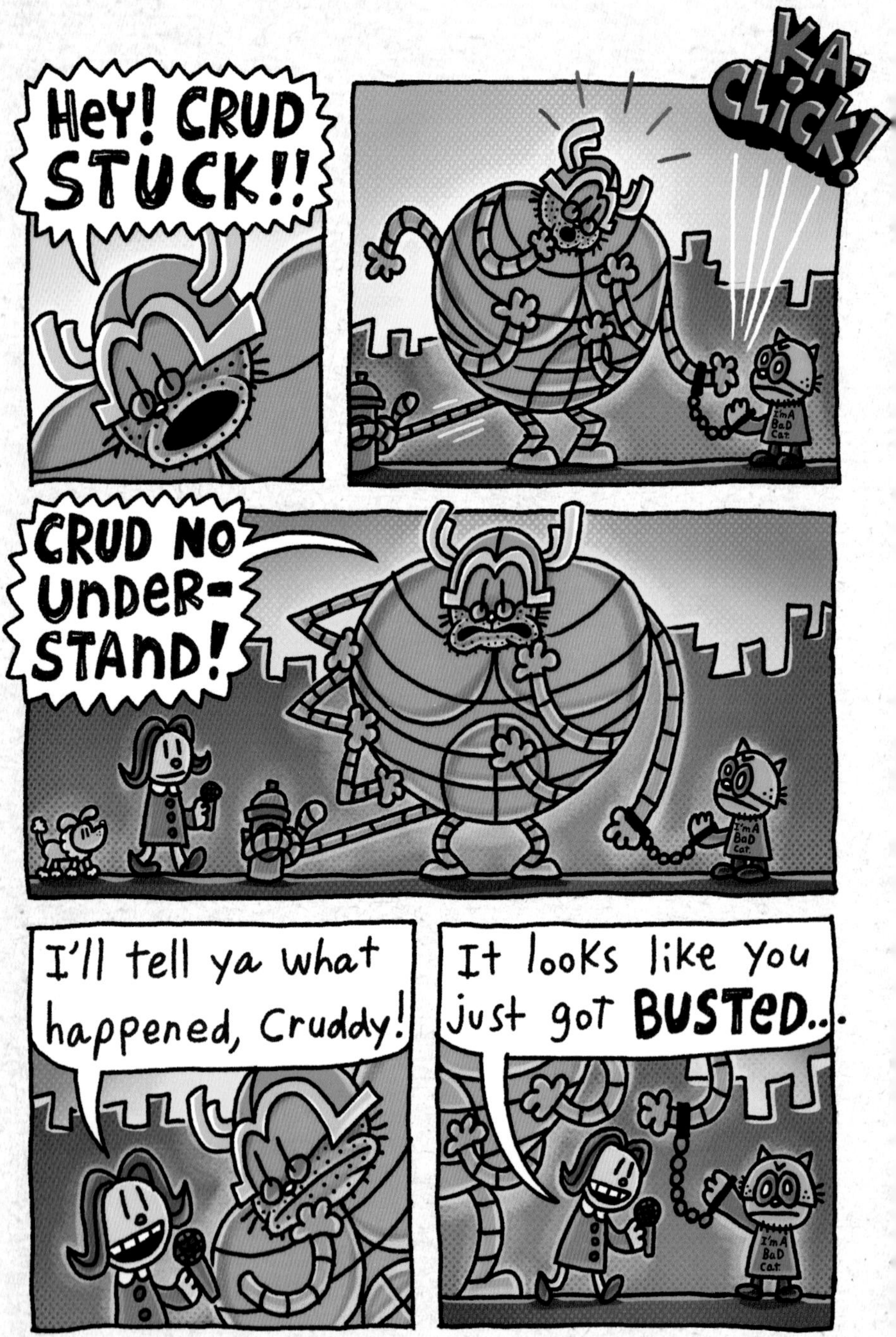
HEY! CRUD STUCK!!
KA-CLICK!
I'm A BaD Cat.
CRUD NO UNDER-STAND!
I'm A BaD Cat.
I'll tell ya what happened, Cruddy!
It looks like you just got BUSTED...
I'm A BaD Cat.

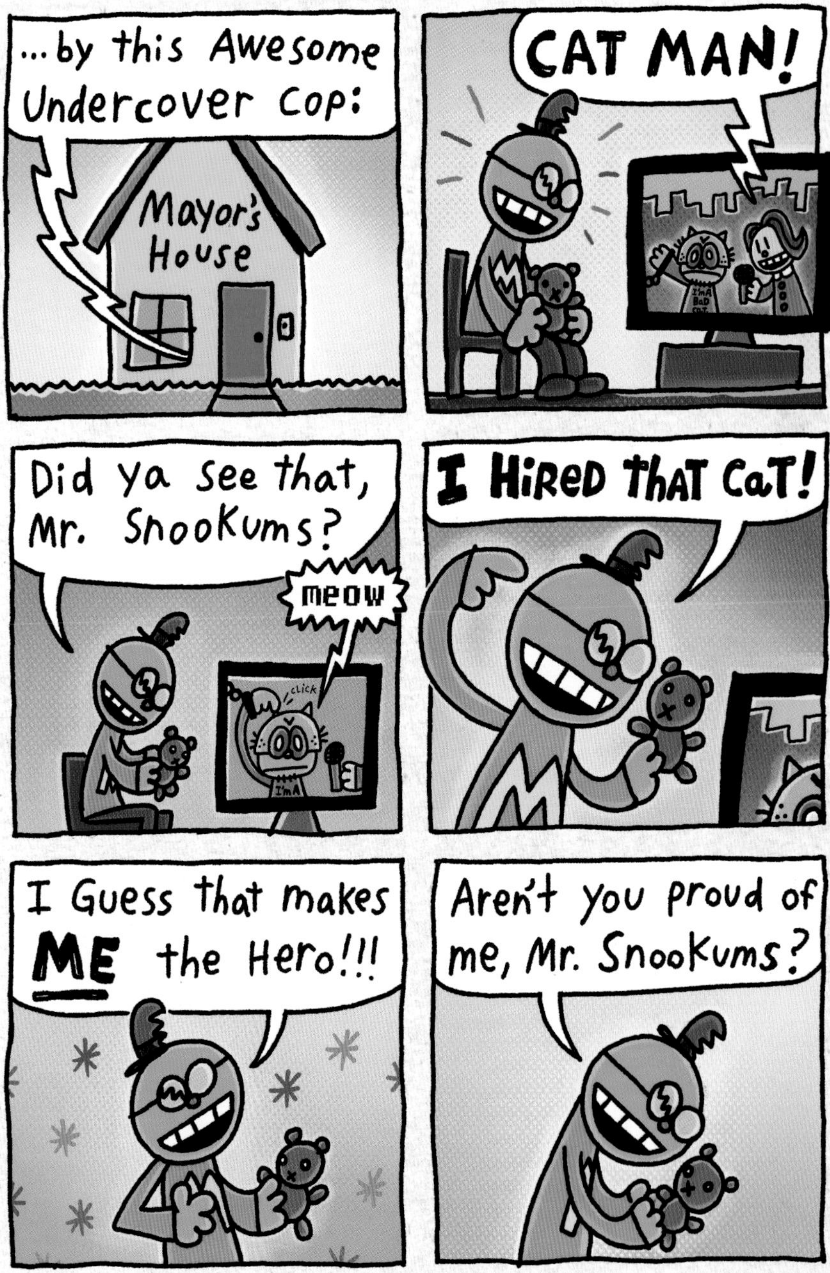
...by this Awesome Undercover Cop:
Mayor's House
CAT MAN!
Did ya see that, Mr. Snookums?
meow
click
I HIRED THAT CAT!
I Guess that makes ME the Hero!!!
Aren't you proud of me, Mr. Snookums?

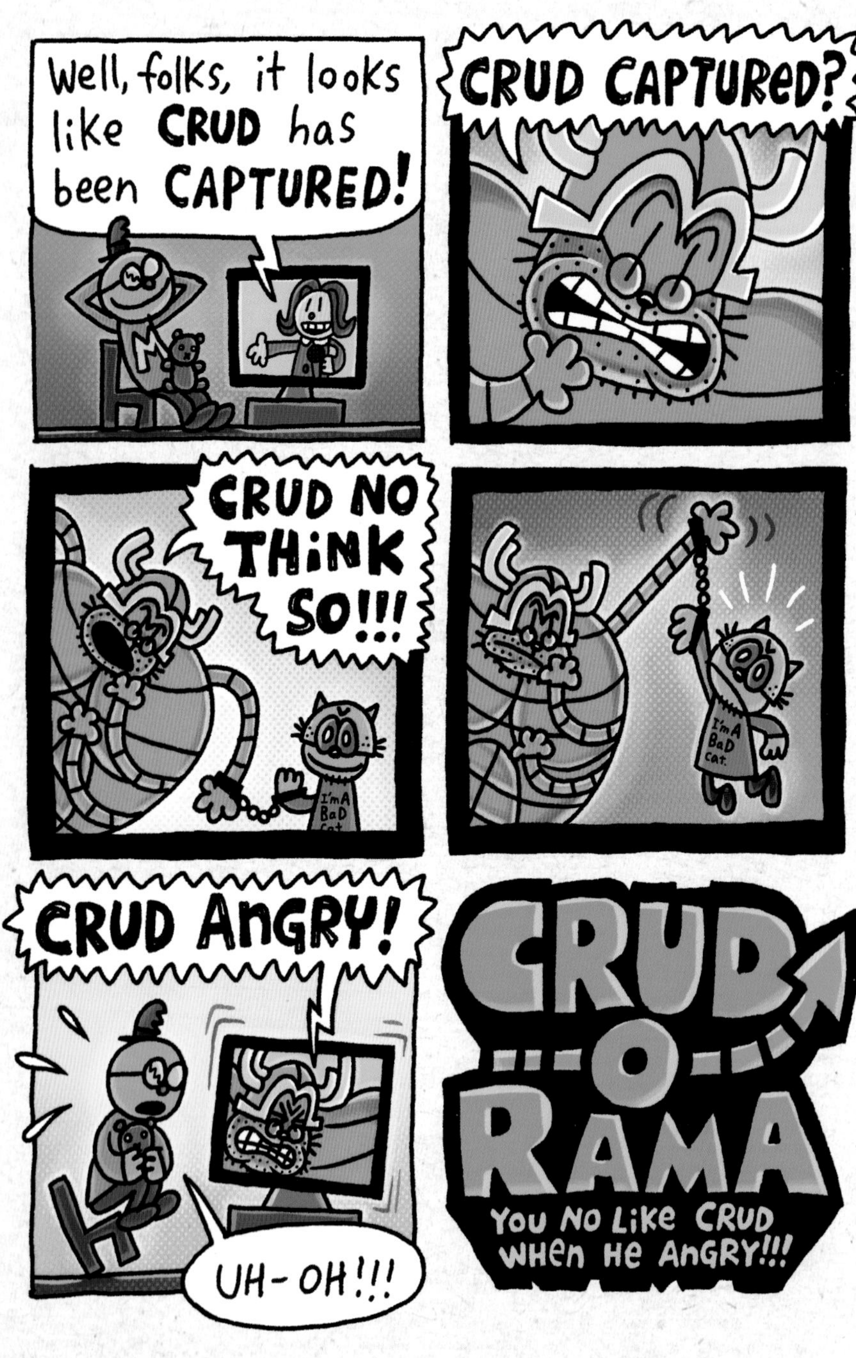
Well, folks, it looks like CRUD has been CAPTURED!
CRUD CAPTURED?
CRUD NO THINK SO!!!
I'm A BaD cat.
I'm A BaD cat.
CRUD AnGRY!
UH-OH!!!
CRUD-O-RAMA
YOU NO LIKE CRUD WHEN HE ANGRY!!!

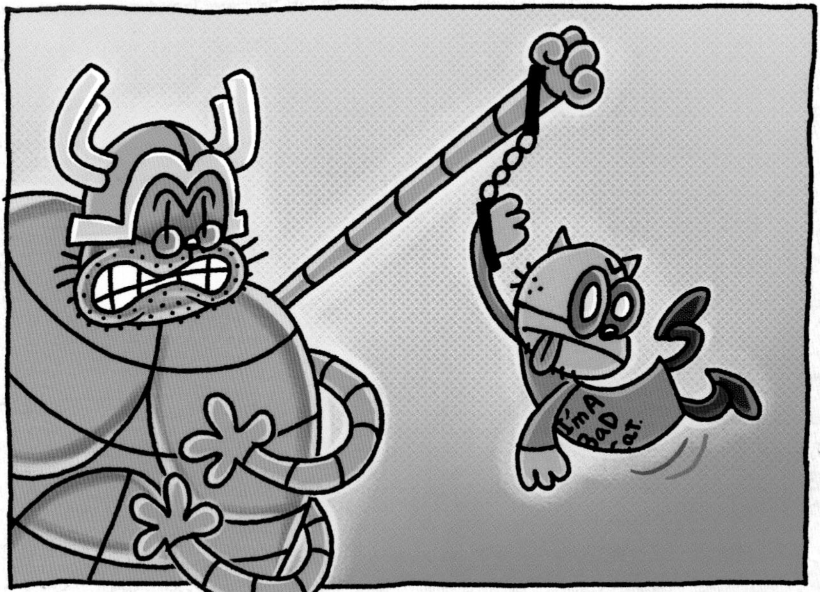
I'm A BaD CaT.

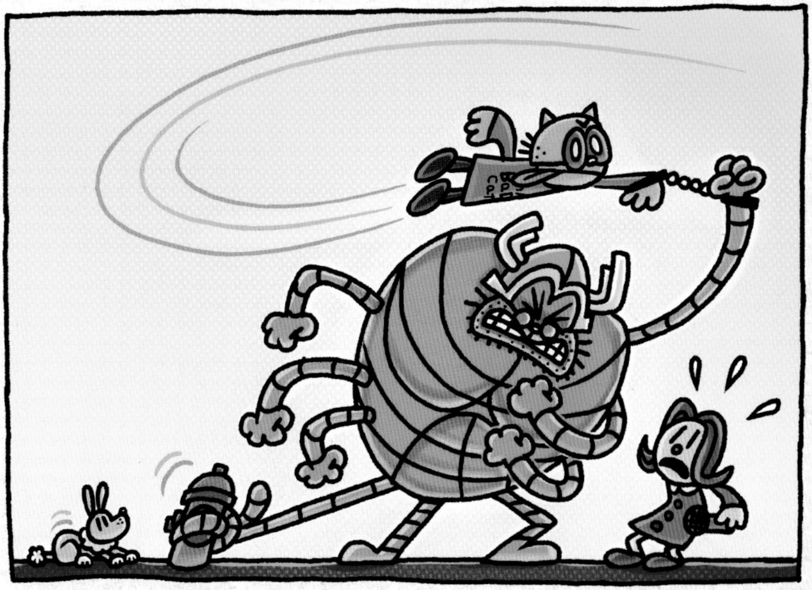

Right Thumb here.

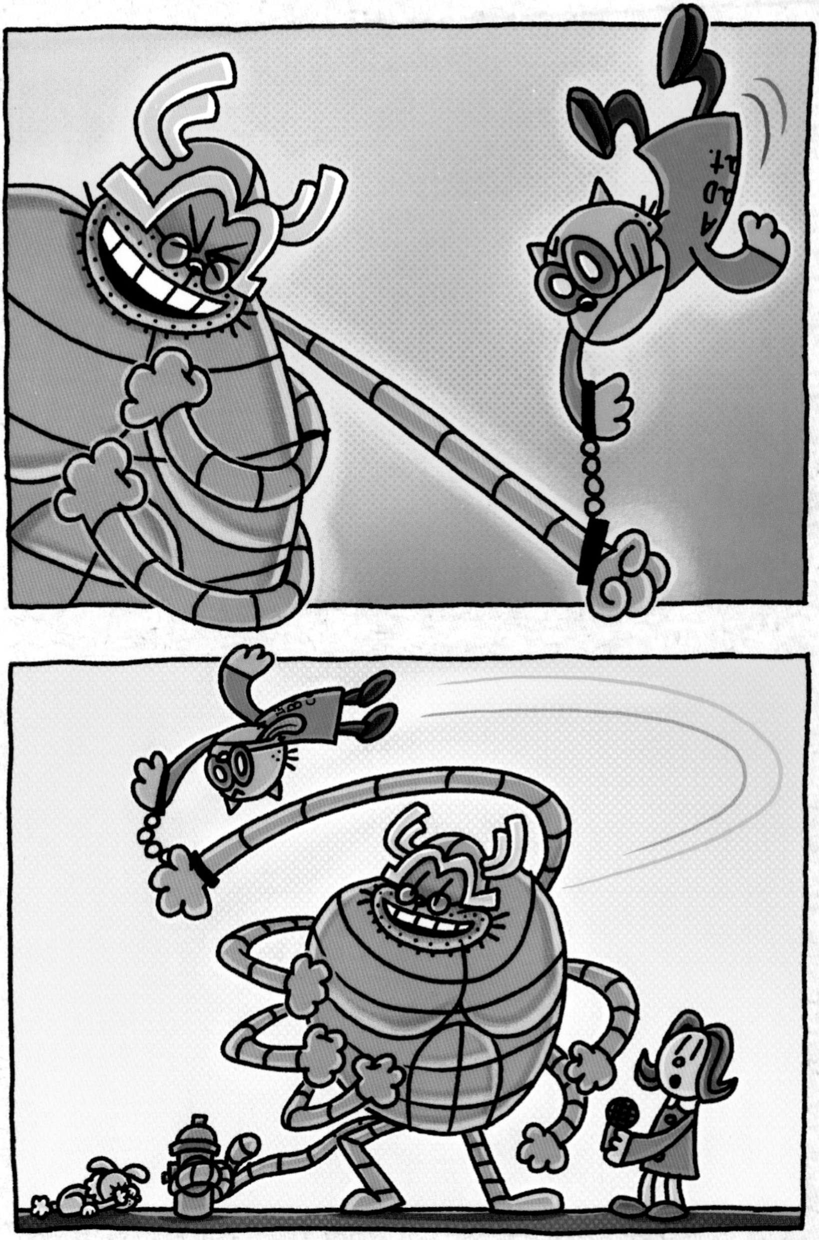

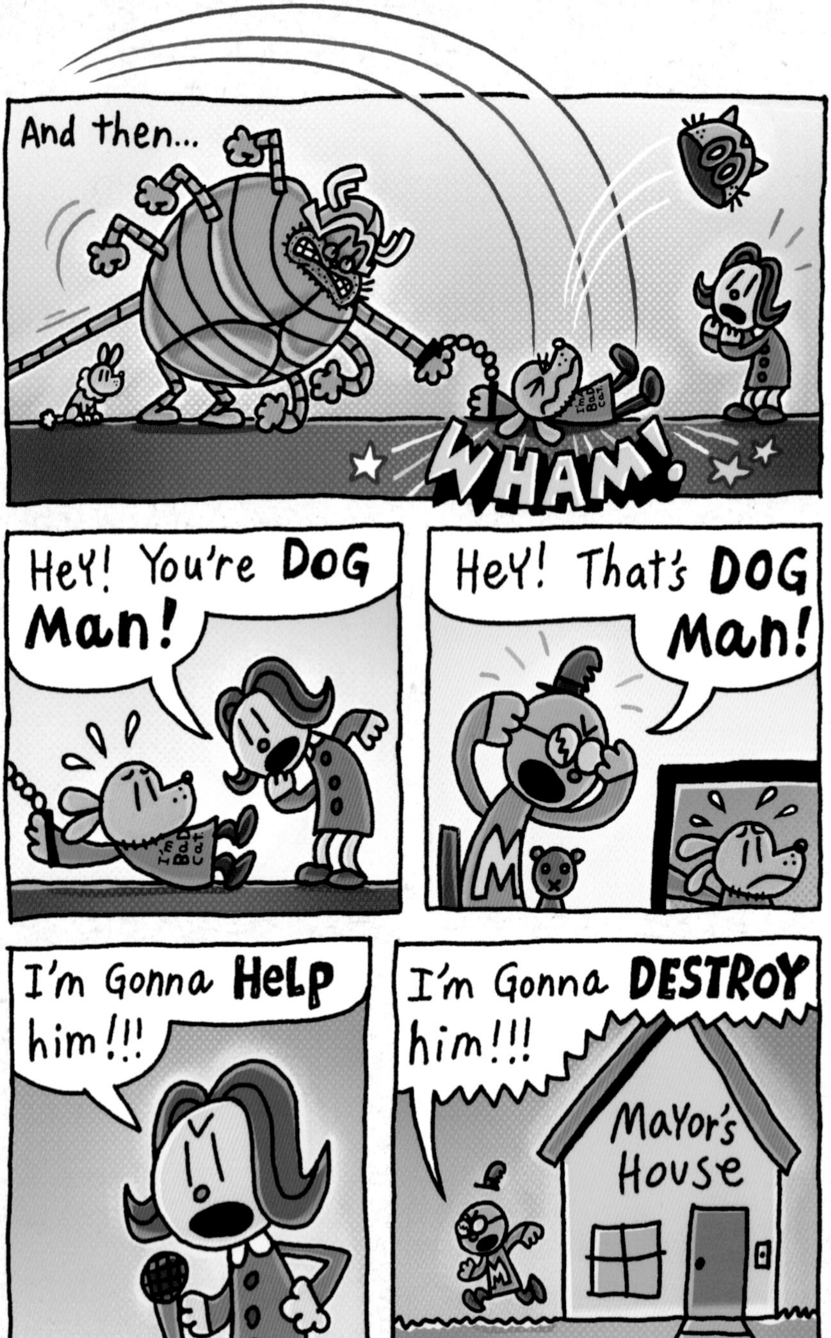
And then...
I'm Bad Cat.
WHAM!
Hey! You're DOG Man!
I'm Bad Cat
Hey! That's DOG Man!
I'm Gonna HELP him!!!
I'm Gonna DESTROY him!!!
Mayor's House

CHAPTER 8

BIG FIGHT

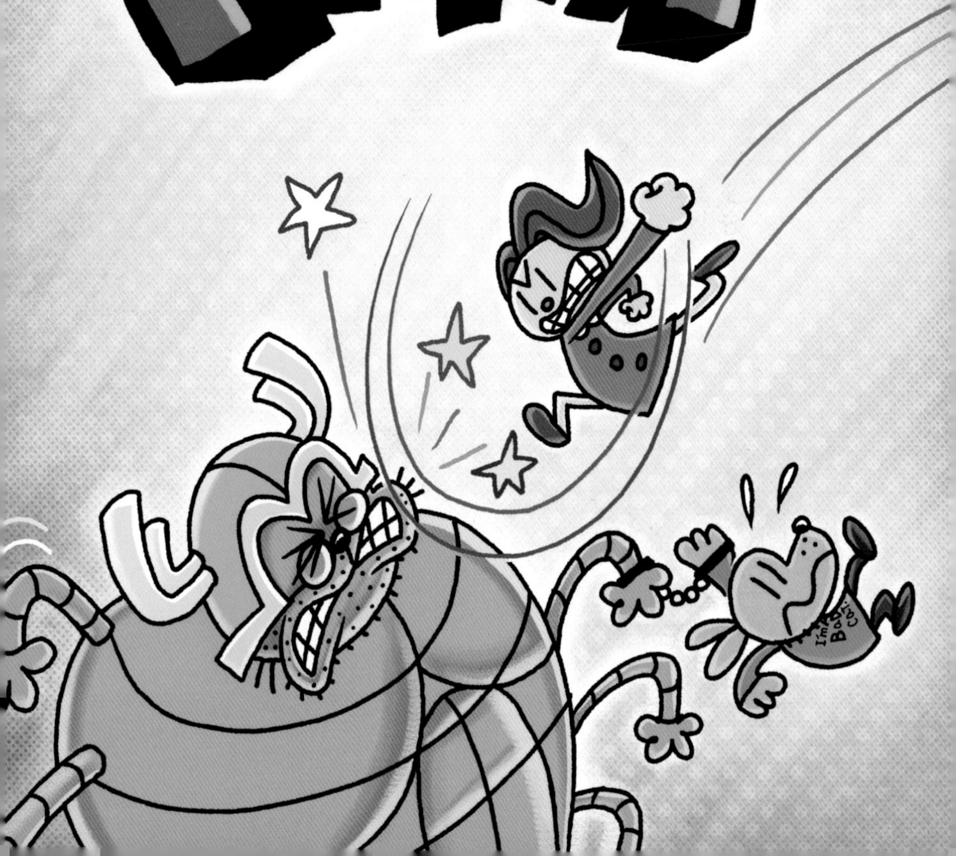

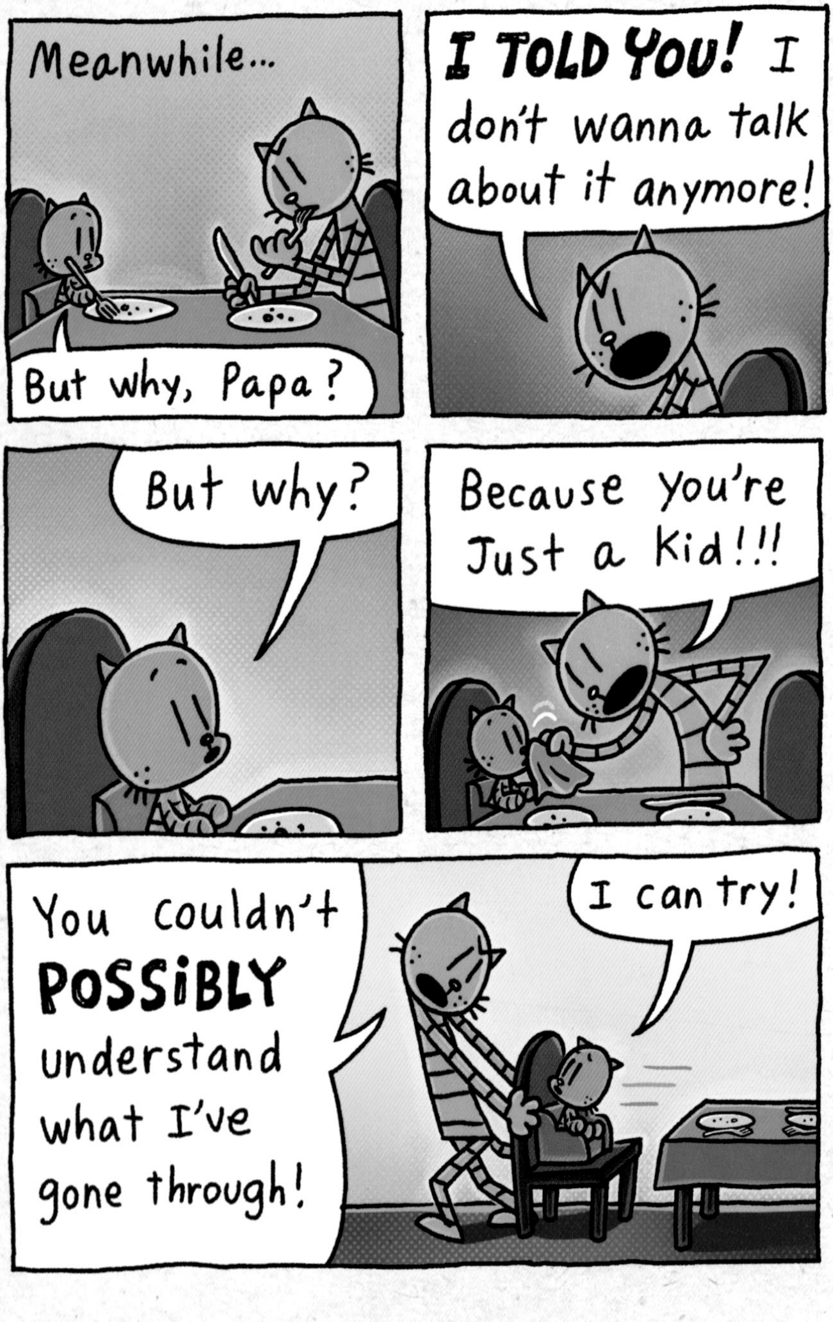
Meanwhile...
But why, Papa?
I TOLD YOU! I don't wanna talk about it anymore!
But why?
Because you're Just a Kid!!!
You couldn't POSSIBLY understand what I've gone through!
I can try!

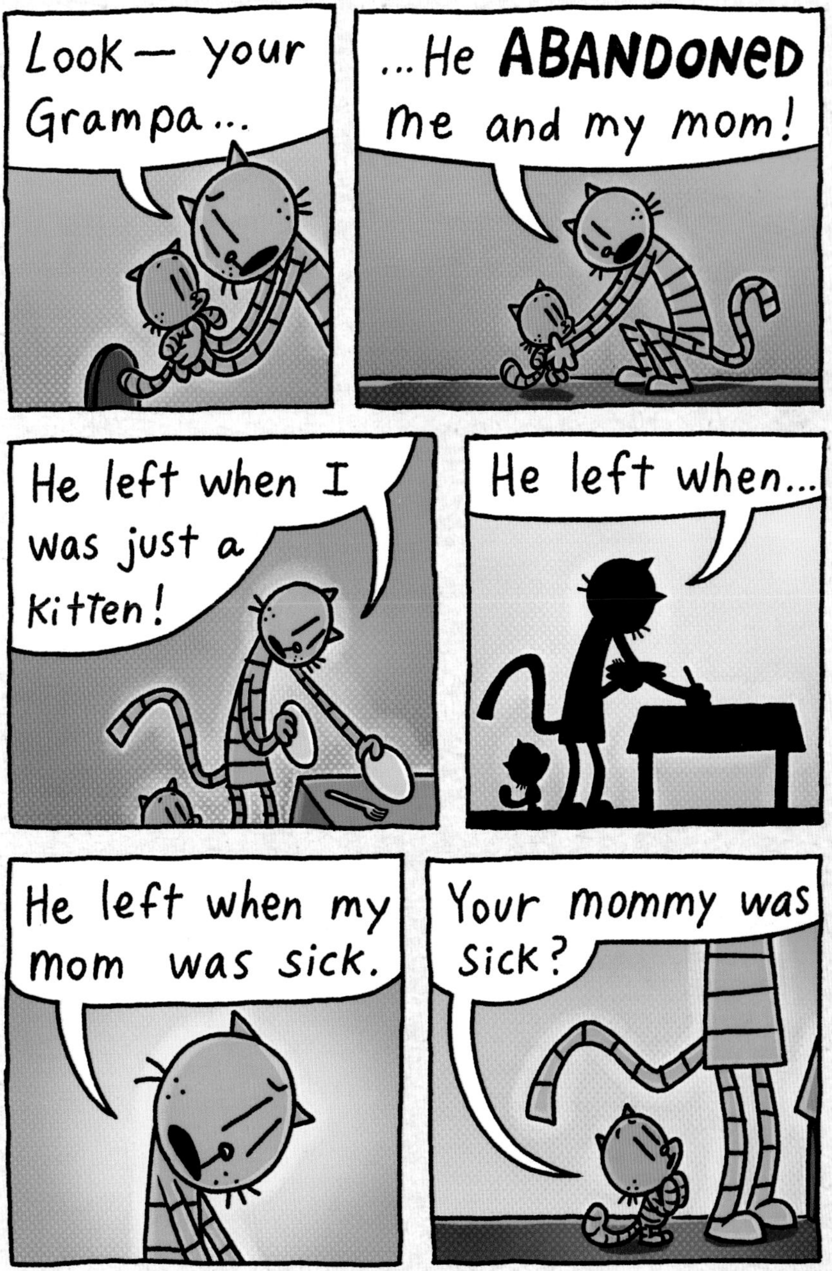
Look— your Grampa...
...He ABANDONED me and my mom!
He left when I was just a kitten!
He left when...
He left when my mom was sick.
Your mommy was sick?

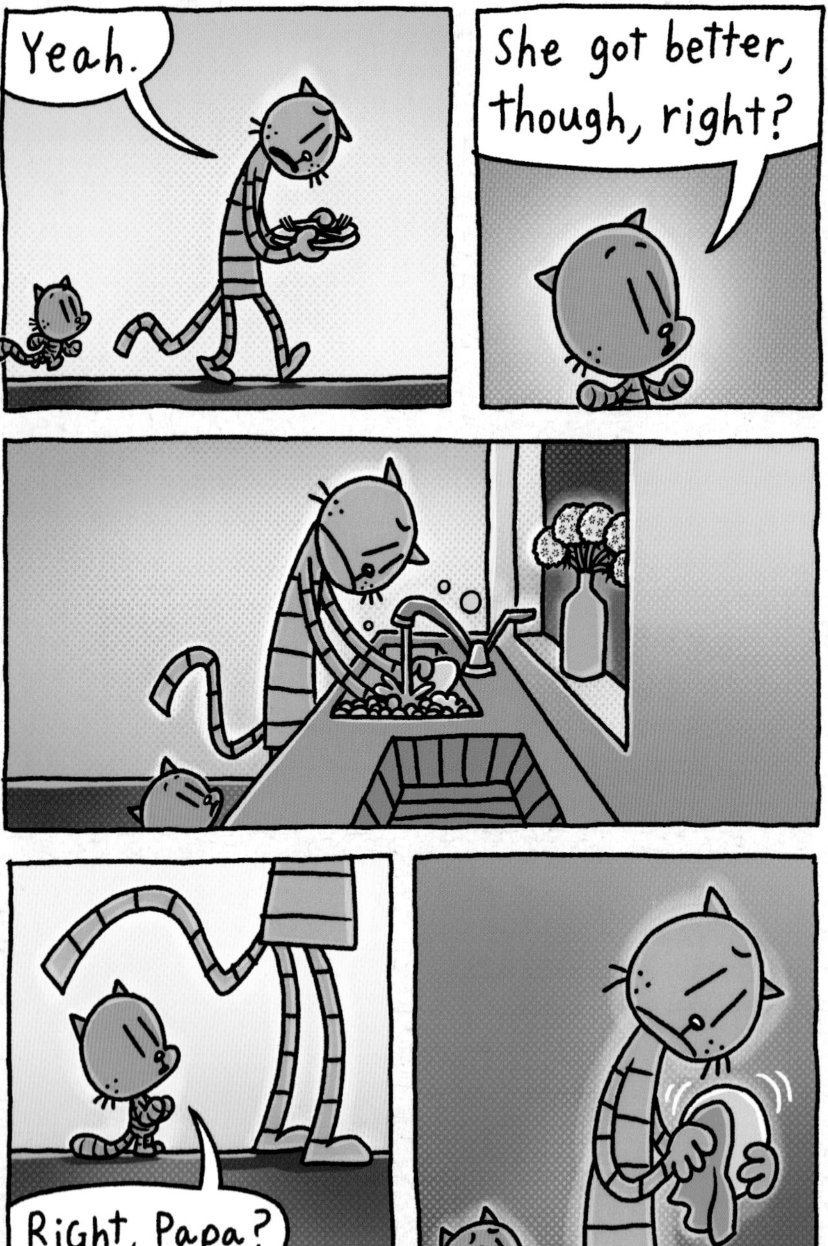
Yeah.
She got better, though, right?
Right, Papa?

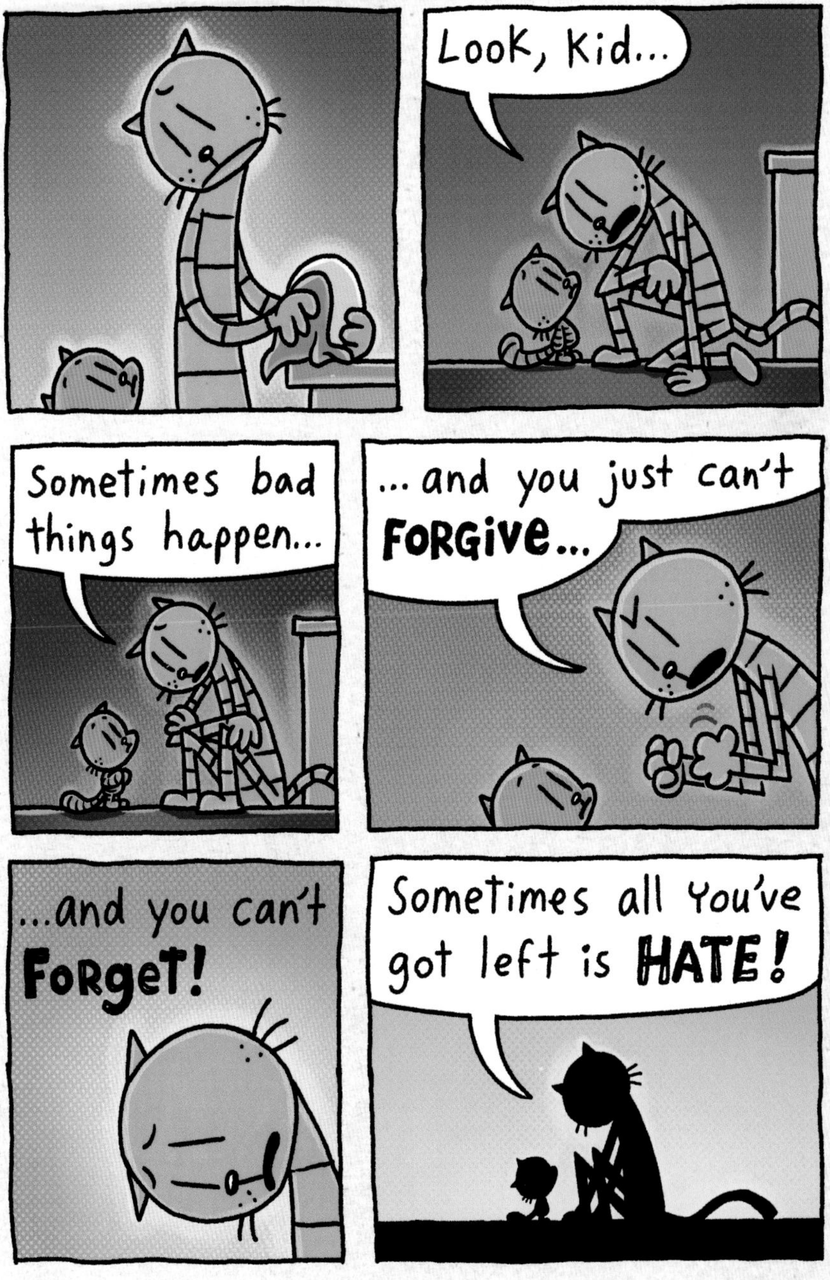
Look, Kid...
Sometimes bad things happen...
... and you just can't FORGIVE...
...and you can't FORGET!
Sometimes all You've got left is HATE!

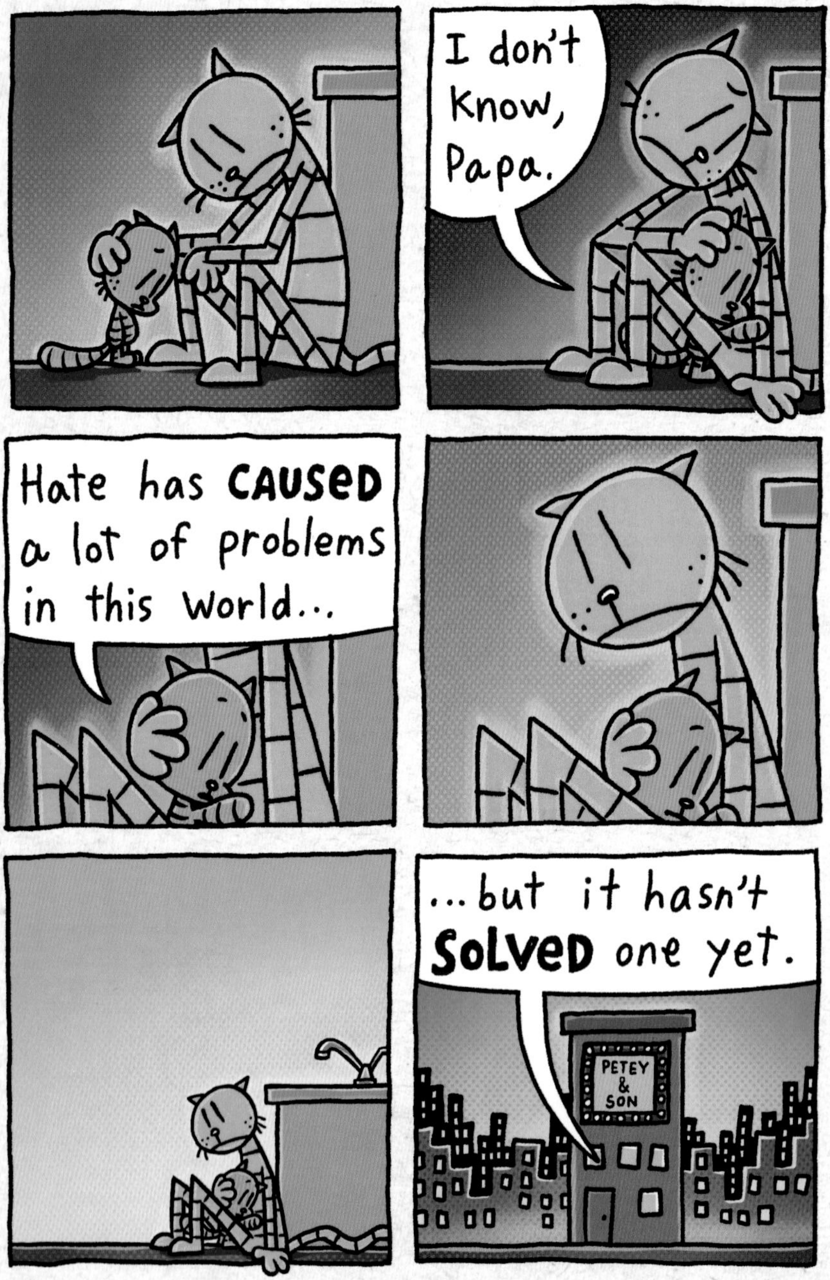
I don't Know, Papa.
Hate has CAUSED a lot of problems in this World...
...but it hasn't SOLVED one yet.
PETEY & SON

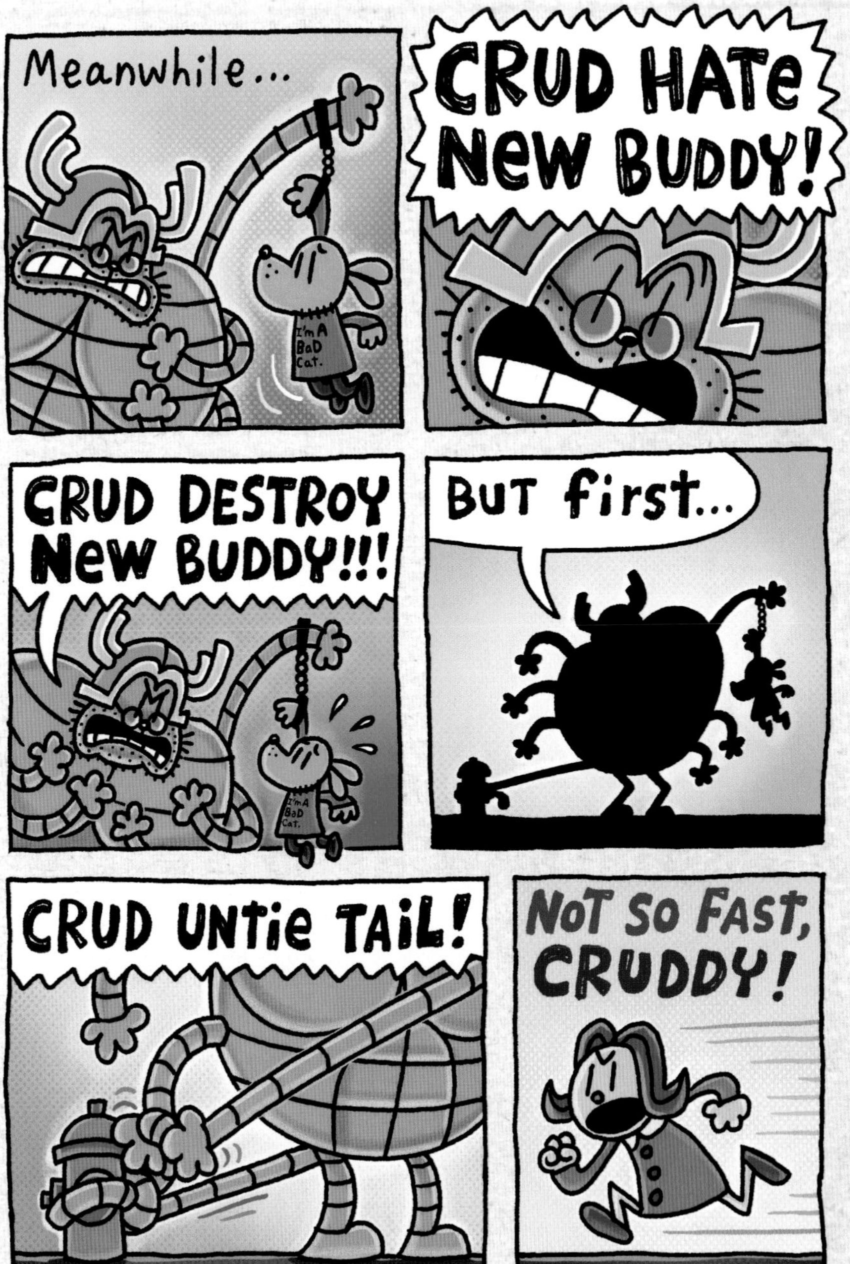
Meanwhile...
I'm A BaD Cat.
CRUD HATE New BUDDY!
CRUD DESTROY New BUDDY!!!
I'm A BaD Cat.
BUT first...
CRUD UNTie TAIL!
NOT SO FAST, CRUDDY!

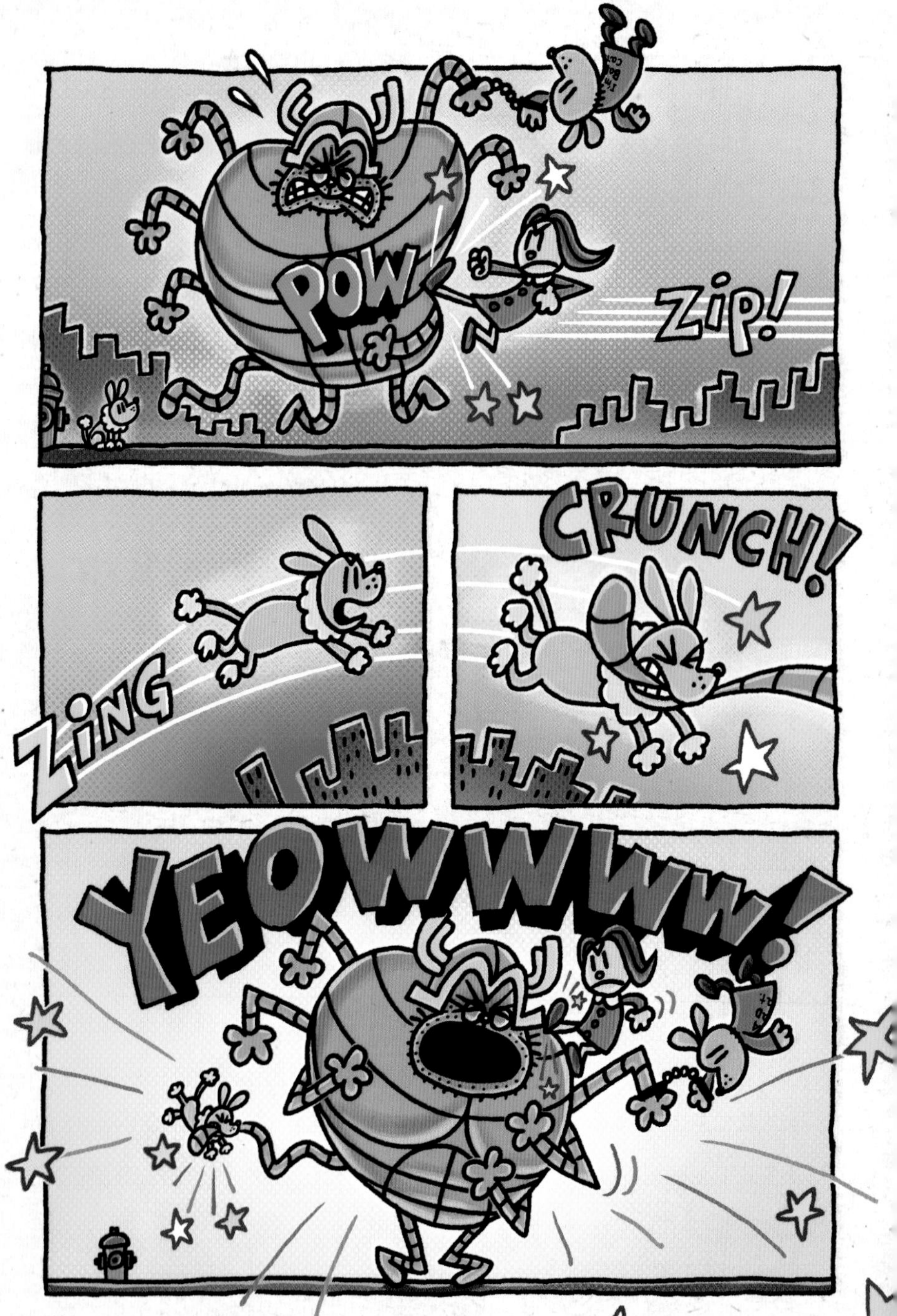
POW
ZIP!
ZING
CRUNCH!
YEOWWWWW!

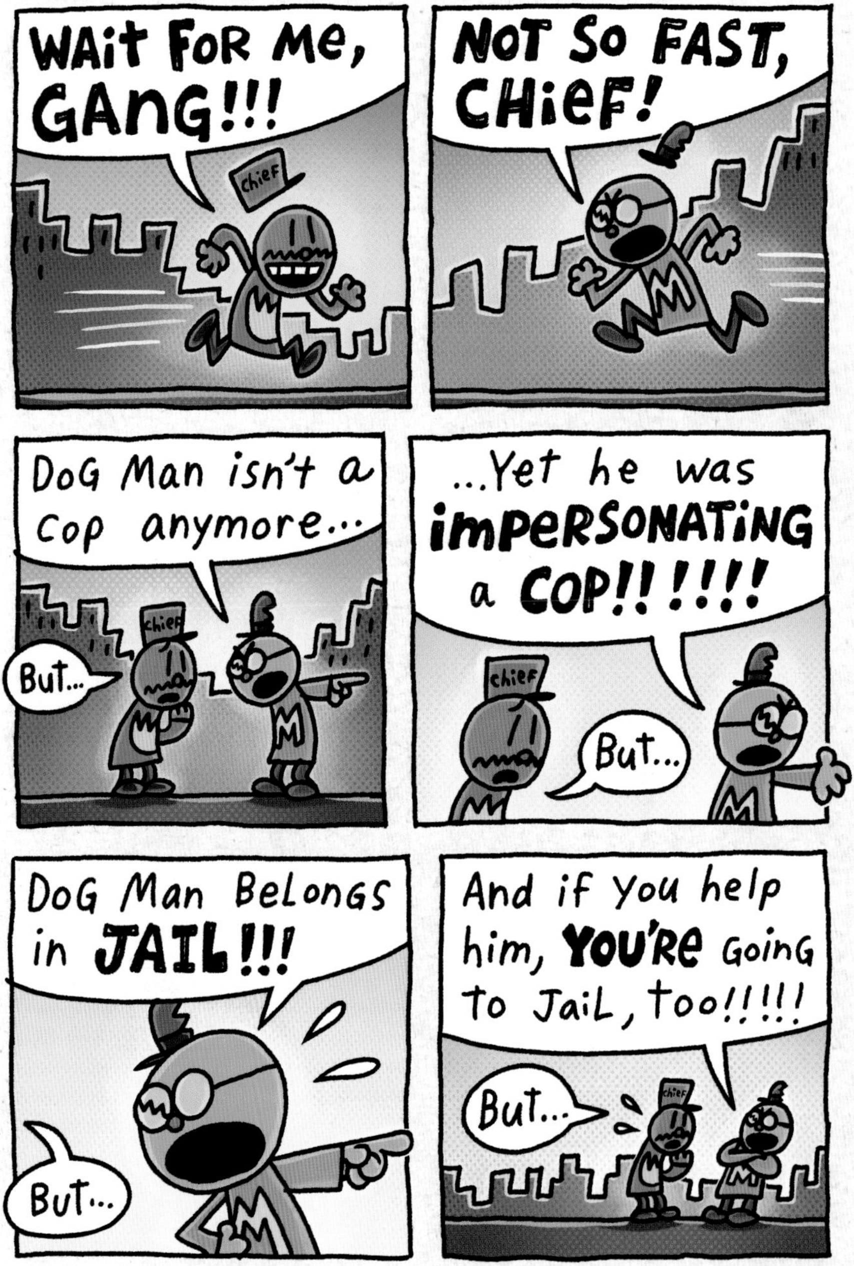
WAit FOR Me, GANG!!!
CHIEF
NOT SO FAST, CHIEF!
DoG Man isn't a cop anymore...
Chief
But...
...Yet he was iMPERSONATING a COP!!!!!!
chief
But...
DoG Man BeLonGS in JAIL!!!
But...
And if you help him, YOU'Re GoinG to JaiL, too!!!!!
But...
chief

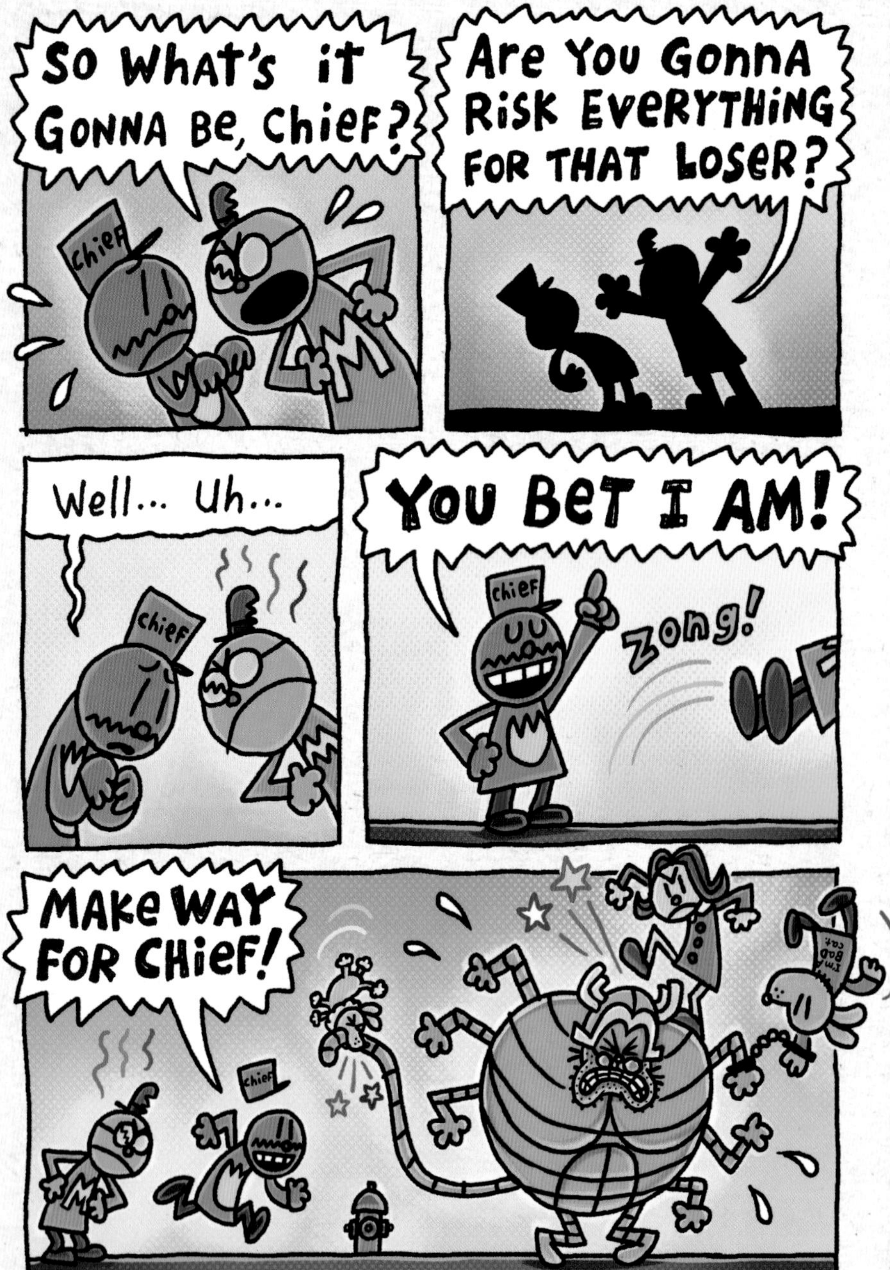
So What's it Gonna Be, Chief?
Are You Gonna Risk Everything For That Loser?
Well... Uh...
You Bet I Am!
Zong!
Make Way For Chief!

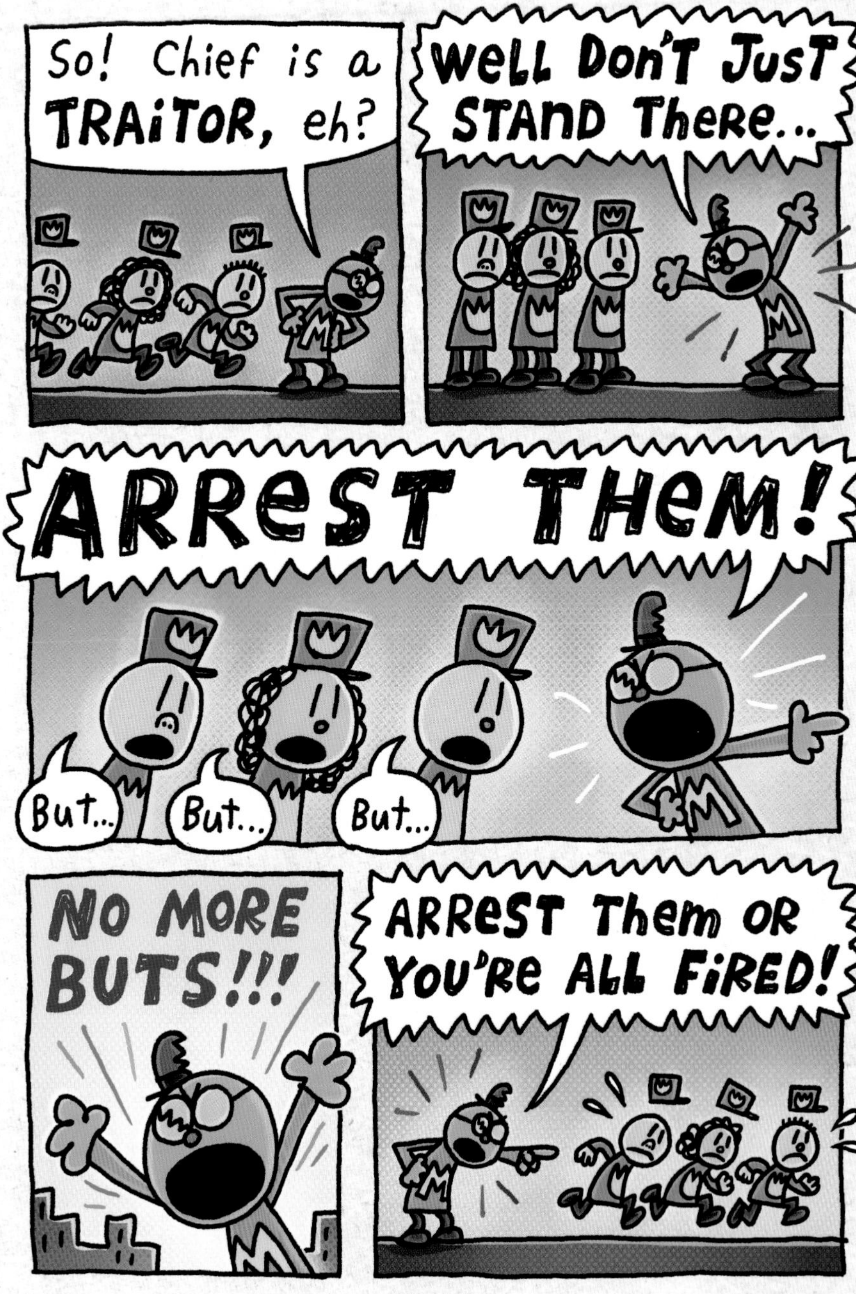
So! Chief is a TRAITOR, eh?
WELL DON'T JUST STAND THERE...
ARREST THEM!
But...
But...
But...
NO MORE BUTS!!!
ARREST THEM OR YOU'RE ALL FIRED!

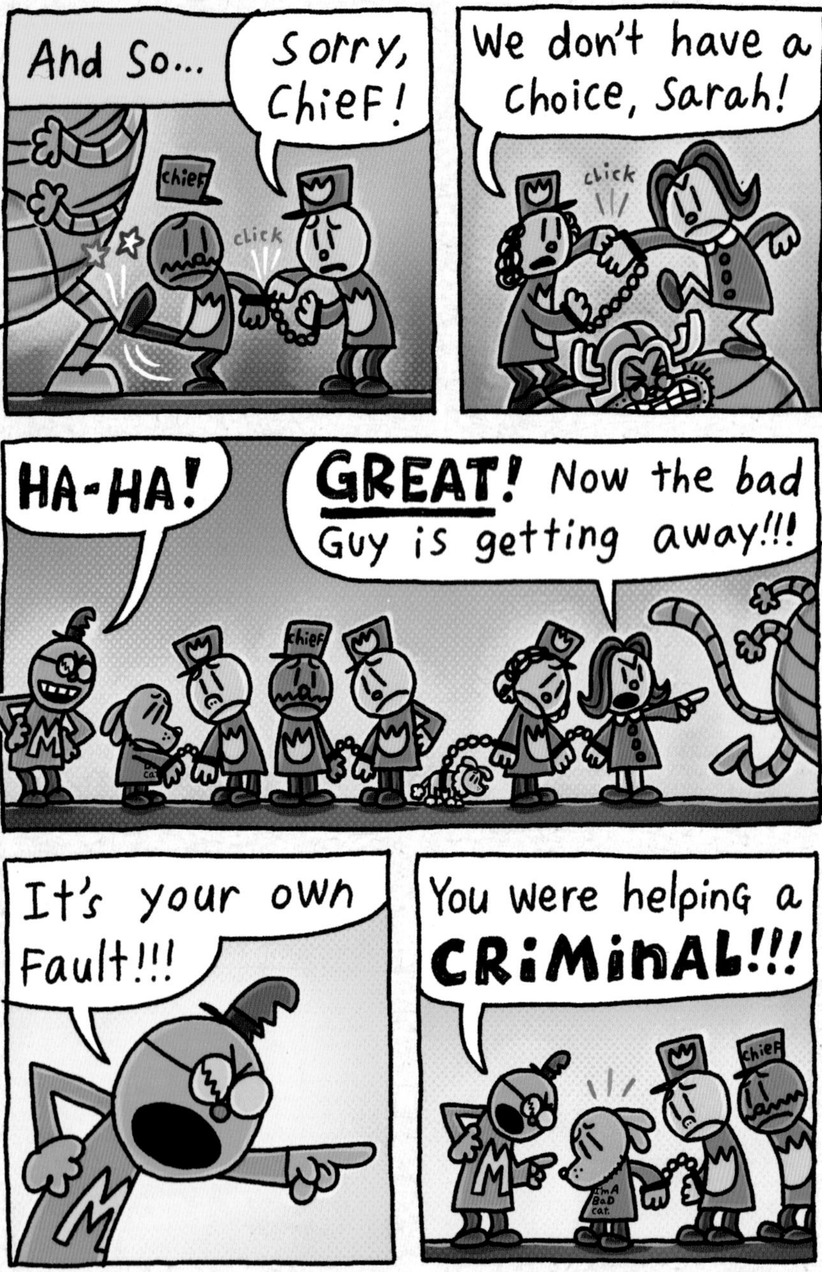
And So...
Sorry, ChieF!
chieF
click
We don't have a choice, Sarah!
click
HA-HA!
GREAT! Now the bad Guy is getting away!!!
chieF
It's your own Fault!!!
You were helping a CRiMinAL!!!
I'm A BaD cat.
chieF

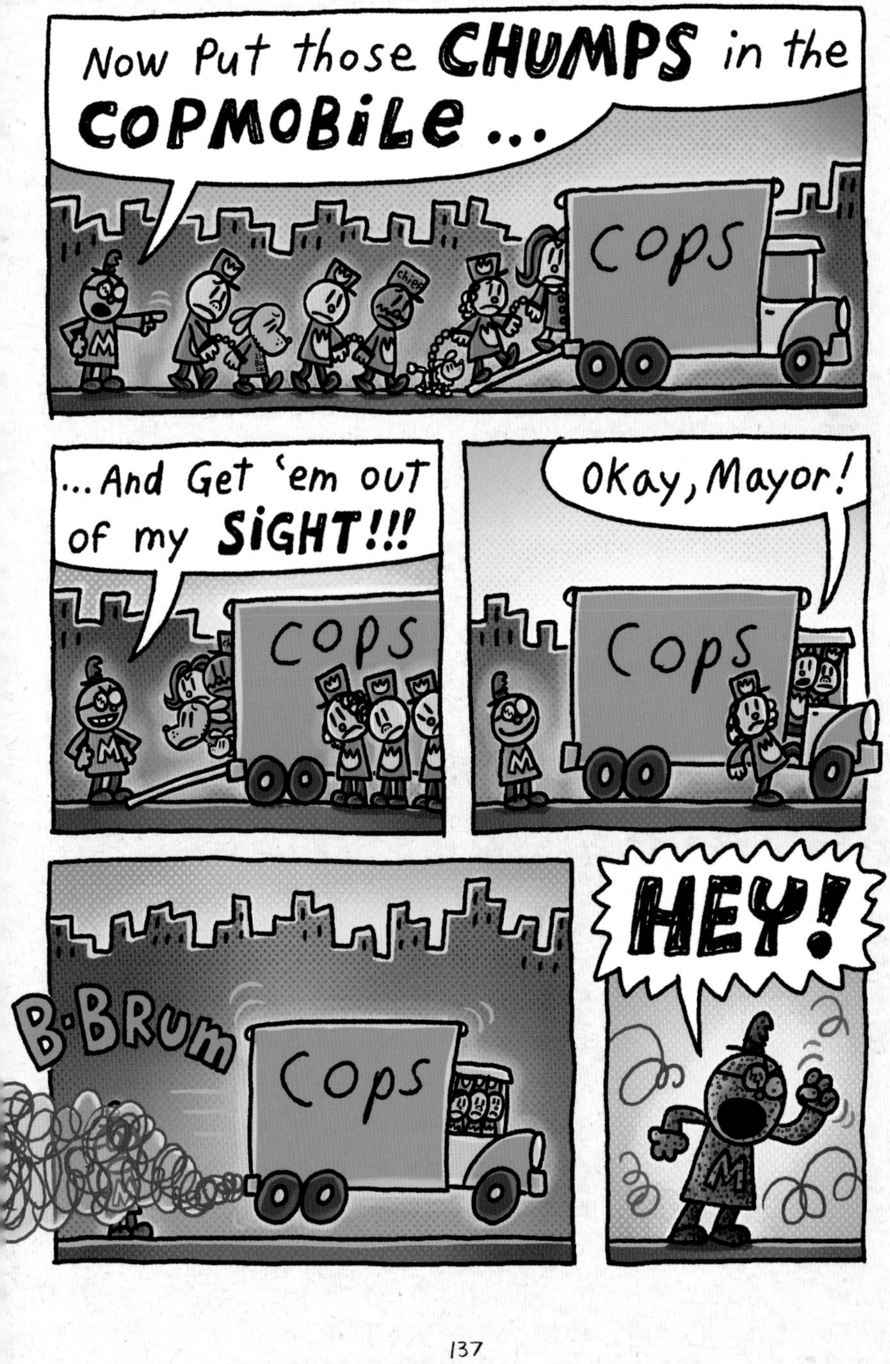
Now Put those CHUMPS in the COPMOBILE...
COPS
...And Get 'em out of my SIGHT!!!
COPS
Okay, Mayor!
Cops
B-BRUM
Cops
HEY!

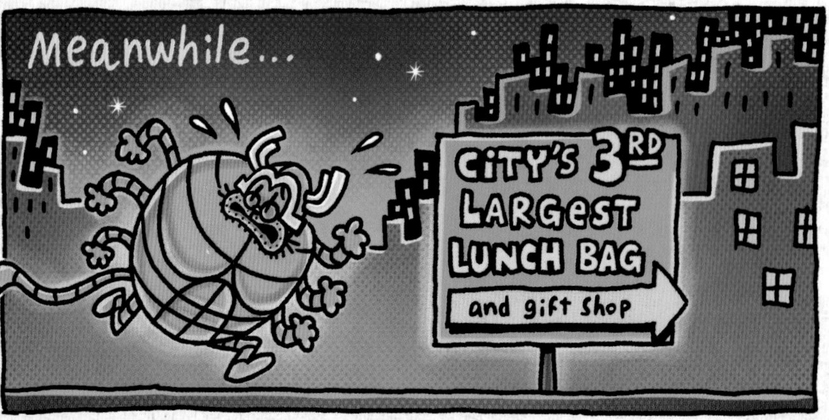
Meanwhile...
CiTY'S 3RD LARGEST LUNCH BAG
and gift Shop

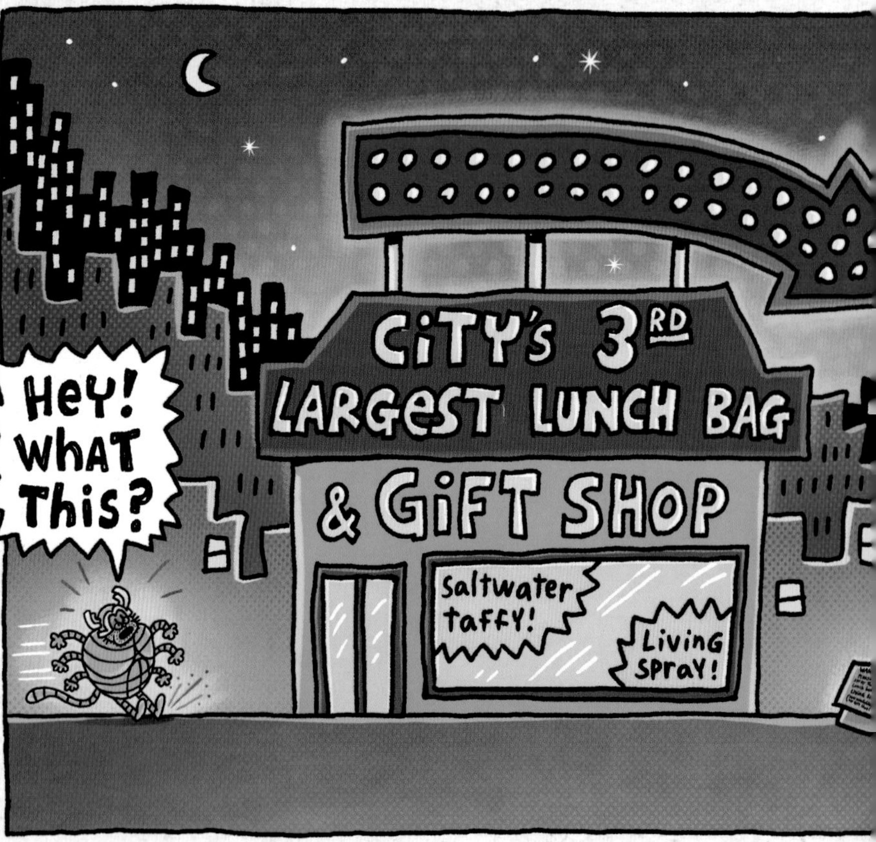
CiTY'S 3RD LARGEST LUNCH BAG
& GiFT SHOP
Saltwater taffy!
Living Spray!
Hey! WHAT This?

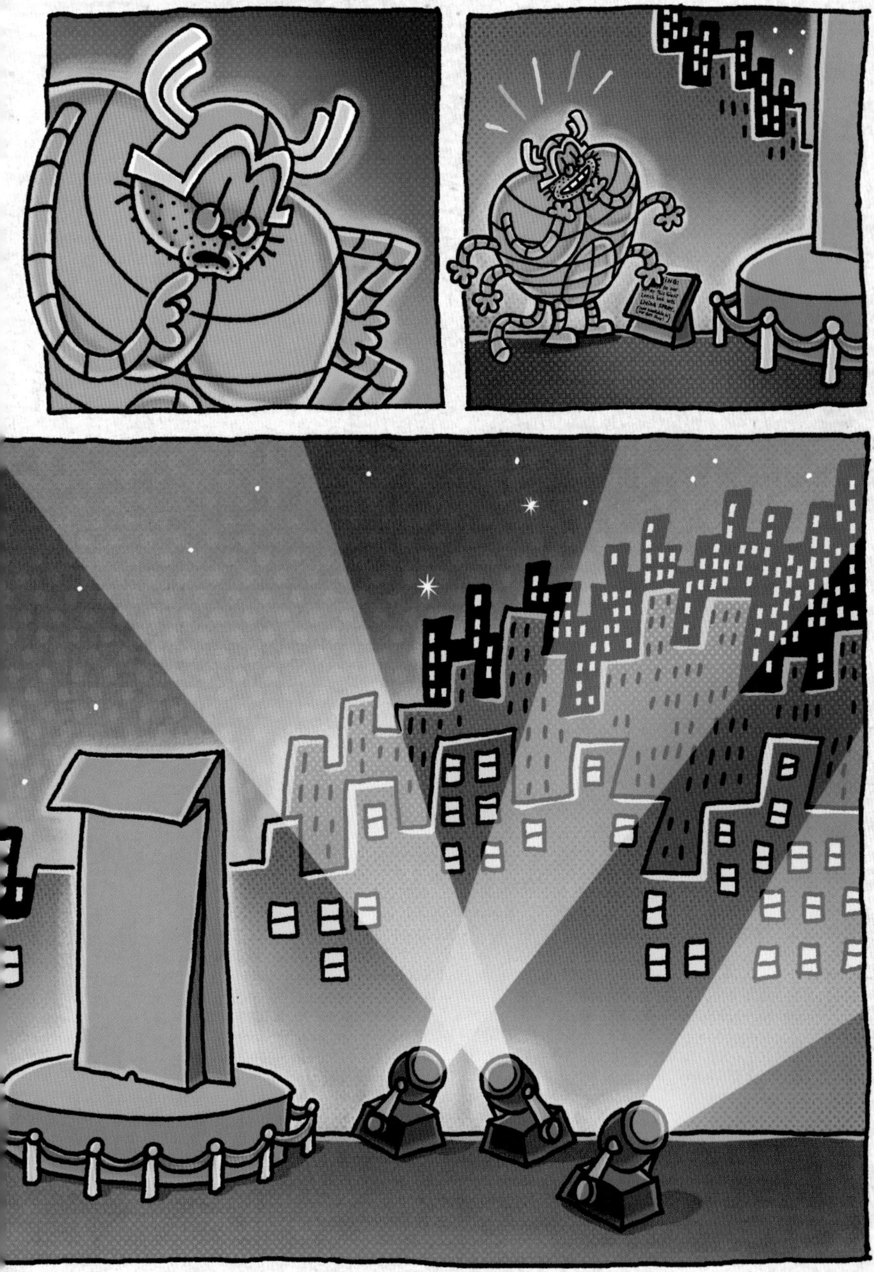

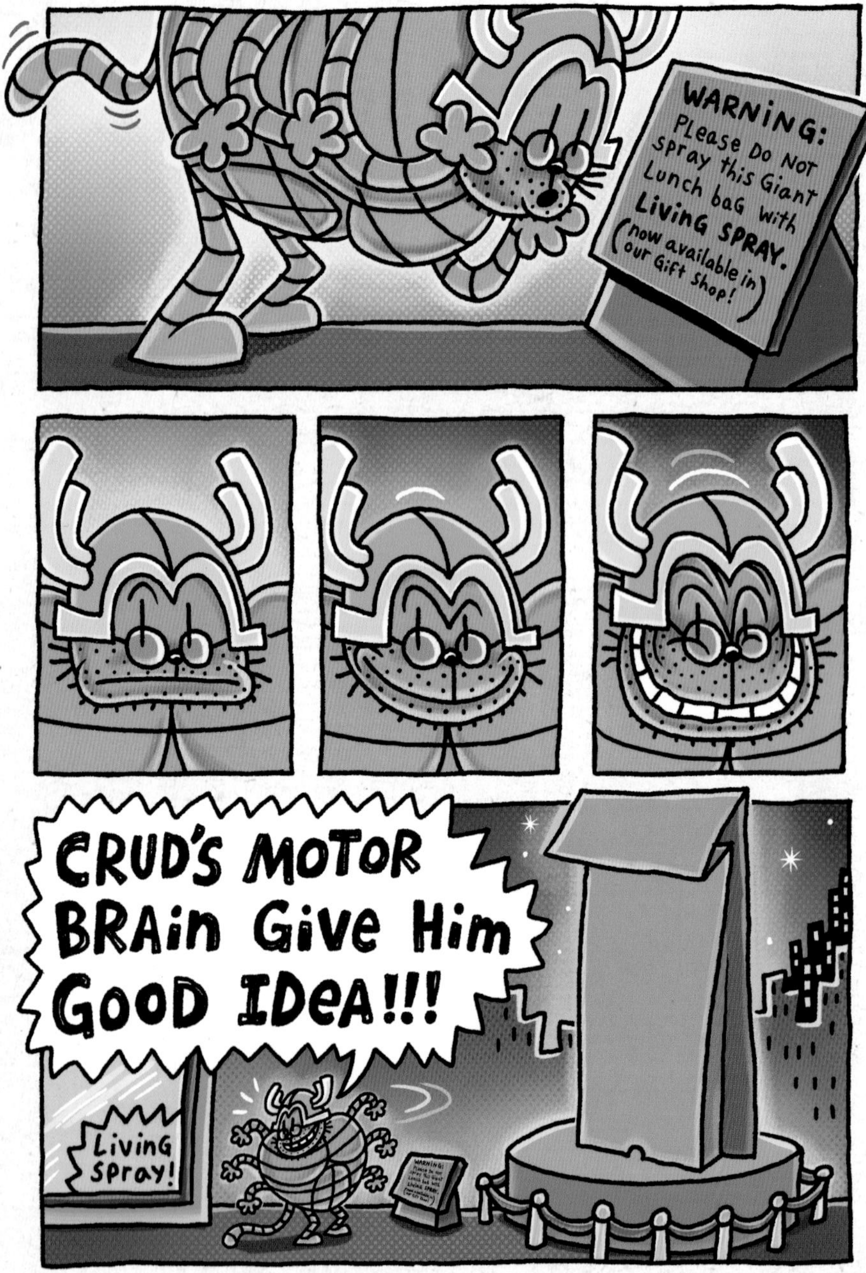
WARNING:
Please DO NOT spray this Giant Lunch baG with LiVinG SPRAY.
(now available in our Gift Shop!)
CRUD'S MOTOR BRAin Give Him GOOD IDeA!!!
LiVinG Spray!

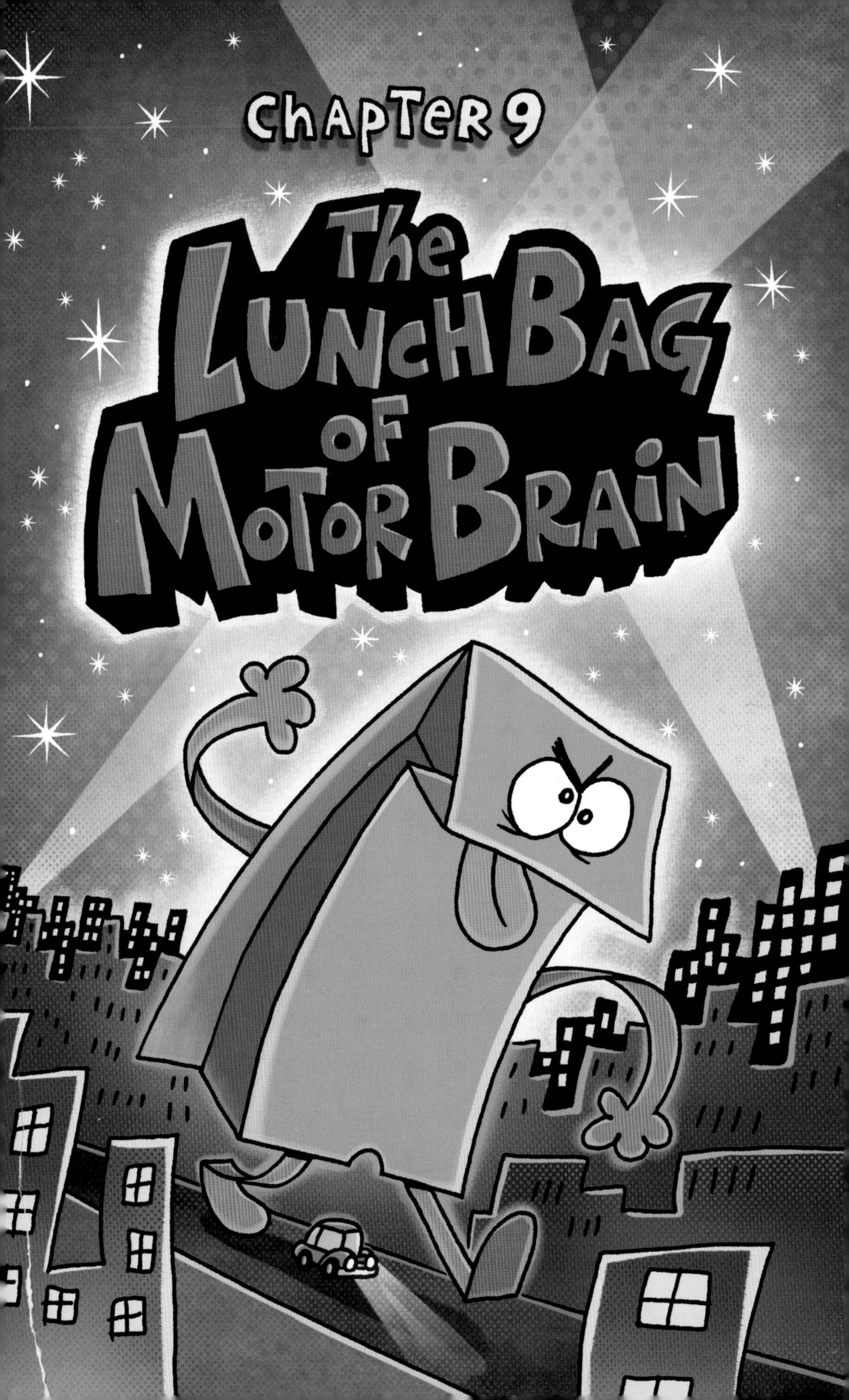
Chapter 9
The Lunch Bag of Motor Brain

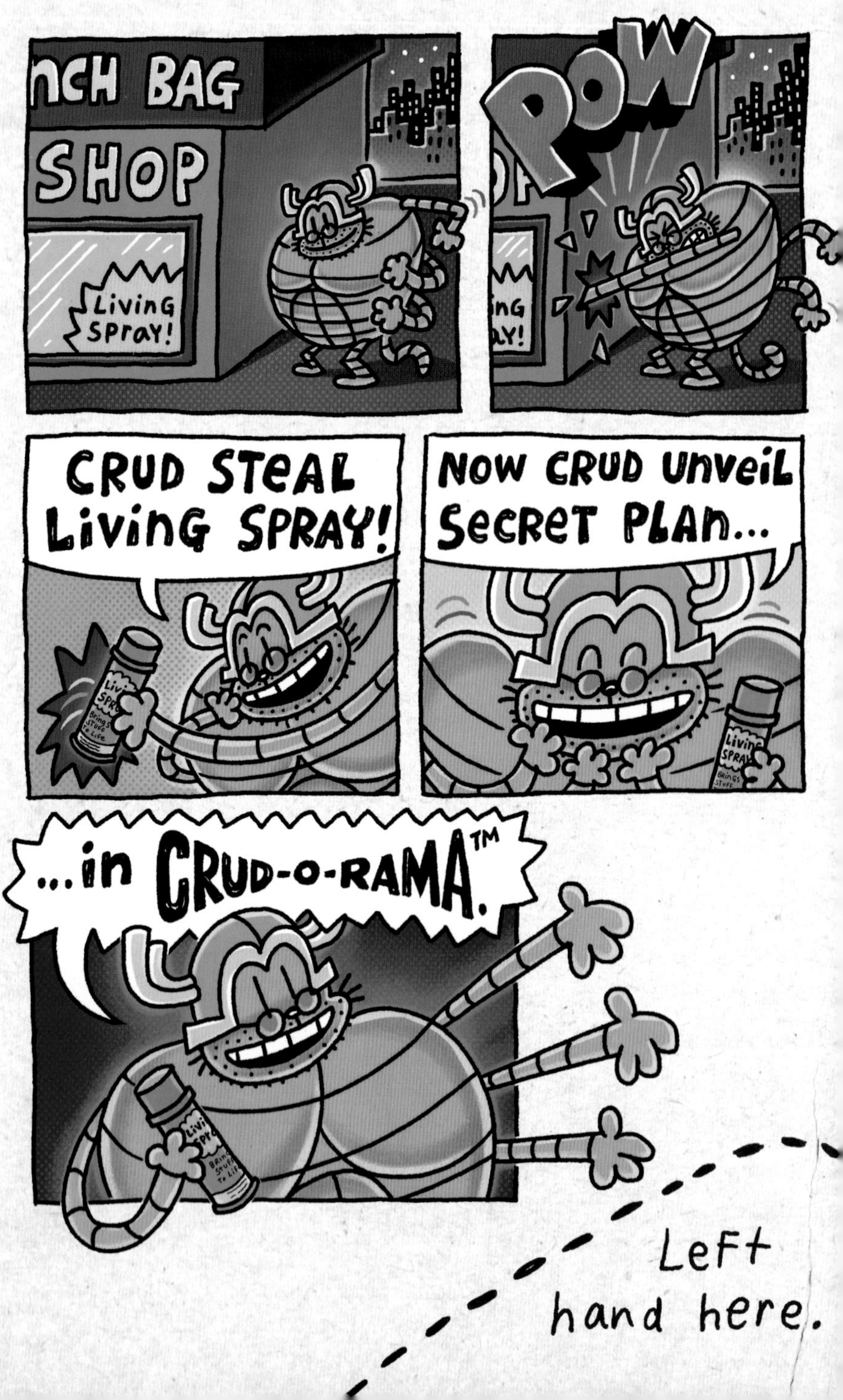
NCH BAG
SHOP
Living Spray!
POW
CRUD STEAL Living SPRAY!
NOW CRUD UNVEIL SECRET PLAN...
...in CRUD-O-RAMA™.
Left hand here.

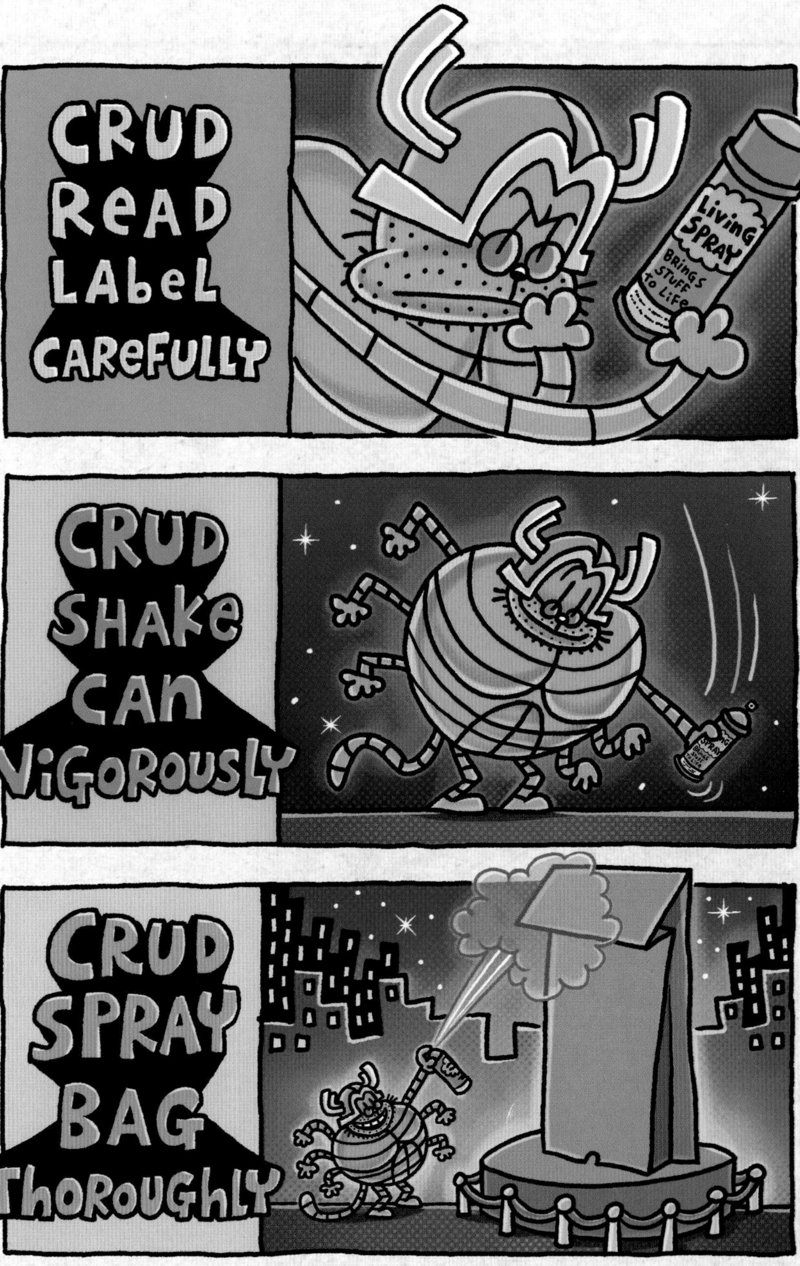
CRUD READ LABEL CAREFULLY
LIVING SPRAY
BRINGS STUFF TO LIFE
CRUD SHAKE CAN VIGOROUSLY
CRUD SPRAY BAG THOROUGHLY

Right Thumb here.

CRUD READ LABEL CAREFULLY

CRUD SHAKE CAN VIGOROUSLY

CRUD SPRAY BAG THOROUGHLY

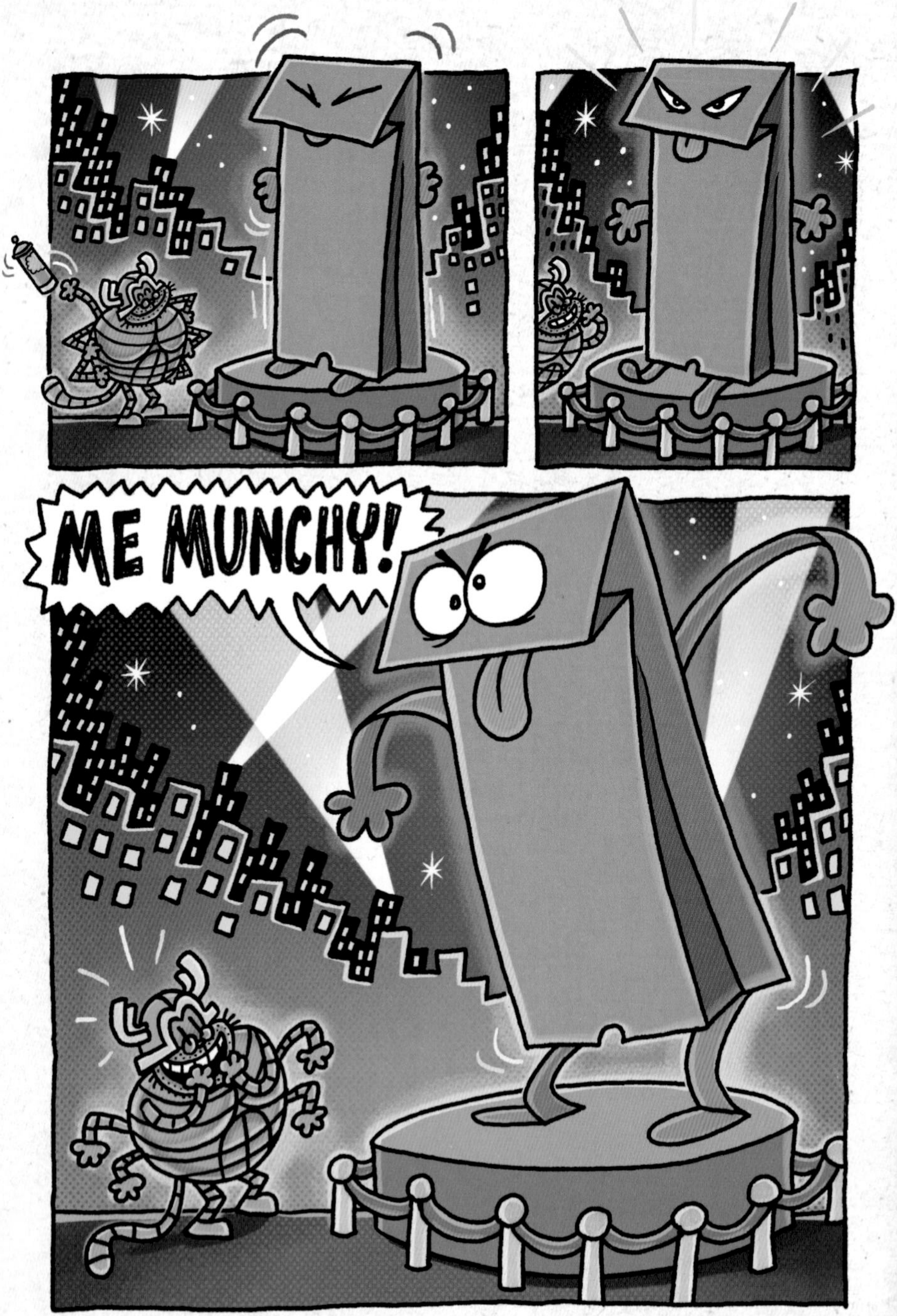
ME MUNCHY!

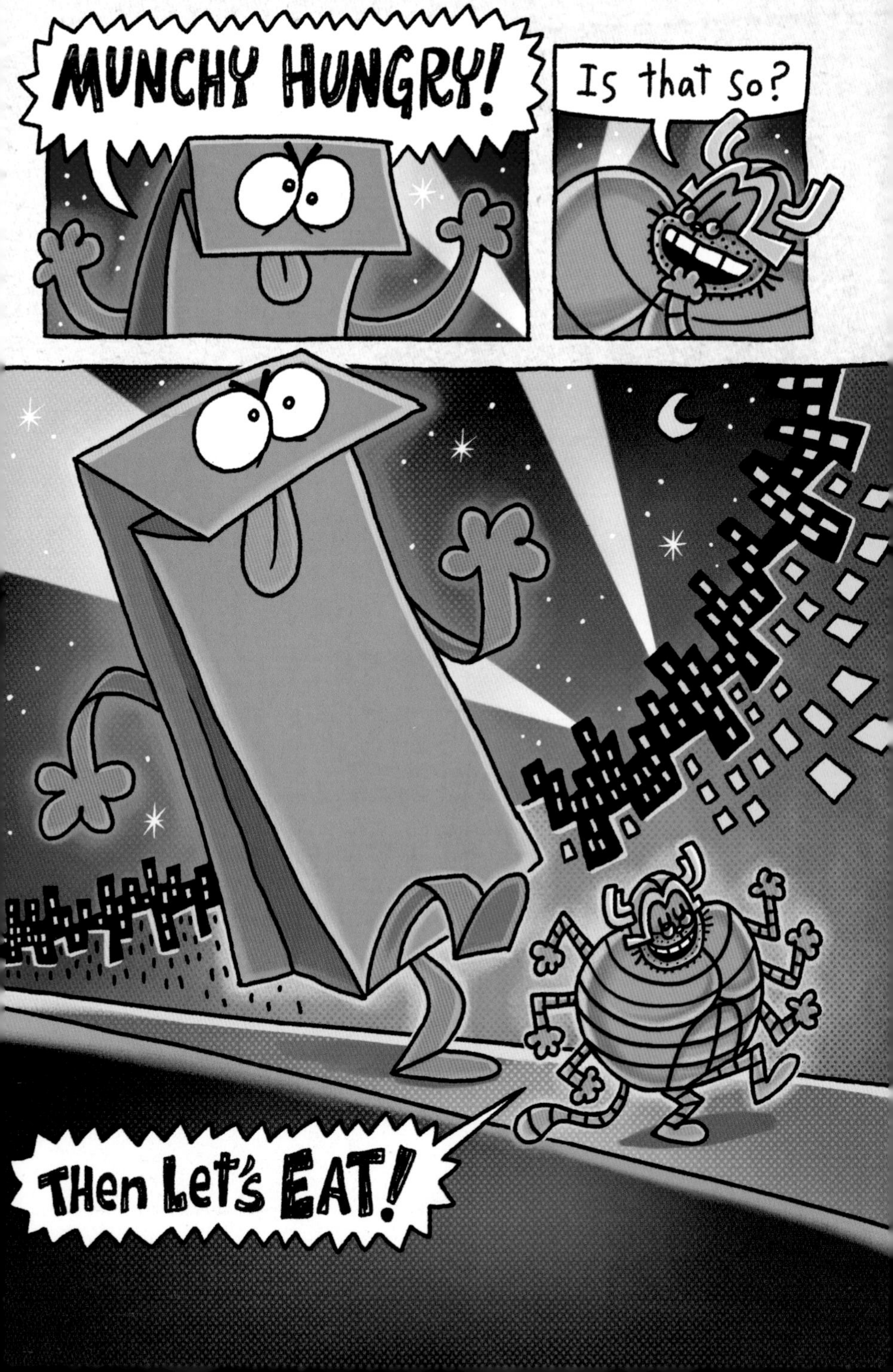
MUNCHY HUNGRY!
Is that so?
Then Let's EAT!

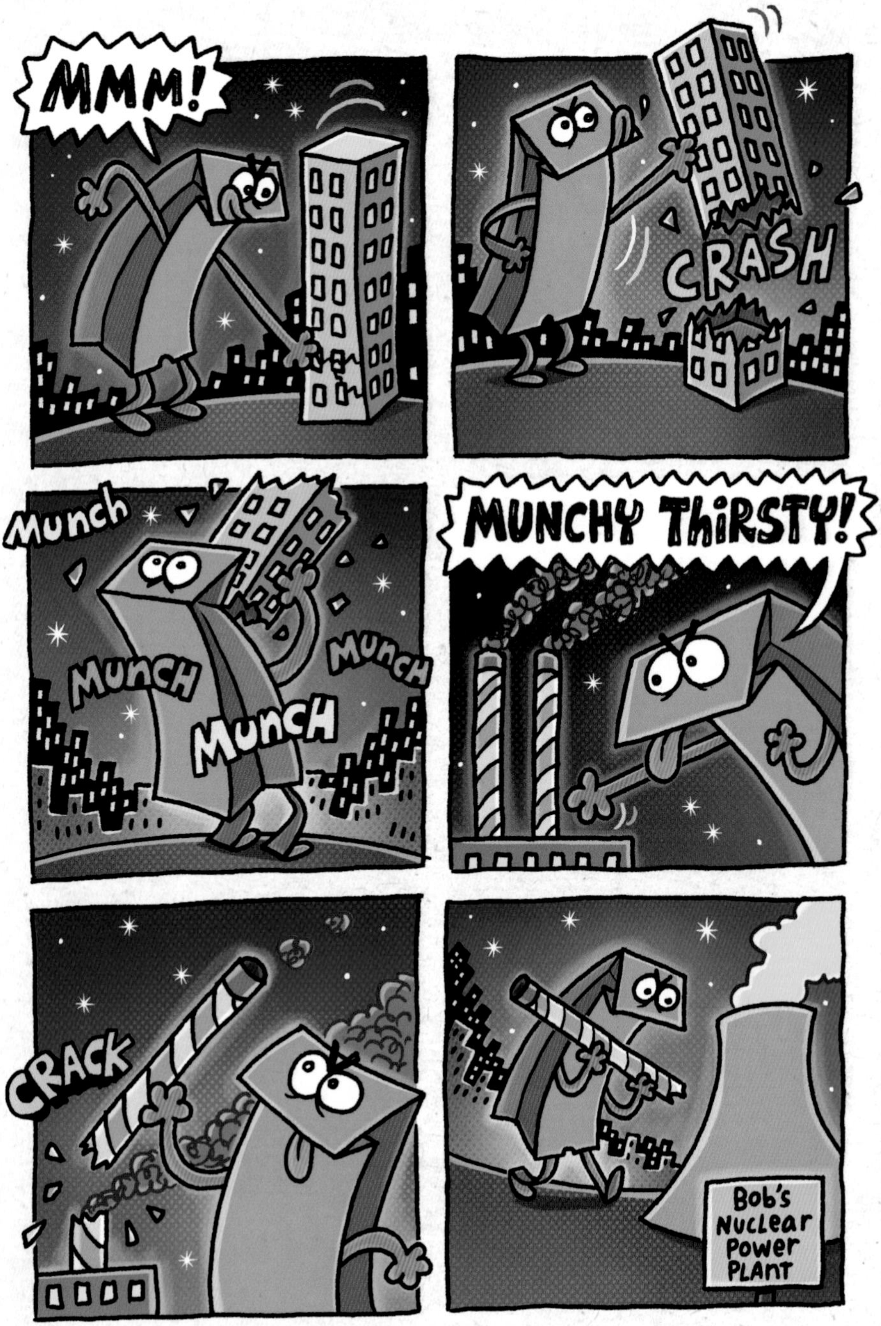
MMM!
CRASH
Munch
MUNCH
MUNCH
MUNCH
MUNCHY THIRSTY!
CRACK
Bob's Nuclear Power PLANT

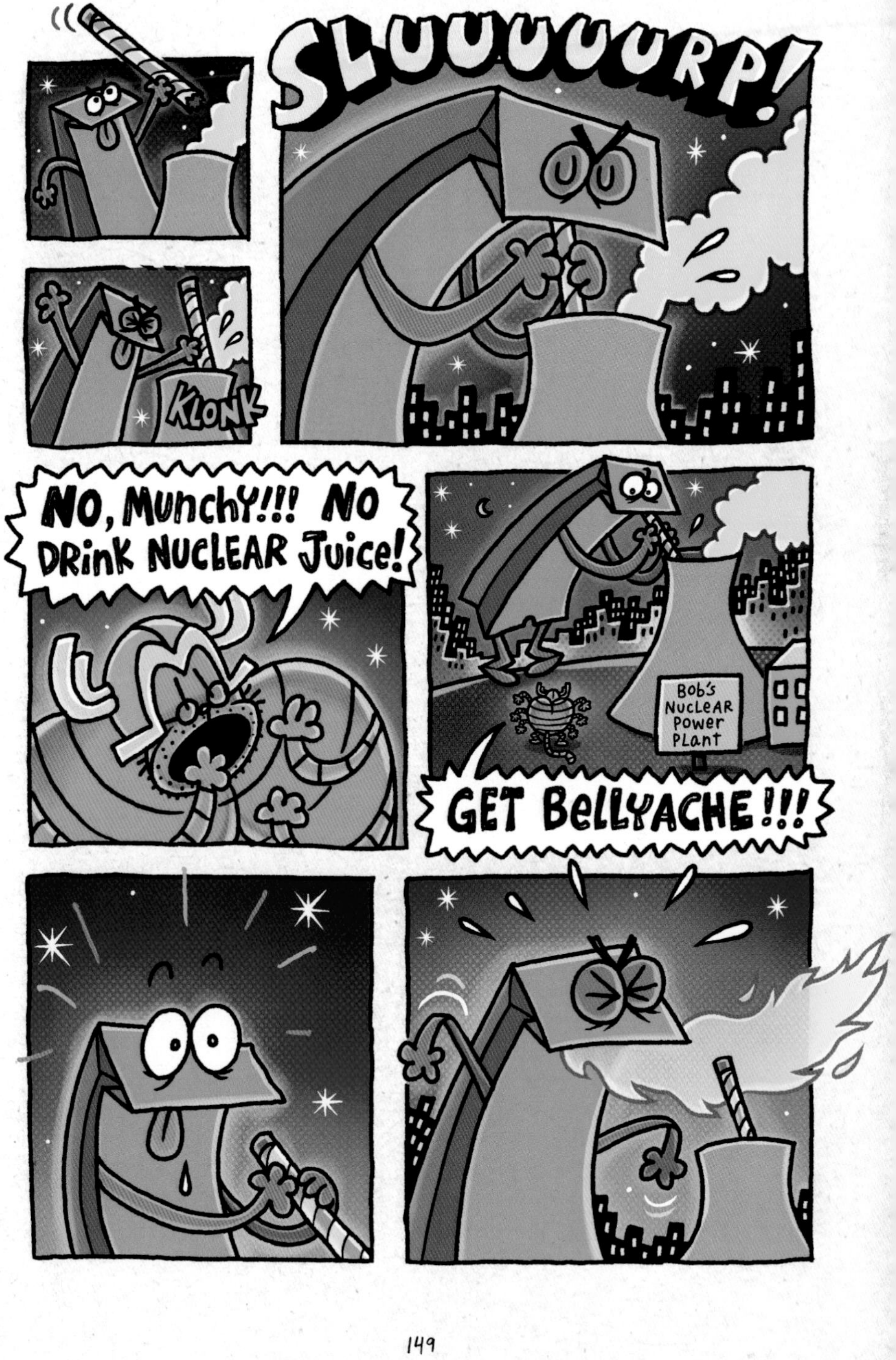
SLUUUUURP!
KLONK
NO, MUNCHY!!! NO DRINK NUCLEAR JUICE!
Bob's Nuclear Power Plant
GET BELLYACHE!!!

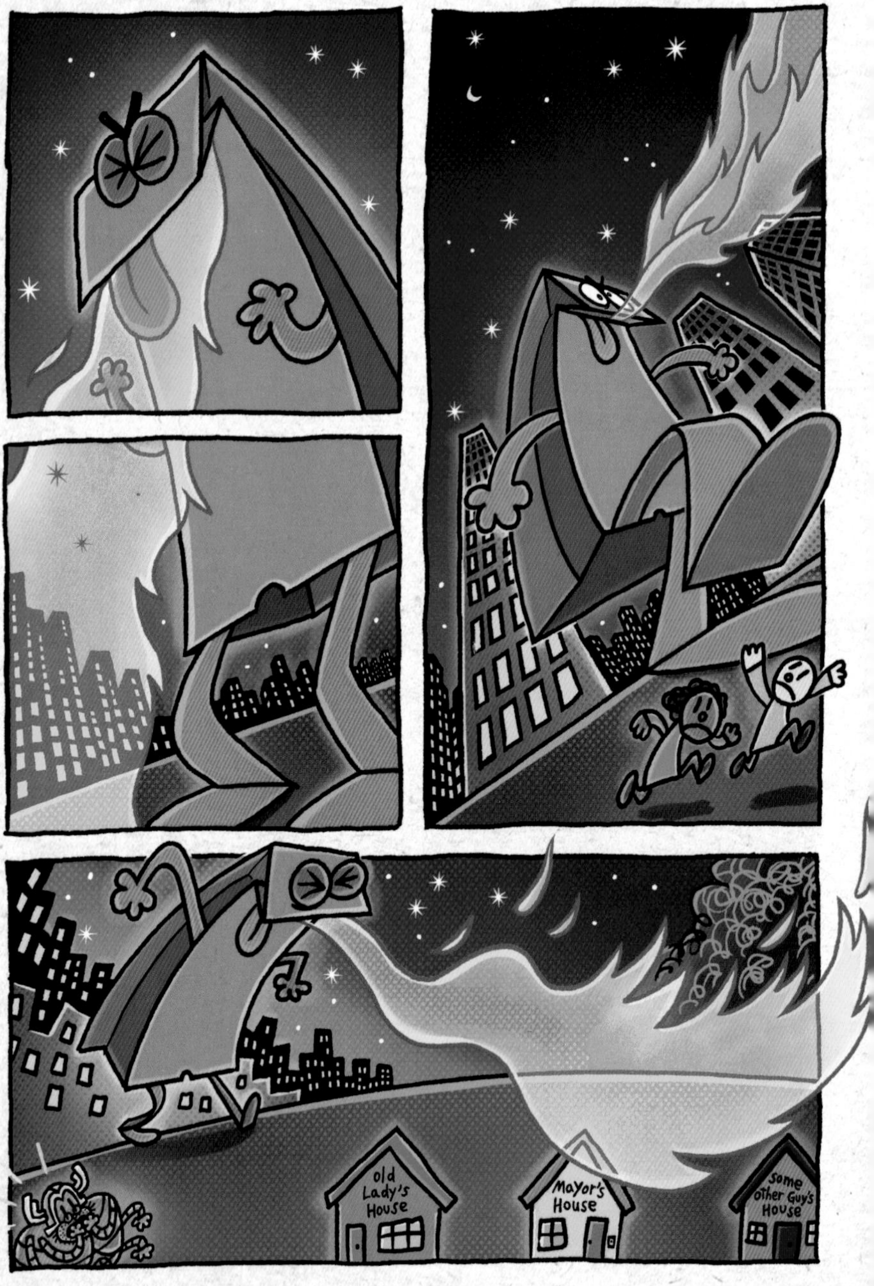

Old Lady's House
Mayor's House
Some other Guy's House

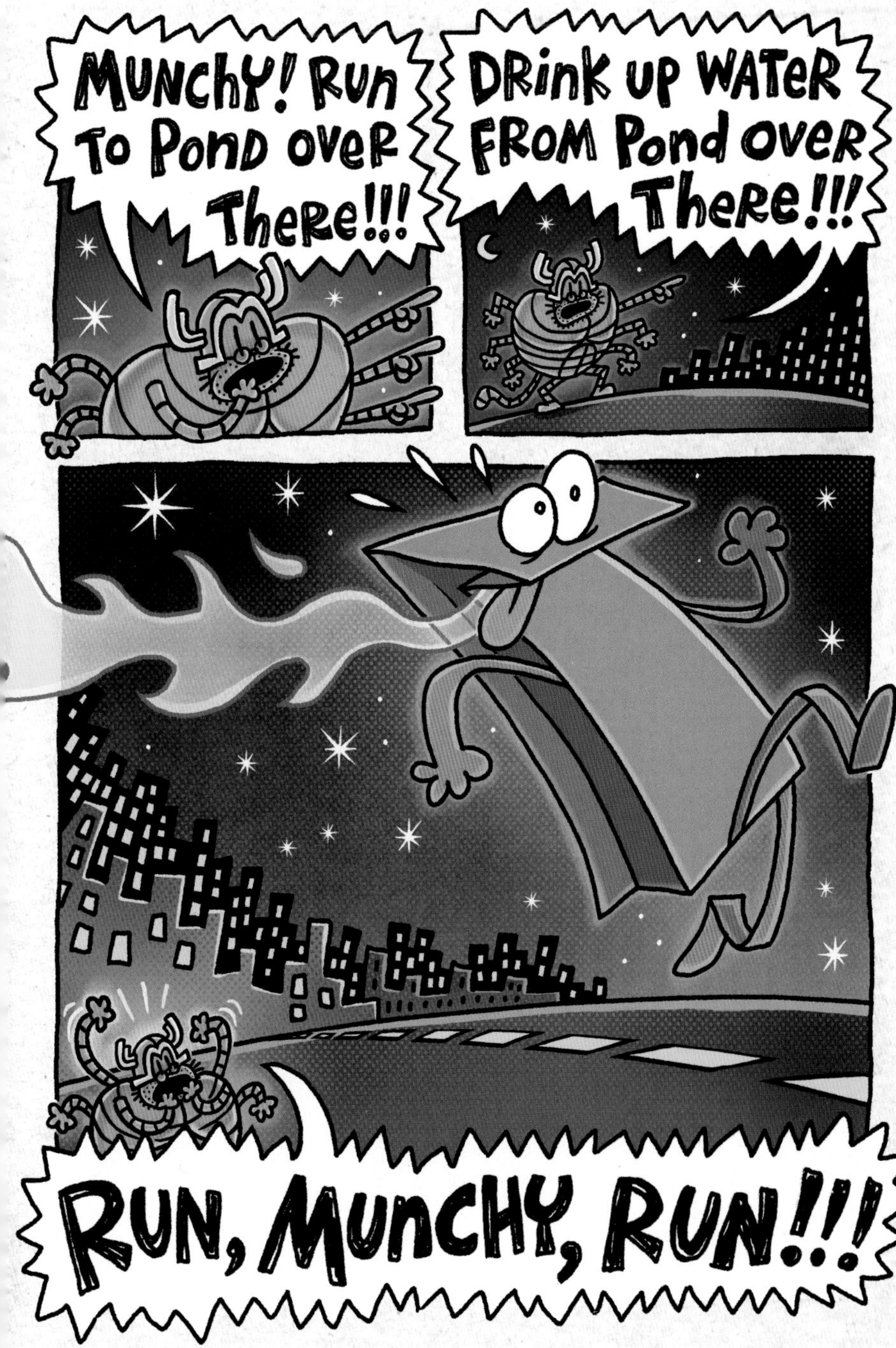
MUNCHY! RUN TO POND OVER THERE!!!
DRINK UP WATER FROM POND OVER THERE!!!
RUN, MUNCHY, RUN!!!

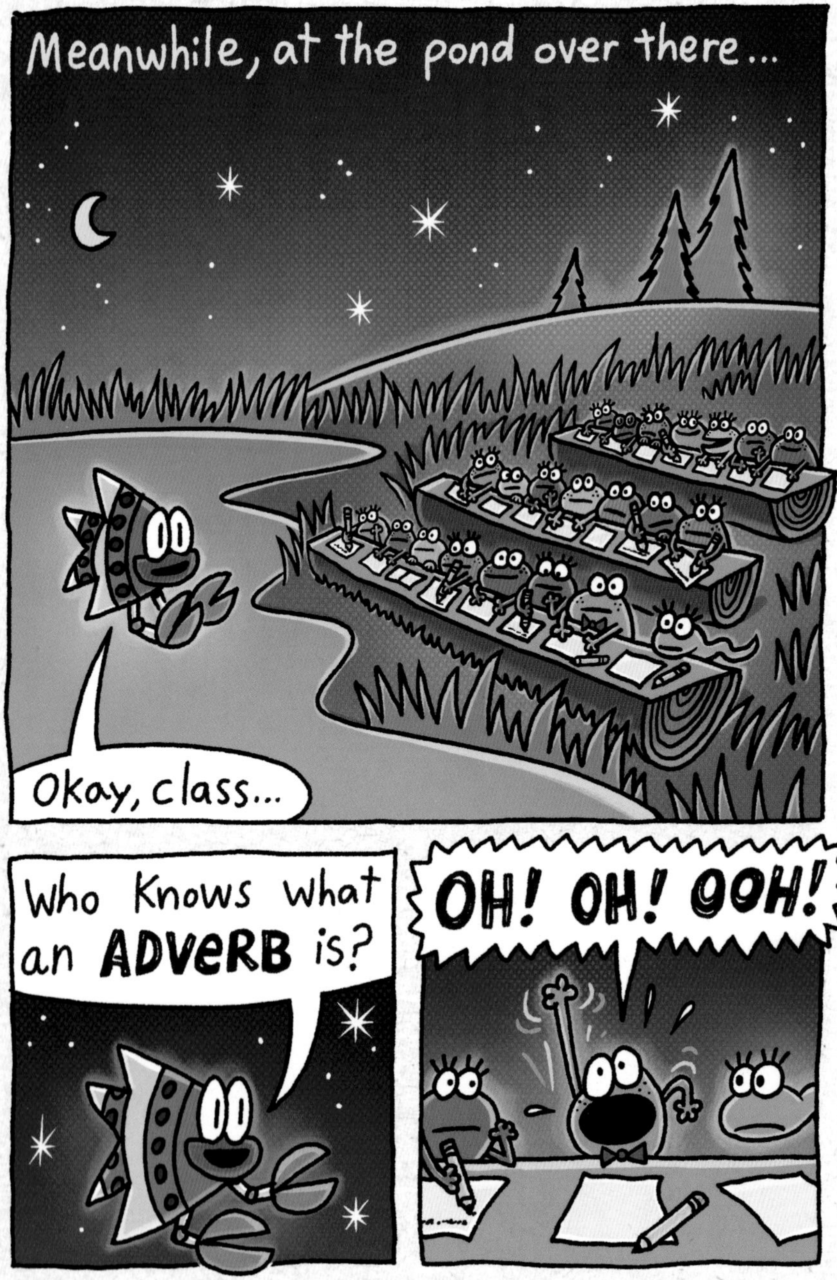
Meanwhile, at the pond over there...
Okay, class...
Who Knows what an ADVERB is?
OH! OH! OOH!

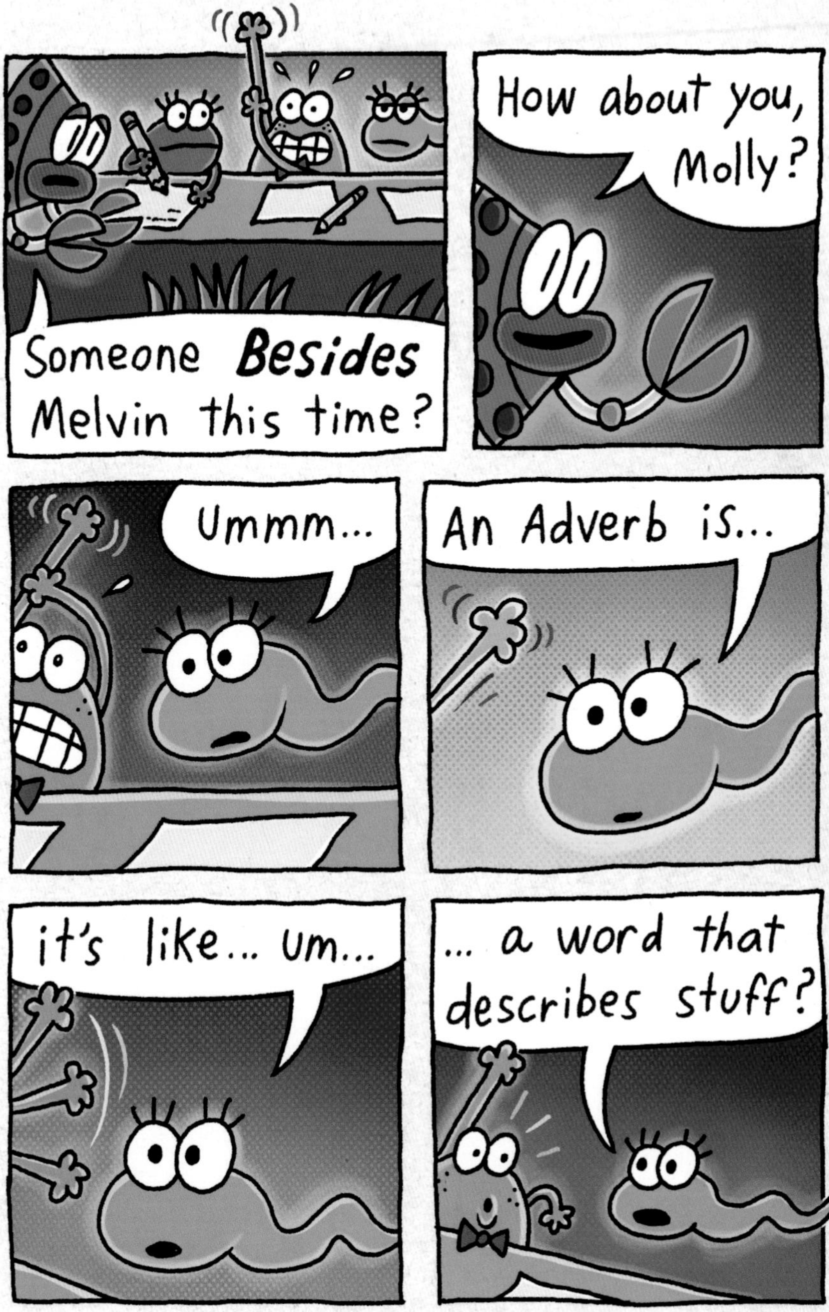

Someone **Besides** Melvin this time?
How about you, Molly?
Ummm...
An Adverb is...
it's like... um...
... a word that describes stuff?

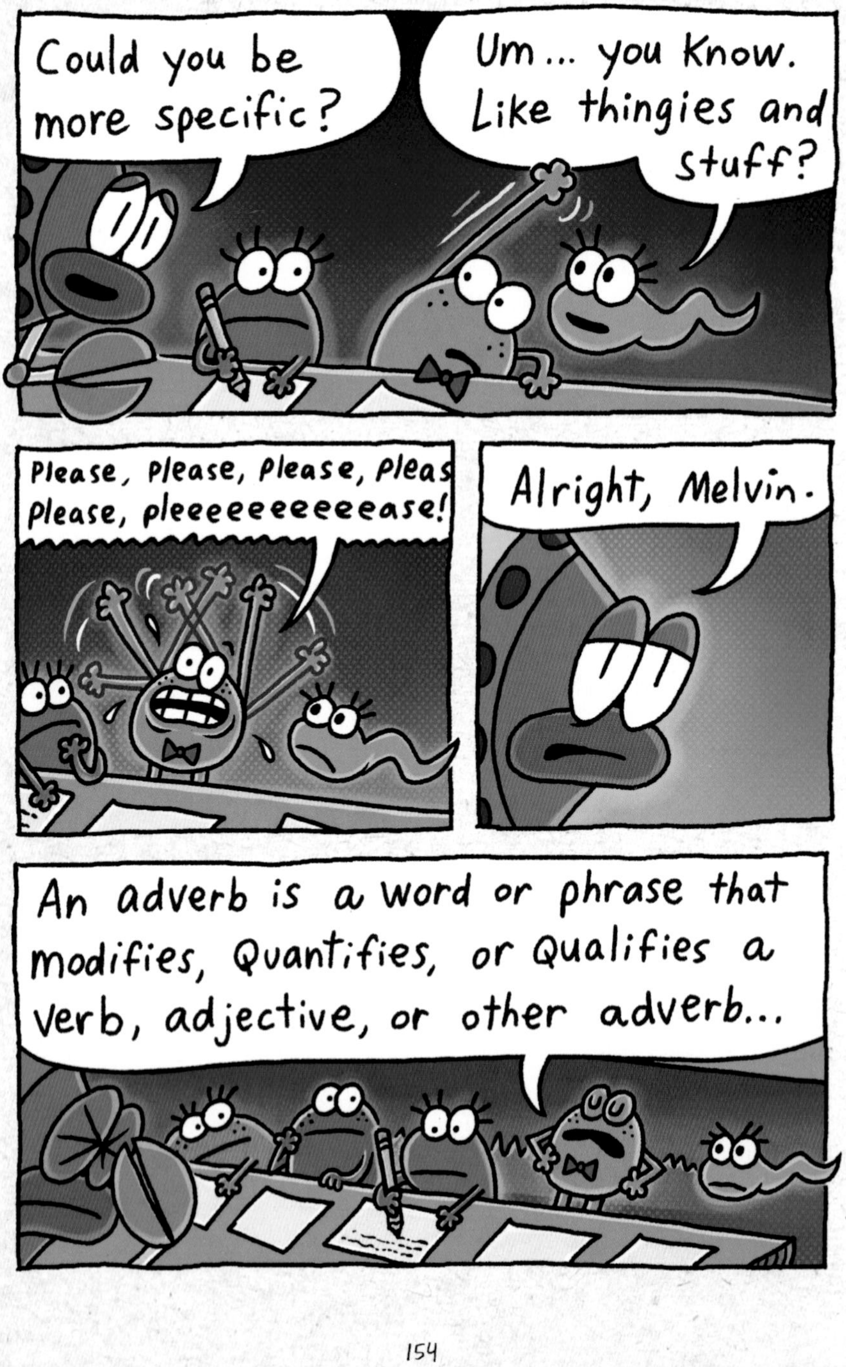

Could you be more specific?
Um... you know. Like thingies and stuff?
Please, please, please, pleas please, pleeeeeeeeeease!
Alright, Melvin.
An adverb is a word or phrase that modifies, quantifies, or qualifies a verb, adjective, or other adverb...

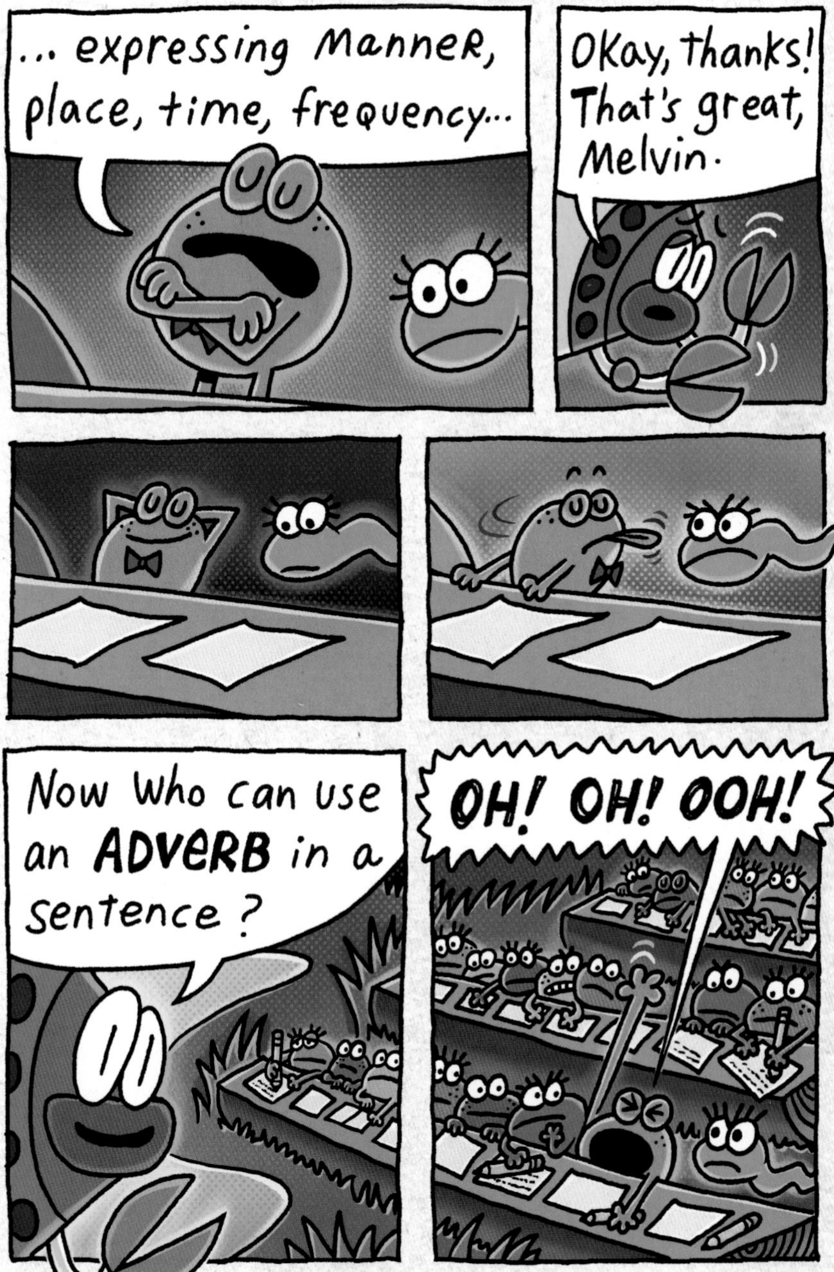
... expressing Manner, place, time, frequency...
Okay, thanks! That's great, Melvin.
Now who can use an ADVERB in a sentence?
OH! OH! OOH!

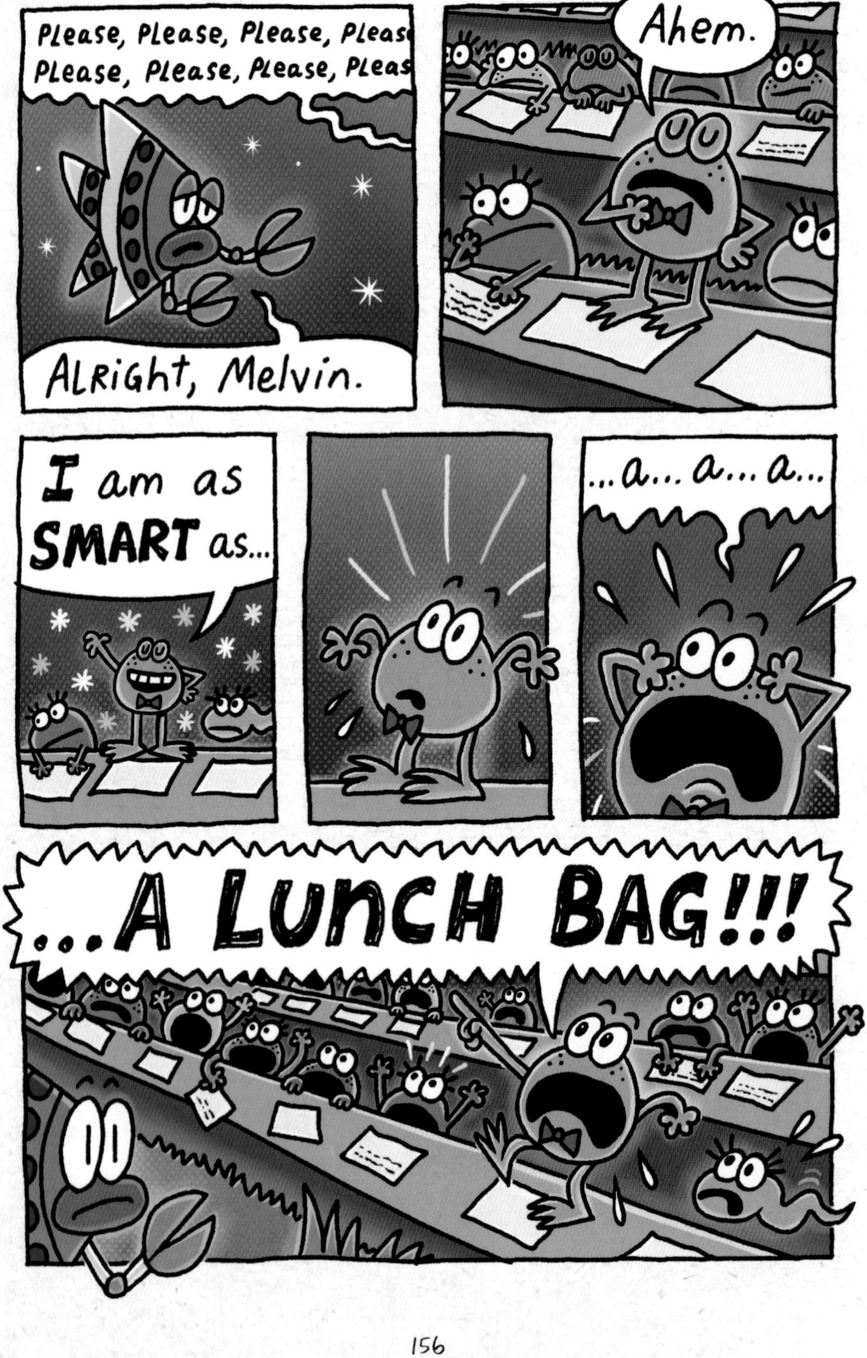
Please, Please, Please, Please
Please, Please, Please, Pleas
ALRIGHT, Melvin.
Ahem.
I am as SMART as...
...a...a...a...
...A LUNCH BAG!!!

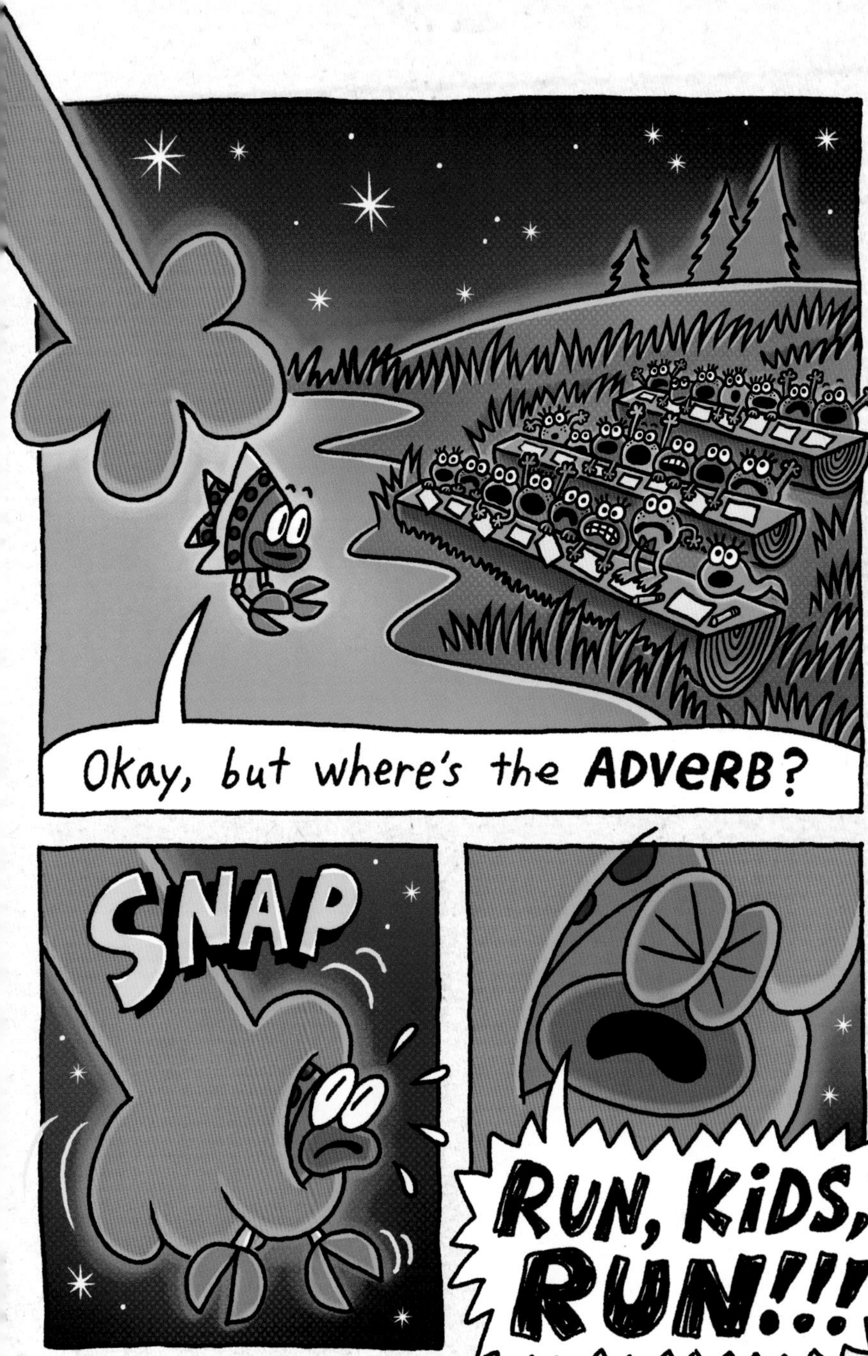
Okay, but where's the ADVERB?
SNAP
RUN, KIDS, RUN!!!

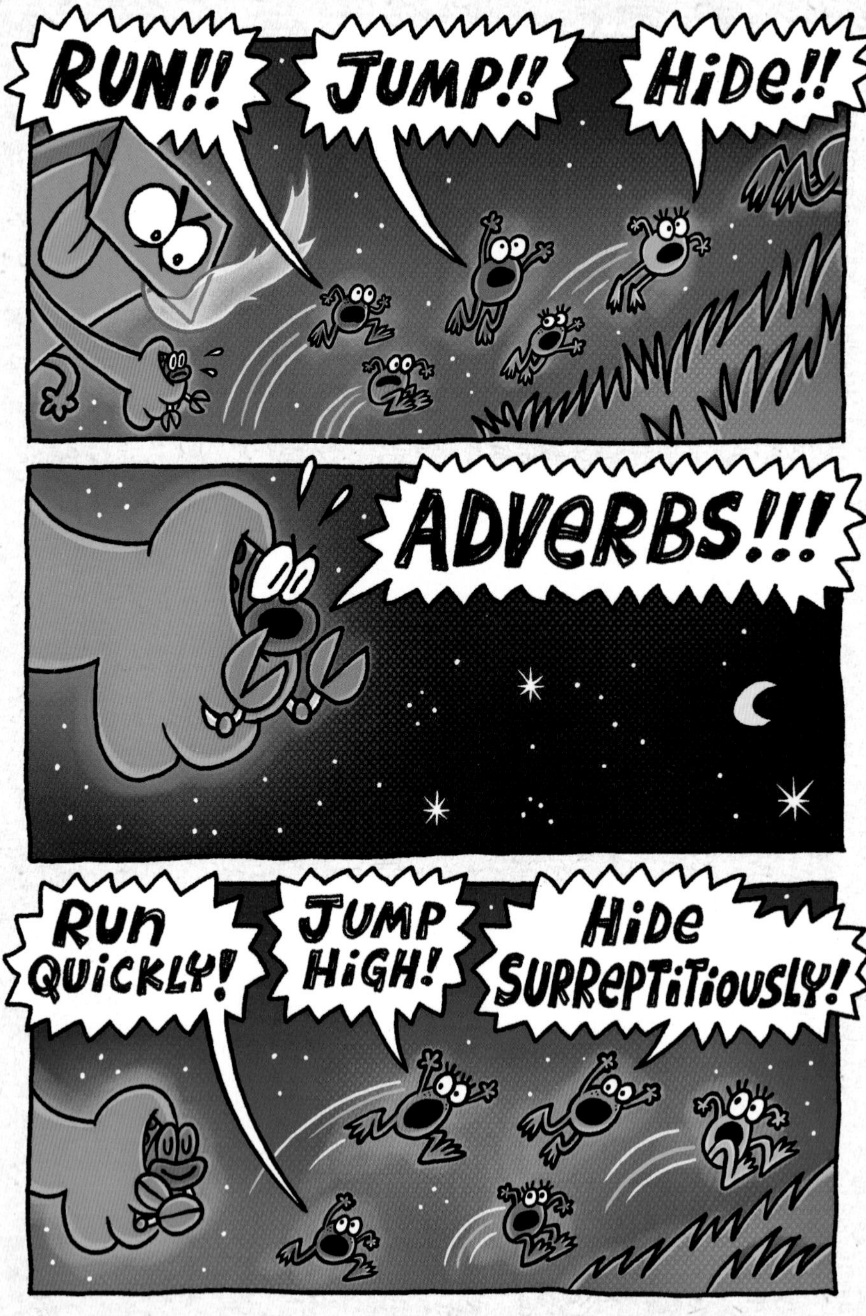
RUN!!
JUMP!!
HIDE!!
ADVERBS!!!
RUN QUICKLY!
JUMP HIGH!
HIDE SURREPTITIOUSLY!

CHAPTER 10

80-HD POWER

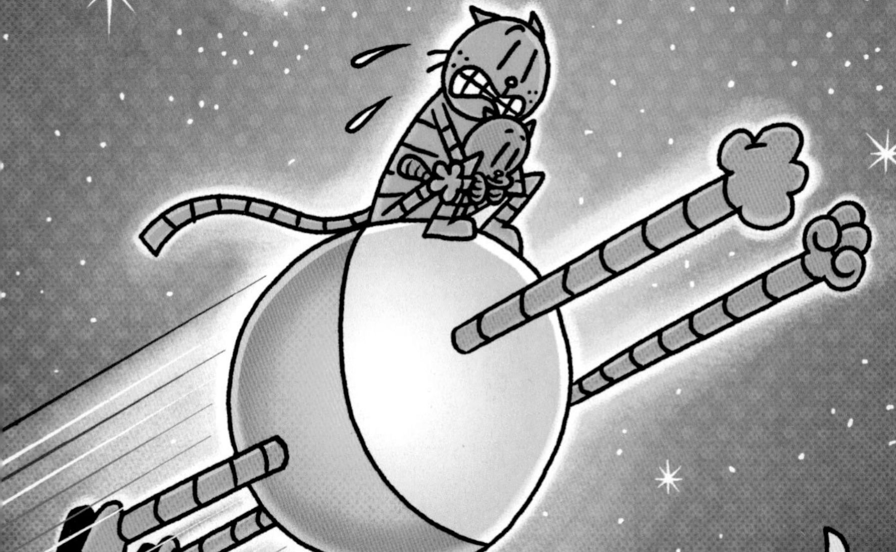

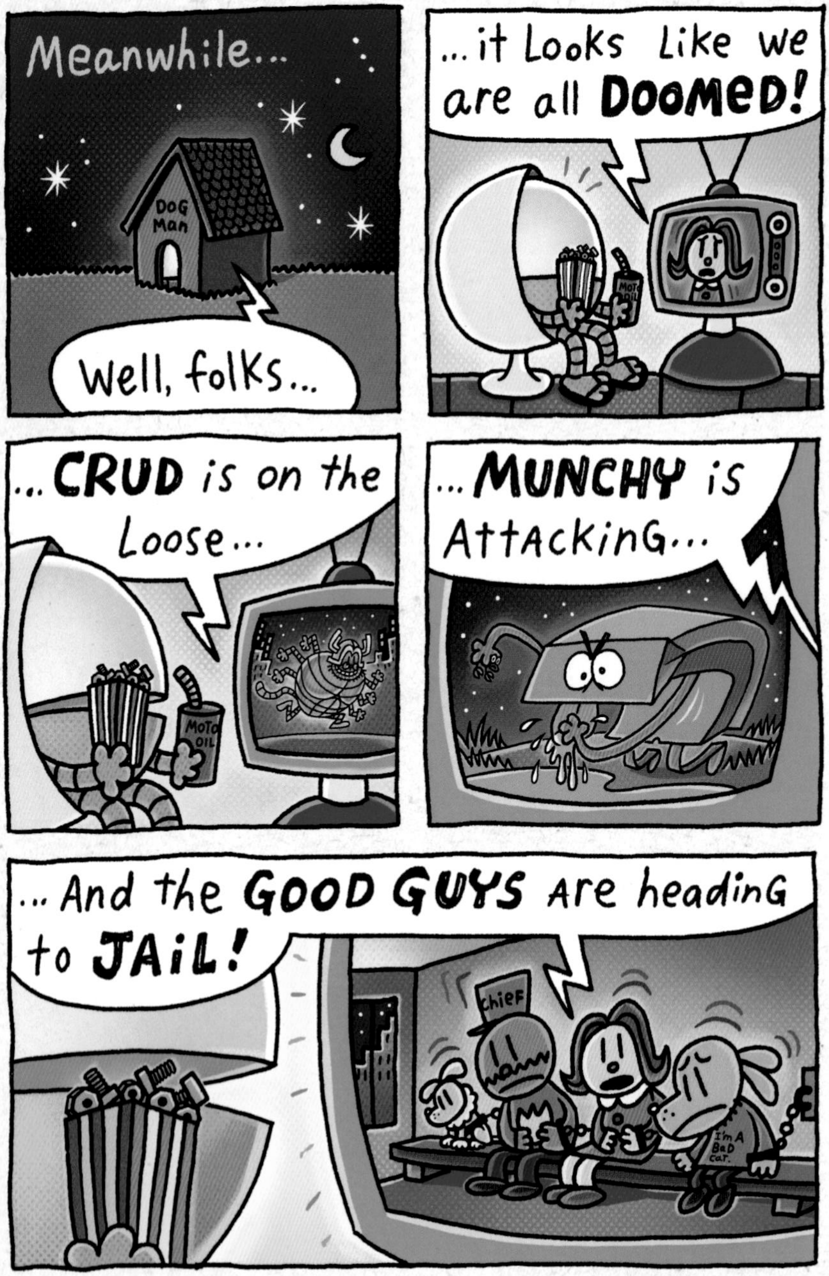
Meanwhile...
DOG Man
Well, folks...
...it Looks Like we are all DOOMED!
MOTO OIL
...CRUD is on the Loose...
MOTO OIL
...MUNCHY is Attacking...
...And the GOOD GUYS Are heading to JAIL!
Chief
I'm A BaD cat.

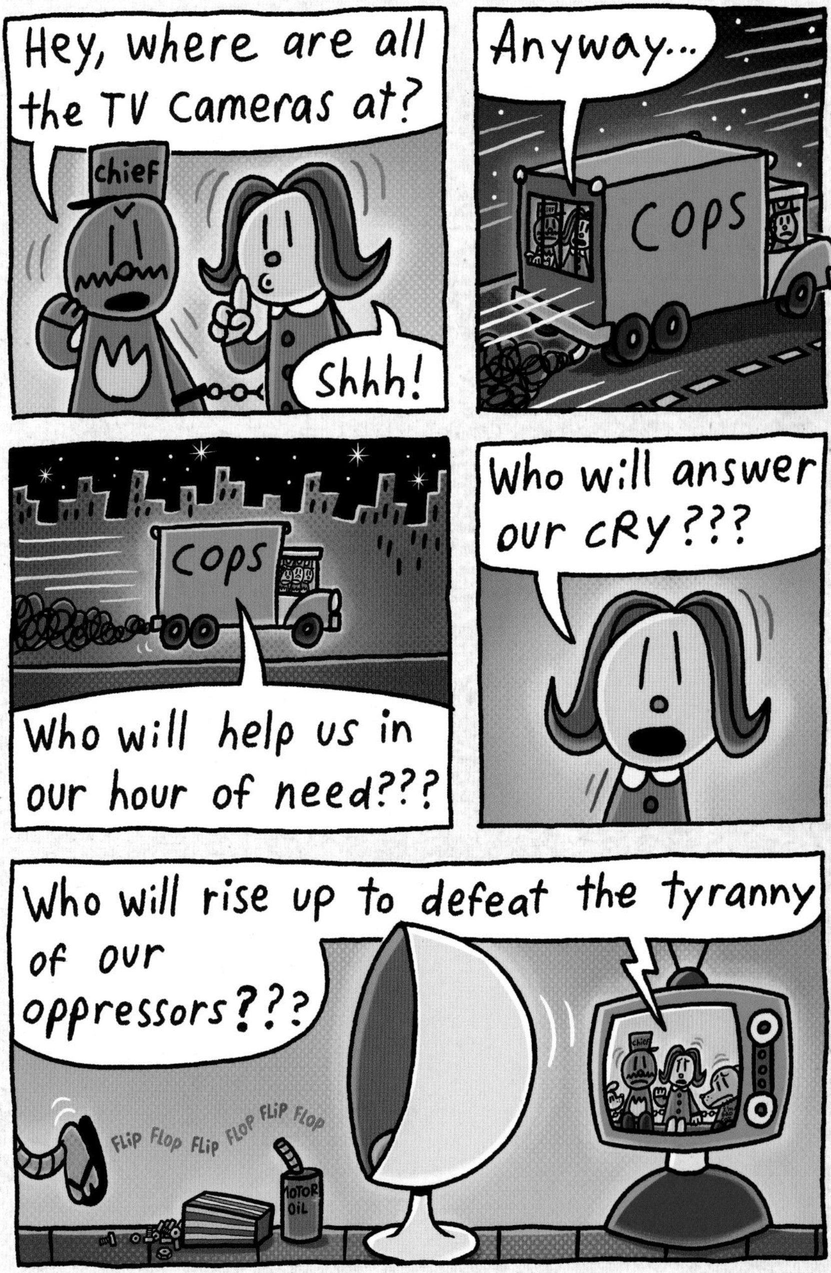
Hey, where are all the TV cameras at?
chief
Shhh!
Anyway...
COPS
COPS
Who will help us in our hour of need???
Who will answer our CRY???
Who will rise up to defeat the tyranny of our oppressors???
FLIP FLOP FLIP FLOP FLIP FLOP
MOTOR OIL

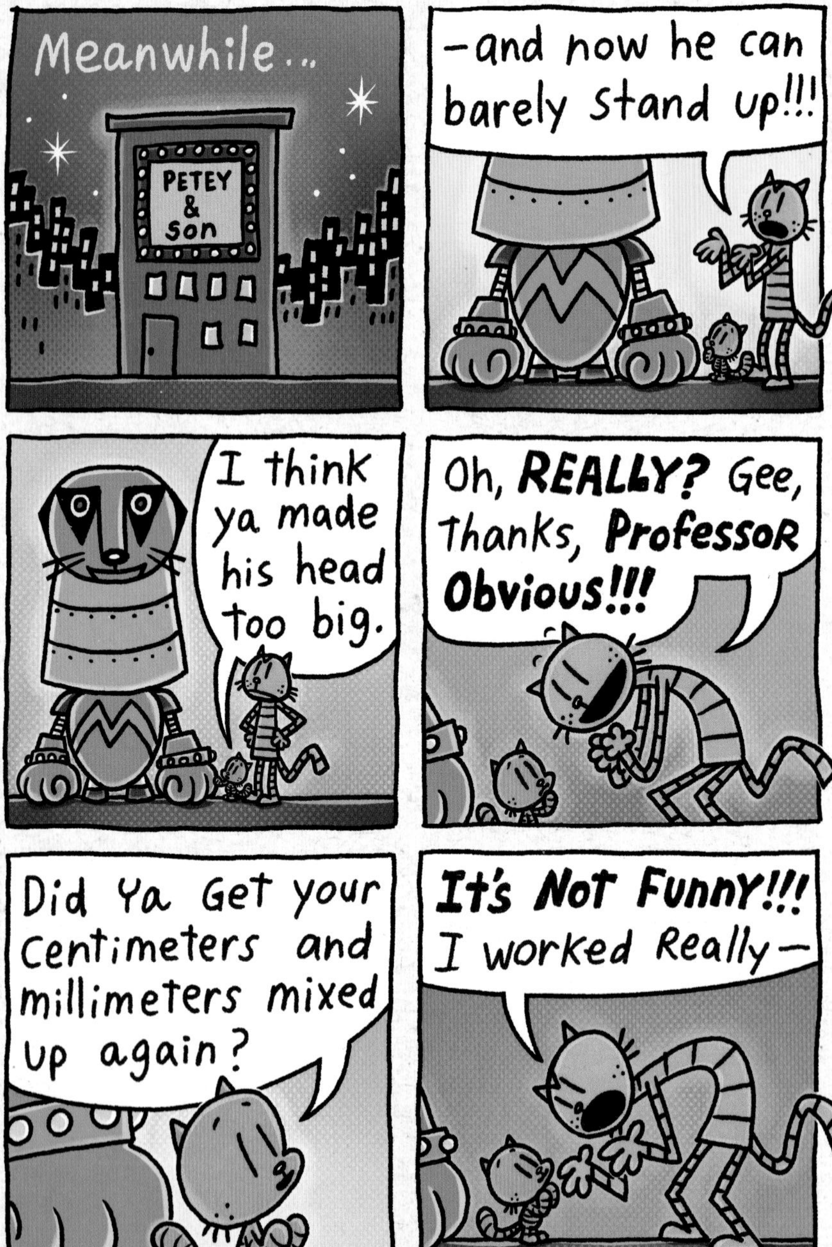
Meanwhile...
PETEY & SON
-and now he can barely Stand up!!!
I think ya made his head too big.
Oh, REALLY? Gee, Thanks, Professor Obvious!!!
Did Ya Get your Centimeters and millimeters mixed up again?
It's Not Funny!!! I worked Really—

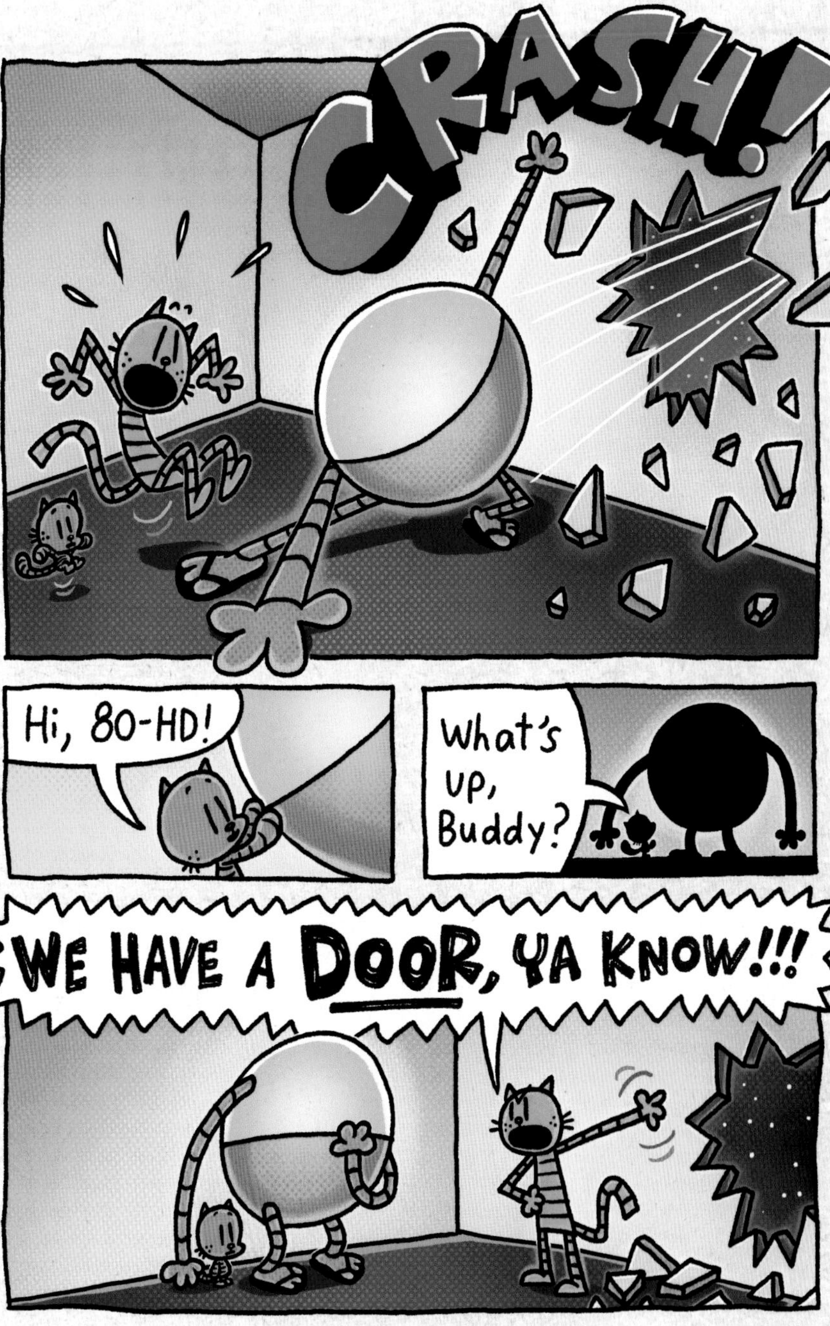
CRASH!
Hi, 80-HD!
What's up, Buddy?
WE HAVE A DOOR, YA KNOW!!!

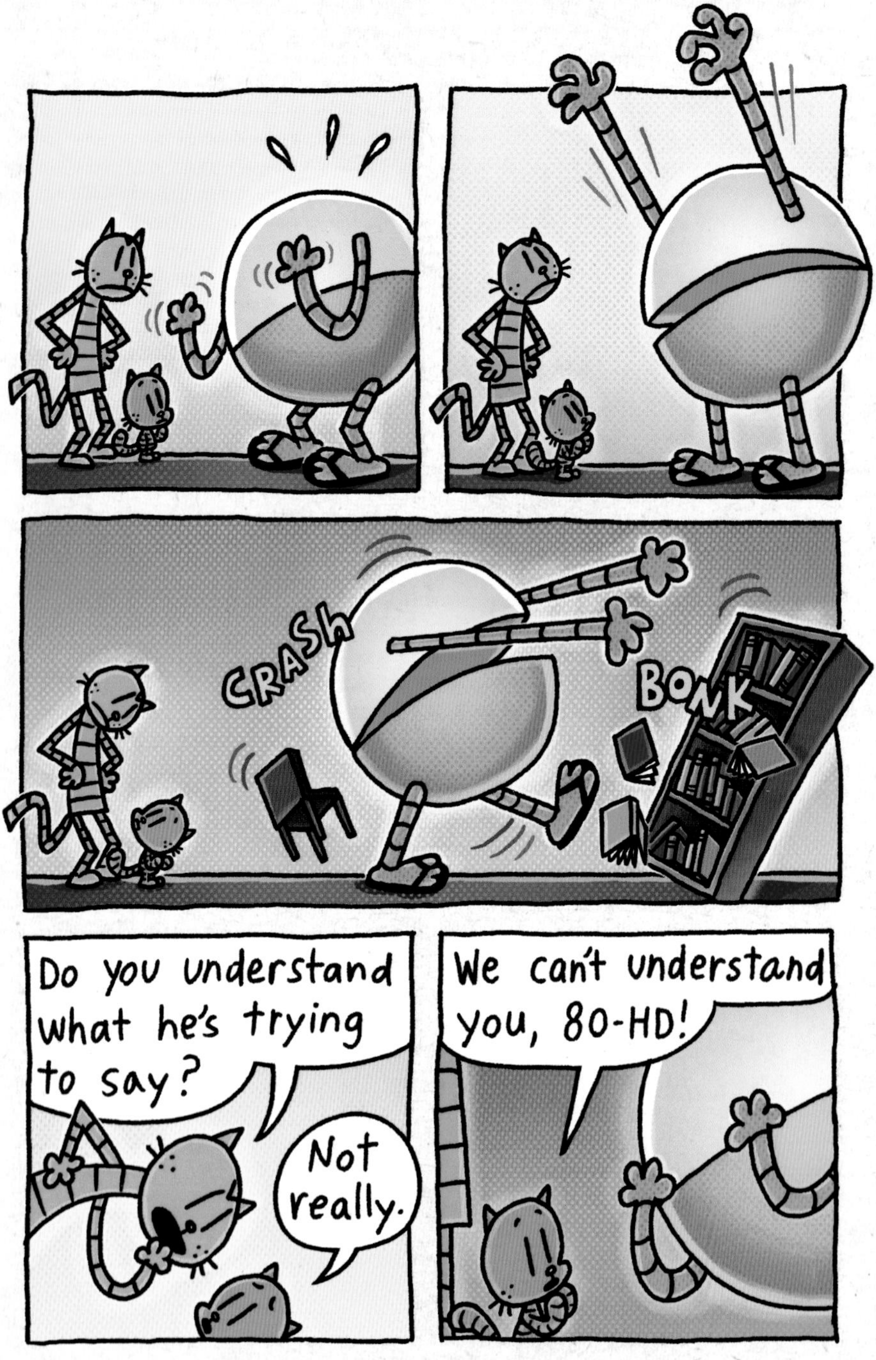
CRASh
BONK
Do you understand what he's trying to say?
Not really.
We can't understand you, 80-HD!

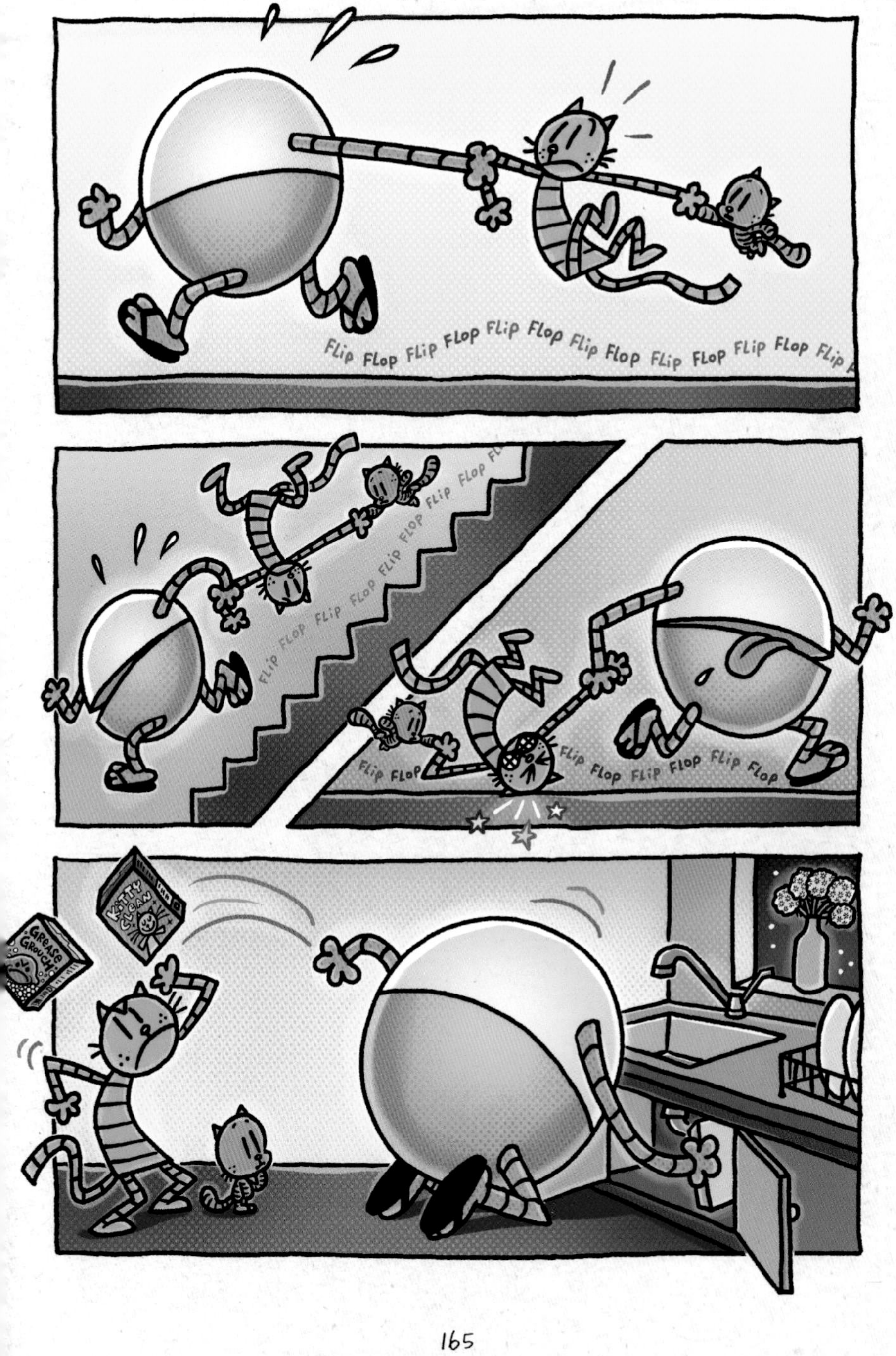
Flip Flop Flip Flop Flip Flop Flip Flop Flip Flop Flip Flop Flip
Flip Flop Flip Flop Flip Flop Flip Flop
Flip Flop Flip Flop Flip Flop Flip Flop
Kitty Clean
Grease Grouch

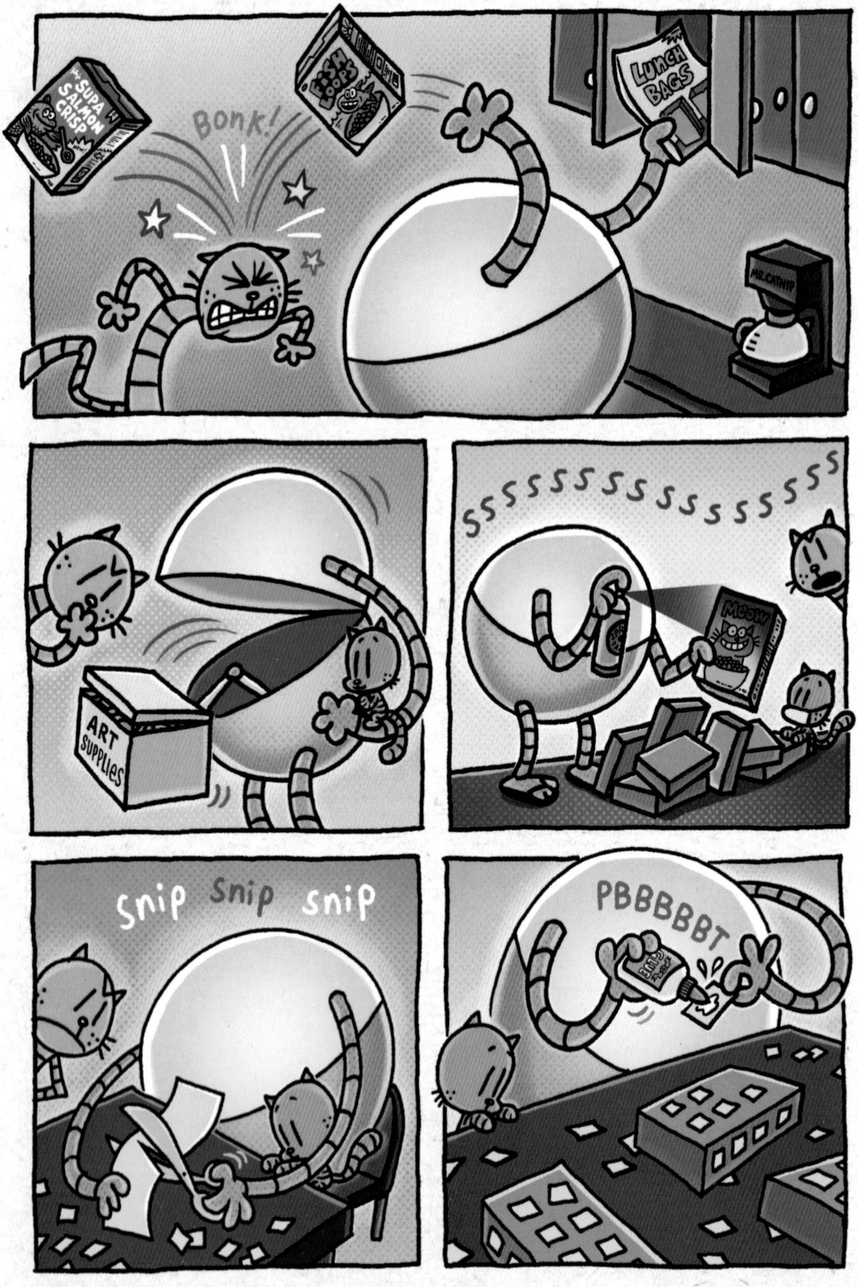
SUPA SALMON CRISP
BONK!
FISH LOOPS
LUNCH BAGS
MR. CATNIP
ART SUPPLIES
SSSSSSSSSSSSSSSS
MEOW
snip snip snip
PBBBBBT

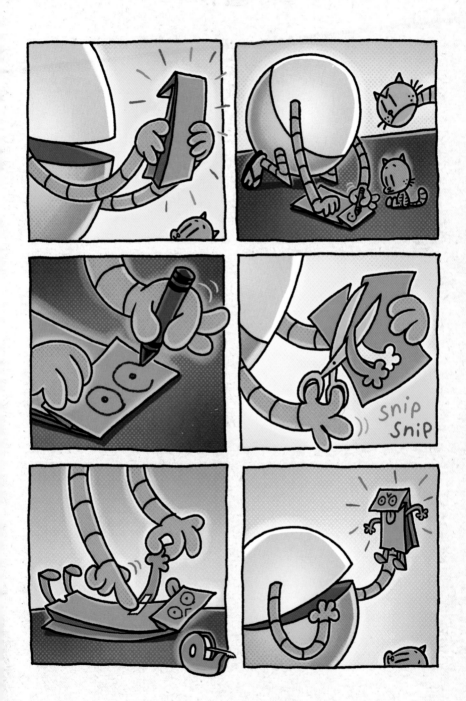

snip
snip

167

MODELING CLAY
6 COLORS
NON-TOXIC

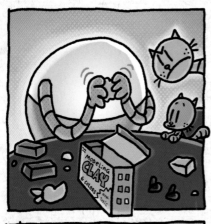

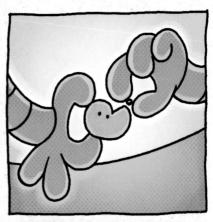

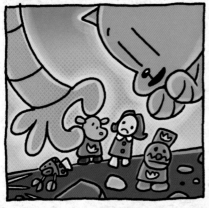

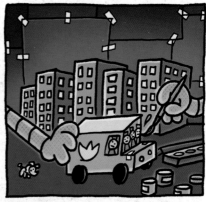

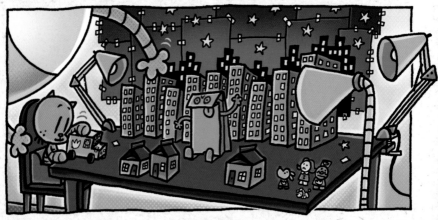

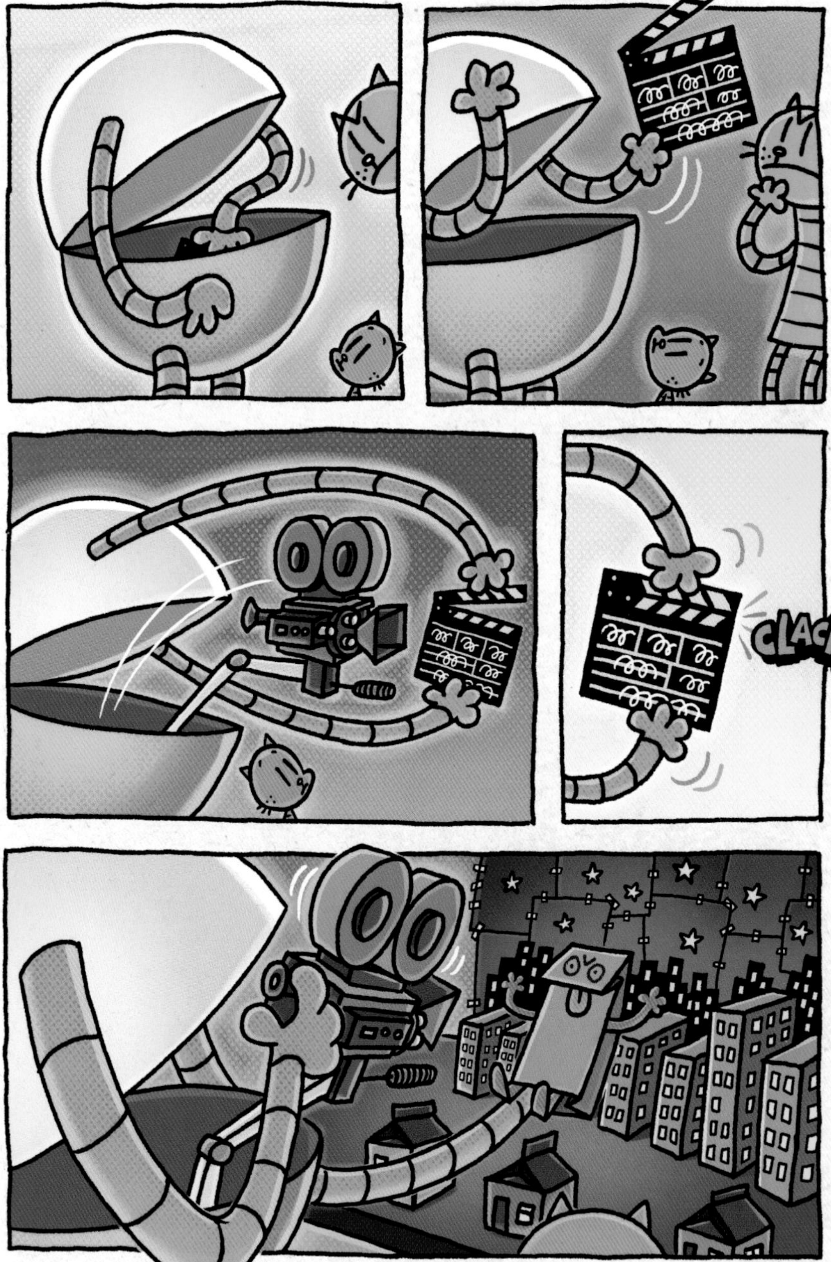
CLACK!

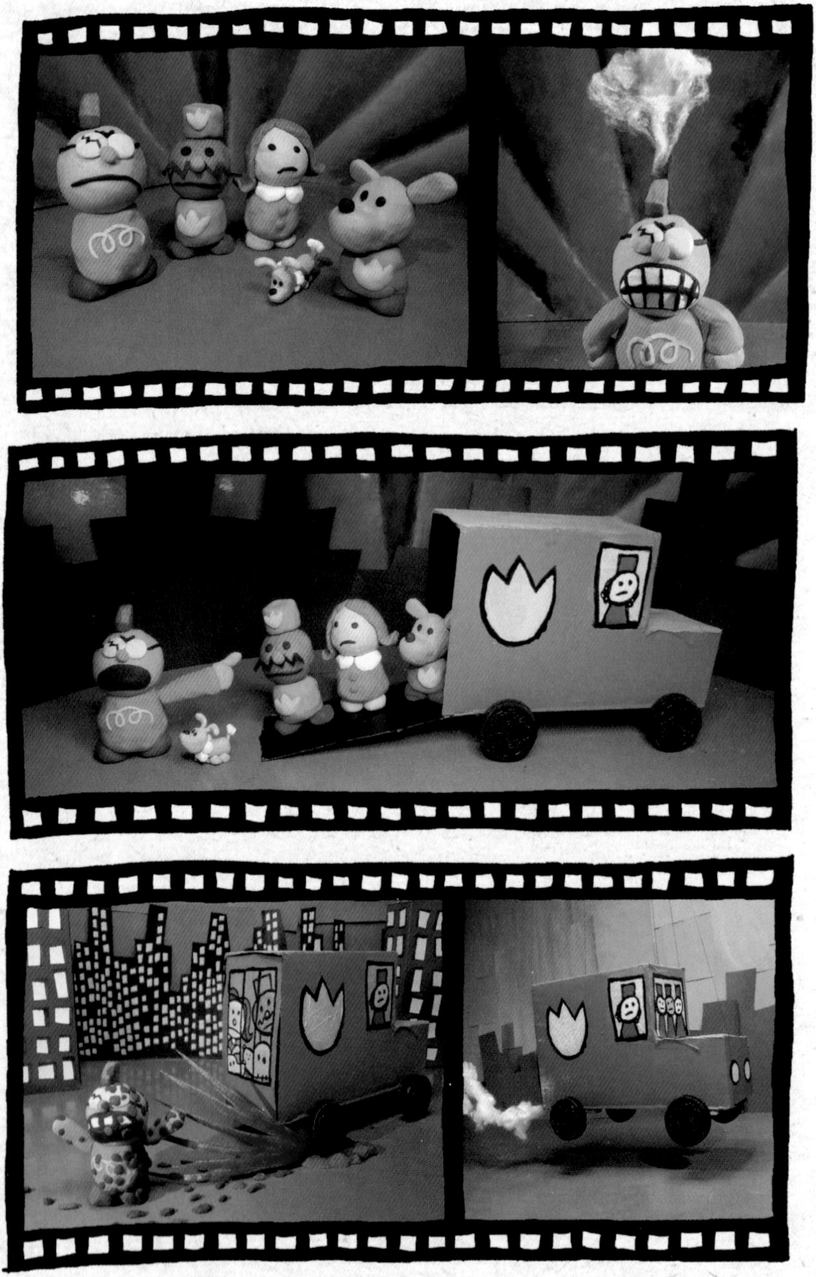

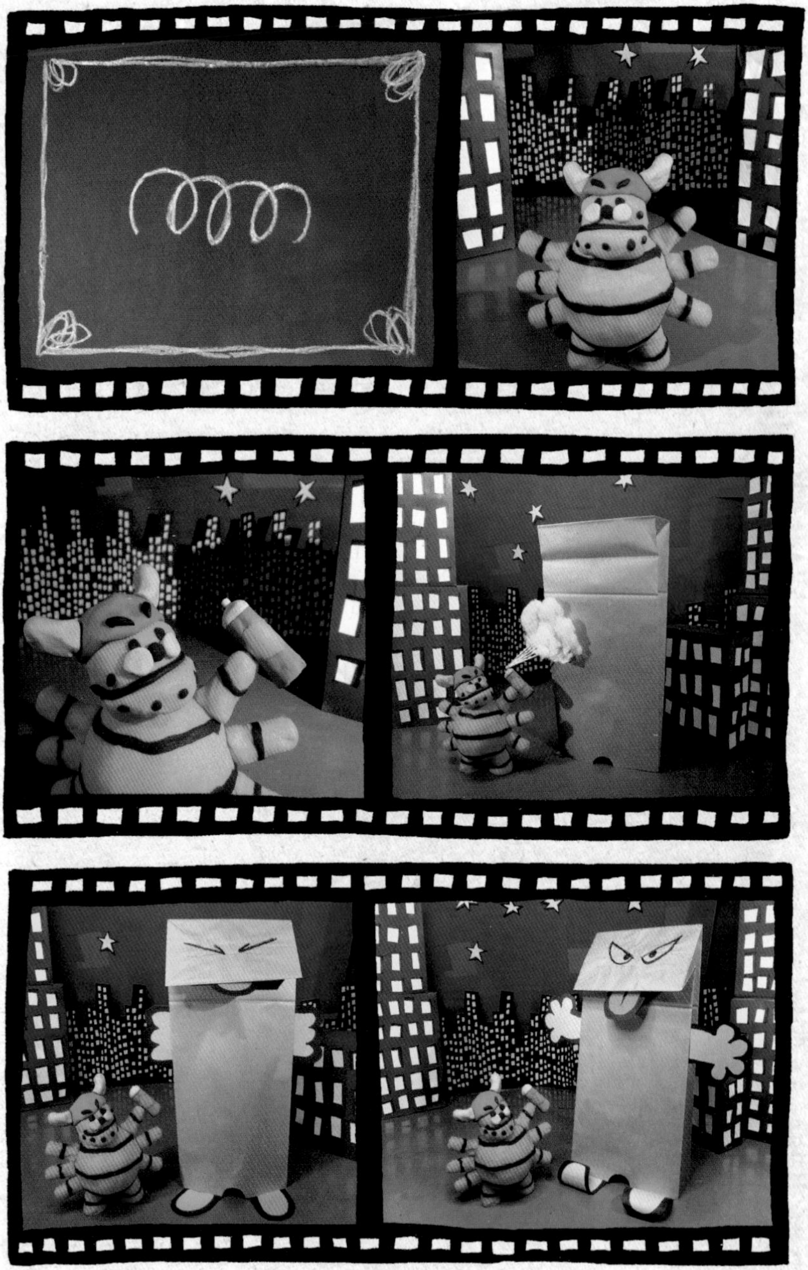

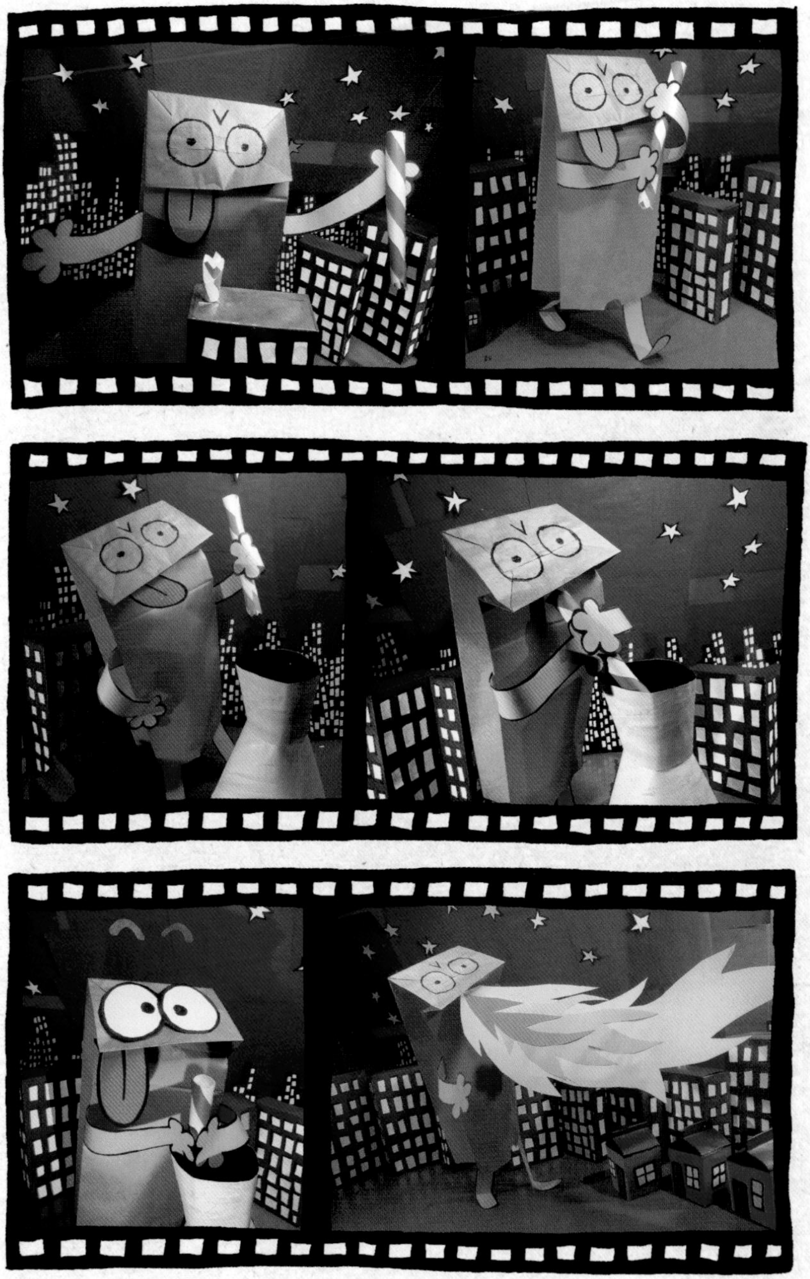

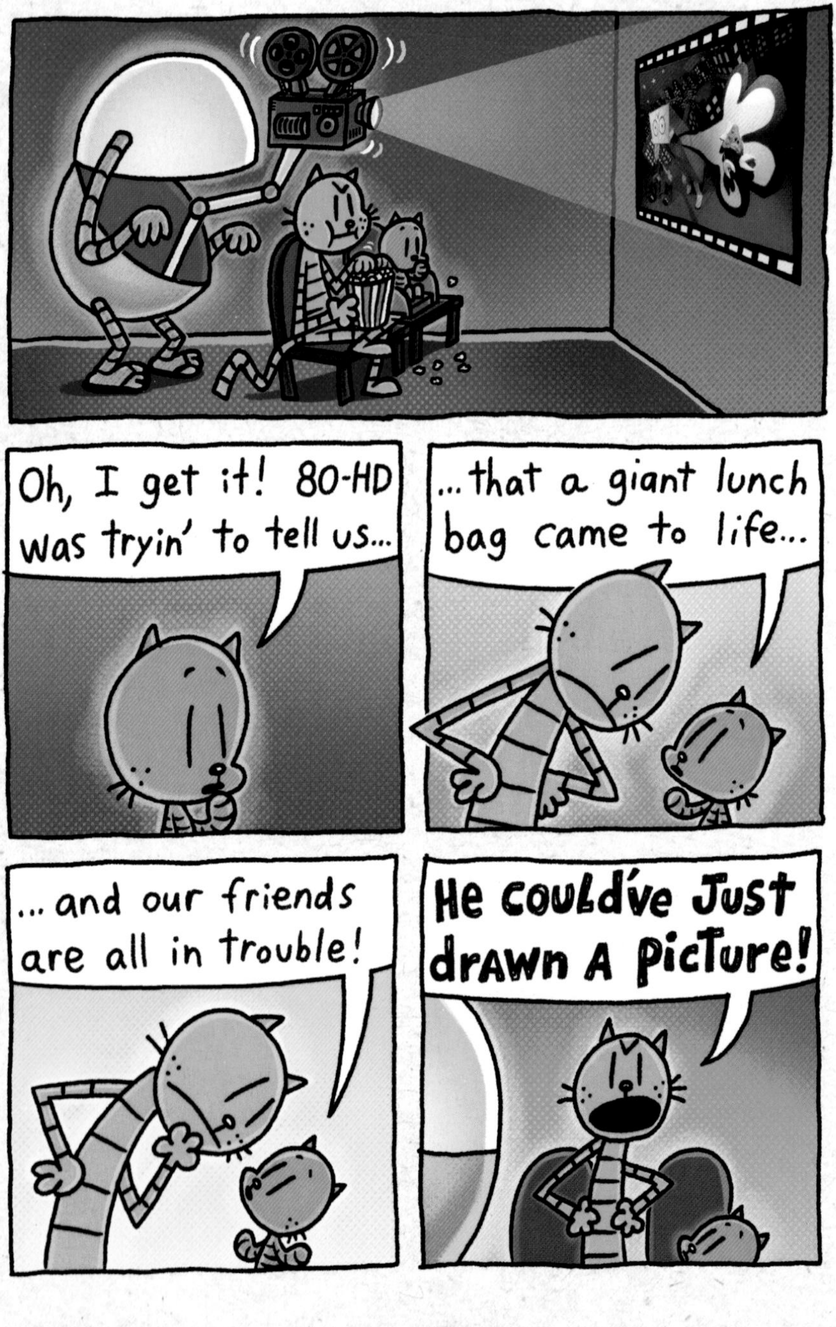
Oh, I get it! 80-HD was tryin' to tell us...
...that a giant lunch bag came to life...
...and our friends are all in trouble!
He could've just drawn a picture!

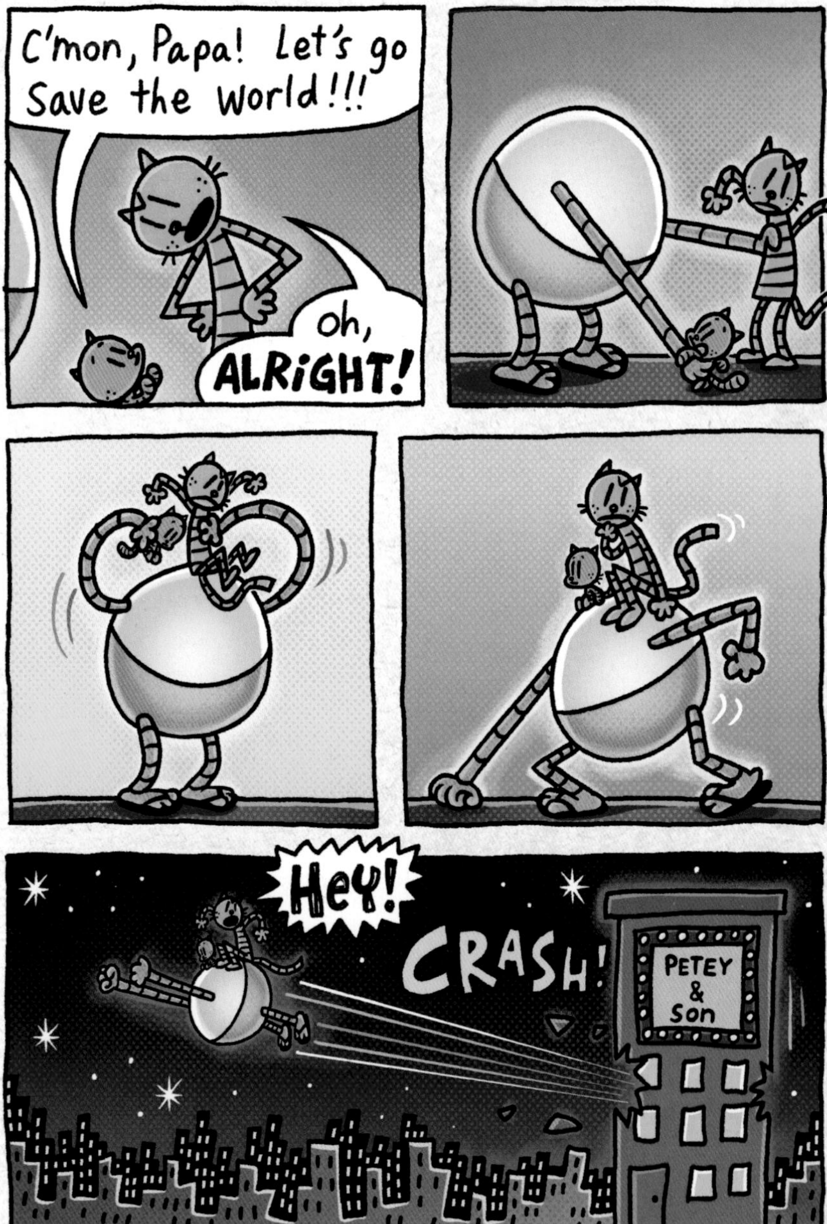

C'mon, Papa! Let's go Save the World!!!
oh, ALRiGHT!
Hey!
CRASH!
PETEY & Son

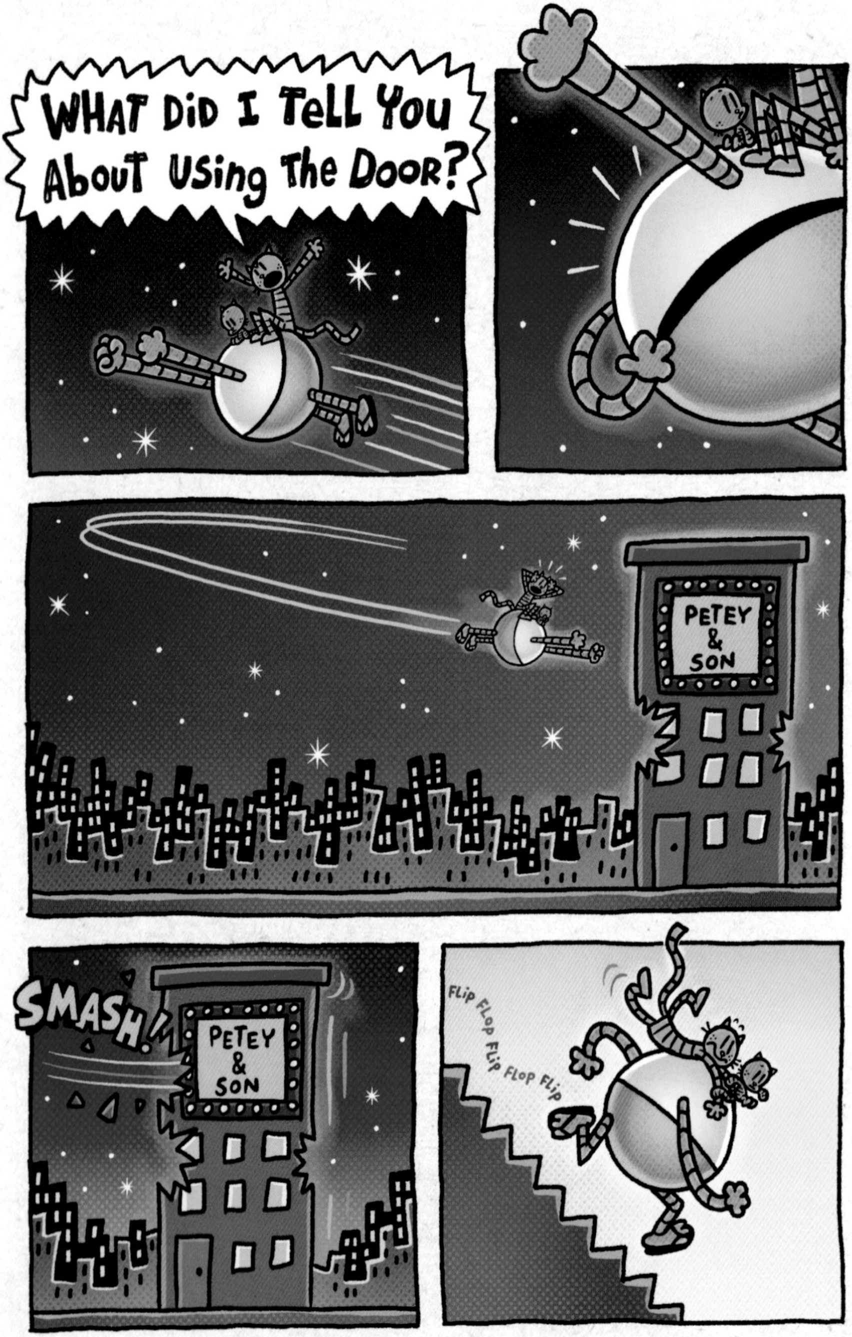
WHAT DID I TELL YOU About USing The DOOR?
PETEY & SON
SMASH!
PETEY & SON
FLip FLop FLip FLop FLip

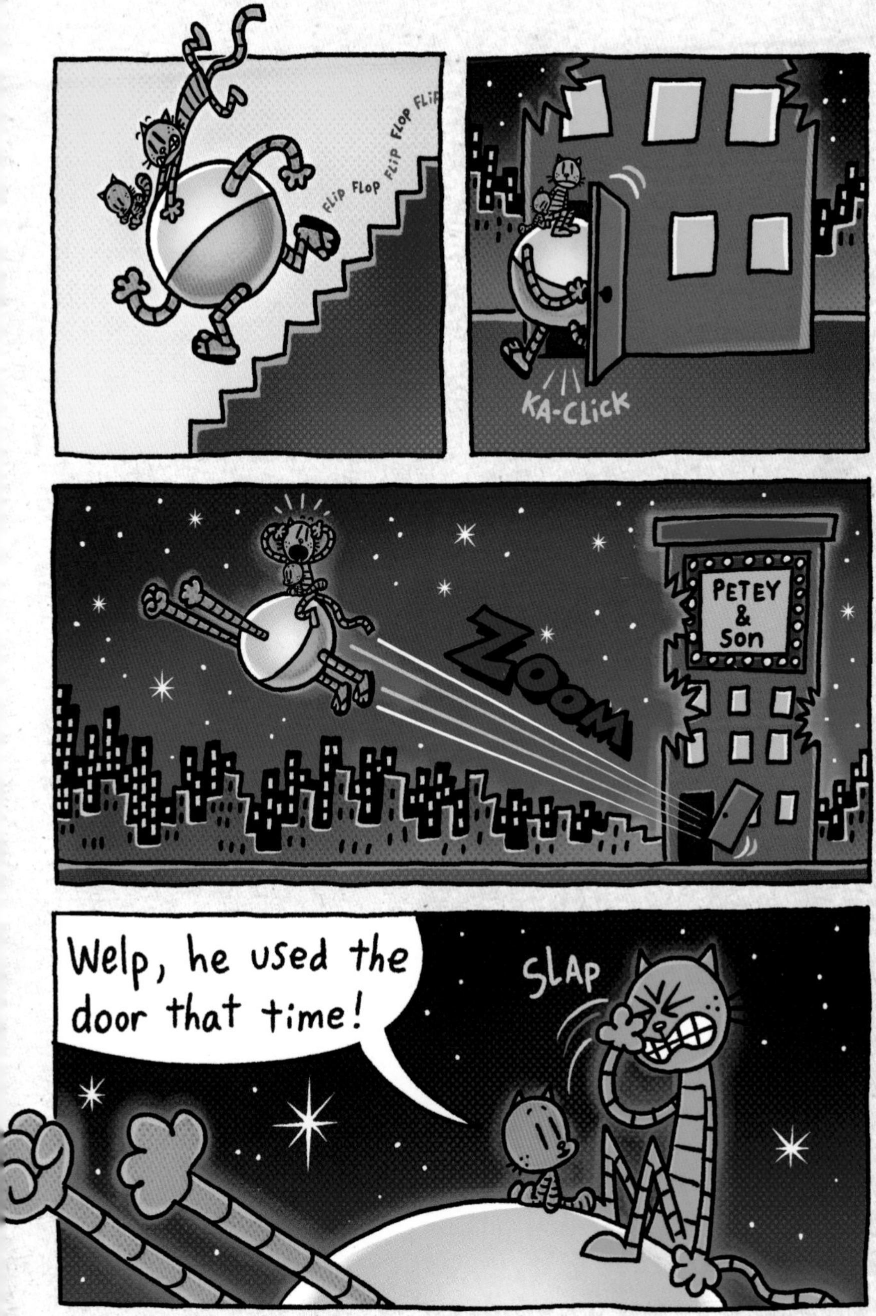
FLIP FLOP FLIP FLOP FLIP
KA-CLICK
PETEY & SON
ZOOM
Welp, he used the door that time!
SLAP

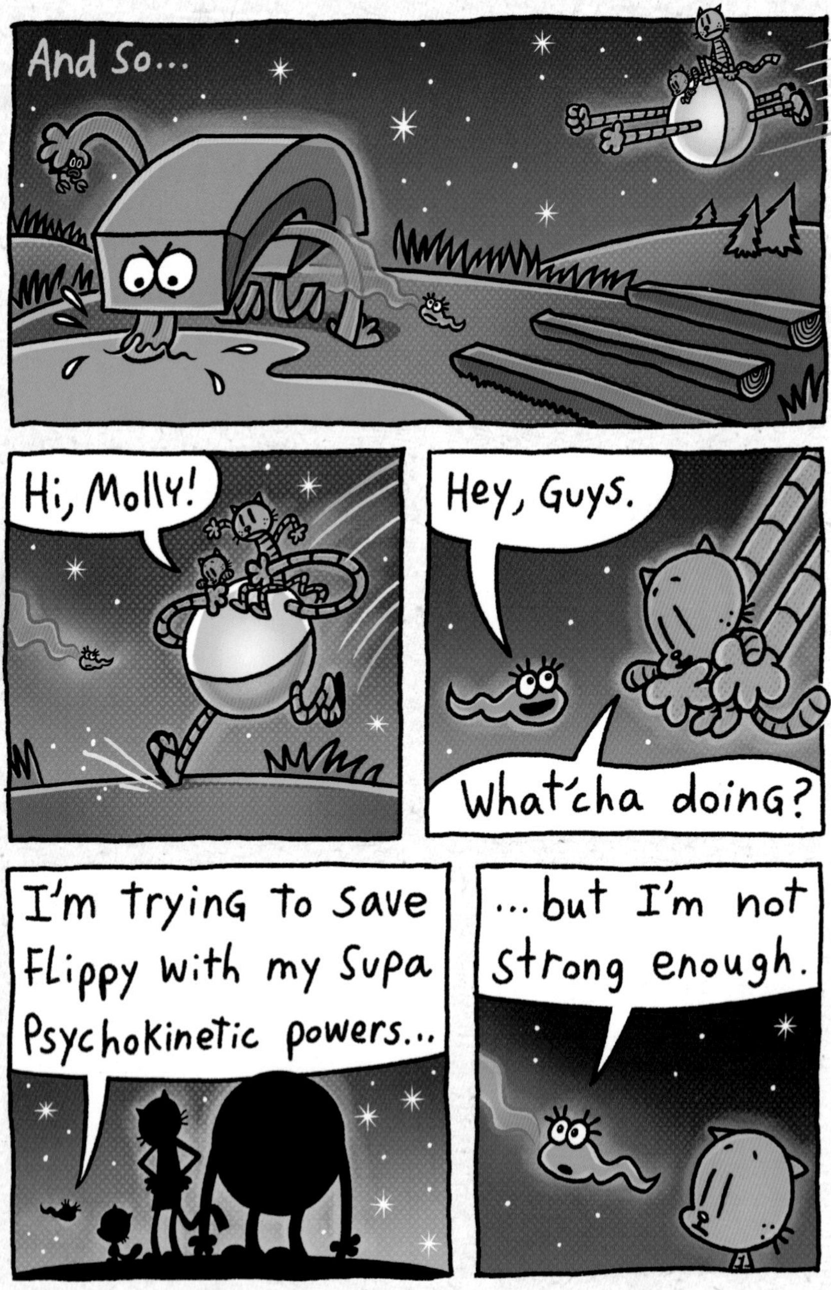
And so...
Hi, Molly!
Hey, Guys.
What'cha doing?
I'm trying to save Flippy with my Supa Psychokinetic powers...
...but I'm not strong enough.

Maybe **we** can help!

Oh, I get it!!!

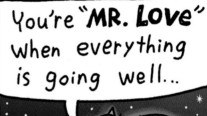

You're "**MR. LOVE**" when everything is going well...

But when something **BAD** happens...

...You suit up and **FiGHT!**

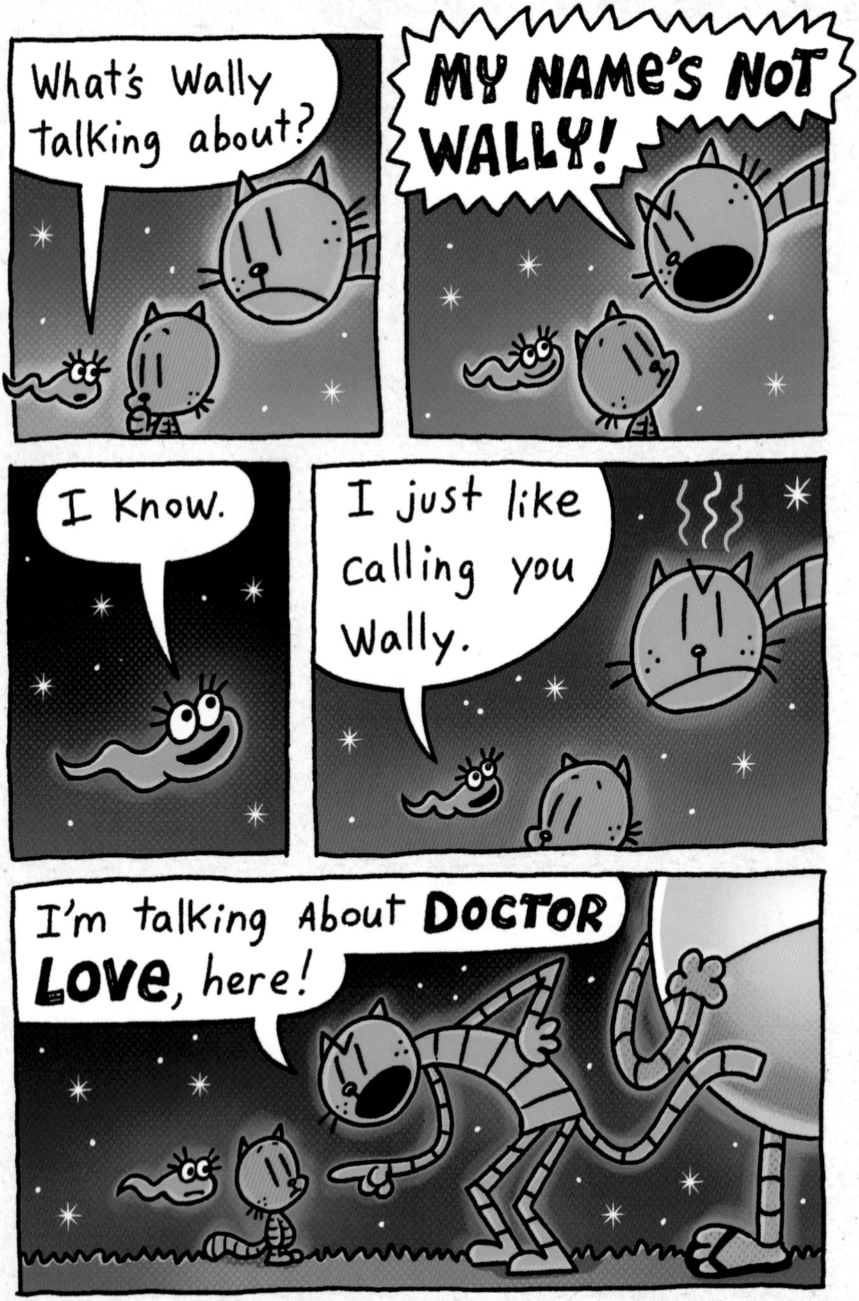
What's Wally talking about?
MY NAME'S NOT WALLY!
I know.
I just like calling you Wally.
I'm talking about DOCTOR LOVE, here!

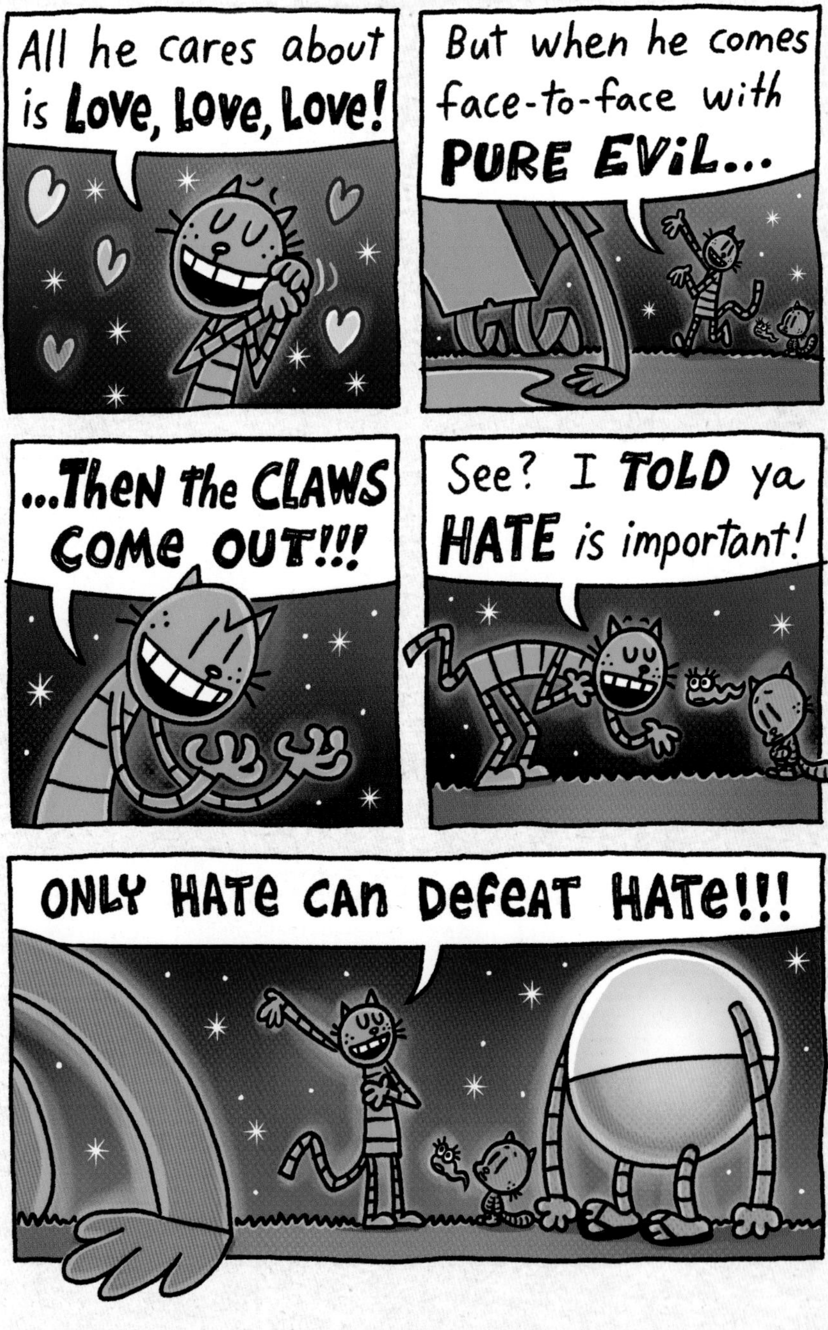
All he cares about is Love, Love, Love!
But when he comes face-to-face with PURE EVIL...
...Then the CLAWS COME OUT!!!
See? I TOLD ya HATE is important!
ONLY HATE CAN DEFEAT HATE!!!

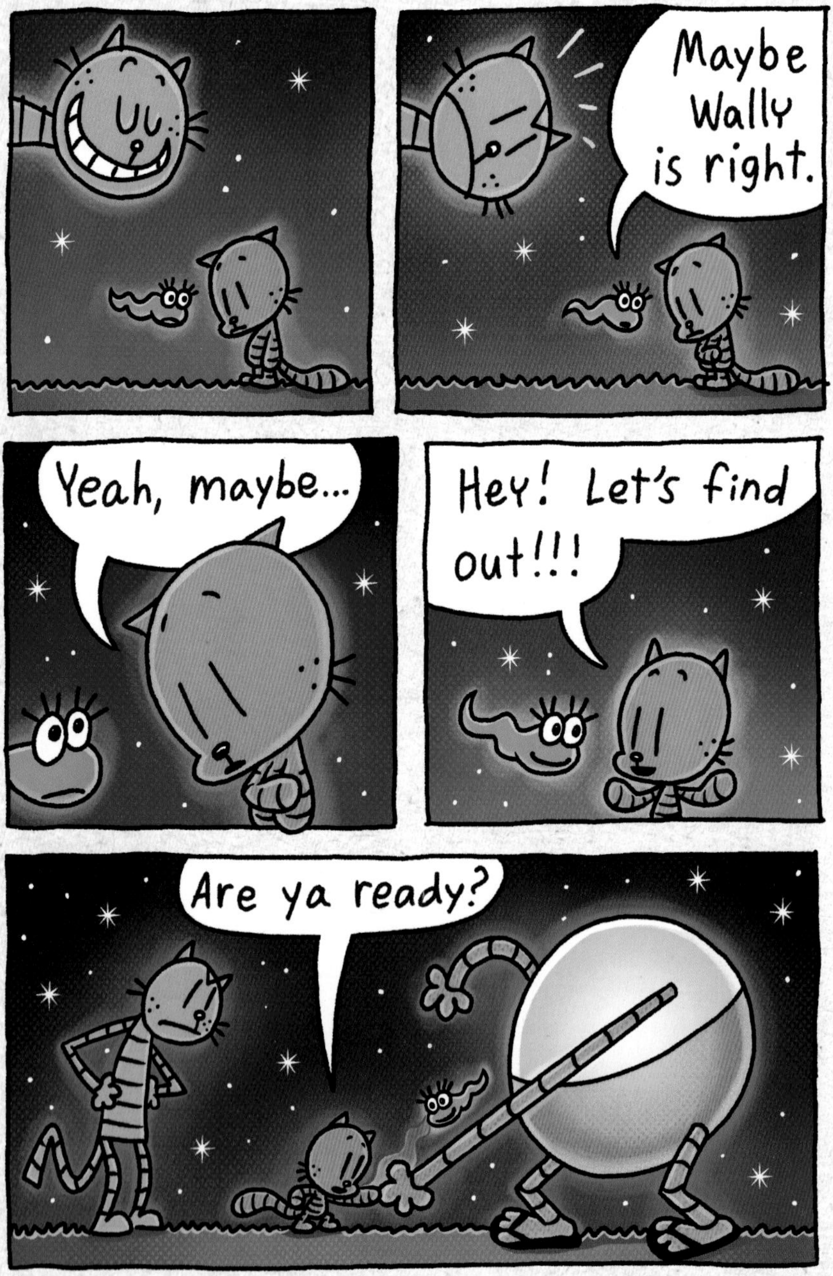
Maybe Wally is right.
Yeah, maybe...
Hey! Let's find out!!!
Are ya ready?

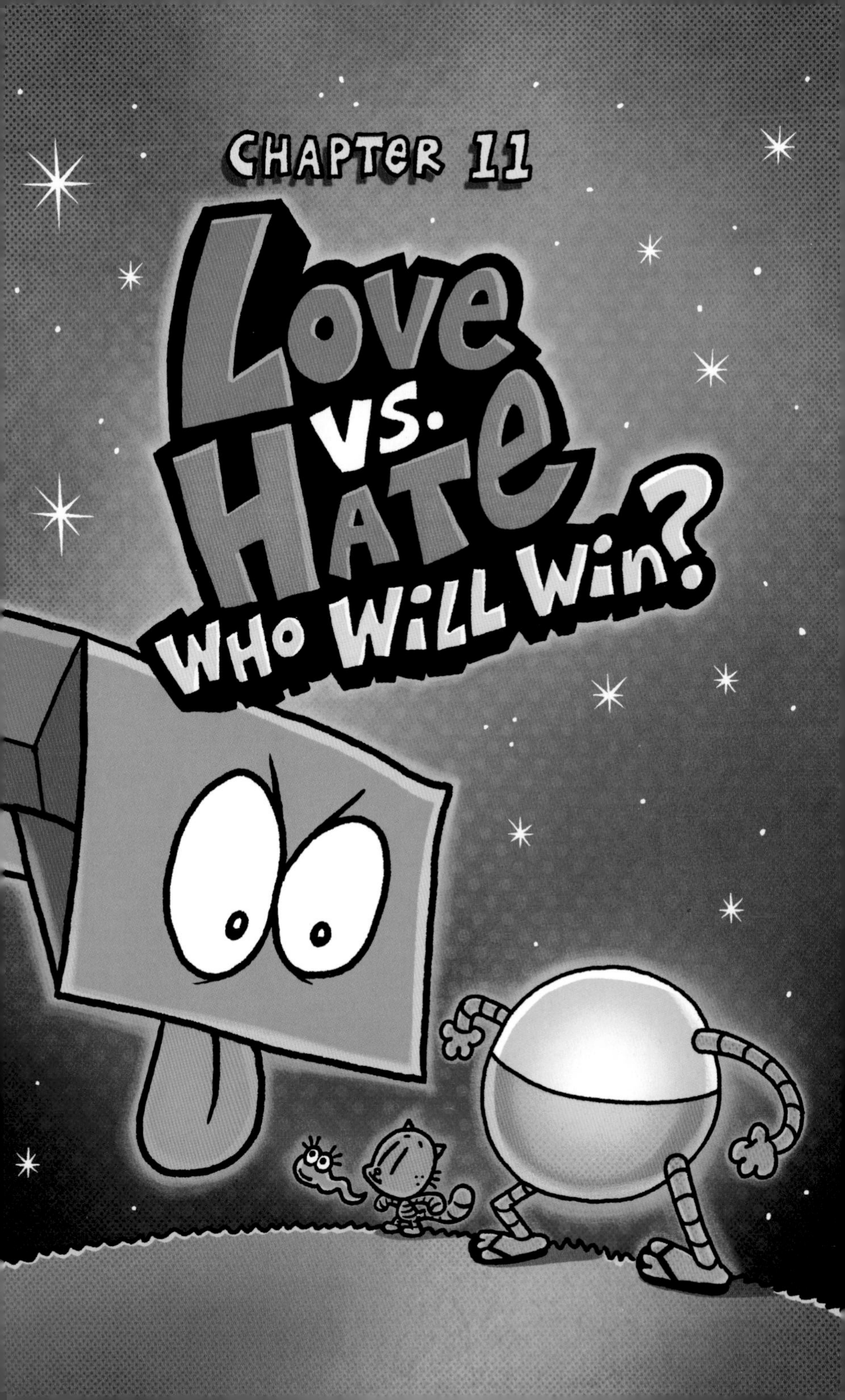
CHAPTER 11
Love vs. Hate
Who Will Win?

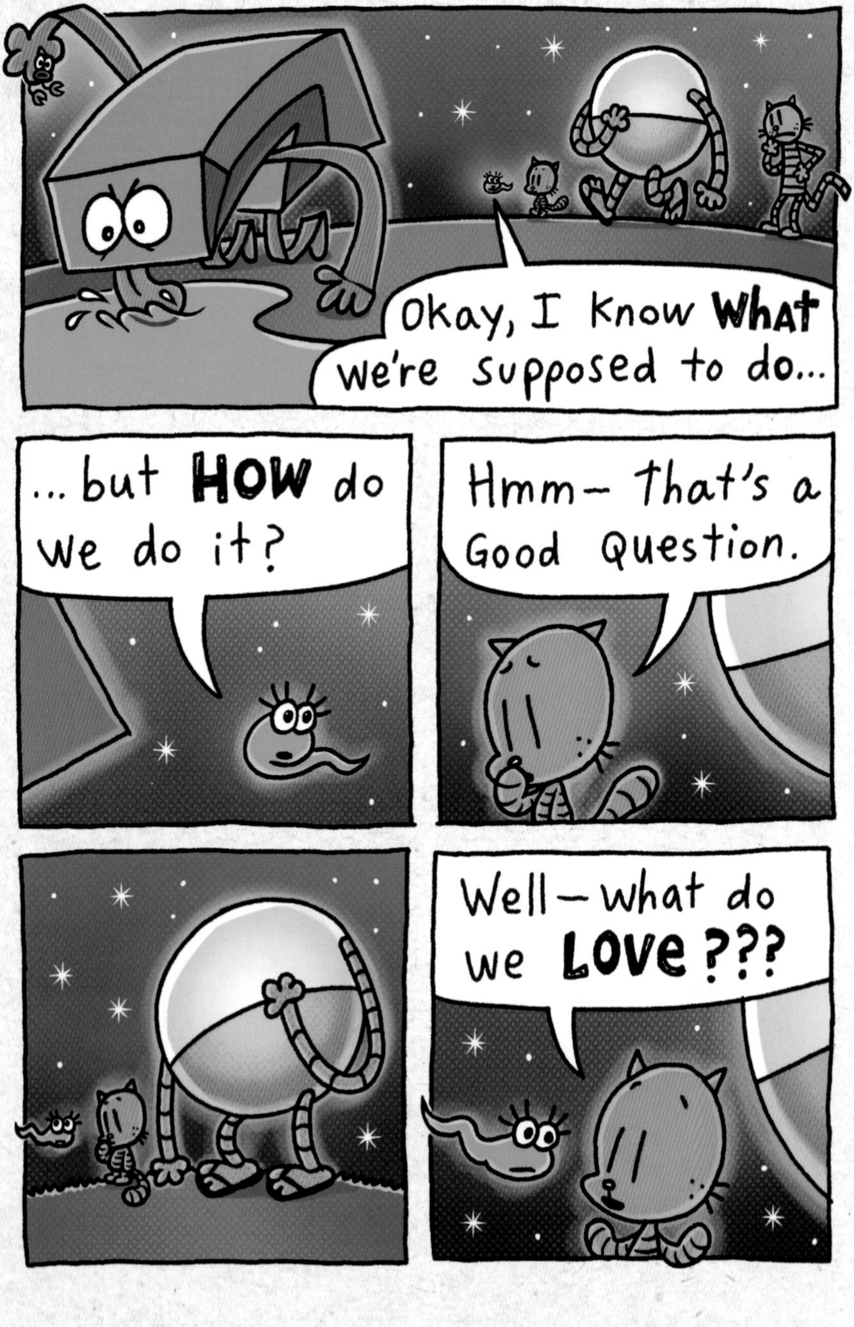
Okay, I know WHAT we're supposed to do...
...but HOW do we do it?
Hmm– That's a Good Question.
Well–what do we LOVE???

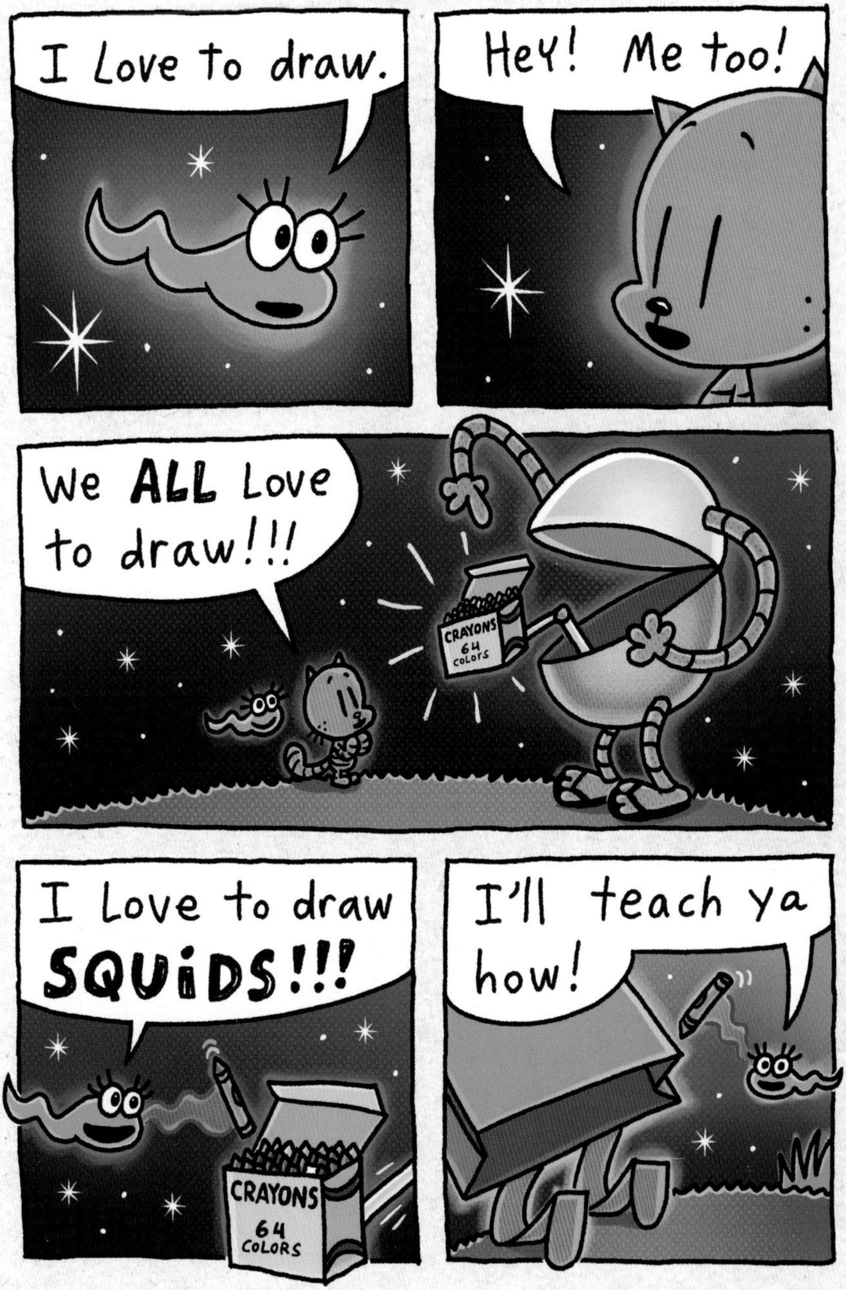
I Love to draw.
Hey! Me too!
We ALL Love to draw!!!
CRAYONS 64 COLORS
I Love to draw SQUiDS!!!
CRAYONS 64 COLORS
I'll teach ya how!

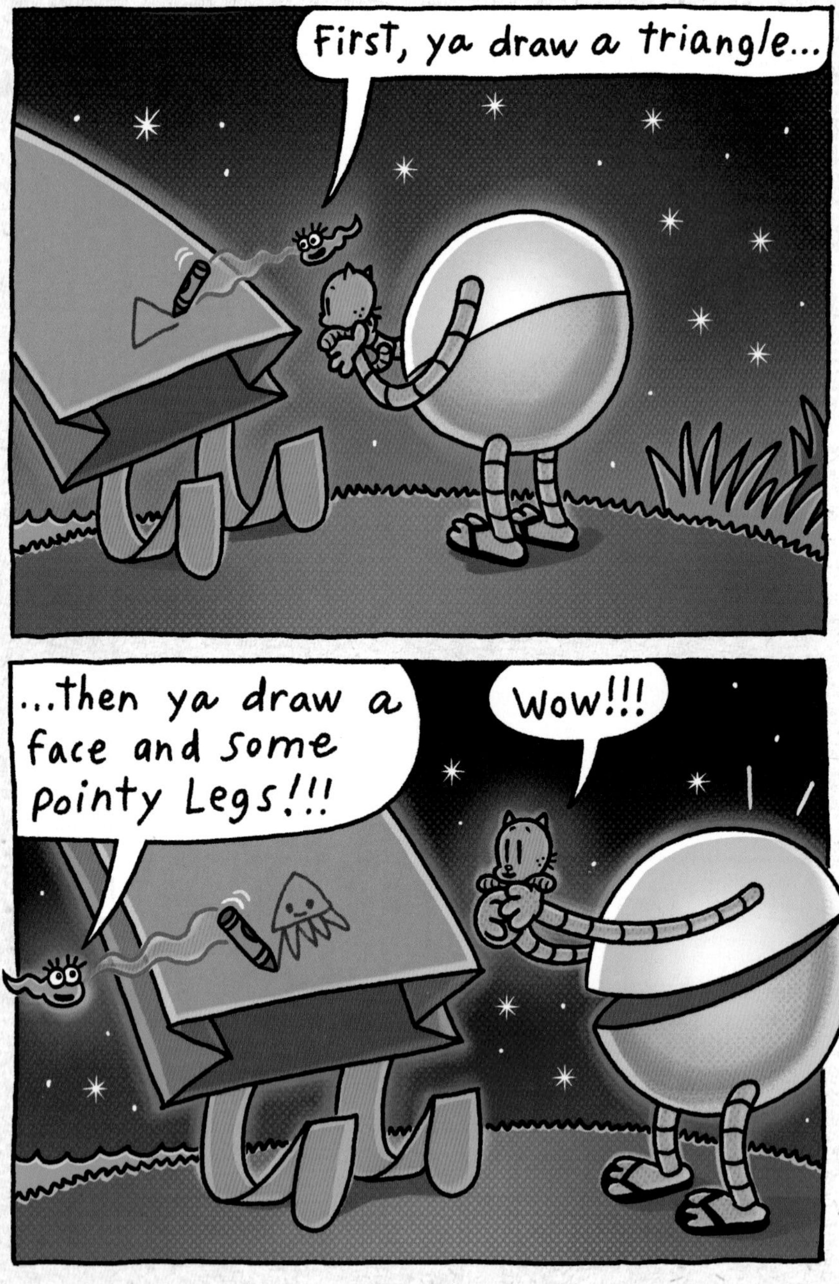
First, ya draw a triangle...
...then ya draw a face and some pointy Legs!!!
Wow!!!

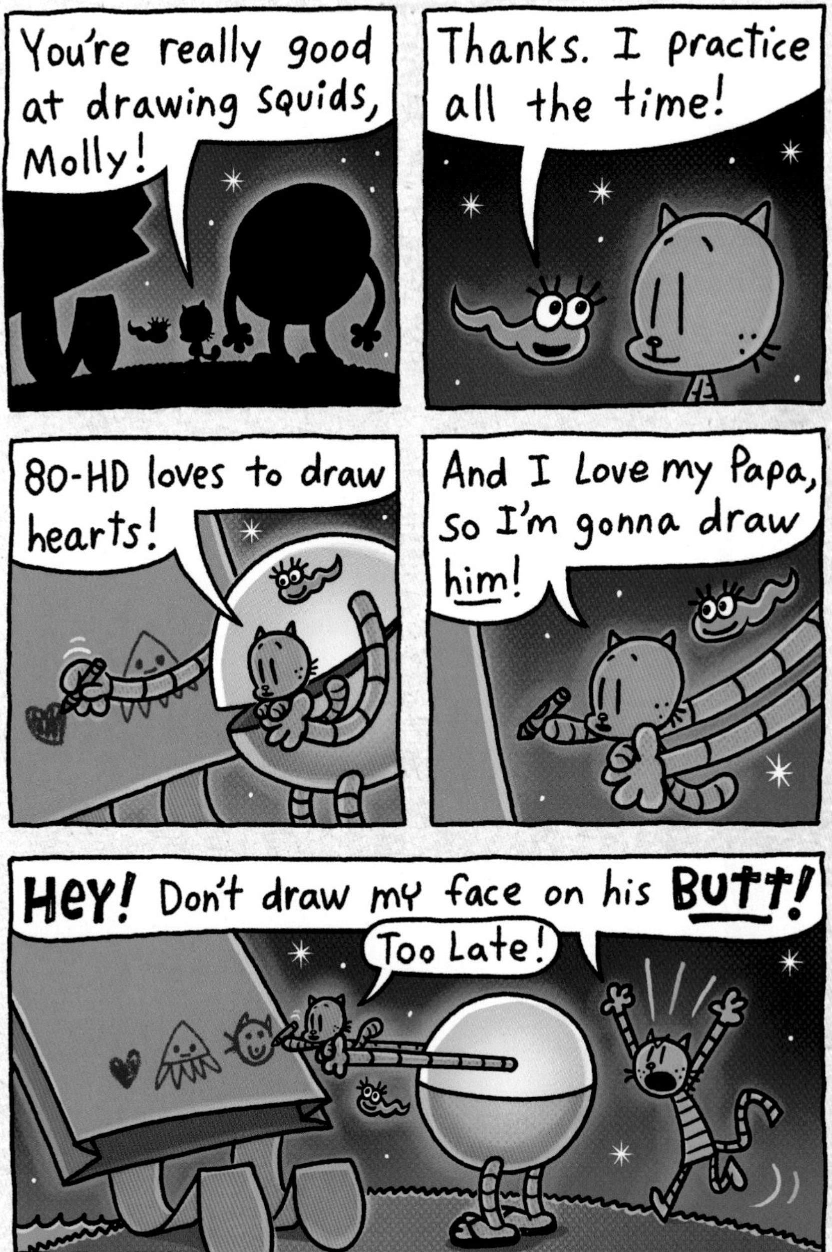
You're really good at drawing squids, Molly!
Thanks. I practice all the time!
80-HD loves to draw hearts!
And I Love my Papa, so I'm gonna draw him!
HEY! Don't draw my face on his BUTT!
Too Late!

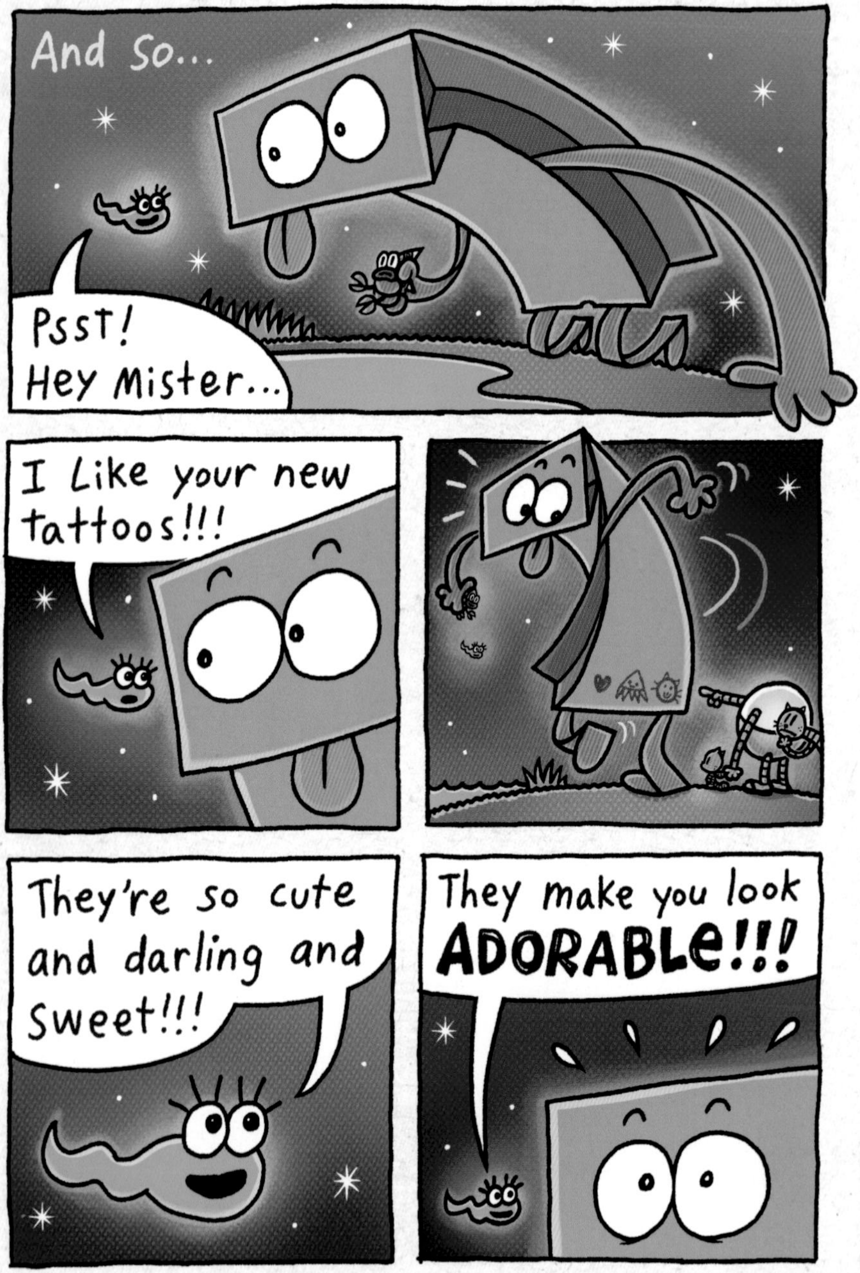
And so...
Psst!
Hey Mister...
I like your new tattoos!!!
They're so cute and darling and sweet!!!
They make you look ADORABLE!!!

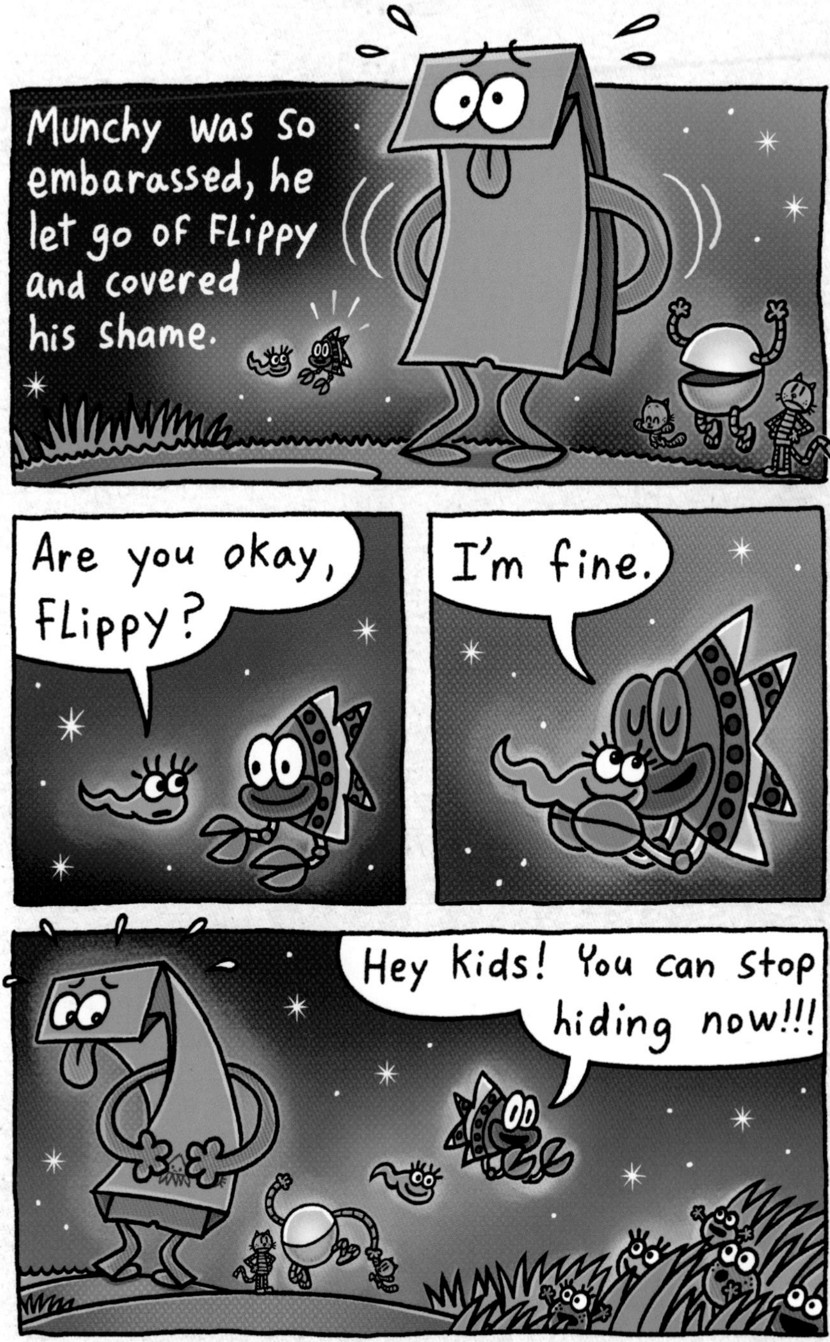
Munchy was so embarassed, he let go of Flippy and covered his shame.
Are you okay, Flippy?
I'm fine.
Hey Kids! You can stop hiding now!!!

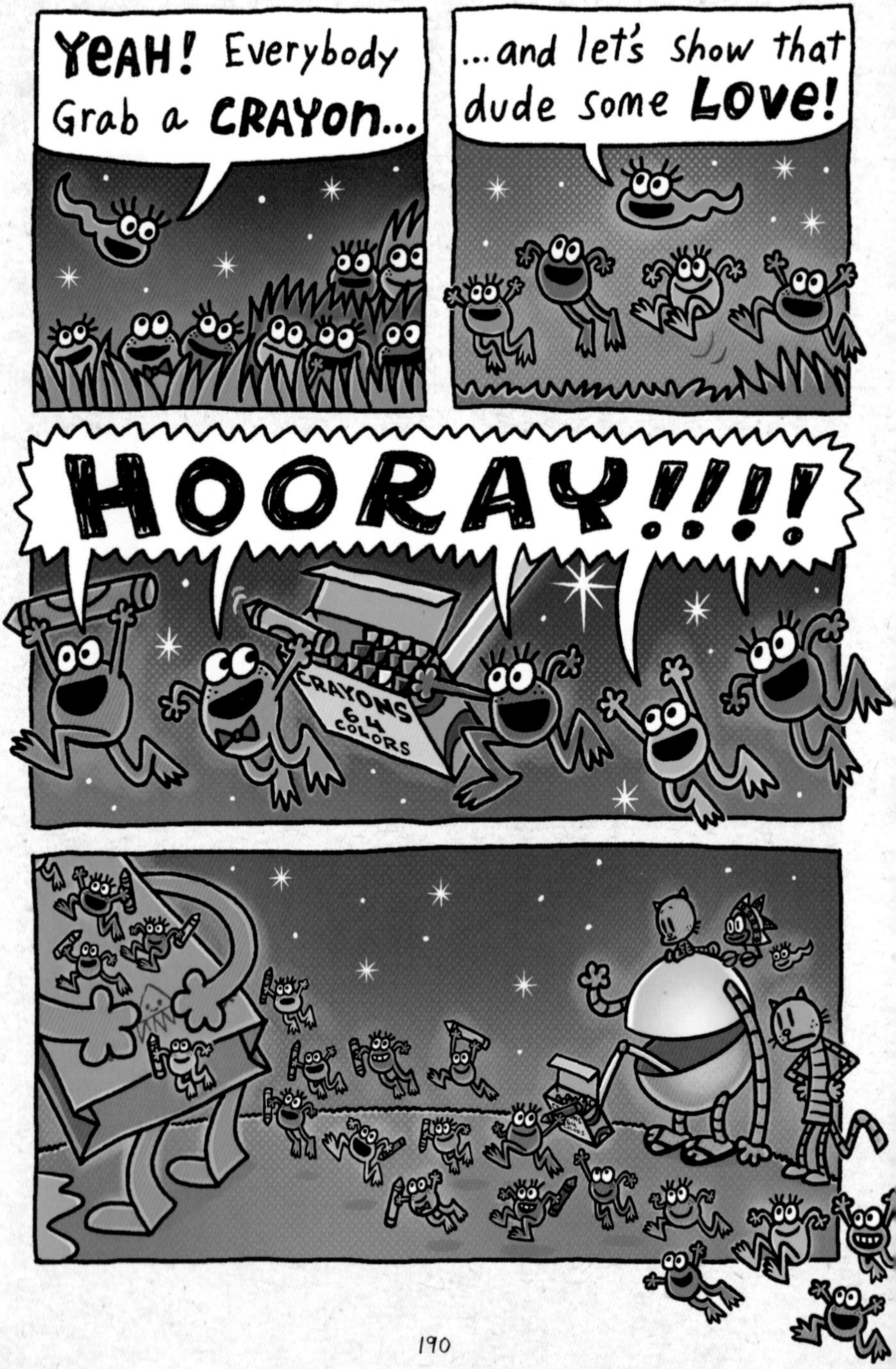
YEAH! Everybody Grab a CRAYON...
...and let's show that dude some LOVE!
HOORAY!!!!
CRAYONS 64 COLORS

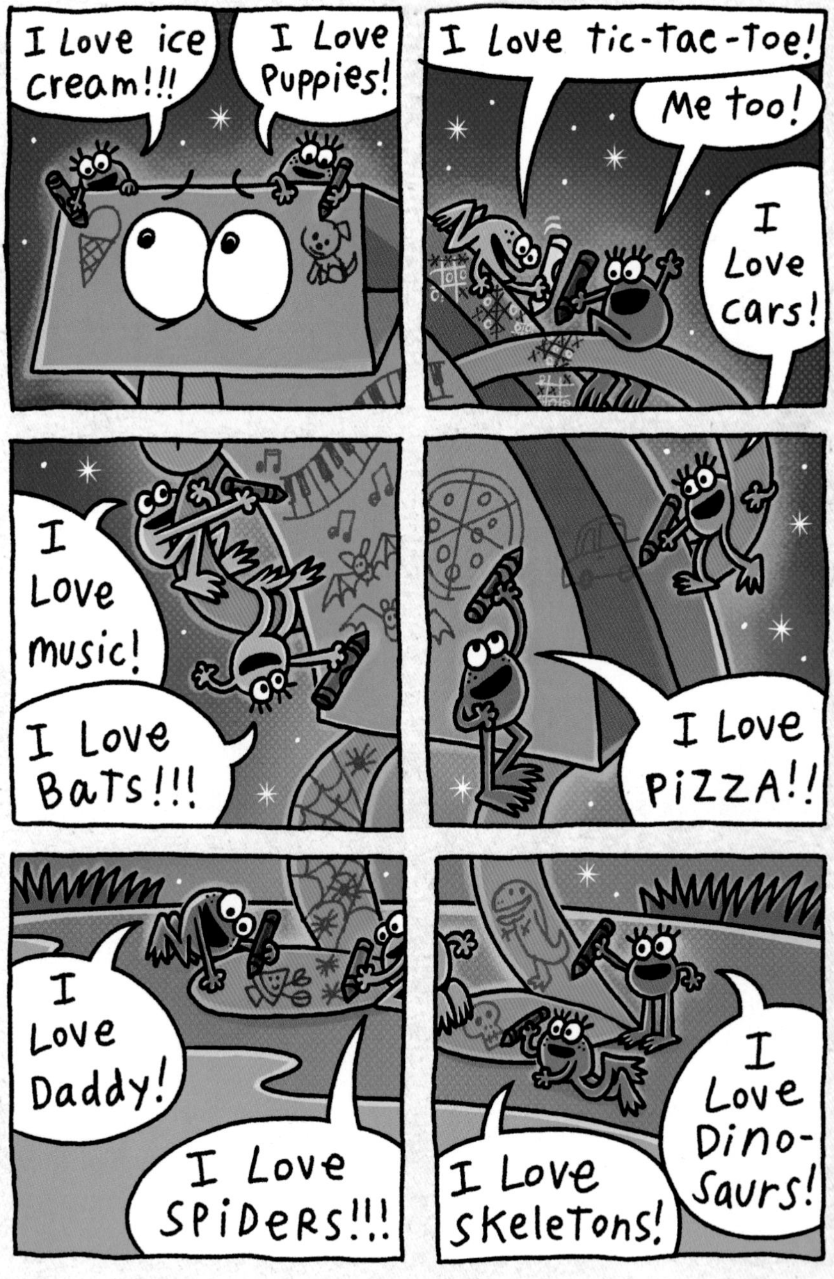
I Love ice cream!!!
I Love Puppies!
I Love tic-tac-toe!
Me too!
I Love cars!
I Love music!
I Love Bats!!!
I Love PIZZA!!
I Love Daddy!
I Love SPIDERS!!!
I Love Dino-Saurs!
I Love Skeletons!

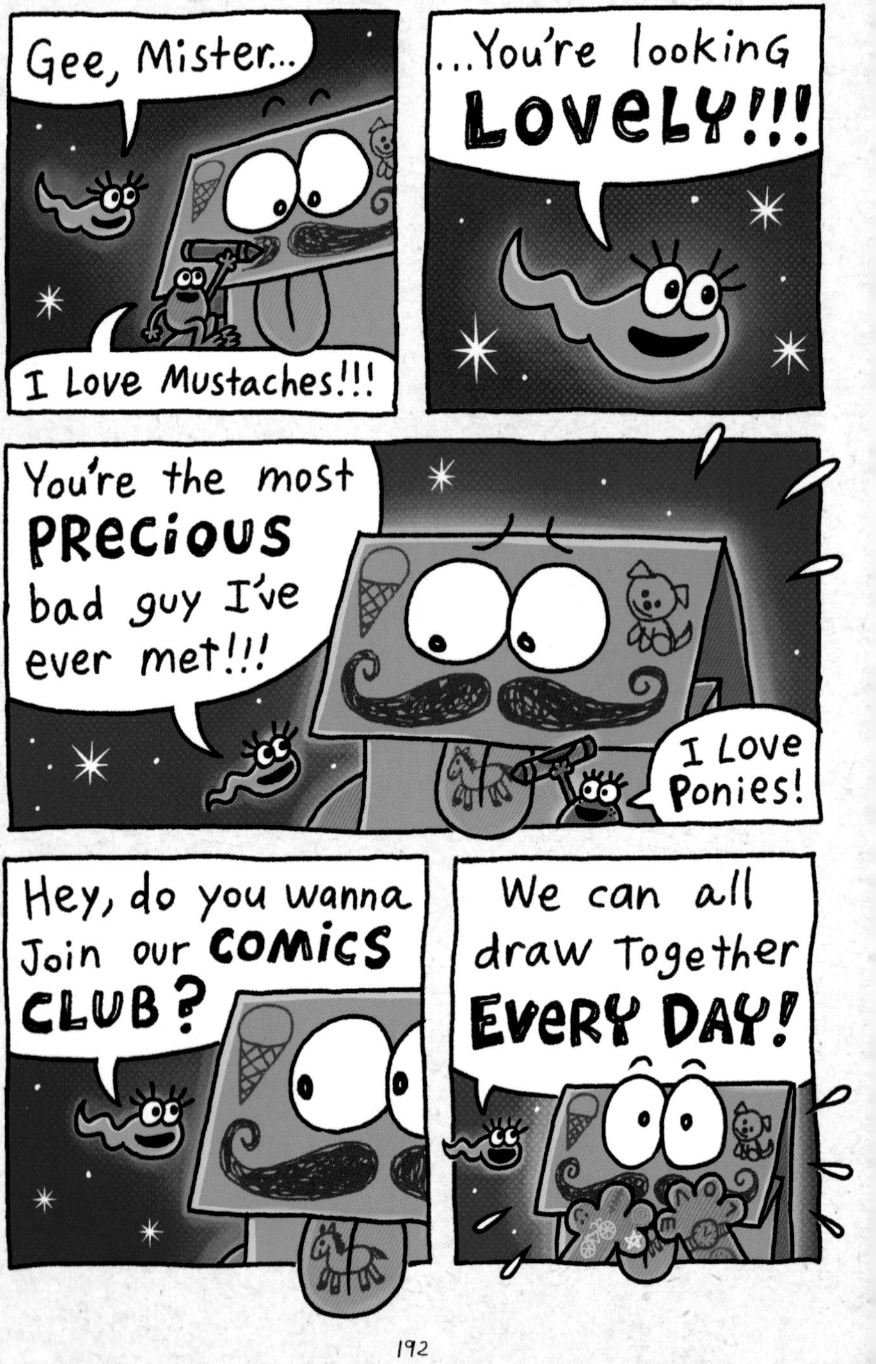
Gee, Mister...
I Love Mustaches!!!
...You're looking LOVELY!!!
You're the most PRECIOUS bad guy I've ever met!!!
I Love Ponies!
Hey, do you wanna Join our COMICS CLUB?
We can all draw Together EVERY DAY!

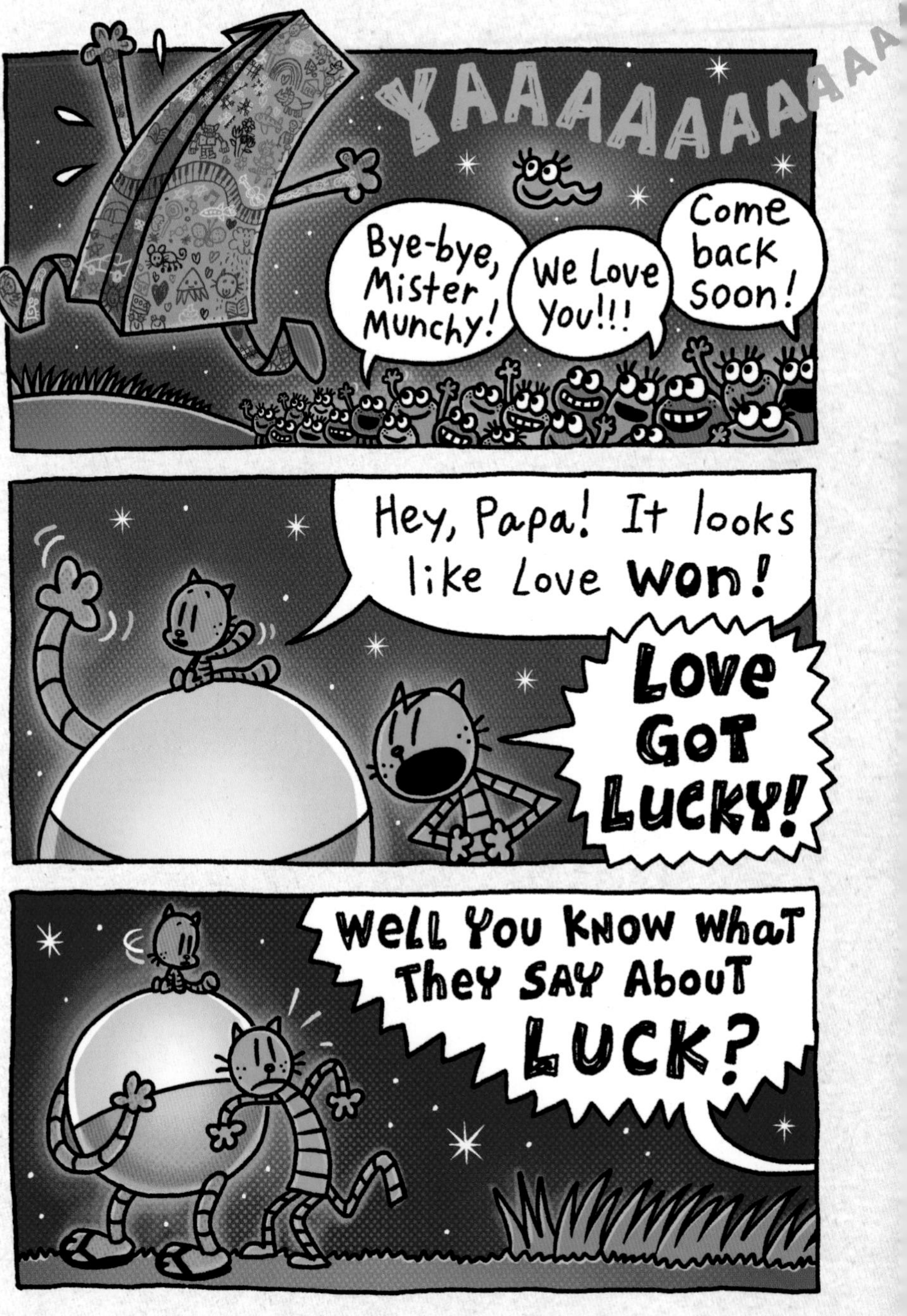
YAAAAAAAAAAA
Bye-bye, Mister Munchy!
We Love You!!!
Come back soon!
Hey, Papa! It looks like Love WON!
LOVE GOT LUCKY!
WELL YOU KNOW WHAT THEY SAY ABOUT LUCK?

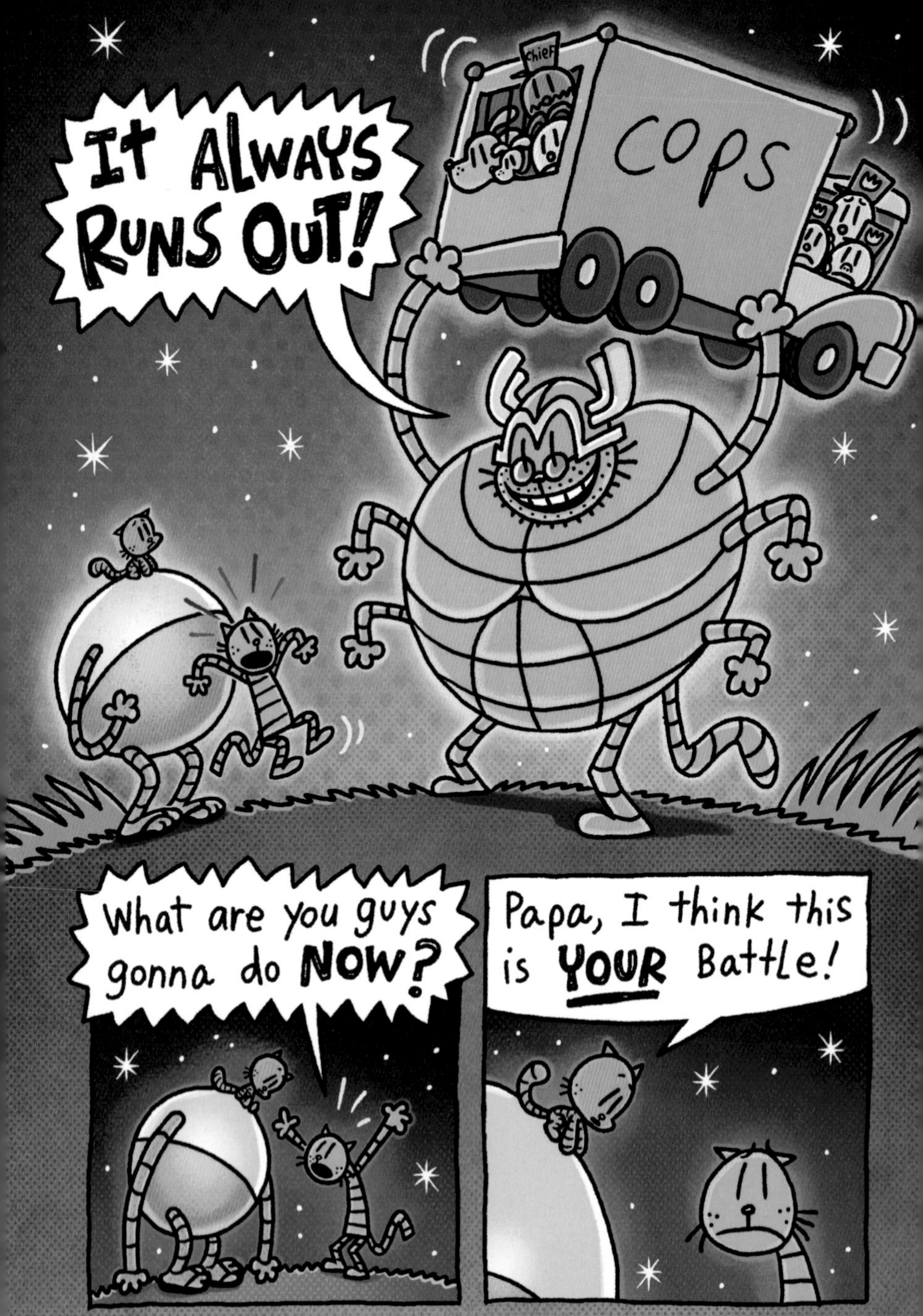
COPS
CHIEF
IT ALWAYS RUNS OUT!
What are you guys gonna do NOW?
Papa, I think this is YOUR Battle!

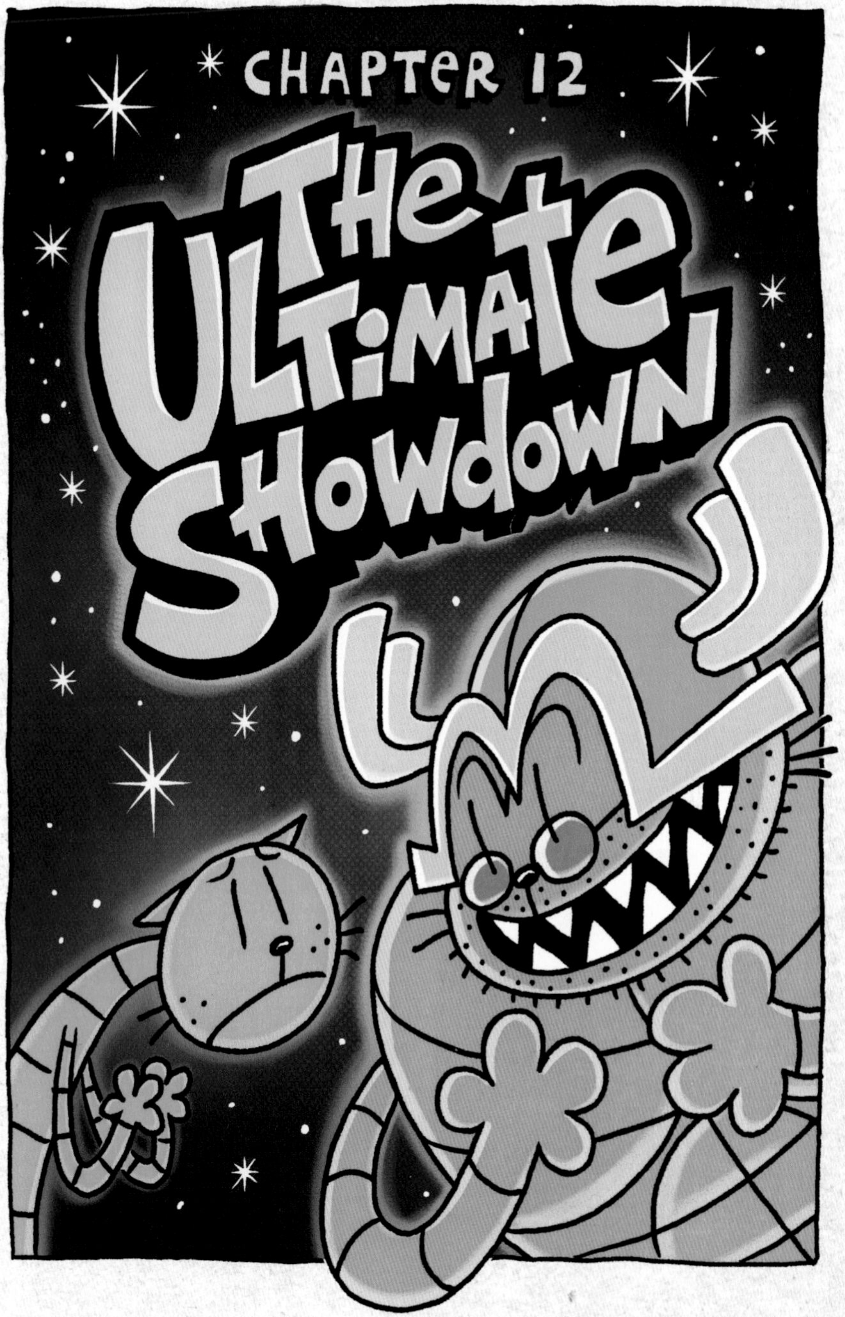
CHAPTER 12
THE ULTIMATE SHOWDOWN

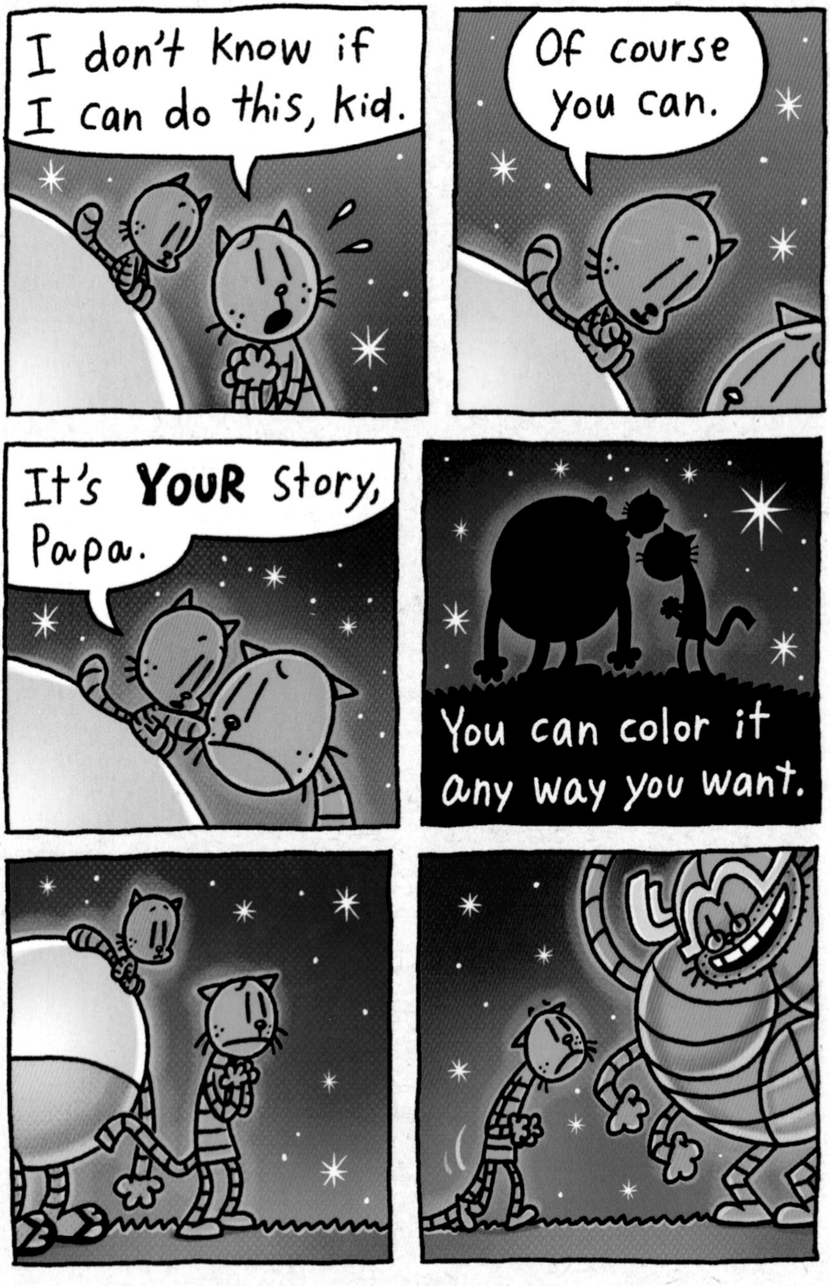
I don't know if I can do this, kid.
Of course you can.
It's **YOUR** story, Papa.
You can color it any way you want.

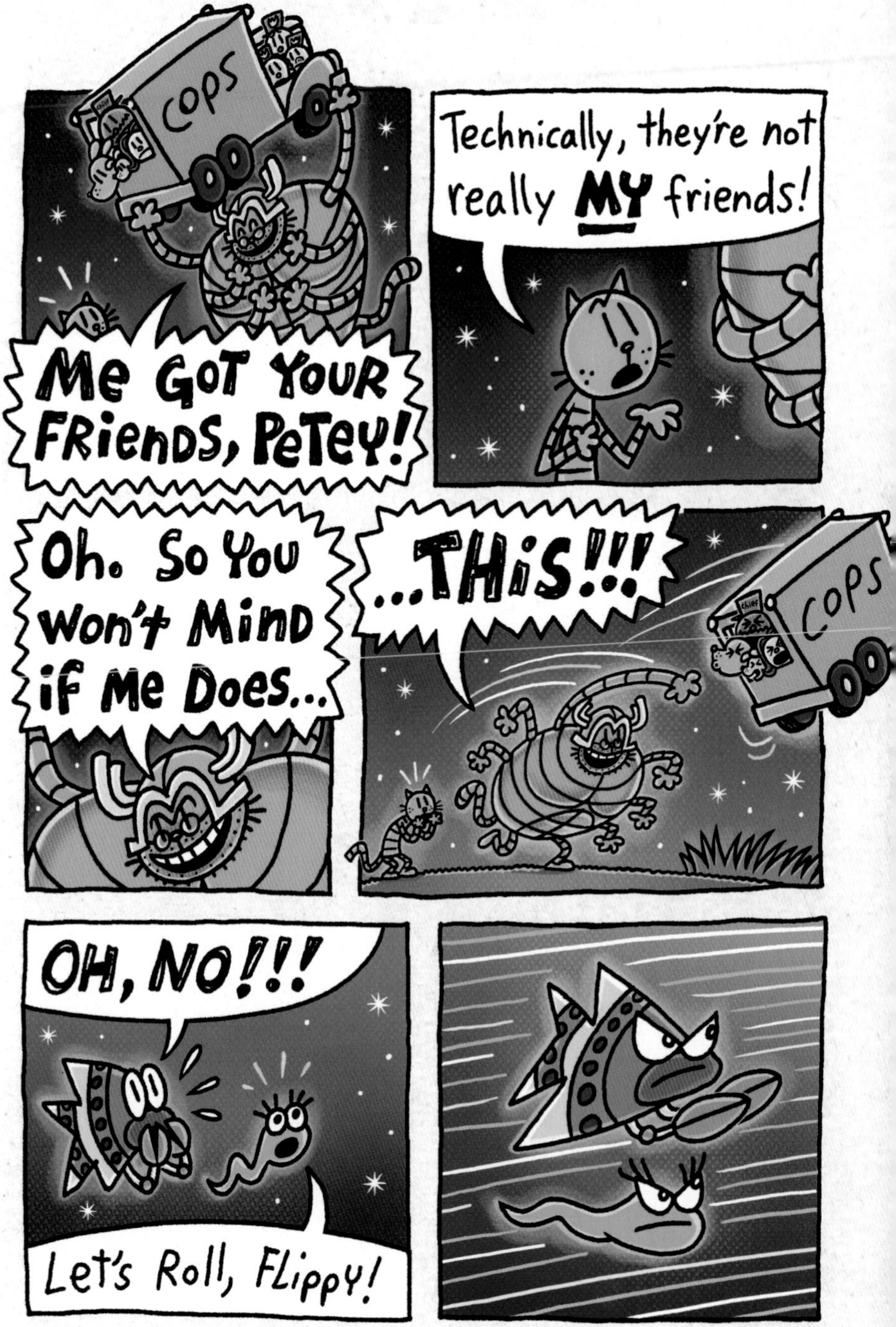
Me Got Your Friends, Petey!
Technically, they're not really MY friends!
COPS
Oh. So You won't Mind if Me Does...
...THiS!!!
COPS
OH, NO!!!
Let's Roll, Flippy!

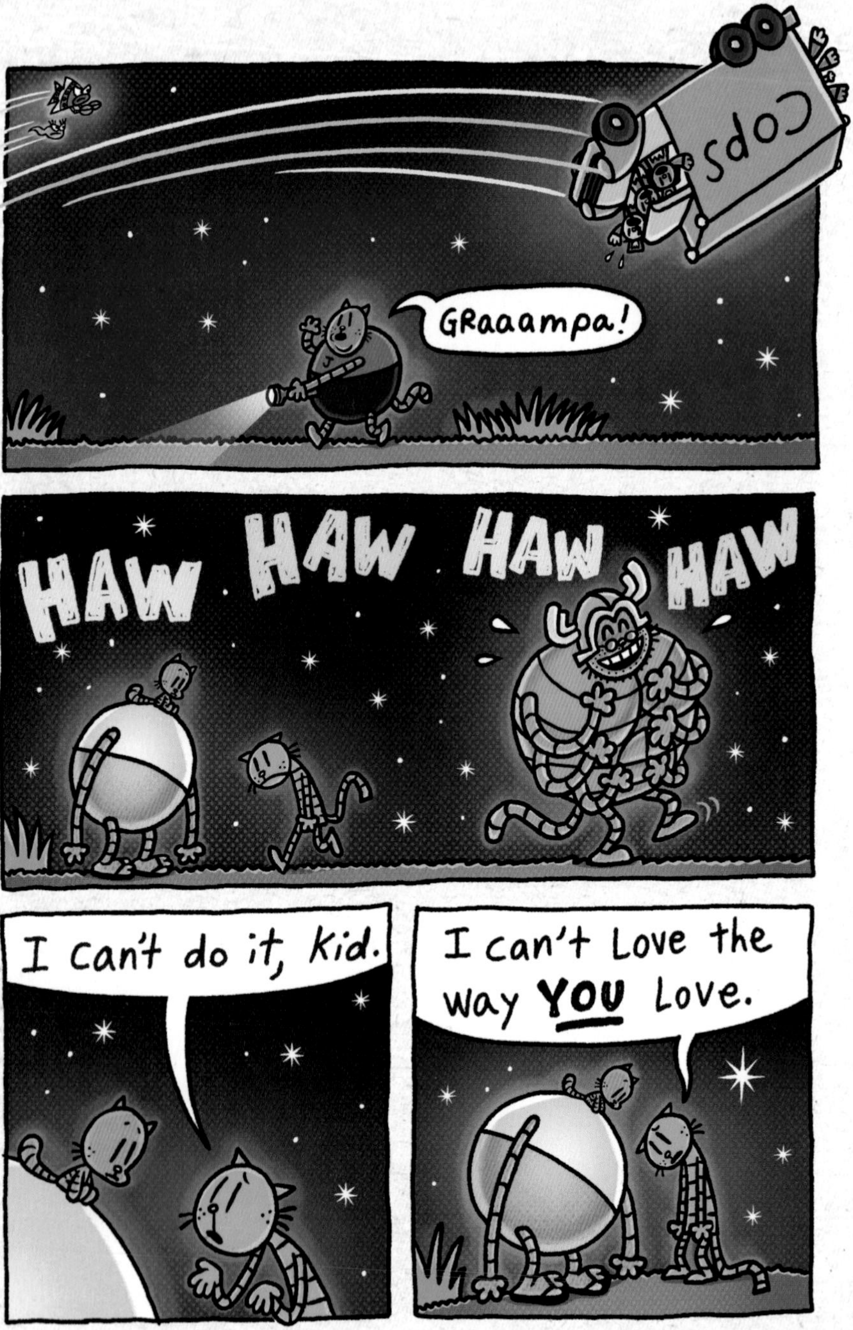
COPS
GRaaampa!
HAW HAW HAW HAW
I can't do it, kid.
I can't Love the way YOU Love.

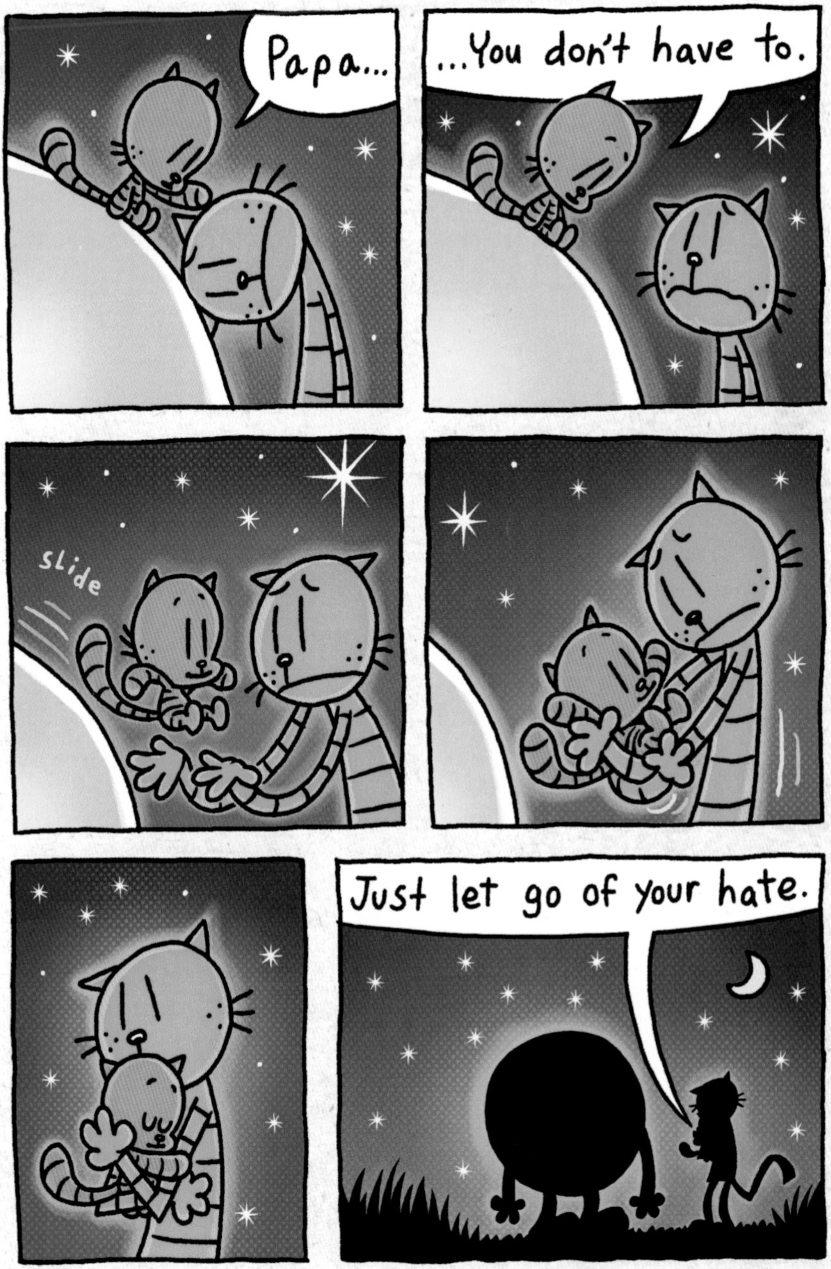
Papa...
...You don't have to.
SLide
Just let go of your hate.

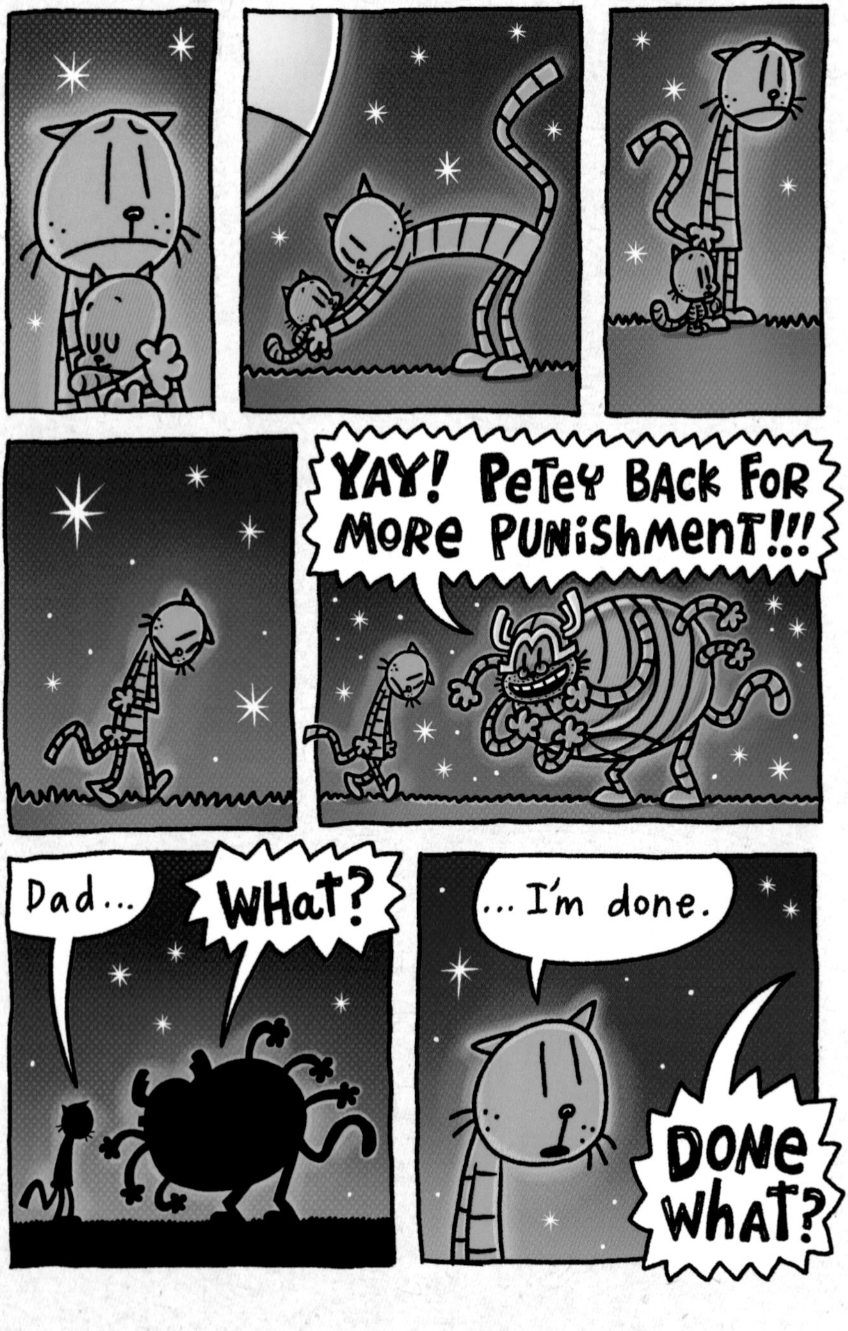
YAY! PETEY BACK FOR MORE PUNISHMENT!!!
Dad...
WHAT?
...I'm done.
DONE WHAT?

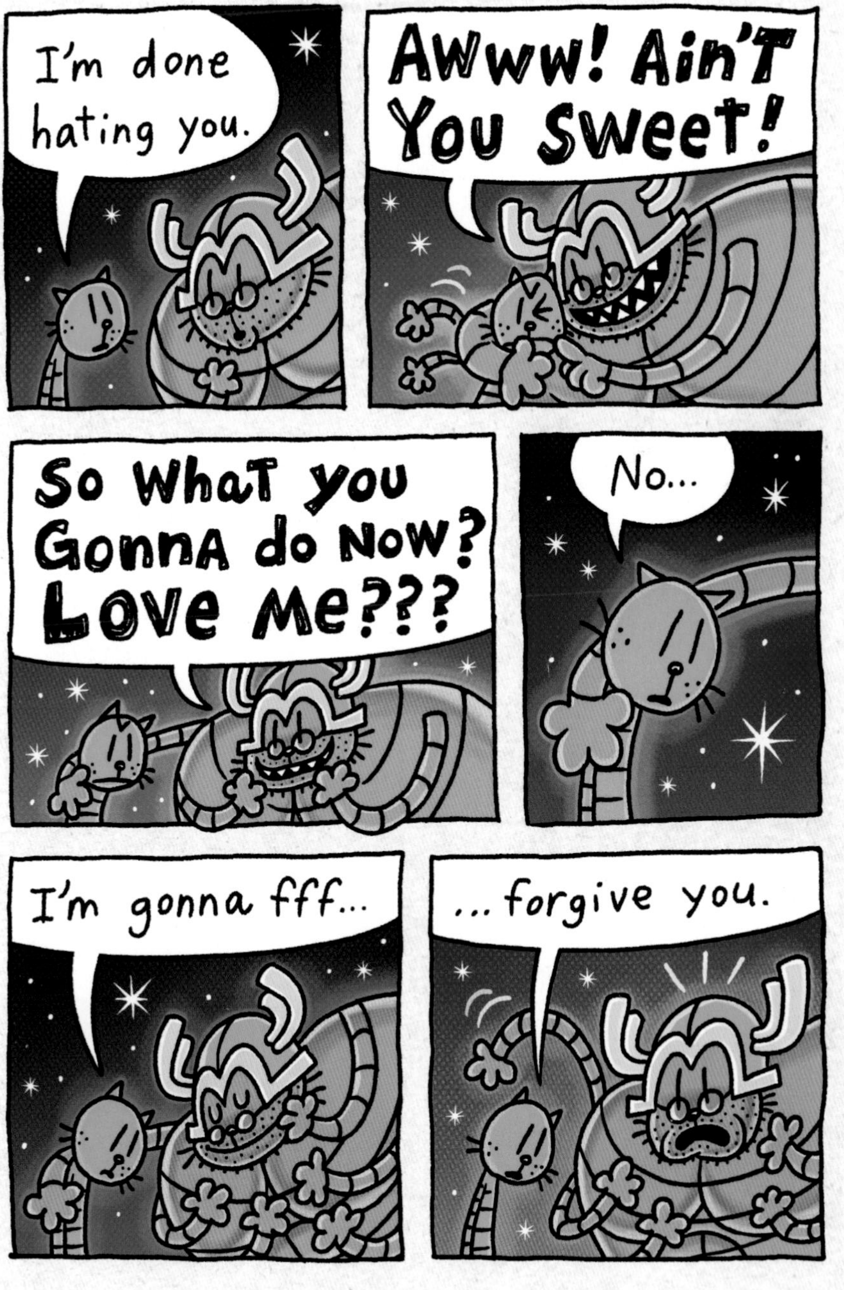
I'm done hating you.
AWWW! AIN'T YOU SWEET!
SO WHAT YOU GONNA DO NOW? LOVE ME???
No...
I'm gonna fff...
...forgive you.

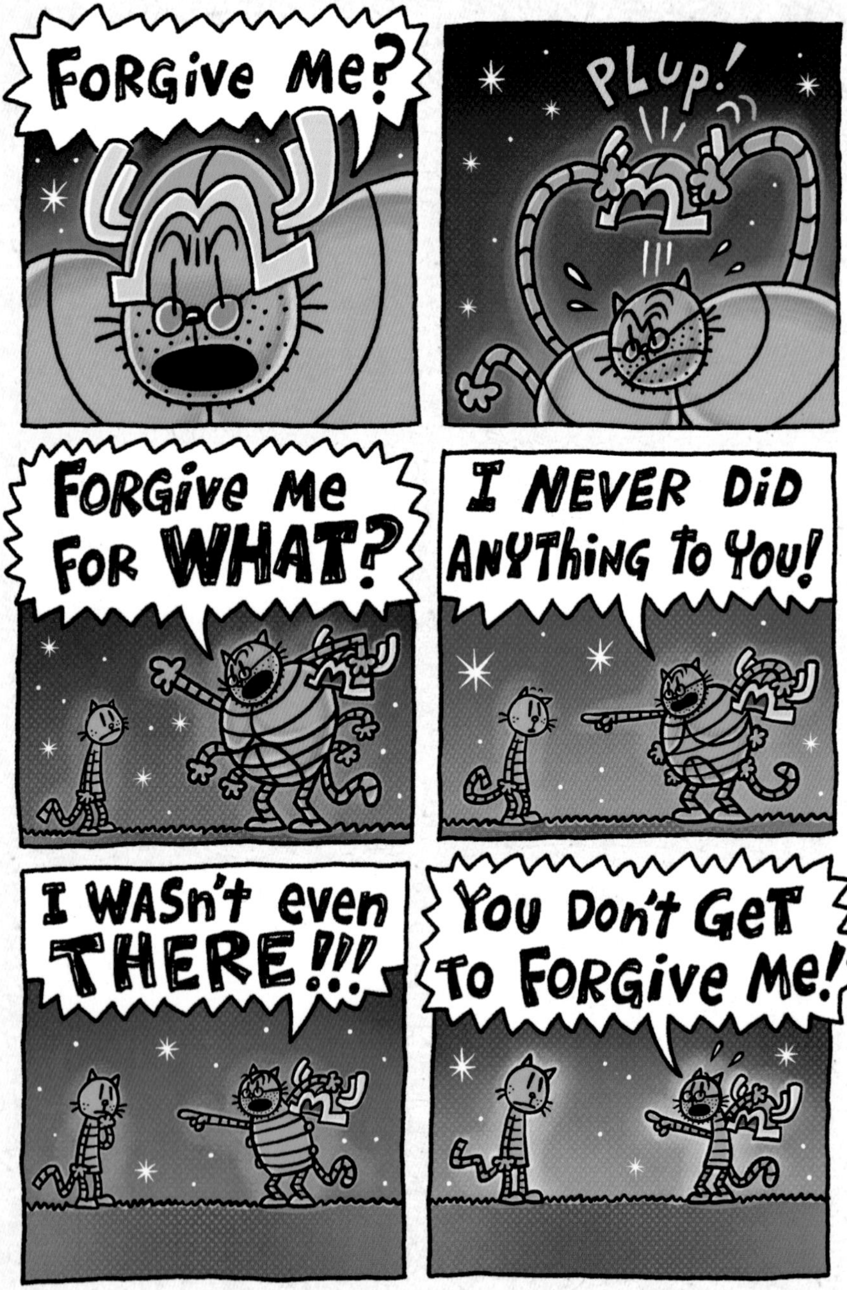
FORGIVE ME?
PLUP!
FORGIVE ME FOR WHAT?
I NEVER DID ANYTHING TO YOU!
I WASN'T EVEN THERE!!!
YOU DON'T GET TO FORGIVE ME!

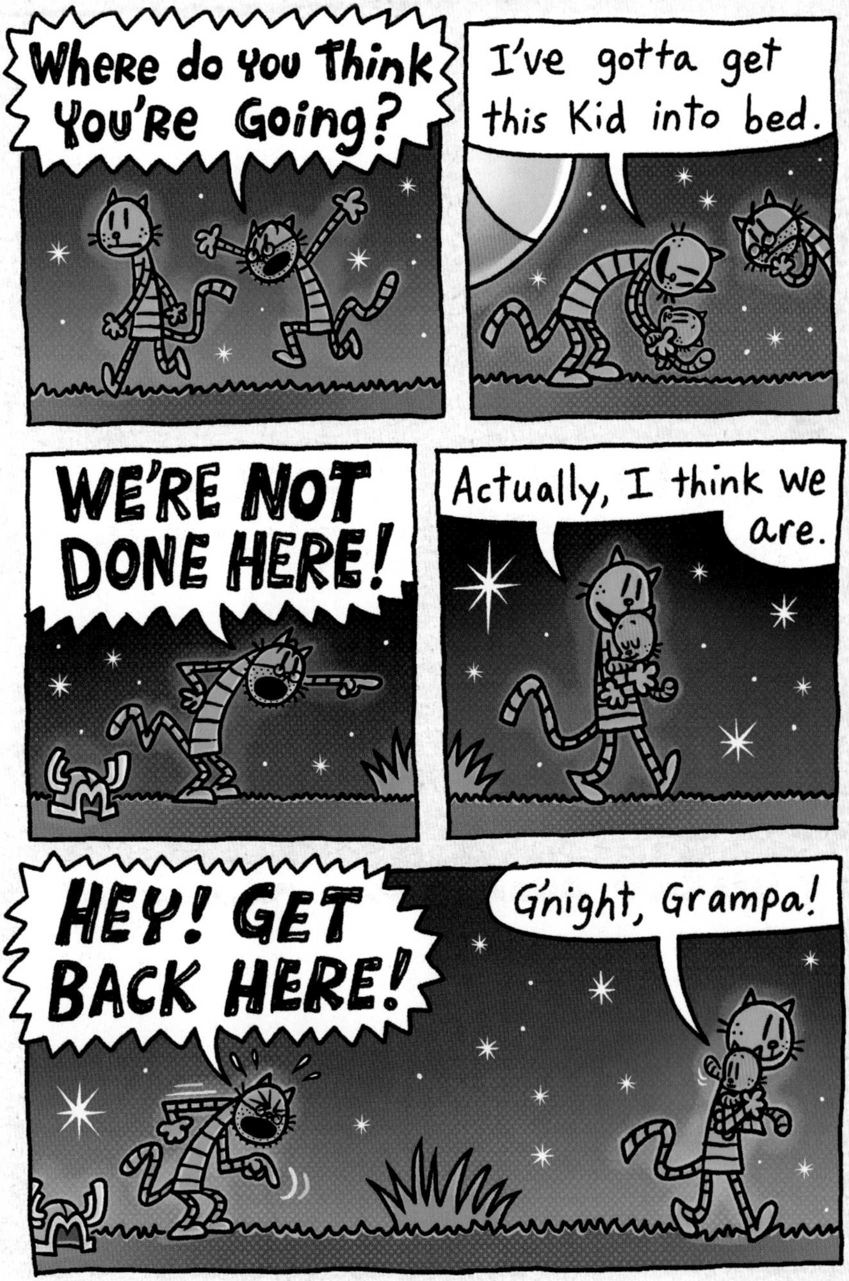
Where do you Think You're Going?
I've gotta get this Kid into bed.
WE'RE NOT DONE HERE!
Actually, I think we are.
HEY! GET BACK HERE!
G'night, Grampa!

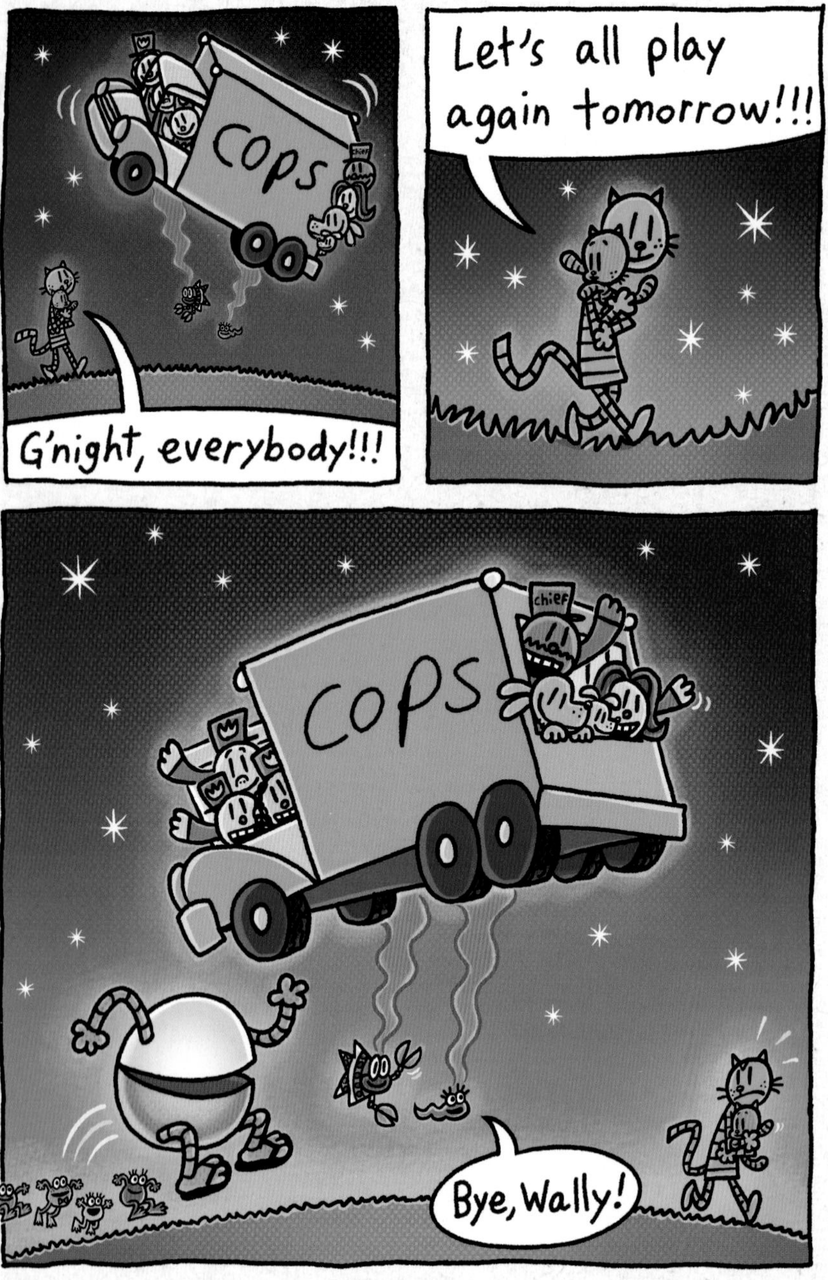
COPS
chief
G'night, everybody!!!
Let's all play again tomorrow!!!
chief
COPS
Bye, Wally!

CHAPTER 13

Three Endings

J

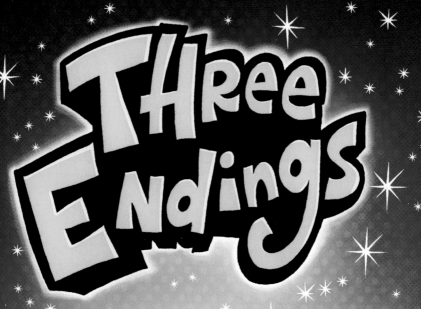

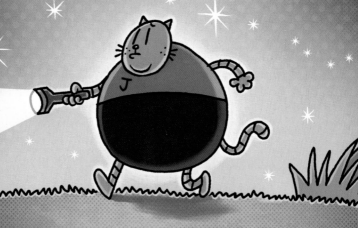

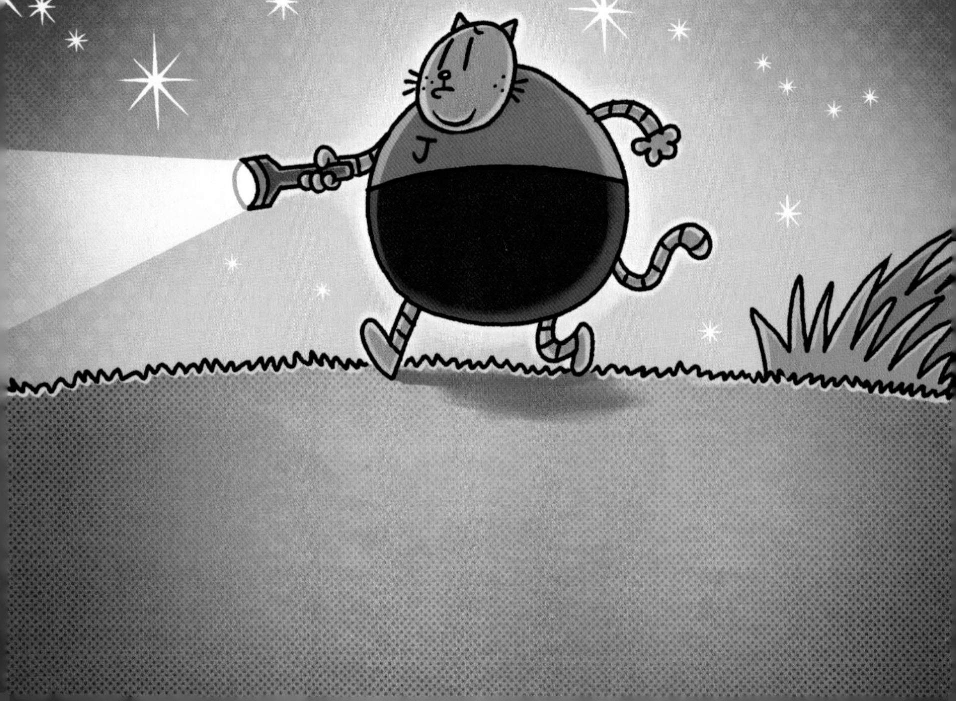

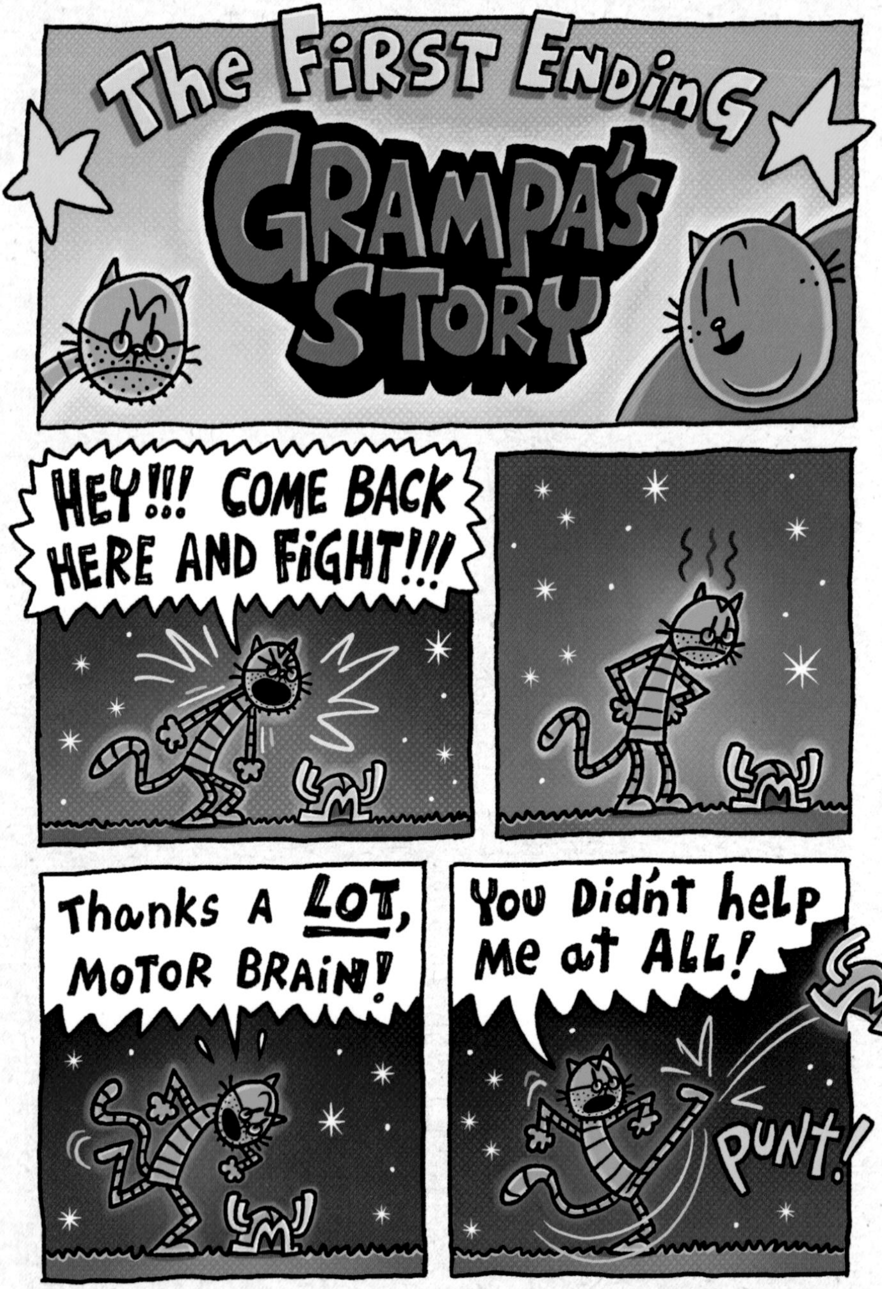
The First Ending
Grampa's Story
HEY!!! COME BACK HERE AND FIGHT!!!
Thanks A LOT, MOTOR BRAIN!
You Didn't help Me at ALL!
PUNT!

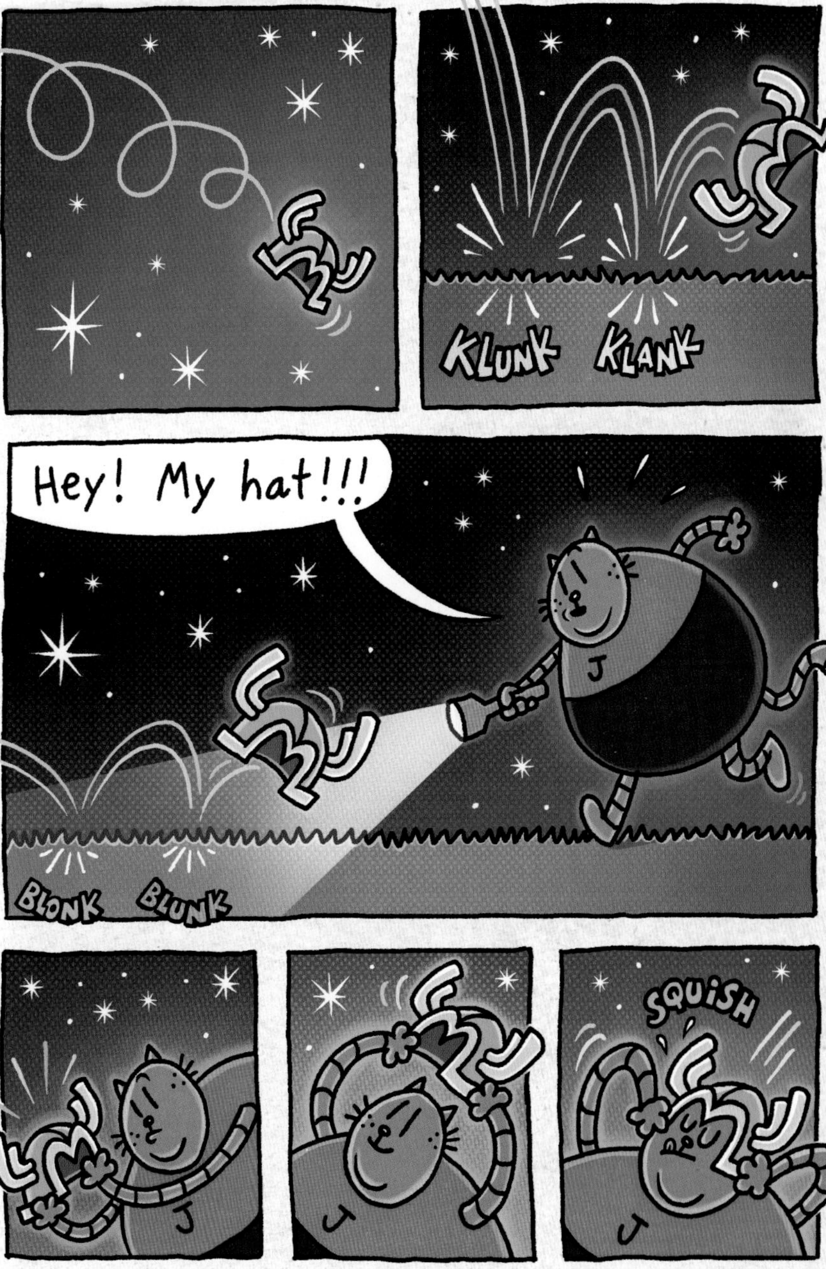
KLUNK
KLANK
Hey! My hat!!!
BLONK
BLUNK
SQUISH

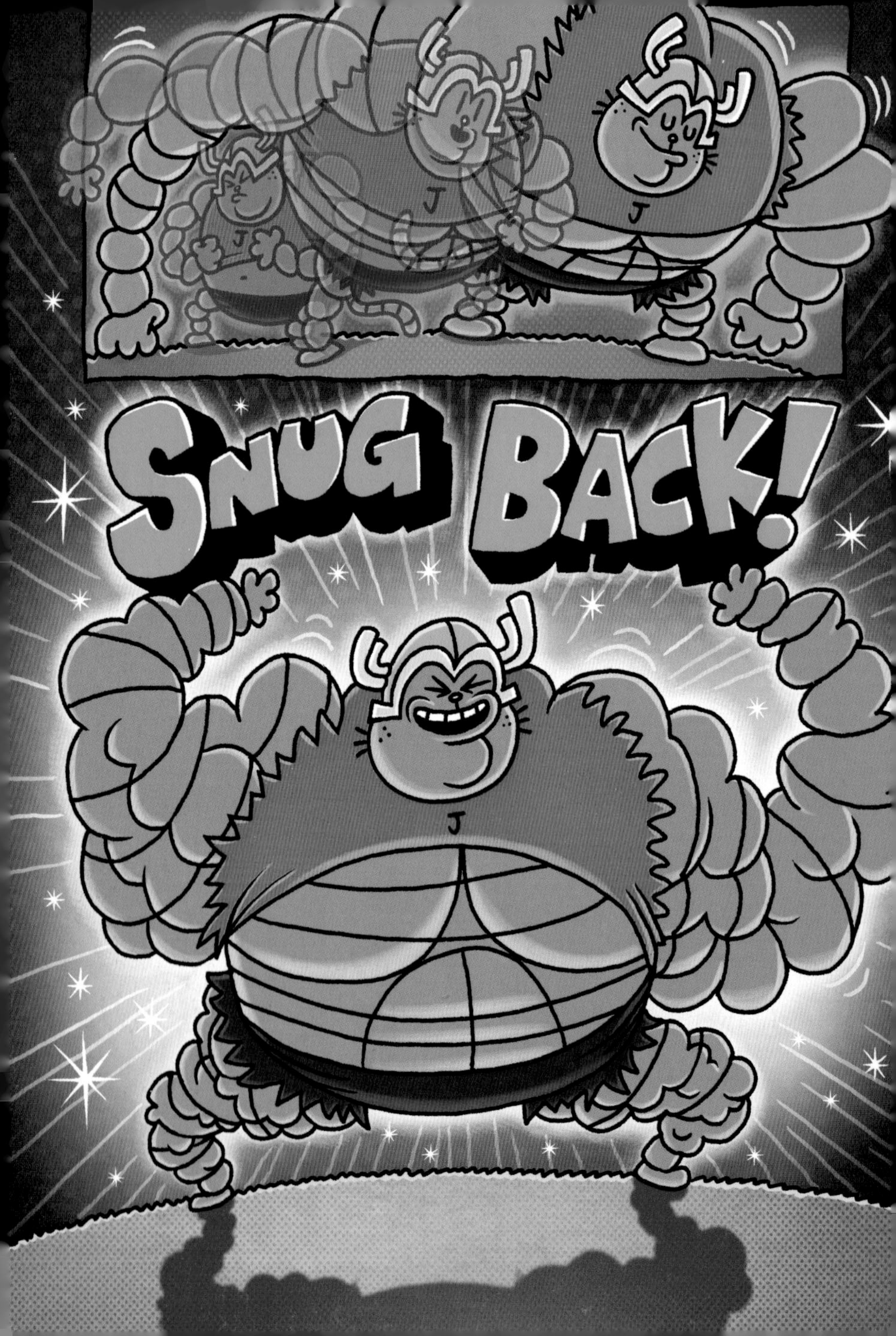
SNUG BACK!

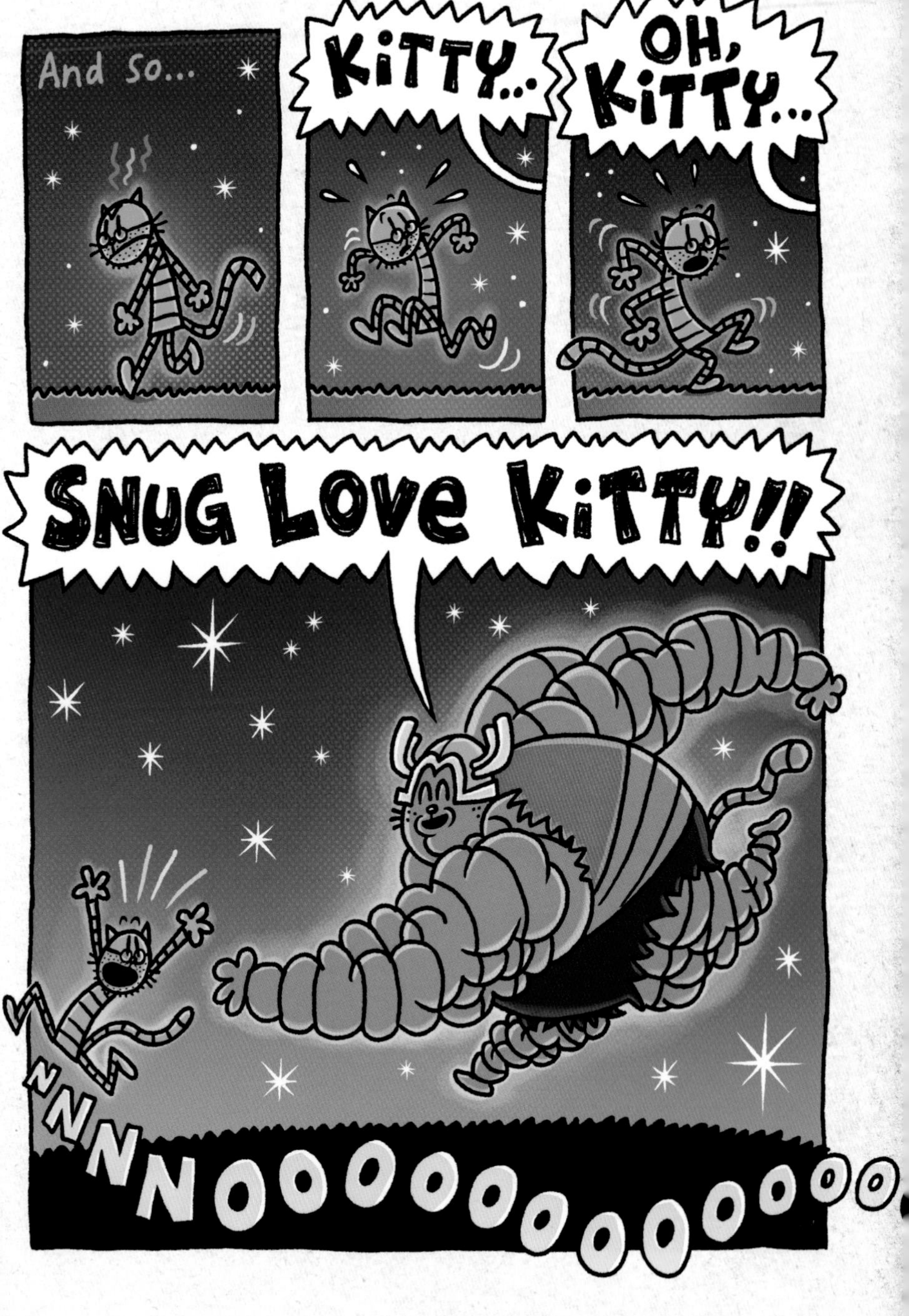
And so...
KITTY...
OH, KITTY...
SNUG LOVE KITTY!!
NNNOOOOOOOOOOOOO...

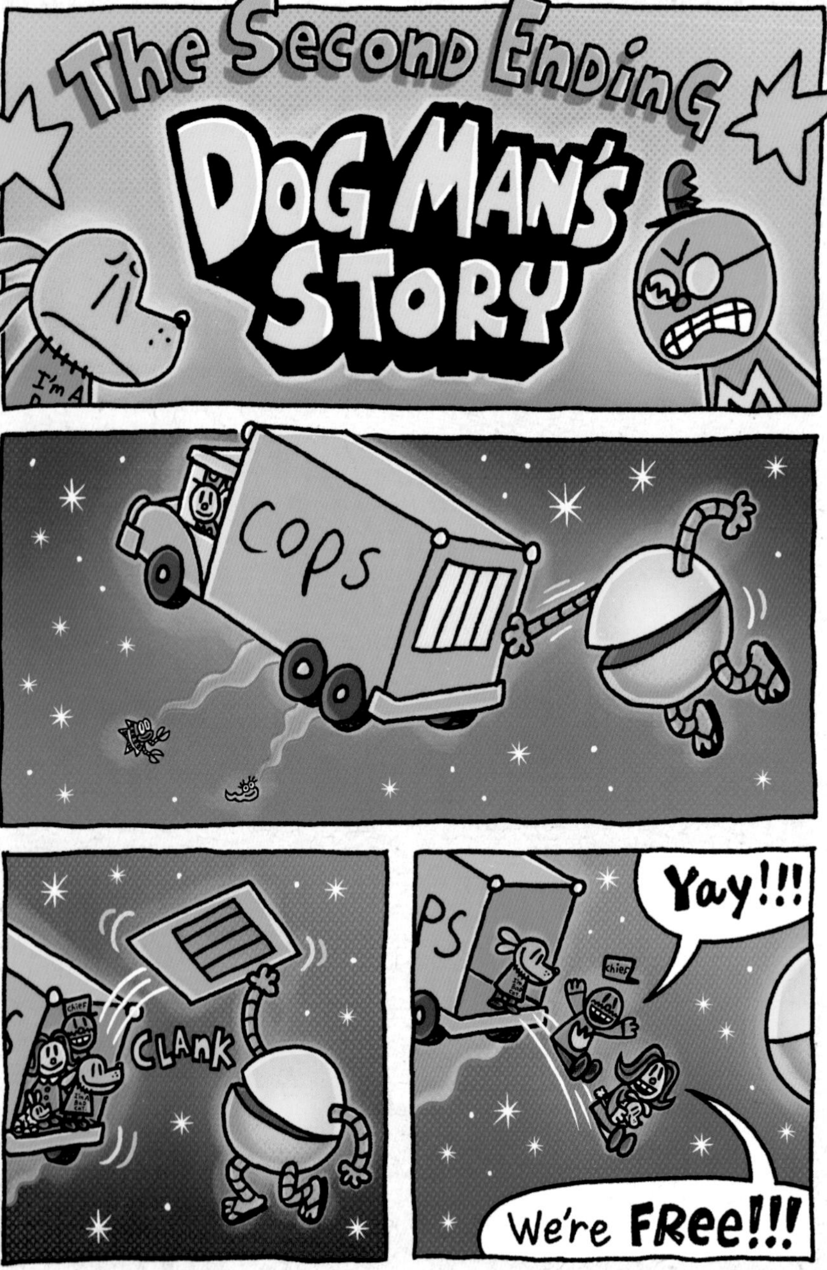
The Second Ending
Dog Man's Story
I'm A
Cops
CLANK
Yay!!!
We're FREE!!!

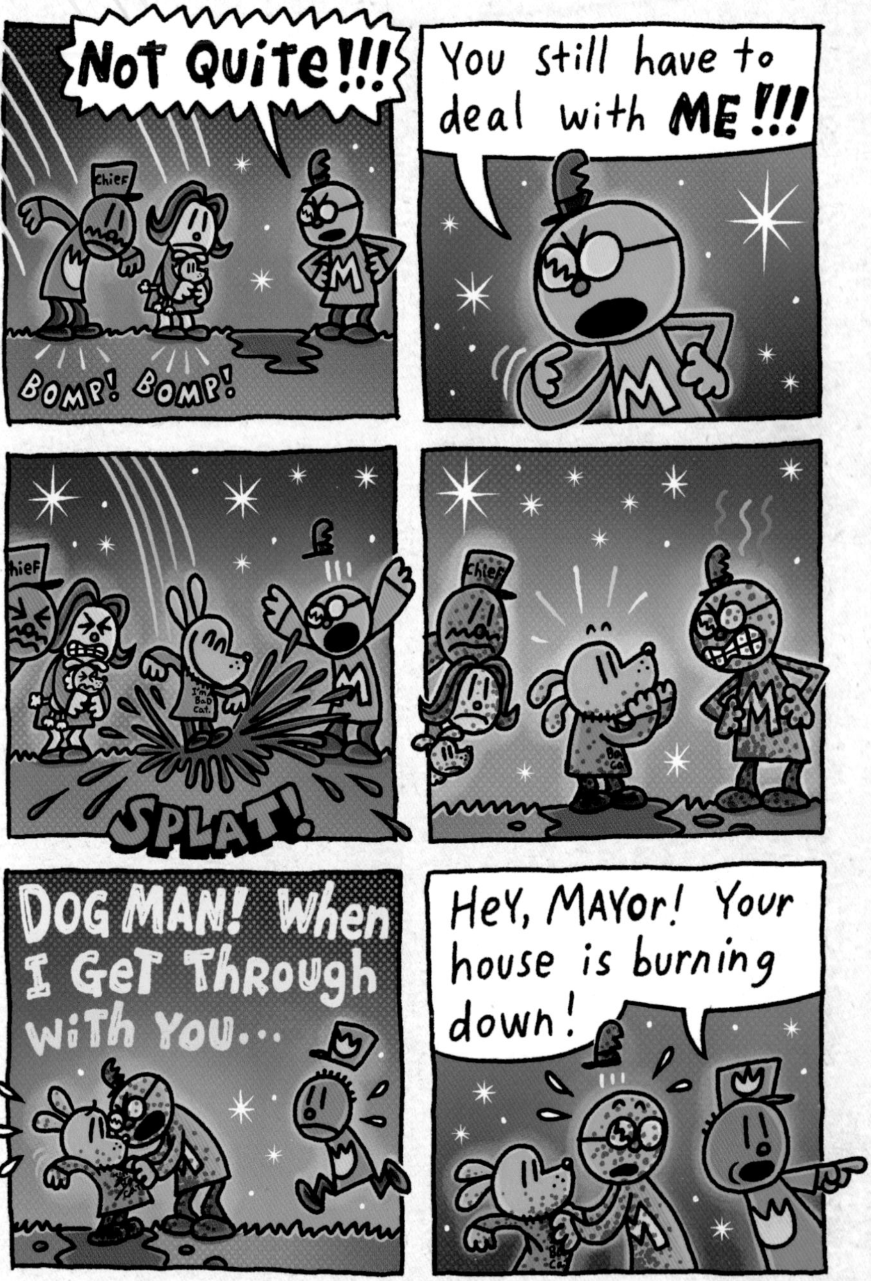

Not Quite!!!
Chief
BOMP! BOMP!
You still have to deal with ME!!!
SPLAT!
Chief
I'm Bad Cat.
Chief
DOG MAN! When I Get Through with You...
Hey, MAYOR! Your house is burning down!

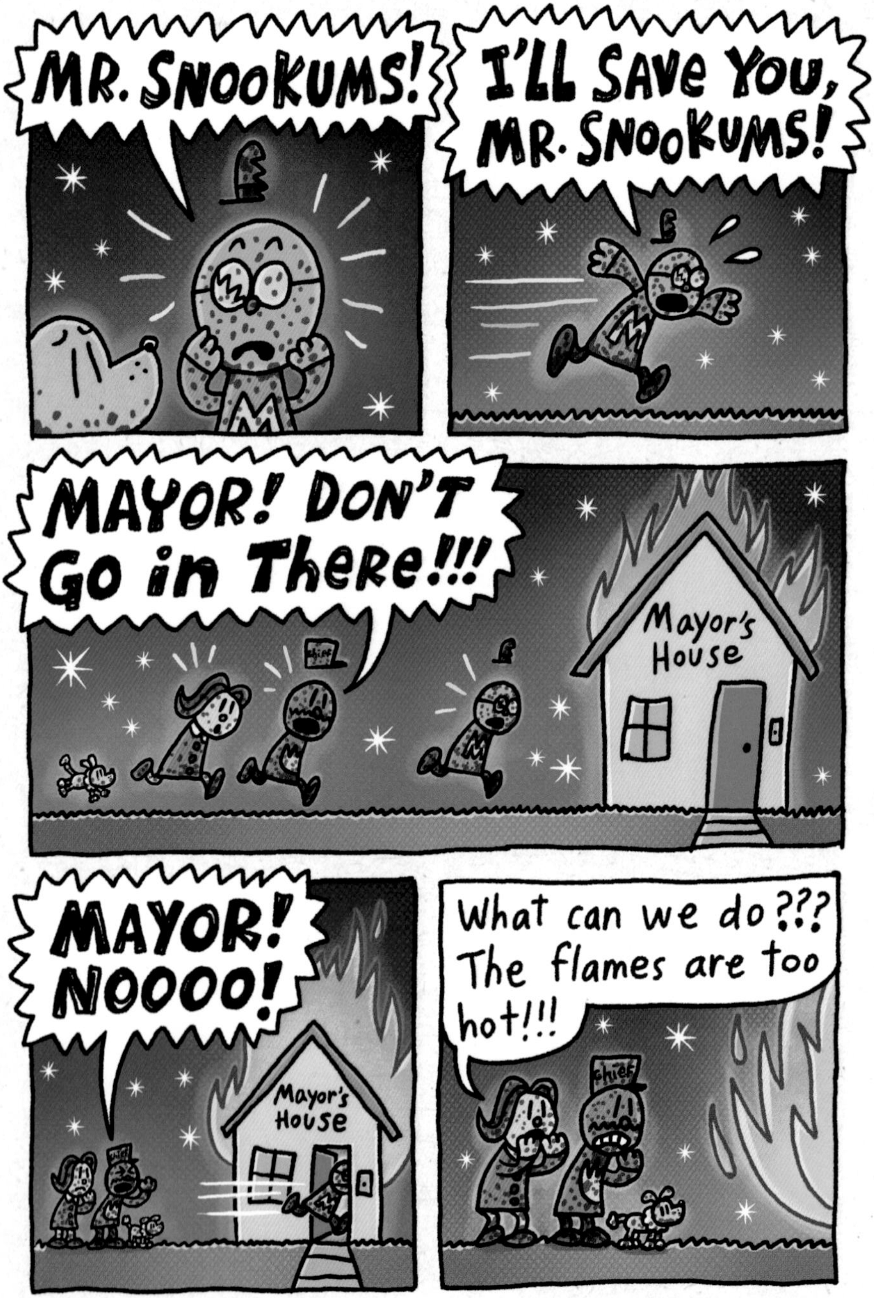
MR. SNOOKUMS!
I'LL SAVE YOU, MR. SNOOKUMS!
MAYOR! DON'T GO IN THERE!!!
Mayor's House
MAYOR! NOOOO!
Mayor's House
What can we do??? The flames are too hot!!!

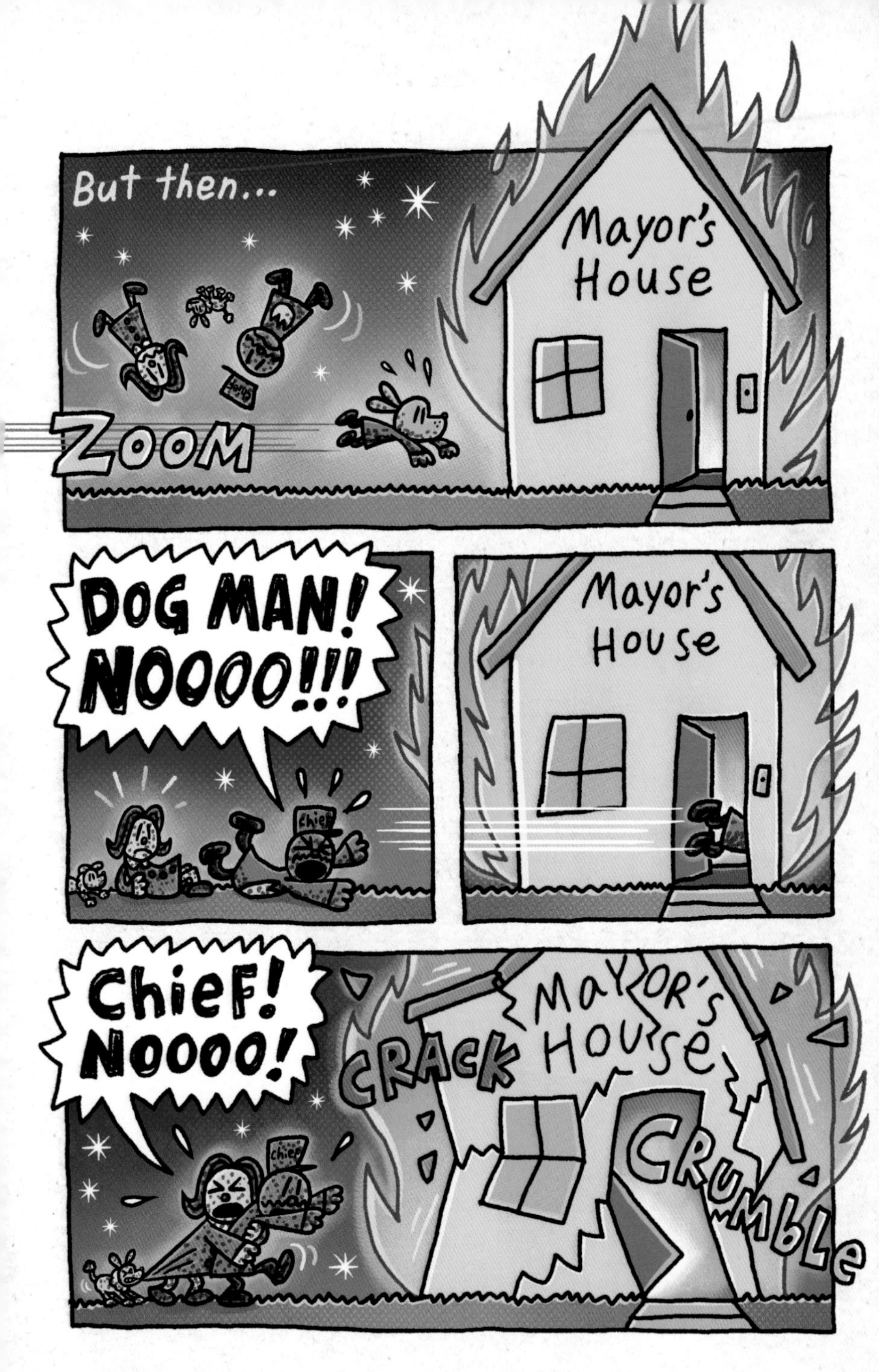

But then...
Mayor's House
ZOOM
DOG MAN! NOOOO!!!
Mayor's House
Chief! NOOOO!
MAYOR'S HOUSE
CRACK
CRUMBLE

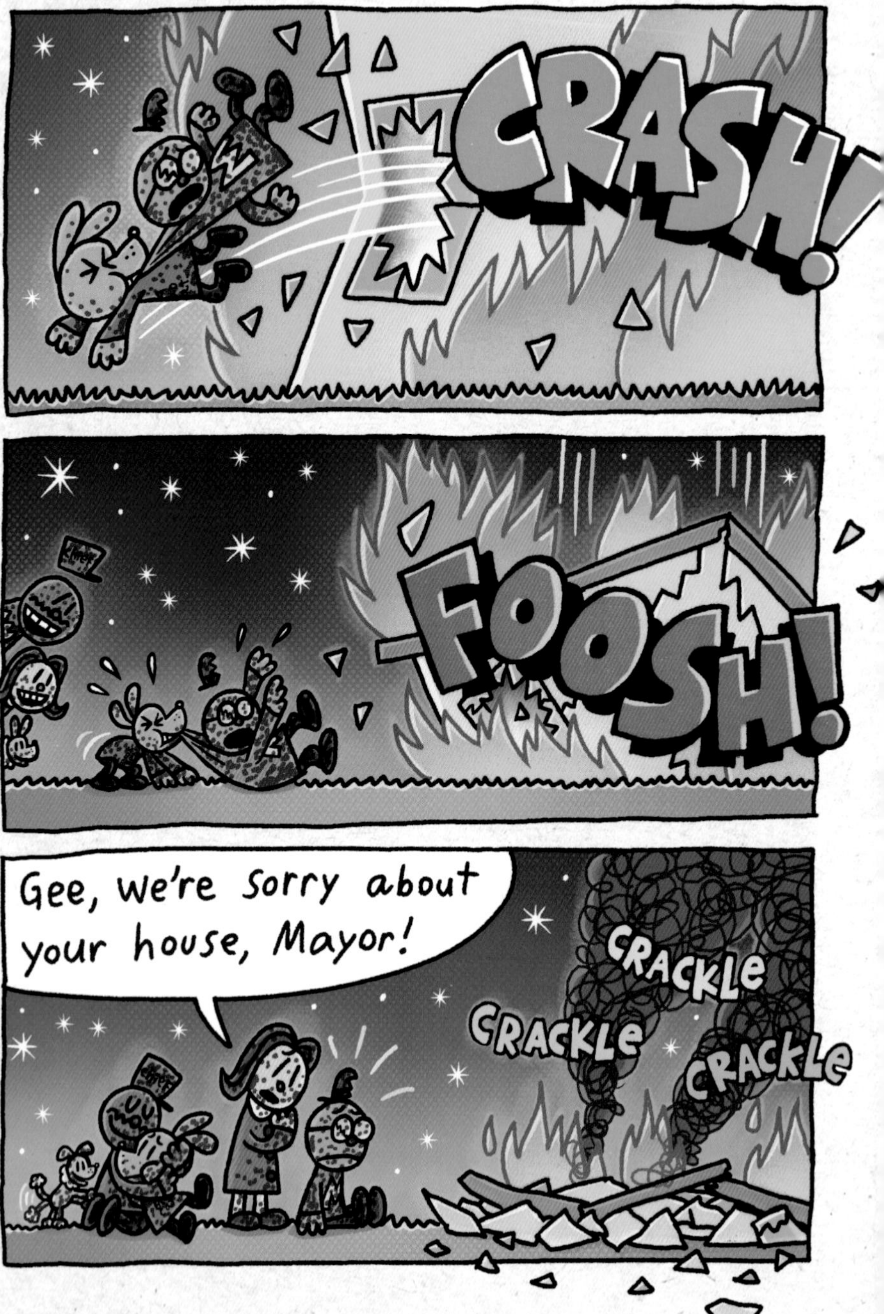
CRASH!
FOOSH!
Gee, we're sorry about your house, Mayor!
CRACKLE
CRACKLE
CRACKLE

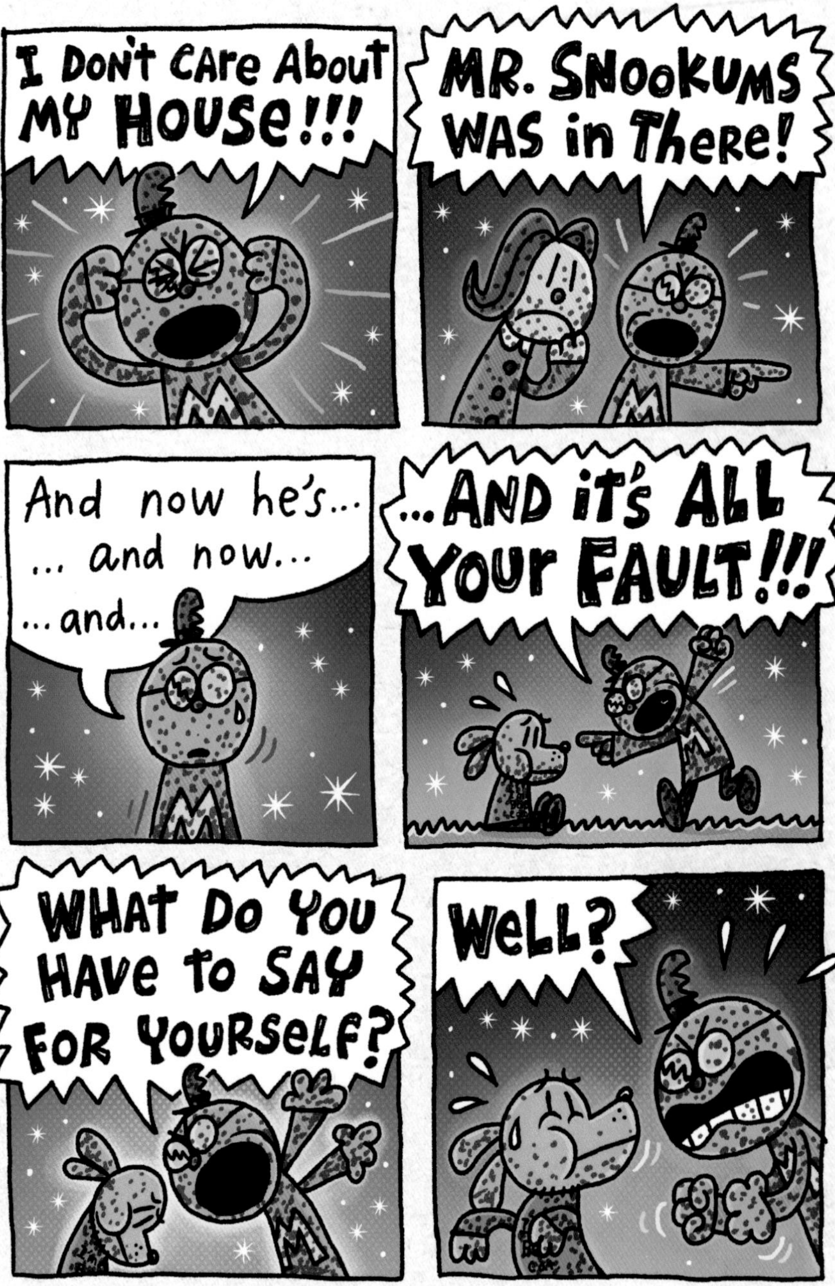
I DON'T CARE ABOUT MY HOUSE!!!
MR. SNOOKUMS WAS IN THERE!
And now he's... ... and now... ...and...
...AND IT'S ALL YOUR FAULT!!!
WHAT DO YOU HAVE TO SAY FOR YOURSELF?
WELL?

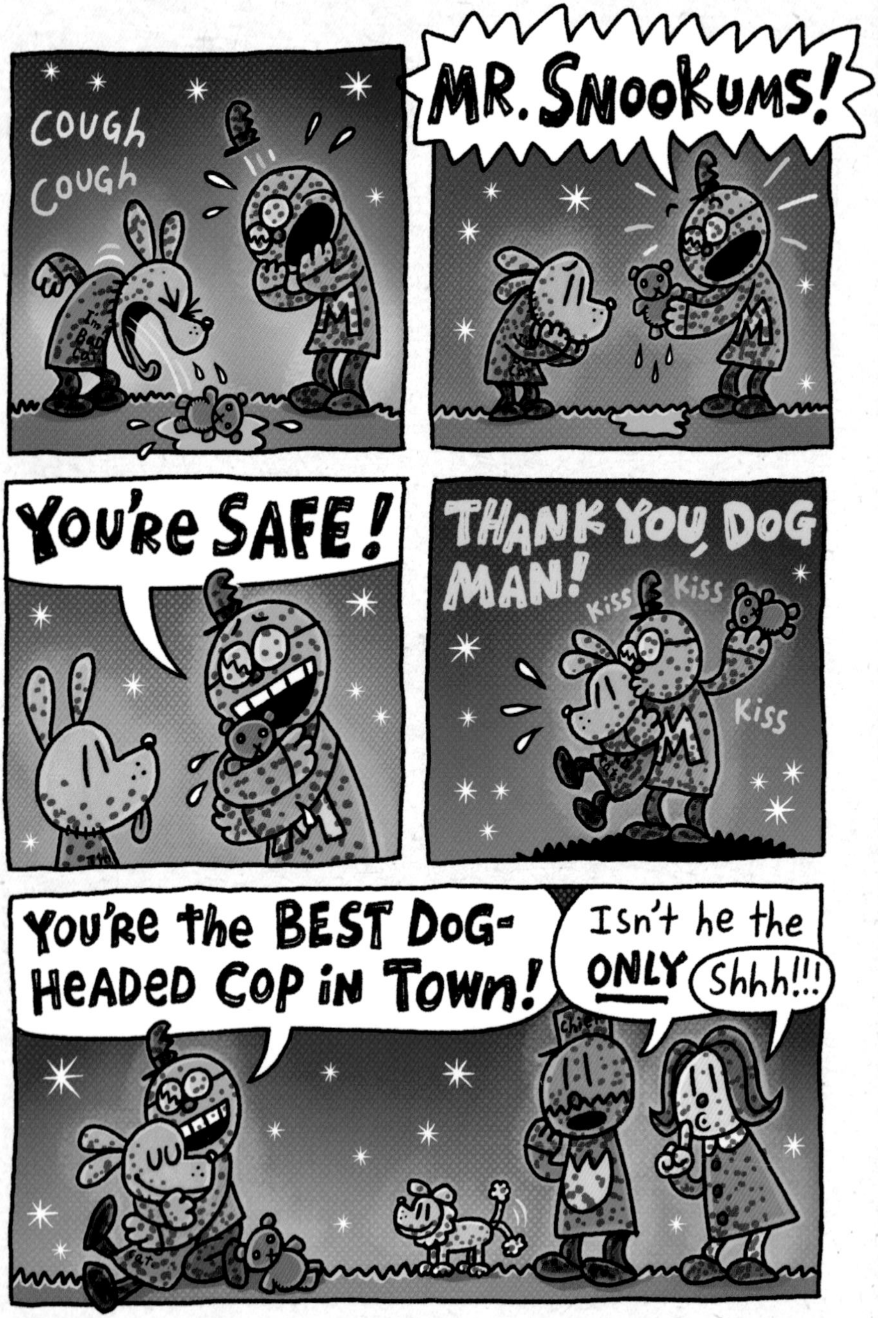
COUGH
COUGH
MR. SNOOKUMS!
YOU'RE SAFE!
THANK YOU, DOG MAN!
KISS
KISS
KISS
YOU'RE THE BEST DOG-HEADED COP IN TOWN!
Isn't he the ONLY
Shhh!!!

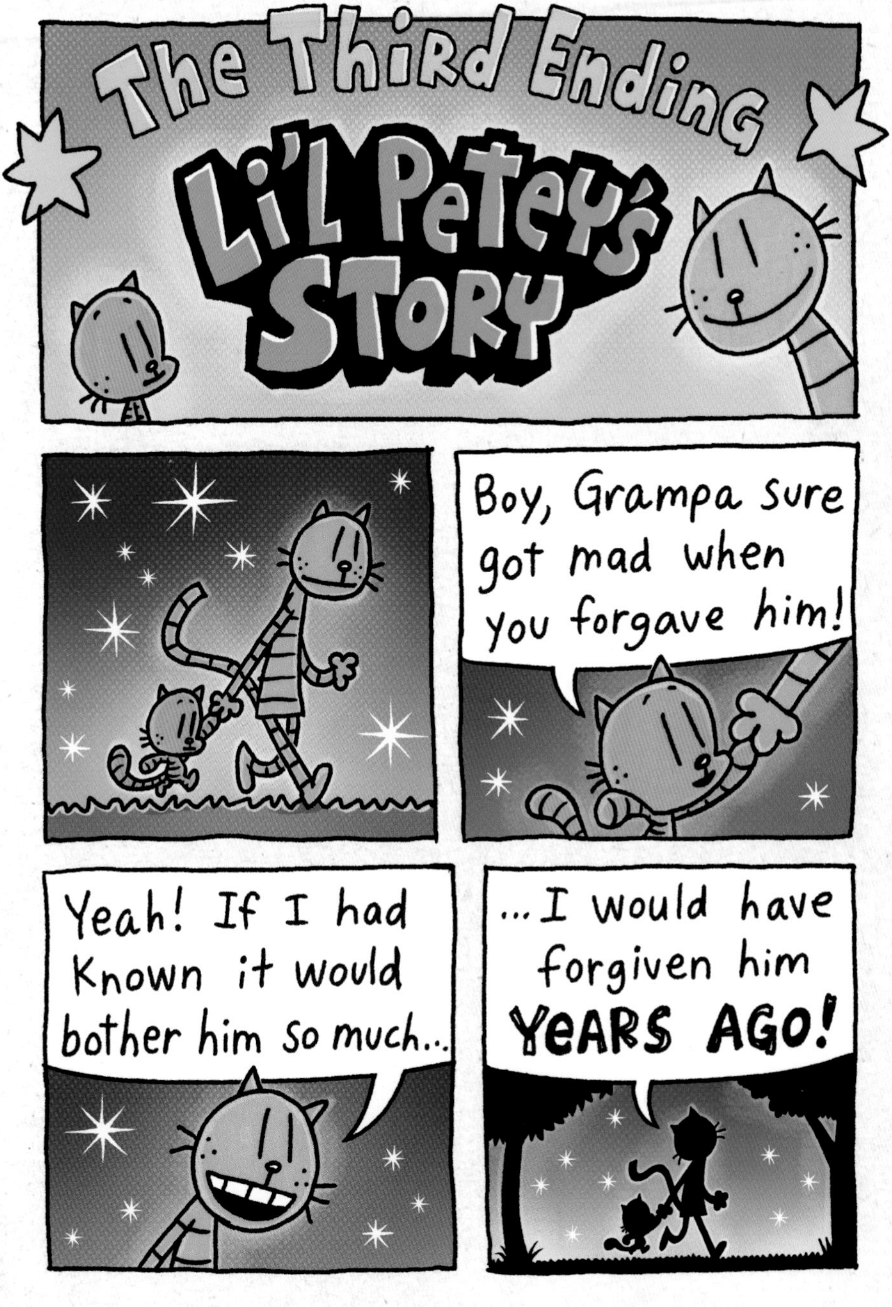
The Third Ending
Li'l Petey's Story
Boy, Grampa sure got mad when you forgave him!
Yeah! If I had known it would bother him so much...
...I would have forgiven him YEARS AGO!

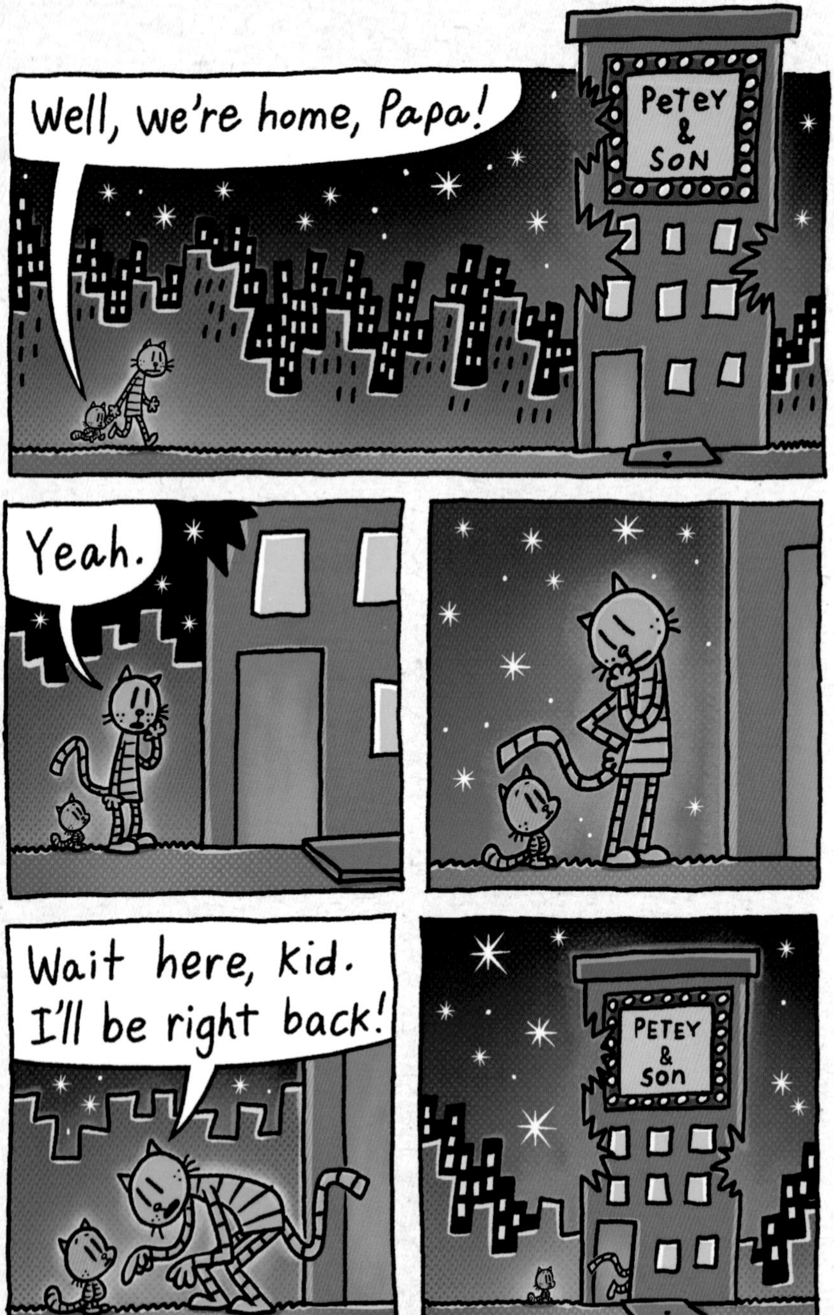
Well, we're home, Papa!
PETEY & SON
Yeah.
Wait here, kid. I'll be right back!
PETEY & SON

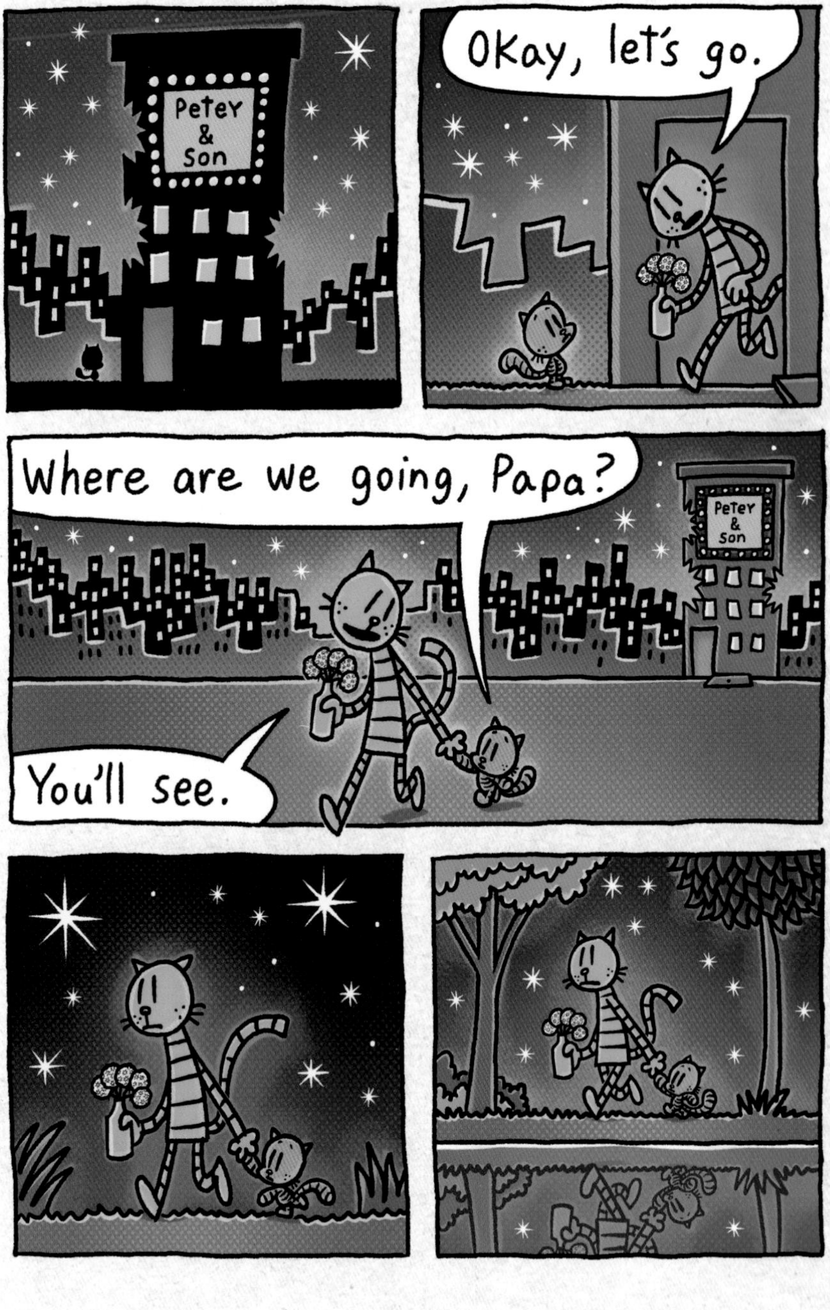
Petey
&
Son
OKay, let's go.
Where are we going, Papa?
Petey
&
Son
You'll see.

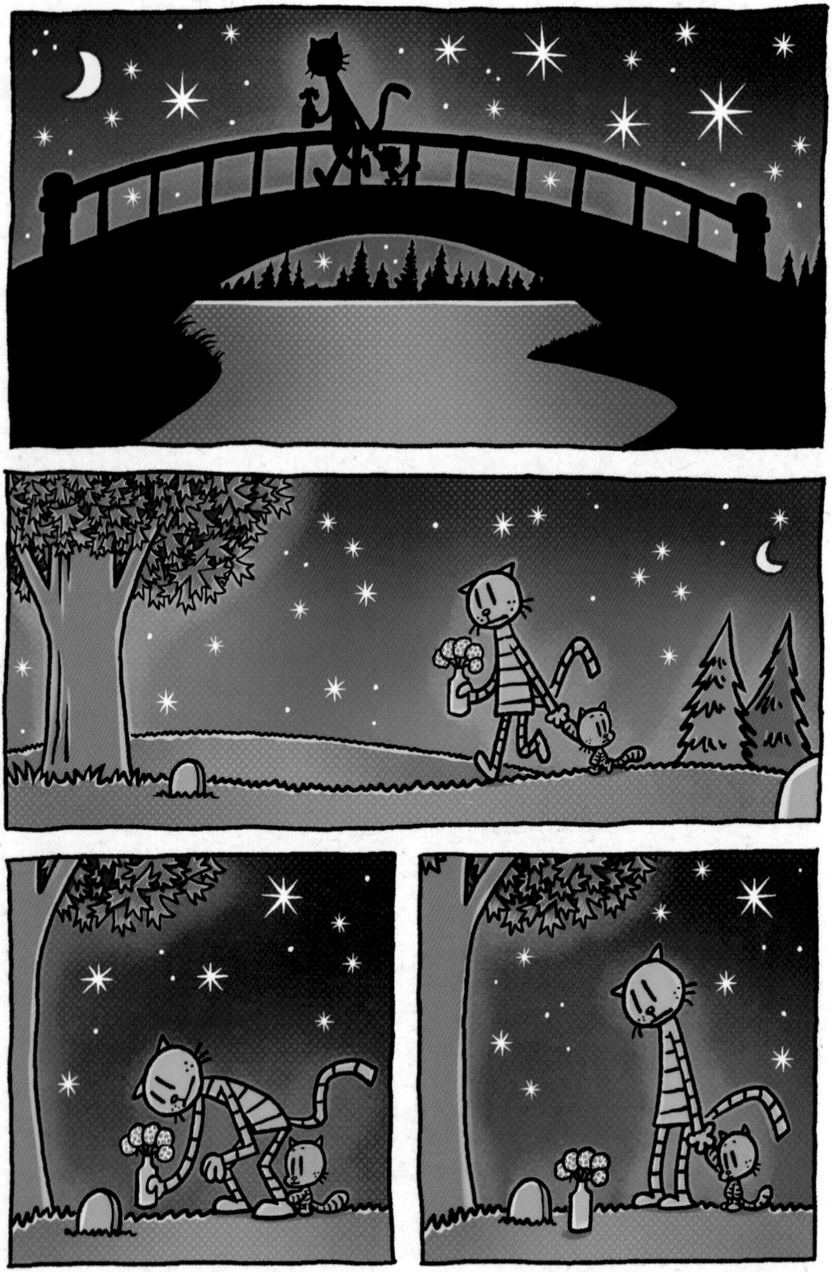

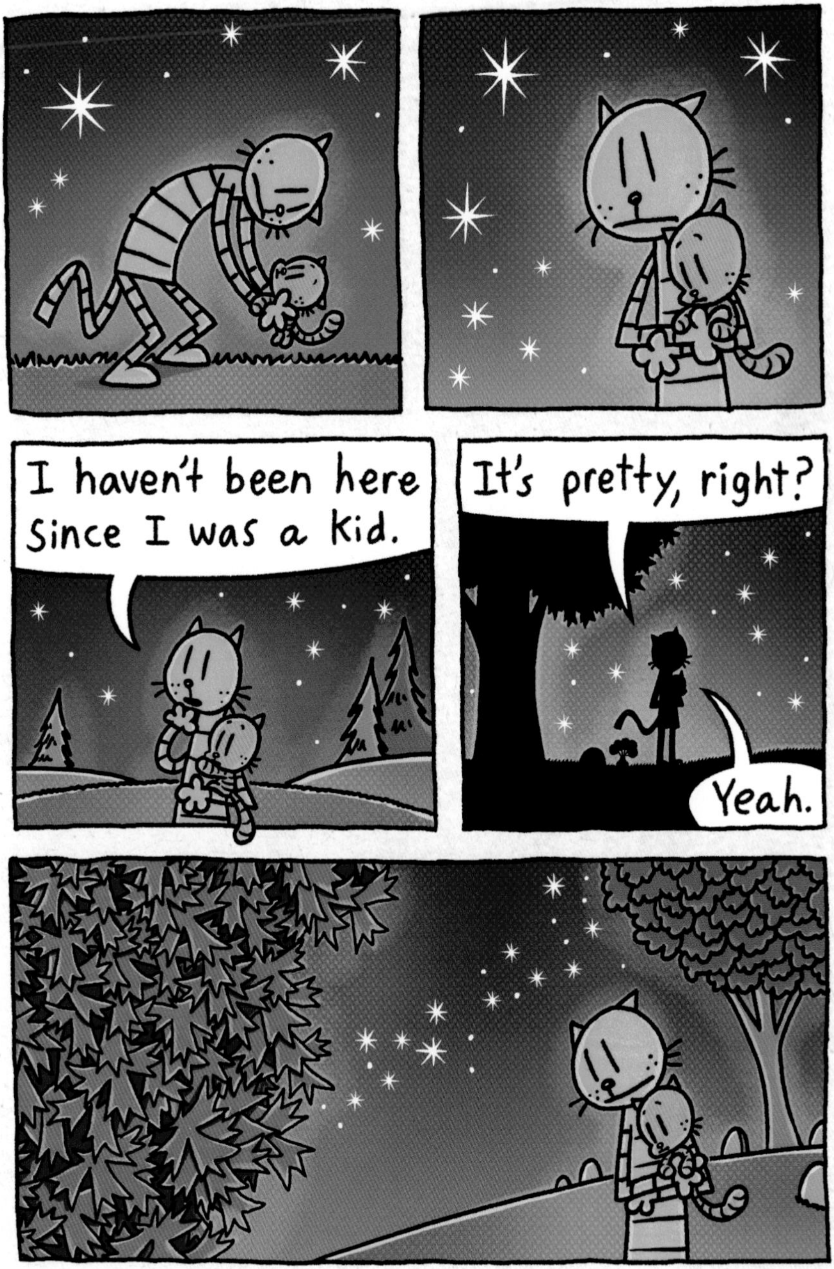
I haven't been here since I was a kid.
It's pretty, right?
Yeah.

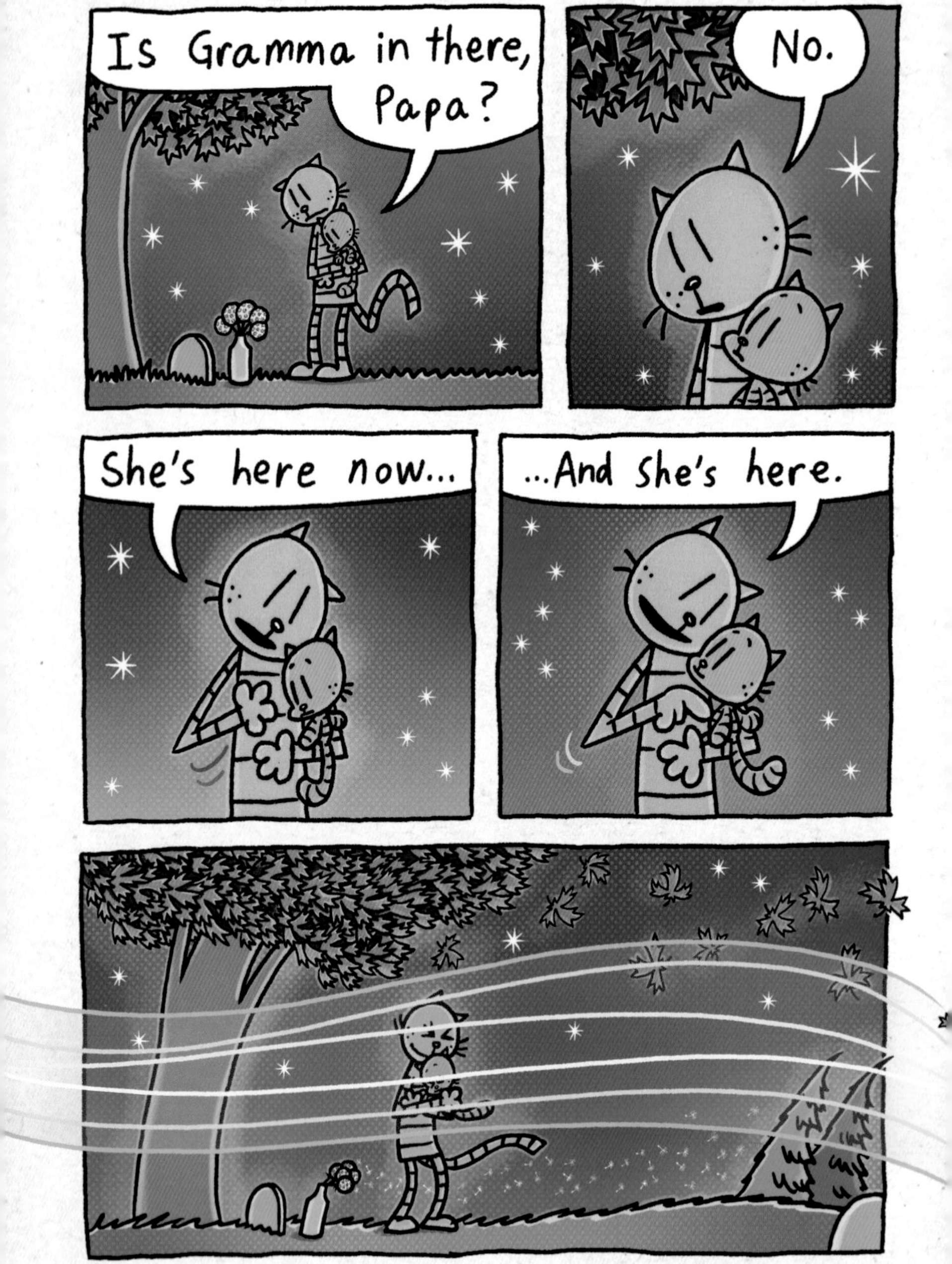
Is Gramma in there, Papa?
No.
She's here now...
...And she's here.

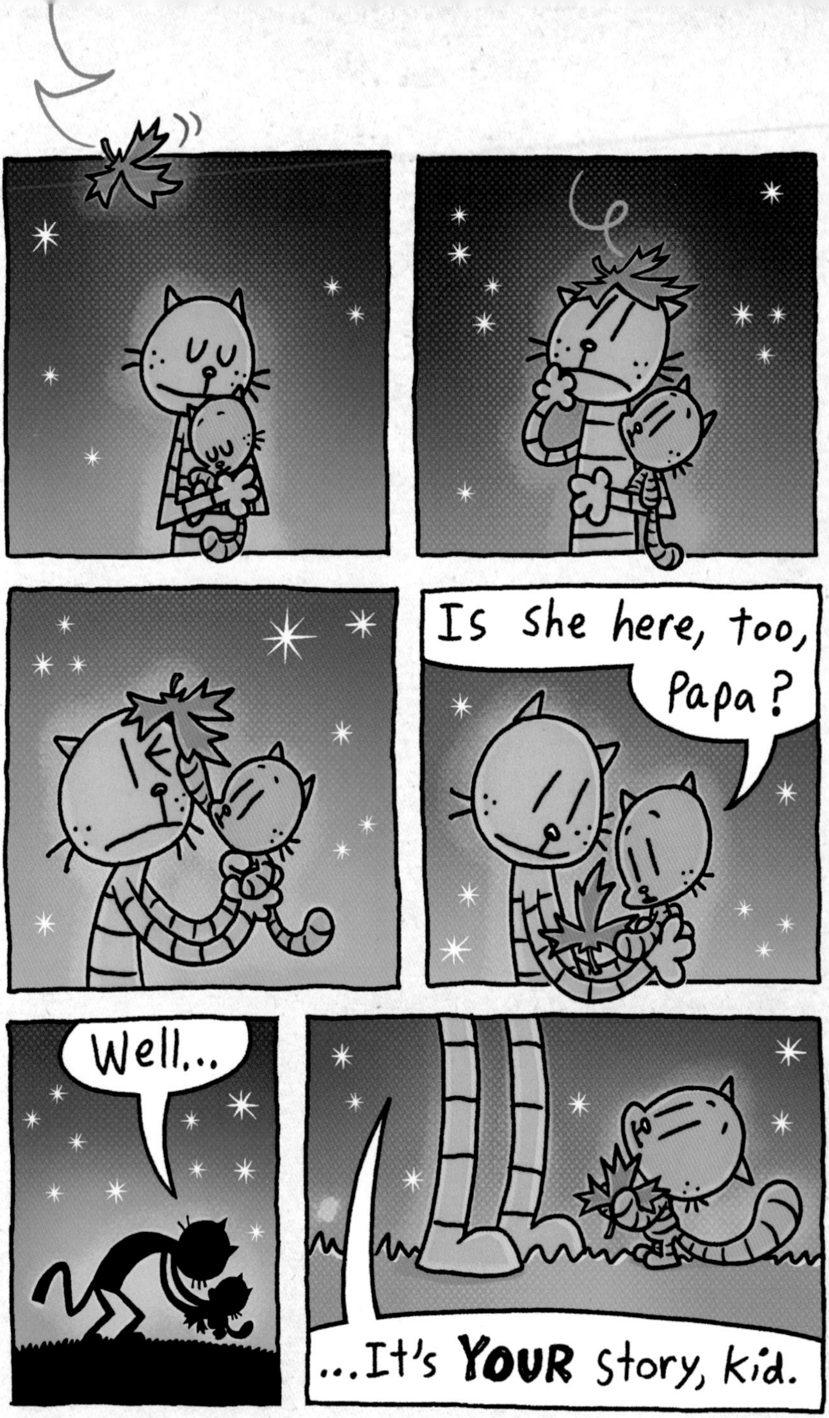
Is she here, too, Papa?
Well...
...It's YOUR story, kid.

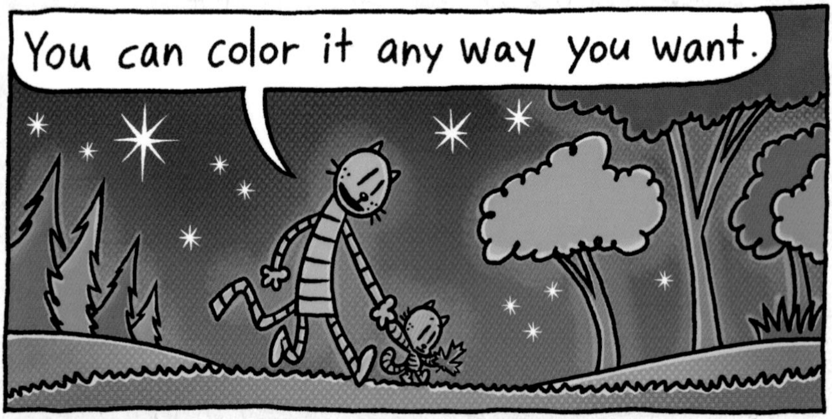
You can color it any way you want.

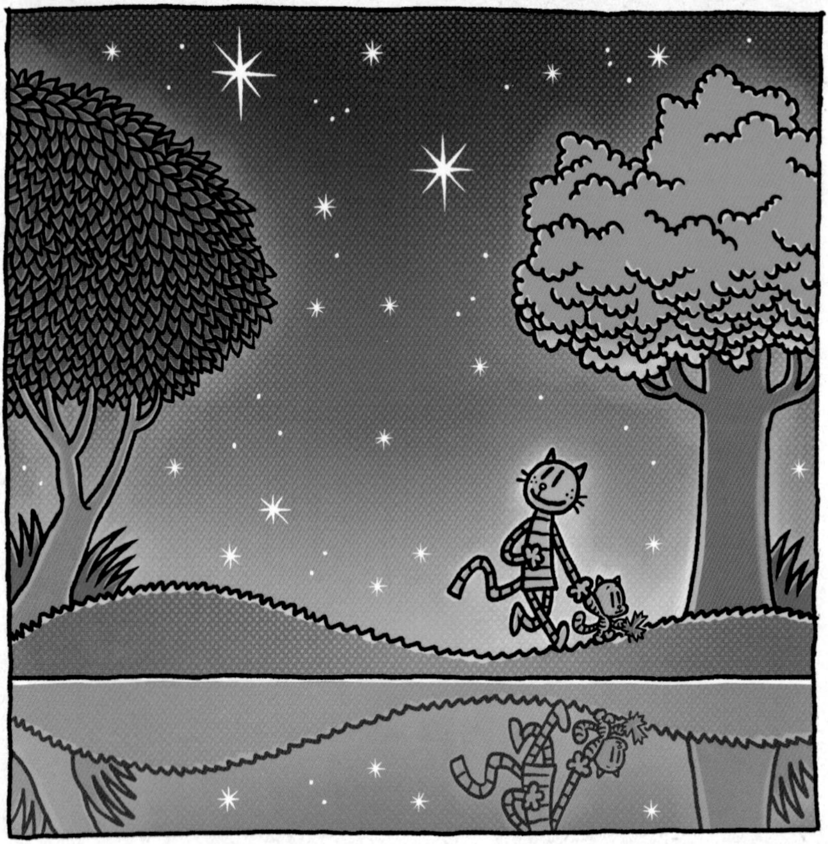

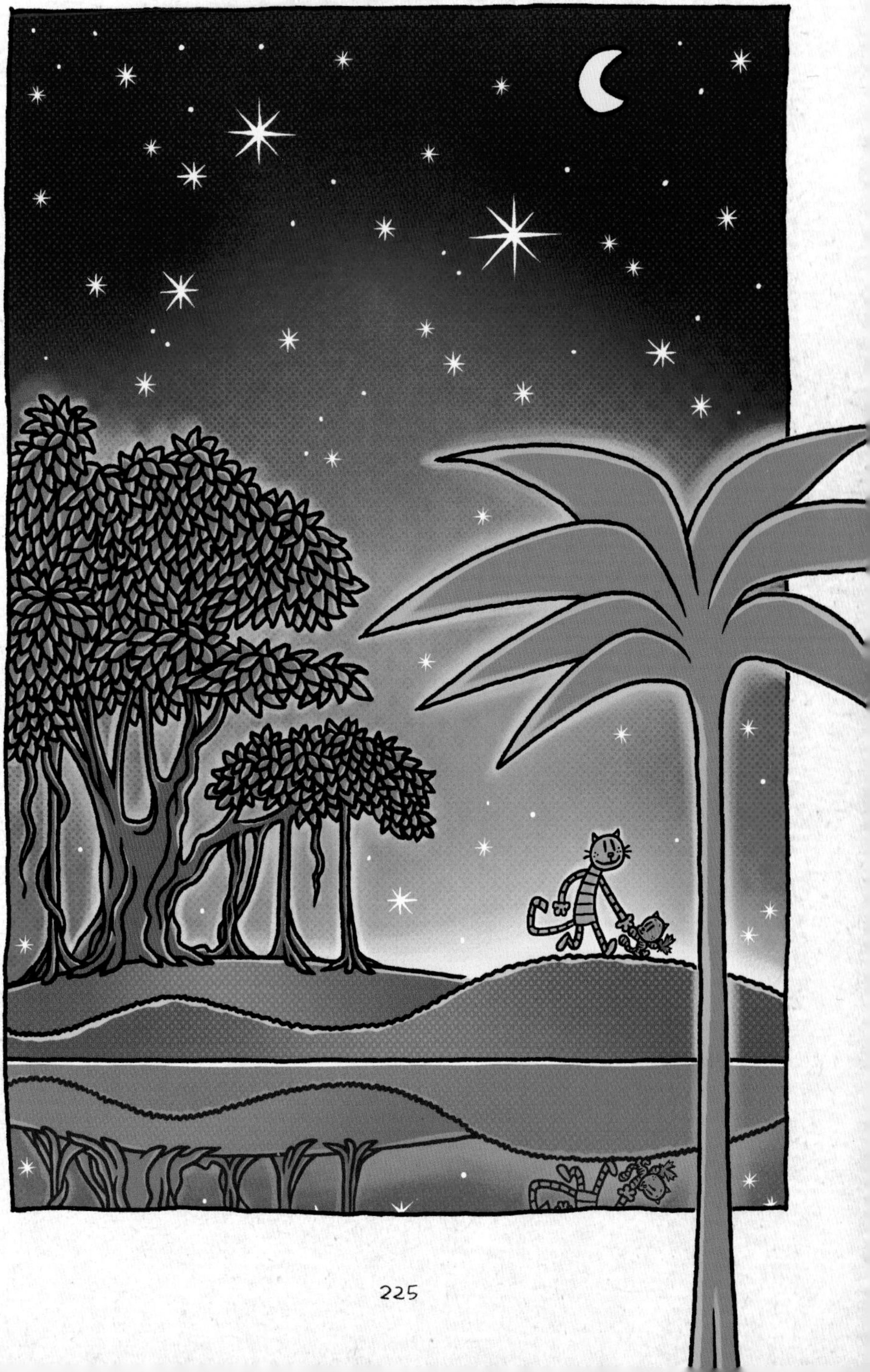

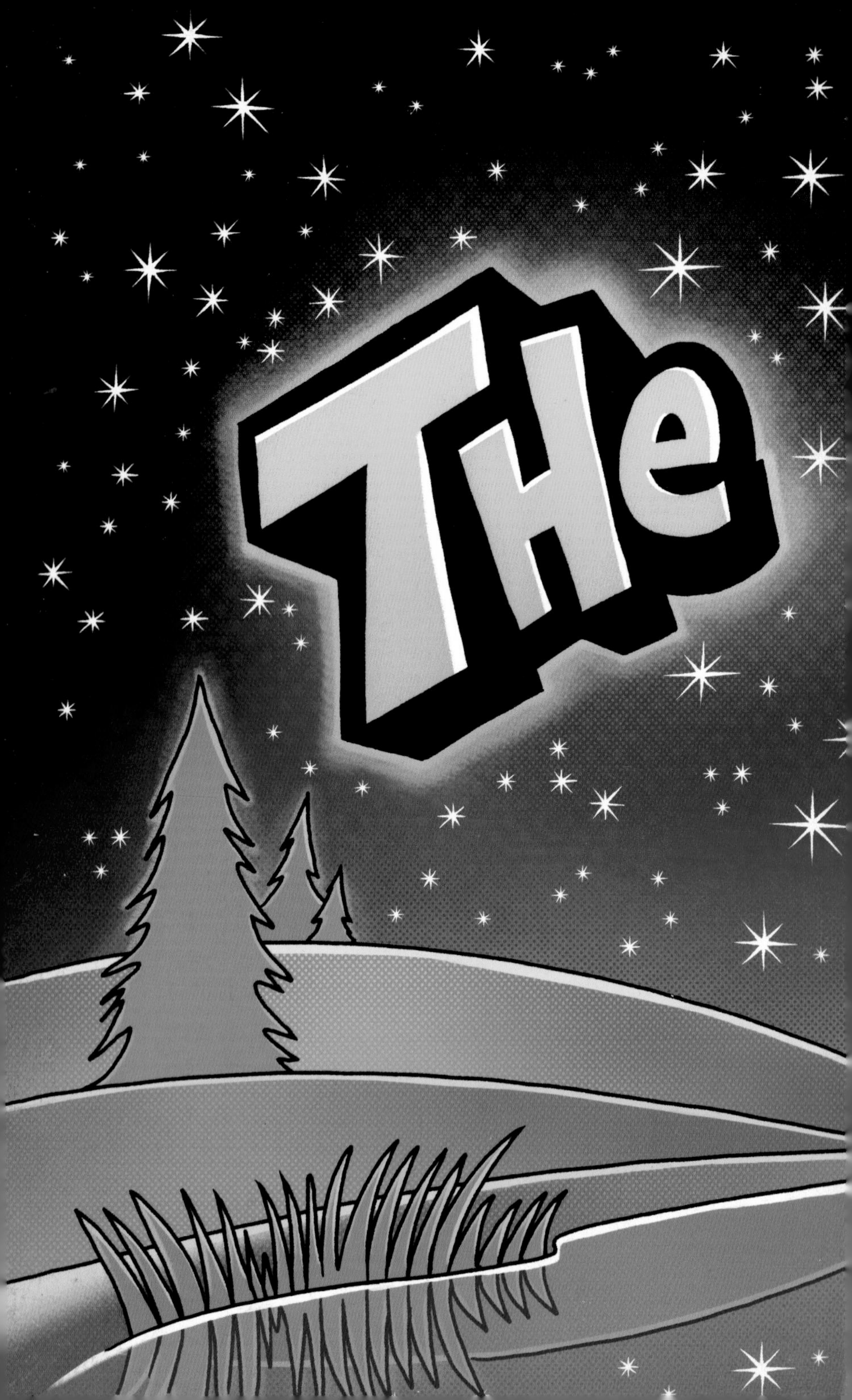
THE

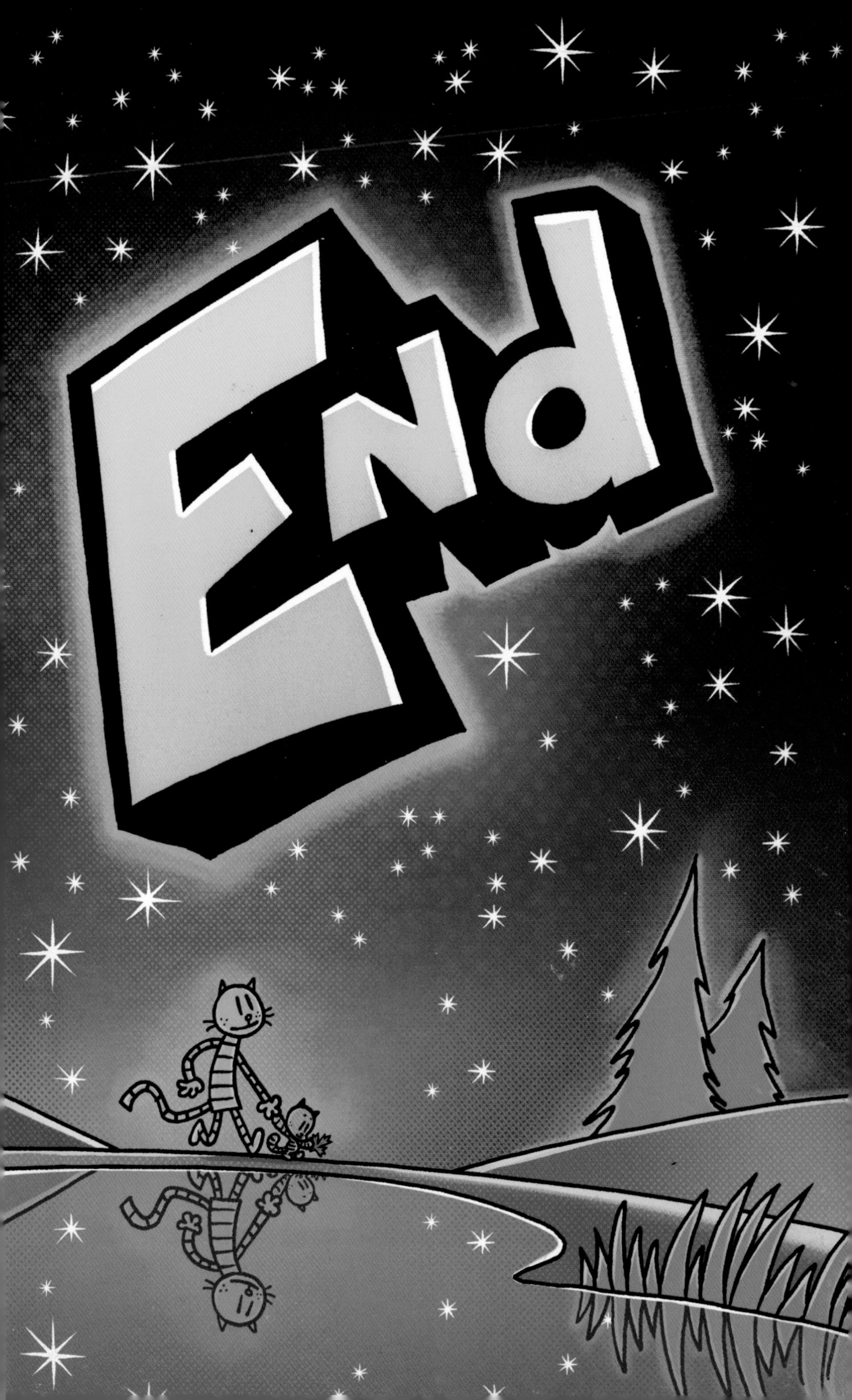
End

by George and Harold

★ Li'l Petey's words on page 130 were taken from the following quote:

> "Hate, it has caused a lot of problems
> in this world,
> but has not solved one yet."
>
> —Maya Angelou

★ Chapter 12 was based on this precept:

> "Resentment is like drinking poison
> and waiting for the other person to die."
>
> —Carrie Fisher

★ Part 3 of the final chapter was inspired by this poem:

> Do not stand at my grave and weep,
> I am not there. I do not sleep.
> I am a thousand winds that blow,
> I am the softly falling snow.
> I am the gentle showers of rain,
> I am the fields of ripening grain.
> I am in the morning hush,
> I am in the graceful rush
> Of beautiful birds in circling flight.
> I am the starshine of the night.
> I am in the flowers that bloom,
> I am in a quiet room.
> I am in the birds that sing.
> I am in each lovely thing.
> Do not stand at my grave and cry.
> I am not there – I did not die.
>
> — Mary Elizabeth Frye

HOW 2 DRAW CATMAN

in 21 Ridiculously Easy Steps!!!

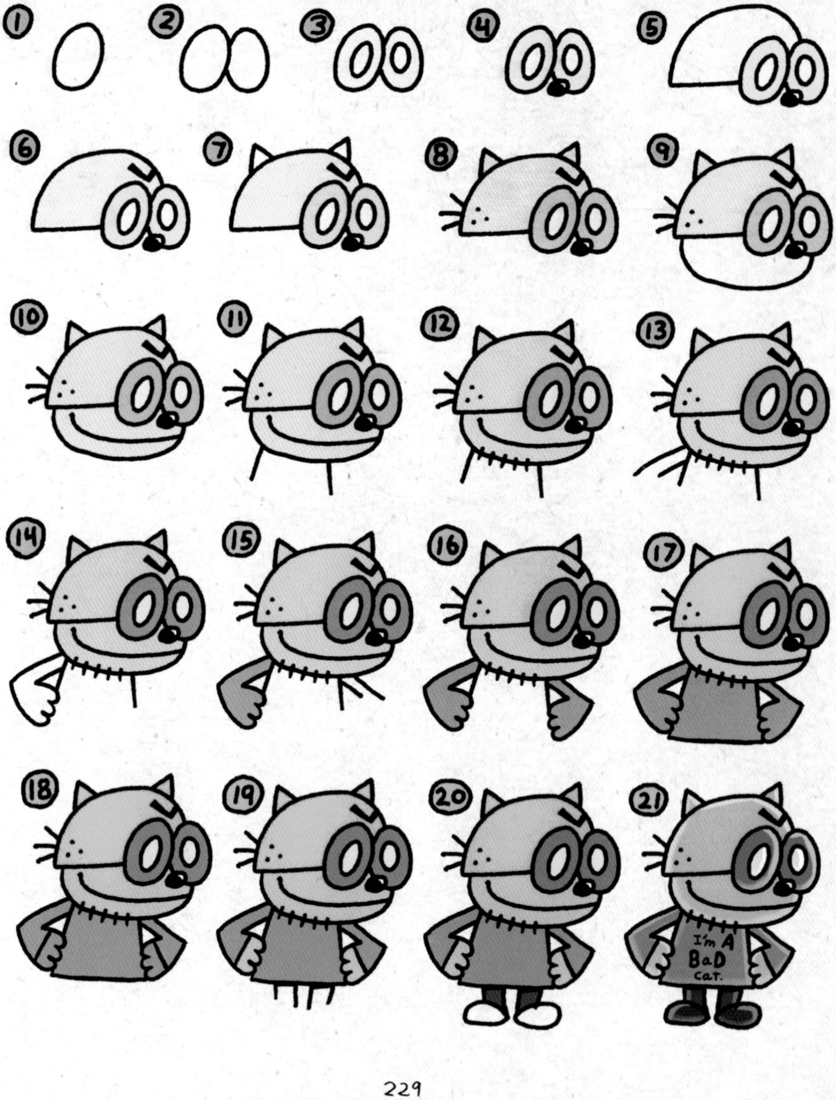
1
2
3
4
5
6
7
8
9
10
11
12
13
14
15
16
17
18
19
20
21
I'm A BaD Cat.

HOW 2 DRAW Melvin The FROG

in 17 Ridiculously easy steps!

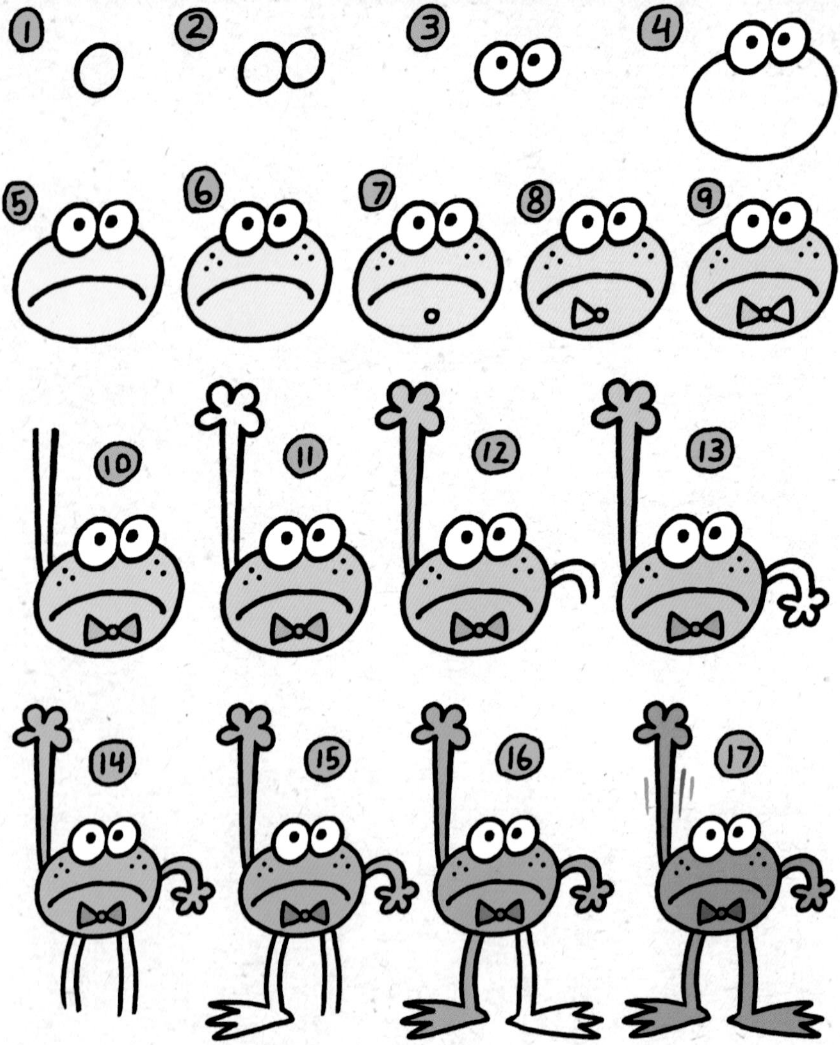
1
2
3
4
5
6
7
8
9
10
11
12
13
14
15
16
17

HOW 2 DRAW SARAH

in 18 Ridiculously Easy Steps!!!

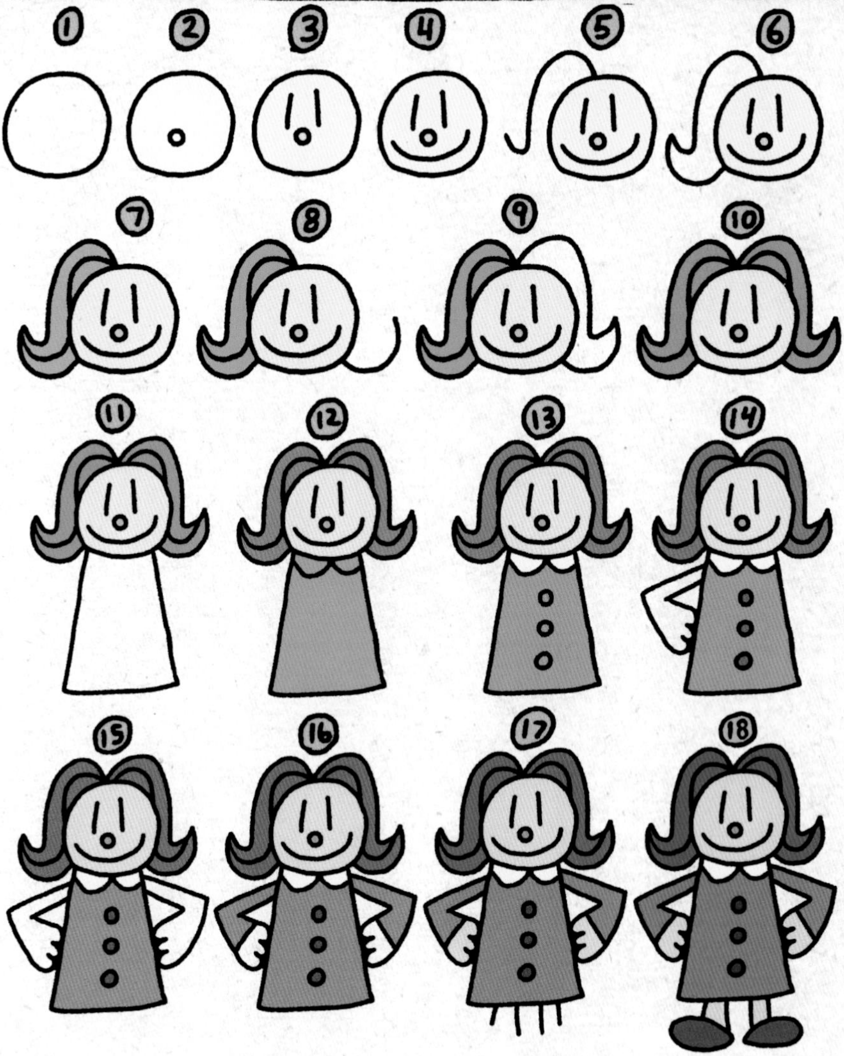

1
2
3
4
5
6
7
8
9
10
11
12
13
14
15
16
17
18

HOW 2 MAKE Munchy The Lunch BAG

in 4 Ridiculously easy steps!

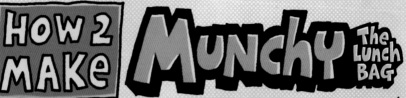

Step 1:

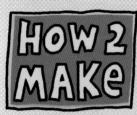

Get supplies:

- ☆ Lunch bag
- ☆ Pencil
- ☆ Tape

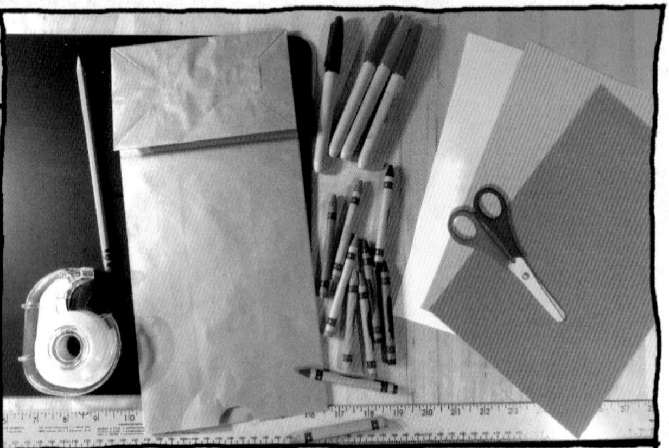

- ☆ construction paper
- ☆ scissors
- ☆ crayons / markers / colored Pencils

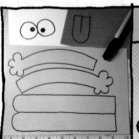

STEP 2:

Draw and cut out the arms, Legs, eyes + Tongue.

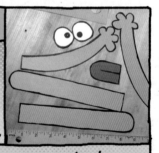

FREE Printable/CoLorabLe template available at: Scholastic.com/catKidcomicclub

STEP 3:

Assemble as shown using tape or glue or paste.

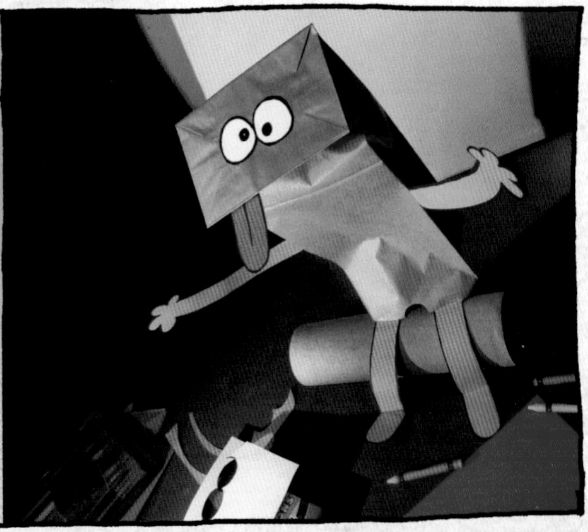

STEP 4:

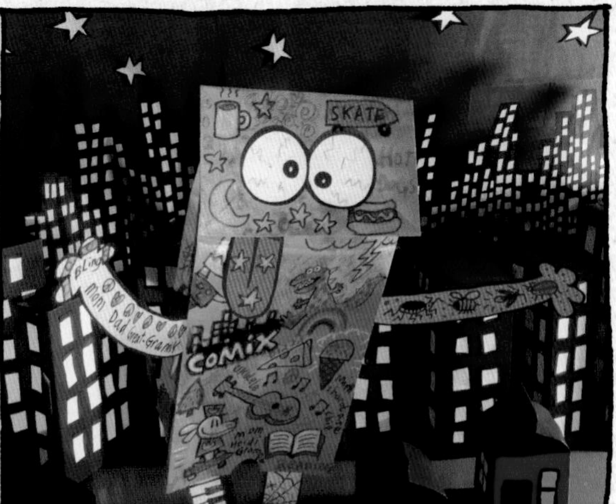
SKATE
COMiX

Take away his evil powers by filling him up with all the people and things you **Love!** Use pencils, crayons, paint, or whatever!!!

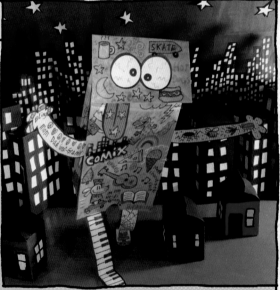

WRITE... DRAW... Be CREATive!

HOW 2 DRAW The INSUPPRESSIBLE SNUG

in 34 Ridiculously easy Steps!

1
2
3
4
5
6
7
8
9
10
11
12
13
14
15
16
17
18
19
20

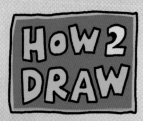

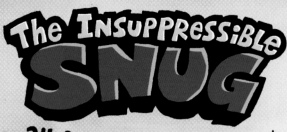

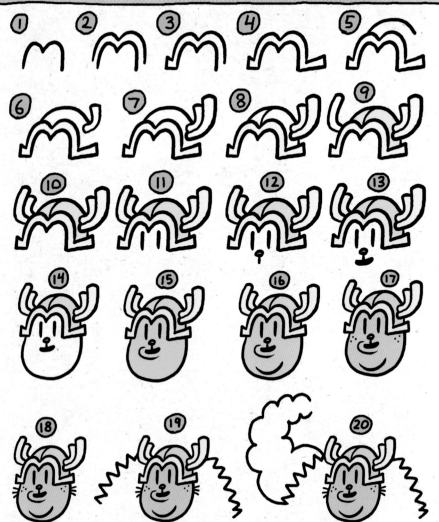

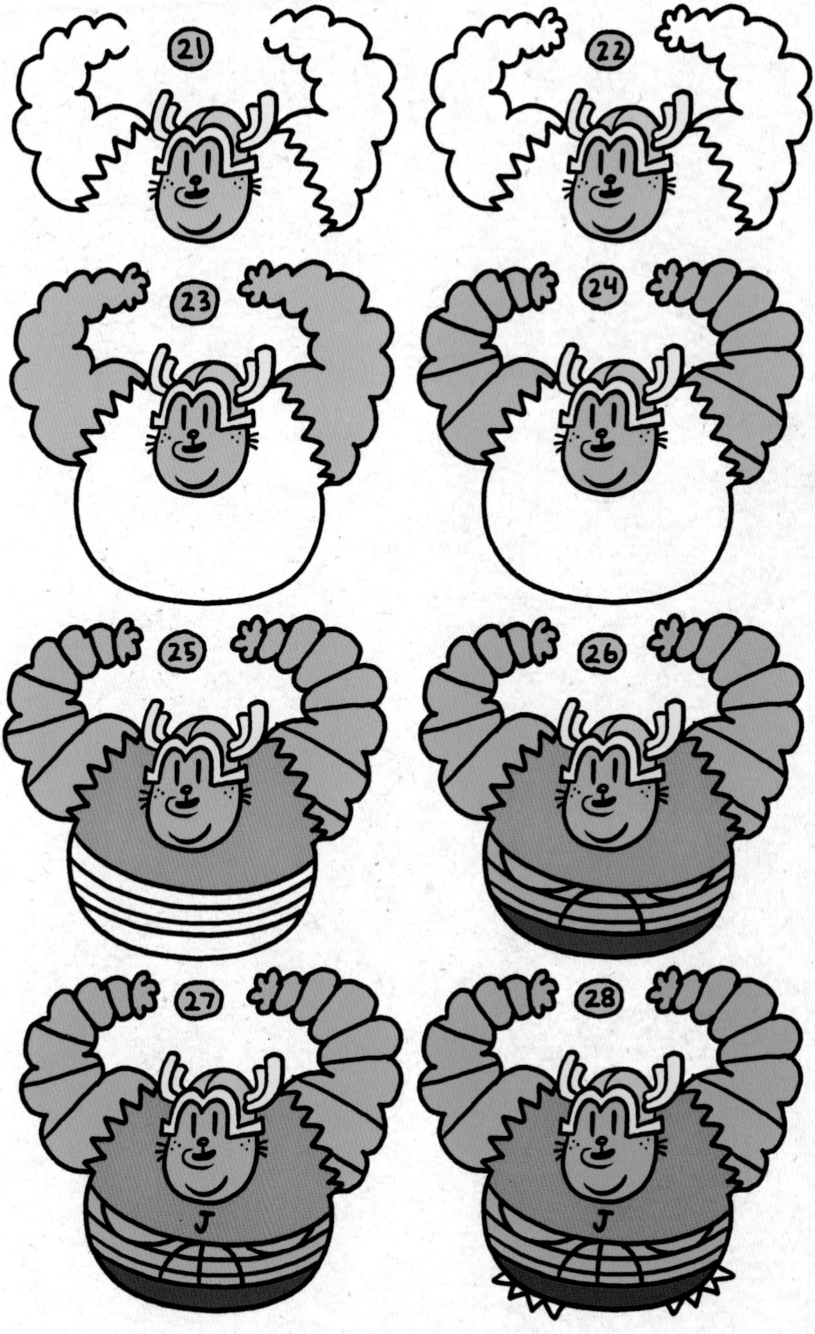
21
22
23
24
25
26
27
J
28
J

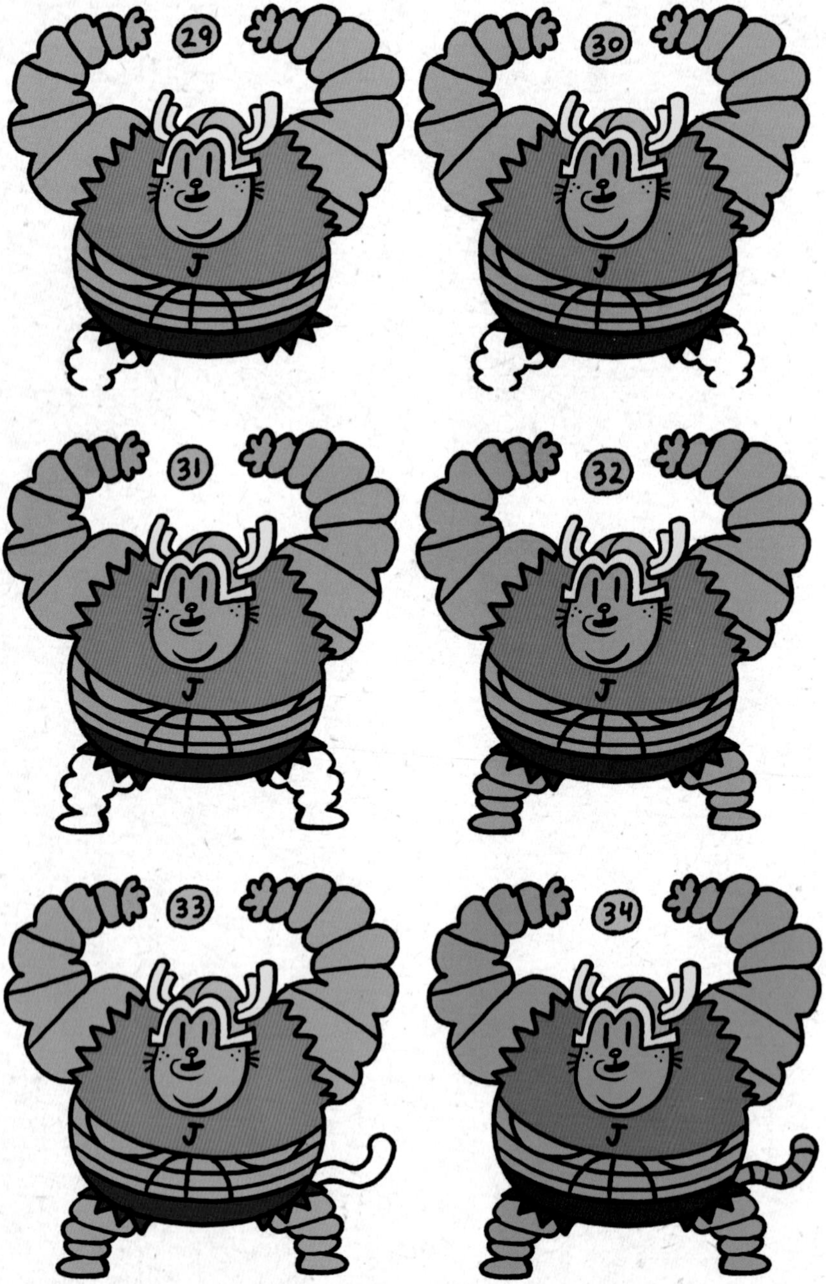
29
30
31
32
33
34

COMING NEXT!
AN ALL-NEW GRAPHIC NOVEL SERIES!
CAT KID COMIC CLUB

GET READING W

The Adventures of Captain Underpants Full Color
The First Epic Novel by Dav Pilkey
Full Color Captain Underpants and the Attack of the Talking Toilets
The Second Epic Novel by Dav Pilkey
Full Color Captain Underpants and the Invasion of the Incredibly Naughty Cafeteria Ladies from Outer Space
The Third Epic Novel by Dav Pilkey
Full Color Captain Underpants and the Perilous Plot of Professor Poopypants
The Fourth Epic Novel by Dav Pilkey
Full Color Captain Underpants and the Wrath of the Wicked Wedgie Woman
The Fifth Epic Novel by Dav Pilkey
Full Color Captain Underpants and the Big, Bad Battle of the Bionic Booger Boy
The Sixth Epic Novel by Dav Pilkey
Full Color Captain Underpants and the Big, Bad Battle of the Bionic Booger Boy
The Seventh Epic Novel by Dav Pilkey
Full Color Captain Underpants and the Preposterous Plight of the Purple Potty People
The Eighth Epic Novel by Dav Pilkey
Full Color Captain Underpants and the Terrifying Re-Turn of Tippy Tinkletrousers
The Ninth Epic Novel by Dav Pilkey
Full Color Captain Underpants and the Revolting Revenge of the Radioactive Robo-Boxers
The Tenth Epic Novel by Dav Pilkey
Caldecott Honor Artist

Dog Man The Musical
Original Cast Recording

The epic musical adventure is now available from Broadway Records!

Meet all your favorite characters on the Dog Man Island in Home Base! Play games, make and share your own comics, and more at scholastic.com/homebase!

Download on the App Store

HOME BASE
SCHOLASTIC

GET IT ON Google Play

TH DAV PILKEY!

ABOUT THE
AUTHOR-ILLUSTRATOR

When Dav Pilkey was a kid, he was diagnosed with ADHD and dyslexia. Dav was so disruptive in class that his teachers made him sit out in the hallway every day. Luckily, Dav loved to draw and make up stories. He spent his time in the hallway creating his own original comic books — the very first adventures of Dog Man and Captain Underpants.

In college, Dav met a teacher who encouraged him to illustrate and write. He won a national competition in 1986 and the prize was the publication of his first book, WORLD WAR WON. He made many other books before being awarded the 1998 California Young Reader Medal for DOG BREATH, which was published in 1994, and in 1997 he won the Caldecott Honor for THE PAPERBOY.

THE ADVENTURES OF SUPER DIAPER BABY, published in 2002, was the first complete graphic novel spin-off from the Captain Underpants series and appeared at #6 on the USA Today bestseller list for all books, both adult and children's, and was also a New York Times bestseller. It was followed by THE ADVENTURES OF OOK AND GLUK: KUNG FU CAVEMEN FROM THE FUTURE and SUPER DIAPER BABY 2: THE INVASION OF THE POTTY SNATCHERS, both USA Today bestsellers. The unconventional style of these graphic novels is intended to encourage uninhibited creativity in kids.

His stories are semi-autobiographical and explore universal themes that celebrate friendship, tolerance, and the triumph of the good-hearted.

Dav loves to kayak in the Pacific Northwest with his wife.